The Fictional Use of History in Shakespeare's English History Plays

莎士比亚英国历史剧的历史虚构研究

许 展—著

河南大学出版社
HENAN UNIVERSITY PRESS
·郑州·

图书在版编目(CIP)数据

莎士比亚英国历史剧的历史虚构研究／许展著. --郑州：河南大学出版社,2021.5
ISBN 978-7-5649-4703-3

Ⅰ.①莎… Ⅱ.①许… Ⅲ.①莎士比亚(Shakespeare, William 1564-1616)-历史剧-文学研究 Ⅳ.①I561.073

中国版本图书馆 CIP 数据核字(2021)第 091328 号

责任编辑　薛巧玲
责任校对　陈晓林
封面设计　李雪艳

出 版	河南大学出版社		
	地址：郑州市郑东新区商务外环中华大厦 2401 号　邮编：450046		
	电话：0371-86059701(营销部)　网址：hupress.henu.edu.cn		
排 版	郑州市今日文教印制有限公司		
印 刷	广东虎彩云印刷有限公司		
版 次	2021 年 5 月第 1 版	印 次	2021 年 5 月第 1 次印刷
开 本	787 mm×1092 mm　1/16	印 张	15.5
字 数	338 千字	定 价	49.00 元

(本书如有印装质量问题,请与河南大学出版社营销部联系调换。)

序　　言

　　许展就读博士前一直在高校进行英美文学教学工作,在英国文学方面具有较好的学术积累。出于对专业领域的热爱和学术进取心,她于2016年考取我的全日制博士,在河南大学外语学院进行博士阶段的学习研究。入校后,她作为研究骨干参与了我的国家社会科学基金项目"莎士比亚英国历史剧的历史叙事研究"工作,发挥了积极的作用。她对莎士比亚戏剧的兴趣浓厚,进行了大量的探索性研究。为了能更好地学习,尽快提高自己的研究能力,她还申请到了国家留学基金委公派留学项目,到莎士比亚故居所在地——斯特拉福小镇附近的伯明翰大学莎士比亚研究中心学习进修了一年。留学期间,莎士比亚研究院院长兼伯明翰大学莎士比亚研究专家迈克尔·道布森(Michael Dobson)教授担任她的导师,与我一起联合指导她的学习,对她的研究工作做出了高度的评价。博士毕业后,她又继续进行相关的博士后研究,此书正是她积累的学术成果。

　　国内外研究界对莎士比亚的研究汗牛充栋,称为"道不尽的莎士比亚",但对其历史剧的研究却远远少于对其悲剧和喜剧的研究,现有的大部分针对历史剧的研究也多从戏剧中的人物形象、君主观、王权观、宗教观等入手,少有对戏剧与历史本身的关系研究。这篇研究题名为《莎士比亚英国历史剧的历史虚构研究》,作者之所以反复强调研究的是莎士比亚"英国"历史剧,是因为莎氏还创作过一些基于其他国家历史素材的戏剧,比如他的罗马剧《尤里乌斯·恺撒》《安东尼和克里奥佩特拉》等。历史本身就是一种虚构,准确地说,真实的已经发生过的历史已经不可能被原原本本地重现,所有被重述或记录的历史都是叙事的重构,这种重构由于叙事的天然性质而不可避免地会有虚构成分。因此,对历史虚构的研究,准确地说,是对历史剧如何虚构叙事以及此种虚构叙事达到了何种效果的研究。故此,许展拟将莎士比亚的历史剧创作放置于社会语境与其他文学文本和历史文本的坐标之中，研讨莎氏作品中历史事实与文学虚构之间的辩证关系，以及莎士比亚历史剧是如何被历史影响又影响历史，从而对莎士比亚研究发表一些个人的见解。整篇研究的重点并非拘泥在莎剧是否真实呈现了历史事实，而是探究莎士比亚如何通过文学虚构控制创作中抽象潜能到历史具象的转变，以及其虚构叙事对历史过程的"塑形"所体现的美学价值。从本书来看，她较好地完成了研究任务。

整体而言，《莎士比亚英国历史剧的历史虚构研究》不同于已有的对莎士比亚英国历史剧的解读，选择从历史事实与文学虚构的辩证关系入手。这篇研究在对莎士比亚的戏剧作品进行论述前，首先追溯了西方思想史中诗（文学）与历史之争，论述视角独到新颖。不仅涉及文学、文论，更是涉及历史、哲学等范畴。通过莎剧研究，探讨了普遍意义上文学与历史的关系。其次，这篇研究追溯了莎士比亚英国历史剧的研究史，并结合文本细读，展示了旧历史主义到新历史主义再到后现代主义理论的发展与流变，提出了一些新的阐释。研究不仅采用了新历史主义研究方法，还采用了利奥塔的小叙述等理论观点，并将文学虚构的叙事学方法引入对戏剧的分析中，于精微之处洞见文本的文化和意识形态意义，帮助理解莎氏历史虚构的可能性与必然性。再次，除了著作权有争议的《爱德华三世》，这篇研究全面地分析了莎士比亚十部以英国国王命名的历史剧，论述较为完整充分。此外，本篇研究的文本细读扎实，较为系统地呈现了莎士比亚历史剧中的边缘人物与女性形象。最后，整体研究材料丰富，细读扎实，观点新颖，对莎士比亚的整体研究具有一定的积极意义，值得推荐。

许展现在洛阳理工学院工作，她在繁重的教学工作之余仍然追求学术科研的发展与进步，为此她到战略支援部队信息工程大学洛阳校区外国语言文学博士后流动站继续开展研究工作。希望她在博士后阶段继续努力，在莎士比亚研究领域取得更好的成果，同时也祝她在今后的学术之路上越走越远，越走越顺利。

高继海

2021 年 3 月

前　言

在约翰·赫明斯和亨利·康德尔于1623年出版的《第一对开本》(实际名称为《威廉·莎士比亚先生的戏剧、历史剧和悲剧》)中,10部以英国历史为素材并以英国君王命名的莎士比亚戏剧被归为历史剧。而莎士比亚基于其他国家历史素材创作的剧作,例如描写罗马共和时期的《尤里乌斯·恺撒》,描写罗马和埃及统治者斗争与联姻的《安东尼和克里奥佩特拉》等则被归到了悲剧之中。《第一对开本》奠定了英国历史剧(以下简称为历史剧)这一莎士比亚戏剧的独特范畴,根据莎士比亚的实际创作时间对这10部历史剧进行排序,分别为《亨利六世》(上、中、下)、《理查三世》、《理查二世》、《约翰王》、《亨利四世》(上、下)、《亨利五世》和《亨利八世》。

本书以这10部历史剧中的历史虚构(这里的"历史"特指戏剧家在写作时依靠的历史文献)为主要研究对象,指出这些历史剧,虽然大部分以霍林希德和霍尔的编年史书为基础,却在人物形象和历史事件两方面进行了一系列虚构操作。具体来说,在人物形象方面是"人物塑造",即对历史人物重新塑形,或虚构新的人物形象;在历史事件方面是"情节化",即对历史事件的重新编排、删减或插入新的材料。

传统史学家认为,在特定的历史时代,有一套占主导地位的完整而稳定的社会思想体系,即时代精神。蒂利亚德即认为莎士比亚的历史剧展现了伊丽莎白时期的世界秩序,他认为自上而下的政治秩序一直存在于莎士比亚历史剧对无序政治状态的描画中。新历史主义则反对将历史文本看作是一种稳定的、统一的文化和思想结构,并提出应该把重点放在颠覆性的而不是文本产生时代的正统力量上。在后现代主义背景下,这种争论被进一步深化,后现代理论家利奥塔反复表达对宏大叙事的怀疑,并提出"小叙述"来对宏大叙事的霸权进行挑战。在这种理论框架下，本书指出，通过历时性考察莎士比亚的历史剧，可以发现其作品中虚构人物与历史人物交汇、互动、不断质疑历史，发出自己的声音，并最终打破了宏大叙事的垄断，构建了"小叙述"的混杂历史。

全书共分六章。第一章简要介绍了莎士比亚英国历史剧的构成、国内外研究现状，指出莎士比亚英国历史剧在国内外学术界的重要地位和国内研究尚未关注的重要内容，以及写本书的主要意图，即希望通过研究莎士比亚的英国历史剧是如何对历史事件和历史人物进行虚构以及这种艺术手法达到的效果来回应历史剧的真实和虚构之争。

第二章着重论述莎士比亚的第一个三部曲《亨利六世》上、中、下，指出这些剧中的历史虚构是对宏大历史叙事的质疑。传统史学家认为，莎士比亚历史剧体现了对等级秩序和君主专制的维护和认同。研究虚构情节和人物则能发现，《亨利六世》第一部通过展现党派斗争和半虚构的女性形象贞德质疑了英雄历史；第二部中，杰克凯德的形象挑战了贵族社会的森严等级，此外，剧中参与起义的底层人民的种种行为是对上层政权斗争的模仿和讽刺；第三部则通过家庭和国家的混乱，质疑亨利对牧羊人精准有序的家国生活的渴望。两个"鼹鼠丘"的虚构场景更是展示了世俗家国历史的破灭。虽然莎士比亚在这些剧中虚构了一批具有代表性的女性和普通民众形象，但这些人物只是对统一专制的宏大叙事进行质疑，未能摆脱王权贵族所展现的历史图景之束缚，标志着莎士比亚对于历史虚构的运用处于早期不成熟的阶段。

第三章主要分析《理查三世》、《理查二世》和《约翰王》，指出这些剧中的历史虚构探索了构建不同历史的可能性。在《理查三世》和《理查二世》中，莎士比亚通过对材料来源进行诗性构建，重塑了两位国王的历史形象。而在《约翰王》中，一些重要的历史史实，如《大宪章》的颁布并未被提及，但莎士比亚虚构出的私生子这一人物在剧中却格外重要，他不但对尔虞我诈的政治行为做了深入人心的评价，且性格忠诚勇敢，在剧中大放异彩；《理查二世》中约克公爵夫人则是莎士比亚历史剧中母亲形象的巅峰。此外，《理查三世》中抄写书记员在海斯丁被无辜处死后誊写早已编撰好的罪状，以及《约翰王》中对亚瑟王子神秘之死的描述，都对历史真实做了挑战和质疑：历史本身即是被书写的，历史真实或无可获得。这些人物和事件标志着莎士比亚对历史虚构的运用逐渐娴熟，预示着他摆脱宏大叙事束缚而自由观照历史和真实的独特虚构模式的出现。

第四章主要分析第二个三部曲,《亨利四世》上、下及《亨利五世》,指出这些剧中虚构人物提供了与宏大历史叙事反向而行的"小叙述"。这些"小叙述"通过普通人的视角和行为呈现了多样化的历史,其中最具代表性的是福斯塔夫。虽然福斯塔夫的原型在历史正典中是个清教的殉道者,但莎士比亚的福斯塔夫早已超越了历史的限制,成为了肉体生命力的象征。野猪头酒吧的快嘴桂嫂和葛洛斯特郡的乡村法官们则给人们提供了一探史书之外平民生活的机会。可以说,"非历史"的福斯塔夫和他的伙伴一起,织就了五彩缤纷的历史画卷,体现了莎士比亚说的"所有人的生活里都有一部历史"。此外,《亨利五世》中虚构的合唱团以及普通士兵的出现则对亨利五世历史上光辉的国王形象提出了质疑,再次展现了与正典历史相悖的普通民众的"小叙述"。福斯塔夫和普通下层民众的"小叙述"所构成的混杂历史,是对正史大叙事的反思、颠覆和重构,标志着莎士比亚独具特色的历史虚构在这一时期已经成熟。

第五章分析莎士比亚最后一部英国历史剧《亨利八世》中对"真实"的理解和呈现。《亨利八世》的副标题为"一切都是真的",这种自我申辩式的真实在剧作中处处达到了反讽的效果。作为一部恳请观众把"故事里的人物/当作真人看待"(开场白:25-27)的历史剧,该剧中不断出现的各种口头报告、言证都在故意掩盖和歪曲事实,来提醒所谓的"历史真实"不过是人们的一厢情愿,历史的传播过程就是一个在言传中失真的过程。此外,剧作通过不同虚构人物的视角呈现同一个历史事件,说明真实是每个人站在自己角度所做的臆想,即便是自称完全真实的正典历史,也不过是主导意识形态下历史真相的冰山一角。虽然"一切皆真"的历史并不存在,但虚构与真实这对矛盾体,在莎士比亚的历史剧中得以奇妙的结合,悖论式地呈现出不是真实、胜似真实的效果。

第六章是本书的小节。此章指出,莎士比亚历史剧通过虚构边缘人物的"小叙述"以及对历史虚构本质的自我指认,挑战了封建贵族秩序和层级的意识形态,质疑了宏大的历史叙事及其真实性,逐步形成了自己成熟的历史虚构模式。同时,本书还讨论了莎士比亚历史剧中历史虚构的归路。关于"文学(诗)之真"的争论几乎从西方文学理论肇始就开始了。柏拉图认为诗人仅仅从事模仿,无法传达真知和真理,而亚里士多德则认为因为诗能够揭示普遍性,因而可以抵达真相。而融合了历史与文学的历史剧更是难以避免被质疑是否"真实"的问题,虽然历史剧无法还原历史之科学真实,但其能够通过艺术加工而贴近真实,产生"审美化"的艺术真实。因此,历史剧描述的真实性是个假命题,因为无论是文学作品或是历史著作,都不能达到所谓的"真实",如果一定要追求"真实",与历史著作相比,莎士比亚历史剧所呈现的对历史事件的拣选和对历史人物的再塑造,则更能体现这种"真实"。因为这种审美化的历史超越了实证主义对真实的要求,达到了人性及精神世界的艺术真实。

许展

2020年12月

Contents

Chapter One　Introduction ･･ (1)
　1.1　Brief Introduction to Shakespeare's English History Plays ･･････････ (1)
　1.2　Literature Review ･･ (8)
　1.3　Three Dimensions of Studying Shakespeare's Fictional Use of
　　　 History ･･･ (21)
　　　1.3.1　Fictional Elements in Shakespeare's History Plays ･････････ (21)
　　　1.3.2　Purposes of Shakespeare's Fictional Use of History ･･･････ (26)
　　　1.3.3　Effects of Shakespeare's Fictional Use of History ･････････ (31)
Chapter Two　Emergence of the Fictional Use of History:
　　　　　　　Questioning the Grand Narrative of History ･･････････ (38)
　2.1　*1 Henry VI*: The Interrogation to the Heroic History ･････････････ (39)
　　　2.1.1　Party Politics: The Deflation of Heroism in the Nation ･････ (40)
　　　2.1.2　Joan of Arc: A Radical Challenge to the Heroic Values ････ (44)
　2.2　*2 Henry VI*: The Interrogation to the National Politics ･･････････ (51)
　　　2.2.1　Jack Cade: An Inversion of the Political Hierarchy ･･････････ (51)
　　　2.2.2　"Infinite Numbers" of Commoners: The Mimicking of the
　　　　　　Political Order ･･ (57)
　2.3　*3 Henry VI*: The Interrogation to the Secular History ･････････････ (64)
　　　2.3.1　Two Molehills: The Subverted Social and Familial Bonds ････ (64)
　　　2.3.2　"Natural Mother" Margret: A Threat to Patriarchy in Family
　　　　　　and State ･･ (71)

**Chapter Three Further Exploration of the Fictional Use of History:
The Possibility of Constructing a Different History**
.... (79)

3.1　Reinvention of History: The Historical Characters Being Refashioned by the Poetic Treatment .... (80)

   3.1.1　*Richard III*: The Deformed Shape of King's Body .... (81)

   3.1.2　*Richard II*: The Different Modes of King's Language .... (87)

3.2　Becoming of History: The Fictional Elements Being Historicised into Plays .... (95)

   3.2.1　Bastard in *King John*: "A Bastard to the Time" .... (96)

   3.2.2　Duchess of York in *Richard II*: The Culmination of Women's Role as Mother .... (103)

3.3　*Meditations on Truth: The Undetermined Truthfulness of History* ... (116)

   3.3.1　*Deaths of Two Princes and Lord Hastings in* Richard III .... (117)

   3.3.2　*Custody and Mysterious Death of Arthur in* King John .... (123)

Chapter Four Maturity of the Fictional Use of History: Making "Petit Récit" of Hybrid Histories .... (130)

4.1　"There is a History in All Men's Lives": Three Related Strata of Histories in *1, 2 Henry IV* .... (131)

   4.1.1　Falstaff's Invented and Subversive "ahistory" .... (132)

   4.1.2　King and Royal Party's Selective and Distorted National History .... (149)

   4.1.3　Commoners' Social History of Quotidian Existence .... (160)

4.2　*Henry V*: Representing History on the World Stage .... (167)

   4.2.1　Drama vs. History: The Chorus' Theatrical Representation of History .... (168)

   4.2.2　Rabbit or Duck?: The Ambiguous Image of the King Presented by His "Band of Brothers" .... (177)

Chapter Five Destination of the Fictional Use of History: An Understanding of the Nature of Truth ⋯⋯⋯⋯⋯⋯⋯ (191)

5.1 "May Here Find Truth": The Scepticism about the Historical Truth in the History Plays ⋯⋯⋯⋯⋯⋯⋯⋯⋯⋯⋯⋯⋯⋯⋯⋯⋯⋯⋯⋯ (193)

5.2 "Our Chosen Truth": The Multiple Perspectives of the Political Motivation ⋯⋯⋯⋯⋯⋯⋯⋯⋯⋯⋯⋯⋯⋯⋯⋯⋯⋯⋯⋯⋯⋯⋯⋯⋯⋯ (201)

5.3 "To Make That Only True We Now Intend": The Ringing Assertion of the Poetic Truth about the Future to Believe ⋯⋯⋯⋯⋯⋯⋯⋯ (211)

Chapter Six Conclusion ⋯⋯⋯⋯⋯⋯⋯⋯⋯⋯⋯⋯⋯⋯⋯⋯⋯⋯ (219)

Bibliography ⋯⋯⋯⋯⋯⋯⋯⋯⋯⋯⋯⋯⋯⋯⋯⋯⋯⋯⋯⋯⋯⋯⋯⋯ (226)

Chapter One Introduction

Serving as a foundation to the book, the Introduction relates four major goals: Firstly, it specifies the history play as a genre and provides a brief introduction to Shakespeare's English history plays. Secondly, it attempts to conduct a comprehensive literature review of Shakespeare's English history plays both at home and abroad. Thirdly, it draws a brief sketch of the basic principles and major issues that the book is trying to illustrate. Finally, it presents the organisation and structure of this book.

1.1 Brief Introduction to Shakespeare's English History Plays

As a great dramatist, William Shakespeare is remembered by the entire world for centuries, and his works are read, put onto the stage, loved and memorised with an intense passion. He occupies a unique place not only in the English literature but also in the World literature. Numerous scholars from all over the world have devoted themselves to the study of Shakespeare's life and works. However, the study of his history plays is far from comprehensive as compared with those of the so-called "Four Great Tragedies" and "Four Great Comedies".

Since this book is about Shakespeare's English history plays, it may be worth looking at the historical context from which the unique category of "English history play" emerges. While we speak about Shakespeare's "history plays", it seems as if Shakespeare wrote them in the categories of "history plays". However, the fact is that when the plays were originally published, they were by no means so clearly identified and distinguished by genre.

The genre of the history play is an Elizabethan invention, which is a hybrid that combines elements of the classical genres of tragedy and comedy. The "history play" lacks a strict definition and causes some to question whether it counts as a genre①. Despite the difficulties associated with determining what precisely defines a history play, there seems little reason to reject the category. One of the critical moments in the process of consolidating the genre occurred in 1623, when the editors of the *First Folio*—John Heminges and Henry Condell regularised the titles of Shakespeare's thirty-six plays and divided them into a tripartite division: "Comedies", "Histories" and "Tragedies", and most editors have followed their practice ever since.

The Folio catalogue makes no room for "Romances" or "Tragicomedies", a fourth category usually found in modern editions of the complete works, but it does set apart the ten plays treating specifically English history. The ten history plays are not, of course, the only plays on historical subject that Shakespeare wrote. There are other history plays written by Shakespeare, such as *Coriolanus*, *Julius Caesar*, and *Antony and Cleopatra*. Instead of grouping the three plays into the genre of "Histories", the *First Folio* groups them as "Tragedies". Coleridge said that "in order that a drama be properly historical, it is necessary that it should be the history of the people to whom it is addressed" (1849: 253), and indeed the Folio's grouping of the ten plays as "Histories" reflects a similar understanding of the particular relationship that such plays can establish with their audience. Therefore, the "English history plays" typically refers to the ten plays that deal with English history and focus on the reign of a particular monarch. In this book, "English history plays" is often referred to in a shorter form as "history plays".

It is also John Heminges and Henry Condell that arrange Shakespeare's ten history

---

① To see this point clearly, please refer to Paulina Kewes. "The Elizabethan History Play: A True Genre?" Eds. Richard Dutton, Jean E. Howard. *A Companion to Shakespeare's Works: Volume II, the Histories*. Oxford: Wiley-Blackwell, 2003. pp. 170-93.

plays according to the monarchical chronology, beginning with *The Life and Death of King John* and ending with *The Life of King Henry the Eighth*. The ten plays in modernised spelling are as follows①:

  1195-1216 *The Life and Death of King John*
  1367-1400 *The Life and Death of Richard the Second*
  1400-1403 *The First Part of King Henry the Fourth*
  1403-1413 *The Second Part of King Henry the Fourth*
  1413-1422 *The Life of King Henry the Fifth*
  1422-1451 *The First Part of King Henry the Sixth*
  1451-1455 *The Second Part of King Henry the Sixth*
  1455-1471 *The Third Part of King Henry the Sixth*
  1483-1485 *The Life and Death of Richard the Third*
  1509-1547 *The Life of King Henry the Eighth*

If we correspond Shakespeare's writing time with each King's reign in different dynasties, the table would be as follows②:

History Plays	Writing Time	Reign Time	Dynasties
1 Henry VI	1590	1422-1451	Lancaster
2 Henry VI	1590-1591	1451-1455	Lancaster
3 Henry VI	1592	1455-1471	Lancaster
Richard III	1592-1593	1483-1485	Plantagenet
Richard II	1595-1596	1377-1399	Plantagenet
King John	1596	1199-1216	Plantagenet

---

 ① In this book, all of them are used in a much shorter abbreviated forms as follows: *King John*, *Richard II*, *1 Henry IV*, *2 Henry IV*, *Henry V*, *1 Henry VI*, *2 Henry VI*, *3 Henry VI*, *Richard III*, and *Henry VIII*.
 ② This table is arranged by the author of this book according to *A Shakespeare Encyclopaedia* and the Arden series of Shakespeare's history plays. Please refer to Bibliography for more publication information of the books.

History Plays	Writing Time	Reign Time	Dynasties
1 Henry IV	1596-1597	1399-1403	Lancaster
2 Henry IV	1598	1403-1413	Lancaster
Henry V	1598-1599	1413-1422	Lancaster
Henry VIII	1612-1613	1509-1547	Tudor

From the table, we can see that the ten history plays, with one exception were all written in the 1590s. The exception is *Henry VIII*, written in collaboration with John Fletcher at the end of Shakespeare's career. Of the other nine plays, *King John* stands by itself and depicts a much earlier reign. The remaining eight plays depict one continuous period of English history from the reign of Richard II in the fourteenth century to the accession of Henry VII, the first of the Tudor Kings, in 1485.

There is no denying that Shakespeare's history plays have a complicated relationship with the "history" as a set of discursive practices in his time. History, in the modern sense, is an umbrella term which relates two related but distinct concepts: One is the actual happenings of the human past which once happened and would never be grasped; the other is the study or inquiry into the nature of the human past, with the aim of preparing an authentic account of one or more of its facets (Ritter 279). Back in Shakespeare's time, the meaning of history was by no means so clearly defined and the term "history" could mean either "history" or "story". Nevertheless, it has been suggested that by the end of the sixteenth century and early seventeenth century, "history had become an autonomous discipline with its own purposes and methods" (Rackin 1990:18-19).

The new sense of history as a distinct discipline was manifested in Shakespeare's time, not only in the practice of historians and the discourse of theorists but also in the invention of those terms "historiographer" and "historiography" (Rackin 1990:33). In *Dictionary of Concepts in History*, Ritter points out that "historiography" is used in two senses by English-speaking historians: broadly, to refer to written history in general or to the act of writing history (historiographer is a synonym for historian, now rare); and, more narrowly, as a technical term to designate the study of the history of historical writing, methods, interpretation, and controversy (Ritter 273). The integration of the two is what we usually call "history". So that is why Phyllis Rackin points out the word "history" refers equally to the signifying text and what the text signifies, to the present record and the absent, and in fact dead life the text attempts to resurrect. Rackin further argues that, strictly speaking, what is written is not history but "historiography", and what historiography writes about is history (1990:33).

Shakespeare's history plays are based on the historiography of the sixteenth century, especially those by Raphael Holinshed and Edward Hall. The second edition of Holinshed's three volumes of *Chronicles of England, Scotland, and Ireland* had been published in 1587. They were thus the most up-to-date and authoritative chronicle of English history to which Shakespeare could have referred. They had supplied him with material for all the English history plays and for *King Lear*, *Macbeth*, and *Cymbeline* (Wells 146). Shakespeare also supplemented his reading by referring most often to one of Holinshed's sources—Edward Hall's chronicles of the English Civil Wars under the title of *The Union of the Two Noble and Illustrate Families of Lancaster and York*. Therefore, in the specific term of this research—the fictional use of history, the word "history" here refers to the historical records, and especially the historiography Shakespeare variously used in creating his history plays.

Since Shakespeare's history plays have a close relation with historiography, it is necessary to refer back to the early historiographical writing in his time. As many early writers of history noted by themselves, the usual practice of historiography at Shakespeare's time was to incorporate the writings of earlier historians wholesale and without question into the work in hand, just as Holinshed incorporated More's *History of Richard III*. Holinshed's "preface to the reader" in volume Two offered this justification for incorporating the work of earlier historians without alteration:

> For my part, I have in things doubtful rather chosen to show the diversity of their writings, than by overruling them, and using a peremptory censure, to

frame them to agree to my liking; leaving it nevertheless to each man's judgment, to control them as he sees cause. ①(Preface)

Similarly, Samuel Daniel described and justified this kind of practice in the "Epistle Dedicatory" to his history of *The Civil Wars between the Houses of Lancaster and York*. He wrote:

> I have carefully followed that truth which is delivered in the history; without adding to, or subtracting from, the general received opinion of things as we find them in our common annals; holding it an impiety, to violate what public testimony we have, without more evident proof; or to introduce fictions of our own imagination, in things of this nature. (qtd. in Pugliatti 33)

In other words, earlier historians depended on their commitment to received opinions in the chronological record. Anything else is fiction②, derived from the author's "own imagination". There is, however, a further context for this thinking besides respect for earlier authorities. Historiography was a notoriously sensitive form

---

① The spelling is modernised by the writer of this book. The original spellings in Holinshed's texts are "for my part, I have in things doubtfull rather chosen to shew the diversitie of their writings, than by over-ruling them, and using a peremptorie censure, to frame them to agree to my liking; leaving it nevertheless to each mans judgement, to control them as he seeth cause". For additional information on citing Holinshed, consult Levy, *Tudor Historical Thought*, pp. ix, 167. Holinshed, "Preface to the Reader", *The Third Volume of Chronicles* (1587), in Patterson, *Reading Holinshed's Chronicles*, pp. 15,40-41.

② In most cases, the word "fiction" denotes only literary narratives used in prose (the novel and short story), and sometimes is used merely as a synonym for the novel. However, M. H. Abrams in his *A Glossary of Literary Terms* points out that the word "fiction", in an inclusive sense, is "any literary narrative, whether in prose or verse, which is invented instead of being an account of events that in fact happened" (188). In this sense, the concept of "fiction" can be found in almost all genres of literary writing—poems, novels, as well as plays. In this book, the word "fiction" means explicitly "something invented by the imagination or feigned specifically". For more elaborations of "fiction", see M. H. 艾布拉姆斯. 文学术语词典（中英对照）. 北京：北京大学出版社, 2009.

of writing in this period, a recognised cover for topical writing. The choice of historical narratives, in fact, brings with it many risks. Those risks are evident in the case of John Hayward, who had been imprisoned in the Tower by Queen Elizabeth I and was only released three years after her death. John Hayward's history *The First Part of the Life and Reign of King Henry Ⅳ* was suppressed because Hayward dedicated it to Essex who rebelled against Elizabeth's rule; but probably also because the deposition of Richard Ⅱ was a topic that much upset Elizabeth, who famously said in a conversation "I am Richard Ⅱ. Know ye not that?"①. It is crucial to realise that history is capable of an endless interpretation, which makes historiography a precarious and risky form of writing.

While writing history is becoming more precarious and risky, dramatising it is becoming more popular. It is self-evident that remaking history as living action, gesture, and dialogue necessarily involves fictional elements, and therefore, history play has more space to adopt a sceptical or questioning stance towards the material of the written history. The genre's reliance on established historical narrative guarantees that they will have a complicated relationship with its sources. Although the dramatist's use of history is bound to observe the significant facts of the received historiography, there is no clear demarcation between the classes of events that stand inviolable and those that are accessible to revision. Shakespeare's history plays invariably reconfigure available historiography, transforming a narrative (or a set of narratives) into a compressed dramatic representation. In every one of his history plays, incidents are selected, from the chronicle accounts, sometimes invented, and always shaped, so that what Sidney called the "bare was" of history is dressed with dramatic fiction and power, or simply cast aside (Shakespeare 2002:12). From this point of view, one can see historical forces at work through the dramatist's re-

---

① The conversation with William Lambarde in which Elizabeth famously said "I am Richard Ⅱ. Know ye not that?" is reprinted in Peter Ure's fifth Arden edition of *Richard* Ⅱ (London: Methuen, 1961. pp. lix).

constructional activities which makes Coleridge put forward: "A historical drama is, therefore, a collection of events borrowed from history, but connected together in respect of cause and time, poetically and by dramatic fiction" (1849:254).

Generally speaking, in the specific term of this research—the fictional use of history, the adjective "fictional" means "feigning or creating with the imagination", while the word "history" refers to the historical records, and especially Holinshed and Hall's historiographies Shakespeare variously used in creating his history plays. It seems that Shakespeare's history plays, on the one hand, are written in close relation to historiography, on the other hand, explore the domain of literary fiction by deviating from historical events and refashioning historical figure, and thus invite constant quests towards the dialectical relationship between "history and fiction". In order to study Shakespeare's fictional use of history in the history plays, one needs to examine exchanges between drama and historiography, which constitute a lasting cultural debate that links to the broader field of literature and history. David Quint has argued that in "Shakespeare's poetic treatment, history ceases to be the didactic instrument of classical humanism and becomes instead an occasion for historicist self-reflection" (50). Graham Holderness takes the matter further by writing: "Shakespeare's historical plays are not just reflections of a cultural debate: they are interventions in that debate, contributions to the historiographical effort to reconstruct the past and discover the methods and principles of that reconstruction" (1985:31). Therefore, before we start it, it is necessary to look at what the previous critics have done and have a piece of comprehensive knowledge about the cultural debates concerning Shakespeare's history plays.

1.2 Literature Review

Almost all criticism of Shakespeare's history plays since the mid-twentieth century has had to take account of E. M. W. Tillyard's *Shakespeare's History Plays*. Tillyard's influential critique argues for sequential reading of the plays as embodying a "whole contemporary pattern of culture"① (1962: 10), "the Elizabethan world picture"②(1943: v). According to E. M. W. Tillyard, there is a historical pattern reflecting the operation of God's Providence and in particular the exaltation of "Tudor Myth" through God's decision to restore England to political stability and economic prosperity (1962: 10-17). According to Tillyard, "Tudor Myth" is a tradition in English history, historiography and literature of the fifteenth century. It serves the political purpose of promoting the Tudor period of the 16th century as a golden age of peace, law, order, and prosperity. Tillyard's critical opinions set a precedent of the once-fashionable notion of "providential history" concurred by many later critics.

Another very influential critic Lily B. Campbell famously argued that history plays are a consistent and considered expression of Elizabethan ideological orthodoxy. Proposing that Shakespeare's "medium was drama, and through the drama, he said what he had to say" (15), Campbell finally settled in the political purpose of Shakespeare:

> His medium made concrete what another man might say of philosophy or political theory in a treatise dealing with abstractions or generalizations. He represented an action with its cause and its results [⋯], because Shakespeare uses the medium of the drama to express what he had to say, there is no reason for denying to him a moral and a political philosophy which motivated first the

---

① The original expression of Tillyard is "He [Shakespeare] writes of God and creation, the universe and the influence of the stars, the soul and body of man, man's mind and its passions. And from his repetitive and indifferently arranged stanzas as completely as from any single source I know of can by extracted the contemporary notion of order or degree which was never absent from Shakespeare's picture of disorder in the Histories". Please refer to Tillyard, *Shakespeare's History Plays*. London: Penguin Books, 1962.

② "The Elizabethan World Picture" is the name of Tillyard's book. In the Preface of the book, he elaborates the meanings of his title as "the pictures of civil war and disorder they present had no meaning apart from a background of order to judge them by". Please refer to Tillyard, *The Elizabethan World Picture*. London: Chatto & Windus, 1943.

choice of story and second the plotting of that story (15-16).

Irving Ribner stepped into Campbell's shoes and proceeded to argue that, history plays share a more profound affinity with prose historiography than they do with other plays. Ribner identified didacticism as the principal purpose of Elizabethan historical writings, whether dramatic or non-dramatic and on that basis argued that the history play is "a separate dramatic genre" (11). A history play, he contended, "was one which fulfilled what Elizabethans considered the purposes of history" (12). In his view, no play without a clearly articulated, coherent message qualified as a history play, and that message could be one and one only: to inculcate obedience and uphold the authority of the Queen.

While many critics hold that Tillyard's "Elizabethan world picture" or the orthodox Tudor political position against disobedience and rebellion is powerful and influential, however, the trouble with this position is that it assumes a unified ideology: firstly, a consensual understanding of the official, consistent and conservative world-view of history; secondly, an ideological uniformity imposed and preached by church and state through government in Elizabethan history plays. This position, which risks reducing a polyvalent drama to the status of a government pamphlet, cannot command full assent and there emerge some new theoretical stances.

The perception of the contradictory impulses in Shakespeare, which composed "that extraordinary fluid compound we call Elizabethan culture" (Sanders 146), started to be clearly formulated and systematically elaborated in the mid-sixties. The old historicism of the orthodox Elizabethan picture is replaced by a new branch of criticism, which proposes the idea of duplicity intrinsic in Elizabethan history play. The ordered, providential concept of history, embodied in Tillyard's seminal study of the history plays and accepted by Campbell and Ribner, had given to recognition that Shakespeare shows a sophisticated and at times problematic understanding of the nature of history. It started from Rossiter's seminal lecture on "Ambivalence" in Shakespeare's history plays.

A. P. Rossiter's influential essay "Ambivalence: The Dialectic of the Histories", in his *Angel with Horns*, argues that the histories are characterised by a "Doubleness":

> In the conflicting values set by the Greatness (the Triumph) of the National Destiny and the Frustration, the inadequacy, of the Individual (the frail Man within the robe)—there is nothing complex in the "Doubleness". It falls just short of the tragic; where Man's greatness is asserted in his destruction. That falling-short is characteristic of the Histories (42).

Part of this duality is an irony on concepts of the order proposed by Tillyard and others:

> The Tudor myth of Order, Degree, etc. was too rigid, too black-and-white, too doctrinaire and narrowly moral for Shakespeare's mind: it falsified his fuller experience of men. Consequently, while employing it as frame, he had to undermine it, to qualify it with equivocations: to vex its applications with sly or subtle ambiguities: to cast doubt on its ultimate human validity, even in situations where its principles seemed most completely applicable (59).

Subsequent studies, such as M. M. Reese's *The Cease of Majesty: A Study of Shakespeare's History Plays*, work within the general framework of this kind of interpretation. He put forward in the Preface that Shakespeare was a poet, not a writer of political tracts; therefore no interpretation of his work can ignore the many-sidedness of his vision, that two-eyed scrutiny in which ideas of good and evil are called to no single account. He believed that:

> An important difference between Elizabethan society and our own is that, whereas we are accustomed to chaos and expect it to continue, the sixteenth

century regarded it as an unnatural departure from a norm that must and would be restored. Order was the supreme political virtue because it was a condition of all other virtue[⋯]. Thus Shakespeare's quest in the histories was not only the ideal king since even the most dedicated ruler must fail when his subjects are corrupt; he was seeking also the ideal social relationship in which the king and people were united in a conception of their mutual duty (vii).

Robert Ornstein, in his *A Kingdom for a Stage*, maintained that Shakespeare in no way attempts to recreate the Elizabethan world picture. Ornstein questioned all the terms of this proposed ideological relationship, arguing that the "inherent bias of the historical method toward what is conventional and orthodox in Elizabethan culture because any search for the 'norms' of Elizabethan thought must lead to a consensus of truisms and pieties" (4).

Robert Ornstein's work led an epoch in the course of the 1970s and 1980s when a whole range of new critical approaches to Shakespeare's history plays emerged. These critical approaches are capable of much more extensive and systematic exposure of the ideological mystification of Tillyard's thesis. Prominent among them was a "new historicism" which offered to reconstitute the chronicle plays in different and politically oppositional ways. "New Historicism", is a critical movement originating in America and strongly influenced by the works of the radical historian and psychological theorist Michel Foucault, and the Marxist theoretician Louis Althusser. The New Historicism starts from the same point as Tillyard, with a will to grasp the relationships between literature and the broader cultural totality of "history", but finally replaces the grand narrative of the old historicism. While Old Historicism relies on basically empiricist form of historical research, confident in its capacity to excavate and define the events of the past, New Historicism draws on poststructuralist theories that history is always "narrated" and therefore the first sense of the "events of the past" is untenable.

What is more, New Historicism examines Renaissance drama as a functional "discourse" in which the ideological conflicts and material power-struggles of the age would be fought out in different forms. Traditionally, discourse means isolated units of language—the sentence, or even single words, phrases, and figures—in abstraction from the specific circumstances of an utterance. After the 1970s, emphasis on discourse shifts to the cultural conditions and particular circumstances. There are a number of investigators and areas of research, including the work of Hans-Georg Gadamer in hermeneutics, the concern of Michel Foucault with the institutional conditions and power-structures. If history is always a contemporary narrative, then what Tillyard sees as the intellectual spirit of age becomes merely a story that Tudor government wishes to have told about its rise to power and continuing dominance. It becomes legitimate for a modern citric to refashion that story otherwise, to disclose a different range of meanings and values. Thirdly, all histories should be foregrounded, and "non-literary" documents produced from different orders of textuality are part of the "intertexts" for discussions of literary history (Zhu Gang 259)①.

These theoretical principles produced an entirely different critical method from that employed by Tillyard and can be exemplified at their most characteristic in the works of the founder of New Historicism, Stephen Greenblatt. Greenblatt's method takes its starting point from an interdisciplinary convergence of literary and historical methodologies②. In an influential essay on Shakespeare's history plays, Greenblatt reads the second tetralogy in relation to Thomas Harriot's *A Brief and True Report of the New Found Land of Virginia*, in order to demonstrate that both the drama and the contemporary political document embody the same ideological structure.

In his 1988 essay "Invisible Bullets", Greenblatt introduced an important pair of concepts in the New Historicism—"subversion and containment" as an instrument to describe Thomas Harriot's report on his experience in the colony of Virginia in 1586. According to Greenblatt, Harriot's two observations in his *Brief and True Report of the*

---

① 朱刚.《二十世纪西方文艺批评理论》.上海:上海外语教育出版社, 2001.
② See Stephen Greenblatt, *Shakespearean Negotiations* (Oxford, 1988).

New Found Land of Virginia drew parallels of the Native Americans' culture to the religion of Christianity. It would seem that Harriot used this to impose Christianity upon the natives. At one point, as the native crop was scarce one year, Harriot suggested that the Christian God would provide better for their land. Thus the subversion was both produced and contained. Greenblatt took pains to stress that the subversion must be invisible to the Subverted just as the name of the essay "Invisible Bullets" indicated.

Throughout Greenblatt's essays, plays, texts, social practices and institutional structures are continually thrown into the interplay of discourses, and thus literature can be seen to enact a type of political discourse. Yet one critic rightly points out: "Wherever in New Historicist readings literature seems to voice subversive or alternative attitudes or emotions, these are always contained within the dominant ideology: the provocation, challenging and defeat of subversion is, in fact, one of the means by which a dominant ideology secures its power" (Holderness 1992: 12).

Besides, the usual practice of the new historicist school that always attempts to place Shakespeare in the historical context elicits many doubts from critics. According to Richard Levin, by "historical context", new historicist critics "almost always [mean] some conception of 'power', defined in term of either class or gender" (92). However, this kind of confirmation of the ideological complicity opens several new lines of thinking which are very insightful. There emerges a line of criticism, taking the views more from the artistic side than from the ideological side, in which S. C. Sen Gupta is a representative. He points out the literary significance of history play has been subordinated "to their ethical and political import". He turns to the aesthetic point by appealing "it is necessary to redress the balance, to reaffirm the purely poetical value of historical drama and to treat the ten plays from *King John* to *Henry VIII* as works of art and not as political and didactic treatises". He also uses the organisation of *Richard III* as a specific example to illustrate the aesthetic structure which he believes inherent in Shakespeare's play (6-7).

Some critics follow the aesthetic line but put their focuses more on the aesthetic figures and plots than on the ideological structures. John Wilders's *The Lost Garden* discussed that in the minds of Shakespeare's historical characters, "personal and political motives are so combined and confused as to be inseparable" (2), and argued that it is in the dramatis personae that Shakespeare locates the forces of historical agency:

> The causes of national unity, of division, of prosperity or decline, are, in Shakespeare's view, to be found not, as some of the fifteenth century chroniclers had believed, in the providential power of God, nor, as we are now inclined to think, in social and economic conditions, but in the temperaments of national leaders and their reactions towards one another. To understand the course of history, we must understand these men (2).

Wilders argued, "Shakespeare portrays history as a struggle by succeeding generations of men to establish ideal world which are beyond their powers to create" (9), hence the "lost garden" of his book's title.

Kristian Smidt followed Wilders' line in *Unconformities in Shakespeare's History Plays*. He argued that plot and character discrepancies develop "gaps between expectation and fulfilment" (3), and he further interrogated these gaps as indications of Shakespeare's sometimes flawed or imperfectly achieved intentions or working processes.

David Scott Kastan's *Shakespeare and the Shapes of Time* draws, not from character and plot but from time and history, a different analogy: "the drama is able to attempt a mimesis of the process, or at least the putative process, of history itself [providing] an analogy to and an experience of the flow of history" (1982:3-4). In the same book, Kastan pointed out two types of historical time at work in history plays: one is the providential and linear and the other is classical and cyclical. Shakespeare's histories are seen as characteristically "open-ended structures" (51), which force us to "confront our fragile existence as 'time's subjects' released into 'a world of contingency and flux'" (55).

The aesthetic line of criticism displays characteristic double movements: restoring the status of the author as a free and independent witness to the historical processes and ideas addressed in his work and at the same time insisting on a more rigorous and complex historical methodology on the part of the critic (Holderness 1992b: 30). Along with the line of aesthetic criticism, there is another line of criticism—the "historiographical" approach to the history plays. Shakespeare's history plays are considered as contributions to the field of historiography, and as phenomena which should ultimately be associated with the practice of historical exegesis. If Tillyard was able to claim every play in the cannon as an illustration of the providential view of history, recent commentators see particular plays (and even characters) as embodiments of rival historiographies.

John W. Blanpied in *Time and the Artist in Shakespeare's English Histories* argued that "the [history] plays show us that Shakespeare was profoundly concerned with the idea of history, that is, as a category of experience with a distinctive nature, simultaneously implacable and ghostly, undeniable and elusive, and that he was determined to find the dramatic form that most truly expressed this special kind of reality" (12). He was concerned with the ways the playwright acts in his historical material—how he manages to transform his own inevitable presence in the histories into the means of sounding out their vast and elusive energies. He also argued that Shakespeare comes to understand that "given the imperatives of his art, 'history' cannot be conceived except dramatically" (13).

Paola Pugliatti, in *Shakespeare the Historian*, proposed that Shakespeare's staging of English history helped to establish a new historiographical outlook. Through close examination of the playwright's varied methods and writing styles, she argued that Shakespeare achieved a radical multi-perspectivism or polyphony through which he was able to challenge the monologic practice of contemporary historical sources and cross-examine political issues, thus inaugurating problem-orientate critical historiography. Her argument is also for the ideological and structural importance of

Shakespeare's cross-examination of history and historical representation, rather than his endorsement of particular positions. Like Norman Rabkin, whose influential application of the *gestalt* optical illusion that is simultaneously a rabbit and a duck to the "irreducible complexity of things" in *Henry V*, Pugliatti stressed the simultaneity of divergent perspectives rather than a single correct reading, thus foregrounding the concurring systems of a "multiplicity of histories" (72). This approach to historical drama places a high value on early modern historiography, and long after the comparison of differences between history and poetry proposed by Aristotle, we are attracted to explore the contemporary relevance between historiography and literary fiction once again.

Though Shakespeare's history plays have attracted considerable attention of the critics all over the world, the study in China is relatively late compared with the research in the West. However, it has also made many achievements and is an integral part of the Shakespearean study in the world. In general, the study of Shakespeare's English history plays in China can be divided into three periods: the initial period—before 1978 years; the outbreak—the 1980s; the sustainable development period—the 1990s to the present.

In the early stage of the study, although the number of output is not large, the research has a relatively high starting point, which had touched on the genres, thoughts, artistic characteristics and main characters of the history play. Unfortunately, during the ten years of disaster, the Shakespearean study stagnated, and the study of history plays had also come to a standstill. After the end of the Cultural Revolution, the Shakespearean study entered into a fast developing period. The study of English history plays mainly appeared in three forms. First of all, as part of the overall study of Shakespeare, it appeared in some research works or monographs. Secondly, there are some independent theses; and then, introductions and comments on the historical play periodically published in Shakespeare's biographies. From the 1990s, the research on Shakespeare's English history plays has been developing into a stable period, and most achievements are published as independent academic theses.

Moreover, there are some excellent theorists and literary criticism practitioners who made a significant contribution to this area of research. One of the prominent young scholars is Li Yanmei, who wrote a monograph named *A Study of Shakespeare's History Plays*①, which was published by China Social Sciences Press in 2009. In the book, she held the opinion that Shakespeare's English history plays have bright humanistic thoughts. Besides, Li Yanmei made innovative research on Shakespeare's methods of characterisation and analysed the images of kings, women and buffoons in his English history plays. However, what should also be noticed is that although she made an overall analysis of Shakespeare's perception of history in the plays, most of Li Yanmei's analysis is based on macro understandings, which makes she fail to go deep on addressing the root of Shakespeare's perception of history. In order to explore why those characters behave like this or that in the plays, we need to examine "the cracks under the smooth ground". The other prominent scholar who made overall research on Shakespeare's English history plays is Ning Ping. She published *On Shakespeare's English Histories*② in 2012. In her book, Ning Ping provided a detailed analysis of Shakespeare's views on the monarchy, royal power and wars in the eleven history plays. Her study is rather systematic and illuminating. Although she emphasises that her focuses are more on history rather than on literature, the final result is that the analysis is more on the political aspects than on either history or literature. It is certain that Shakespeare's history plays shed light on politics by inviting people to explore complex political situations both in Shakespeare's era and contemporary society. However, one cannot go deep into Shakespeare's history plays without the understanding of the text and the grasp of the literary characteristics.

There are also a limited number of theses about Shakespeare's English history plays in CNKI. Liu Yuehong's master thesis "The Limited Royalty in England of the

---

① 李艳梅.《莎士比亚历史剧研究》.北京:中国社会科学出版社,2009.
② 宁平.《莎士比亚英国历史剧研究》.北京:外语教学与研究出版社,2012.

Late Middle Ages: A Perspective from Shakespeare's Chronicle Drama"① is to investigate the limited royal power in England and its political development by utilising the historical analysis methodology. This research only uses Shakespeare's history plays as a background, and the main research objects are the political factors of legislation, parliament and church. Wang Weichang's "On the Artistic Principles of Shakespeare's History Plays"② analyses artistic principles such as continuity, serialising, and the dramatisation of historical events. This research mainly focuses on the theatrical characteristics of Shakespeare's plays. Wei Lijie's master thesis " A Study on the Images of Usurper King in Shakespeare's History Plays"③ is about the images of the Kings and tries to use the socio-historical criticism to investigate Shakespeare's conception of history and his political view. Ning Ping's thesis "The Initial Study on Shakespeare's History Plays in China"④ points out although the study on Shakespeare's history plays in China slowly come into being; the general context of the study is still at its initial stage. Aiming to deepen and broaden the research in the academic circle, she reviews the major research areas, the process of the study, as well as the research approaches' characteristics. Besides, there are many famous scholars who devoted themselves to the critical paradigms of Shakespearean study, among whom Professor Sheng Ning has made a significant contribution to Chinese literary critics' awareness and recognition of literary theory⑤, but since these critical essays are not related to the specific texts of Shakespeare's history plays, this book is not going to give details.

As shown above, the current studies in the West all focus so much on the ideological sub-contexts rather than explore the narration in Shakespeare's dramatic

---

① 刘岳红. "从莎士比亚历史剧看中世纪后期英国的有限王权". 湖南大学,2008.
② 王维昌. "论莎士比亚历史剧创作的艺术原则". 安徽师范大学学报(人文社会科学版), 1999(3): 362-368.
③ 卫丽杰. "莎士比亚历史剧中的篡位君王形象研究". 华中师范大学硕士论文,2009.
④ 宁平. "中国莎士比亚历史剧研究之滥觞". 大连民族学院. 2006(2):34-37.
⑤ 盛宁. "新历史主义·后现代主义·历史真实". 文学理论与批评, 1997(1):48-58.

texts, which makes their argument not only narrow in scope but also short of thickness. Although they achieve politic and antiquarian varieties, it is hardly convincing to accept history as they described, and the question of "truth" is suspended still on the undermined relevance between history and fiction in Shakespeare's history plays. Besides, almost all of them rely so much on the extra-textual influences (biography or other kinds of contemporary texts) to shed light on the study of the history plays. Furthermore, most of the studies only focus on part of Shakespeare's works and lack systematic interpretations of the whole series of history plays. Therefore, the current study invites further discussions that not only can study Shakespeare's ten history plays more systematically but also can combine the exploration between the historical past and the dramatic representation in a more general sense.

There are some common characteristics in the previous studies of Shakespeare's history plays in China: firstly, there has been an increasing amount of scholarly attention devoted to Shakespeare's history plays. However, the criticisms, being taken from multiple perspectives, are at uneven levels. Secondly, the research on Shakespeare's history plays has not yet formed a structured and systematic investigation, and there is a lack of in-depth study.

In conclusion, the literary critics all held different views on the interpretation of Shakespeare's history play. Nonetheless, no matter what kind of literary theory we use in the study on Shakespeare's history plays, there is no denying that Shakespeare combines the historical characters and past events based on historical records with the literary fiction based on shared knowledge and imagination so well. Therefore, this book tries to give a relatively complete analysis of Shakespeare's ten history plays by taking Shakespeare's fictional use of history as its primary concern.

1.3 Three Dimensions of Studying Shakespeare's Fictional Use of History

Shakespeare's ten history plays, on the one hand, are written in close relation to historiography; on the other hand, explore the domain of literary fiction by rearranging historical events and refashioning historical figures. This book aims to examine the deviation Shakespeare's history plays takes from the historical sources, and accounts for that deviation by using the critical perceptions and theories that tackle the relation between history and literature. The main questions of the study are: what are the fictional elements Shakespeare uses in history plays, what are the purposes of Shakespeare's fictional use of history and to what effect Shakespeare's fictional use of history achieves.

1.3.1 Fictional Elements in Shakespeare's History Plays

The long tradition defining literature in opposition to history dates back at least to the time of Aristotle. According to Aristotle, the cardinal difference between poetry (literature) and history is that "one relates what has happened, the other what may happen. Poetry, therefore, is a more philosophical and a higher thing than history" (2004: 17). Here Aristotle makes some clear distinctions straightaway. First of all, history, "relates what has happened" as opposed to poetry, which discusses "what may happen". History addresses that of the particular, and it is a way of cataloguing our past. Poetry, to Aristotle, addresses that of the universal, then is, "more philosophical and a higher thing". After Aristotle, there was a long time that the aims and methods of literature and history remained intertwined, and it was not until the eighteenth century that history and the philosophy of history came to be viewed as "respectable, well-defined disciplines distinct in aim, content, and method, from poetry" (Kamps 12). Over the years, most Western thinkers assume that the essence of proper historical narratives—their pattern, or progress, or direction, or system of causation—is contained in the historical events themselves. This essence is not considered to be the product of the historian's imagination; the essence of history is in the historical data themselves. On this account, it seems fair to conclude that the operations that lead to the production of history and that of drama differ fundamentally. Such a conclusion, however, is no longer compelling under the light of the more recent theoretical experiences of both literature and history.

New Historicism, in the growing calls to the "textuality of history" and "historicity of text", breaks down the traditional barriers between historical contexts and literary texts, which hence explains the dynamic process of the interaction between literature and history in the cultural systems adequately. Abandoning older conceptions of history as a "background" to literature or of literature as transcending the historical conditions that produced it, most New historicism critics argue for cultural equality between literary text and its socio-historical context which traditionally held to be extra-literary. While the New historicists promote the interplay or "exchanges" between literature and its cultural-historical milieu, it is also true that in their analysis the literary text is often overdetermined by a tangle of cultural/historical forces.

A new historicist essay will typically read a work by Shakespeare in conjunction with a contemporary account of New World exploration, such as a medical text, or a treatise on witchcraft. In doing so, it skips the analysis of the literary form and the artistic characteristics of the literary works. Theorists like Fredric Jameson have shown that literary forms and artistic conventions do not constitute static rhetorical paradigms that transmit without alternation through history; they are themselves social and ideological constructs with varying patterns and serve as significant registers of cultural transformation at distinct historical moments[①]. Therefore, despite New Historicism explores the

---

① Jameson elaborates this idea in different places in his book. Jameson, Fredric. *The Political Unconscious: Narrative as a Socially Symbolic Act*. London and New York: Methuen, 1981. See "identification of the ideologeme", pp. 77; "textual object is constructed by the third horizon of cultural revolution with the other two horizons—the symbolic act, and the ideologeme or dialogical organization of class discourse", pp. 84; "different generic confinement to the existent has a paradoxically liberating effect on the registers of the text", pp. 90.

hermeneutic freedom to the utmost, it still fails to provide a satisfactory interpretation of the nature of literature's relationship to history. We need to refer to a more comprehensive interpretive model which is sophisticated enough to explore this epistemological puzzle and to account for the fictional forces active in Shakespeare's creation of his dramatic texts.

In recent years, a number of postmodernism theoreticians, Hayden White among them, have called into question any stable distinction between the domains of the literature and history. For White, history and literature are not two distinct and opposed activities. History is about past events, which once were and are now gone. History is often understood in terms of its relationship to historical facts. According to Ritter, the editor of *Dictionary of Concepts in History*, historical fact is the factual basis that is generally believed to set history apart from fable, legend, and myth (225). Ritter further elaborates that "historical facts consist of historical events and historical figures. Both the historical events and the figures are the primary sources of history records" (226). Although the truth about the past is elusive and hard to achieve, we must confirm that the historical facts will always be there and cannot be denied.

Even though we all believe that historical facts exist, we can only know it through narrative. After all, history does not speak for itself, and all history is made by interpreting what we call historical facts that are deeply affected by the present time. Hayden White points out that the "facts" of history, "in their unprocessed, make no sense at all" (1978:82). In his book *Metahistory*, Hayden White further suggests that all historical "facts" come to us only in the form of narrative or language. Also, he treats the historical work as what it most manifestly is: a verbal structure in the form of a narrative prose discourse. Histories, he believes, combine a certain amount of the historical facts and the narrative structure for the presentation of the sets of events (1973: ix).

White further points out that the narrative can only make sense by using a literary technique "emplotment". Also, by using "emplotment", he means the encodation of the facts contained in the chronicle as components of specific kinds of plots.

According to White, the historian does not find his narrative in the historical facts; instead, he imposes a plot on the facts that will make the past accessible to the present, which is essentially a "literary" or "fiction-making" operation in literature (1978:85).

Since historiography and literature are both narratives, there are many common features between historians' practice in recording history and writers' use of the past in the postmodern context. "Emplotment" is precisely one of the methods Shakespeare applied in his writing. In his history plays, historical records are at once necessary and subject to revision and reshaping. We can see in *1 Henry VI* that Shakespeare simplifies and rearranges historical events in such a way as to arrange battles between Talbot and Joan of Arc. We can also see the insertion of a wholly fictional garden scene in *Richard II* mounting a critique of the King in the play. Not to mention, he also omits so many important historical events in his history plays. For example, Magna Carta, one of the essential constitutional achievements in English history, does not get a mention in Shakespeare's *King John*. So the first element of Shakespeare's fictional use of history is "emplotment", which includes the rearrangement, omission of historical events, and the insertion of new episodes from the historiographical writing.

Secondly, historiography, lacking the kind of "formal terminological system for describing its objects" that physics and chemistry have, rely on rhetorical or figurative language to construct its narratives in much the same way literature does (White 1978: 95). The language of both historiography and literature thus presuppose "figurative characterisations of the events they purport to represent and explain" (White 1978: 94). In this manner, both history and literature gain the revelation of the deeper meaning of the events that they depict through their characterisation. Georg Lukács, through careful examination, also advocates that the "characterisation" is one of the decisive factors in dramatist's representation of history. He articulates: "The struggle of true historical drama with the obstacles formed by what for art is the abstract appearance of things in history shows very clearly, in positive and negative examples, that the individuality of the **dramatic hero**①is the decisive problem" (112).

The characterisation in history plays can be split into two subsets: one is constituted by fictional persons having historical counterparts; the other consists of fictional persons without such counterparts. In the first subset, historical persons transform into fictional counterparts, thus becoming participants of interaction and communication with fictional persons. Dolezel argues, "In history plays, the historical migrants need to adjust to the semantic and pragmatic conditions of the fictional environment" (264).

In Shakespeare's history plays, Kings and most of the noblemen belong to the first subset of fictional characters. For example, Prince Hal and Hotspur are not the same age, and Shakespeare's sources Holinshed and Hall, do not present them as such. The historical Hotspur was about twenty years older than the Prince. Shakespeare deliberately makes them the same age to set the two young men in rivalry for dramatic contrast. Another example is *Richard III*. There are accounts for Richard III that do not present him as a villain, do not give him a hunchback and a withered arm. Shakespeare makes Richard a deformed villain and tyrant, exulting in his wickedness in *Richard III*, and that is the way Richard is remembered.

Although Shakespeare's history plays are named after kings, we should bear in mind that the kings themselves cannot put on a monologue or monodrama all through the theatrical performance, so there must be a great many characters to create the dramatic collision and promote the development of the plot. Here comes the second subset of characterisation—those fictional persons without counterparts in history. If we examine Shakespeare's history plays carefully, we would find out most of them are marginal people. The marginal characters can be further subdivided into two subsets: the first is the commoners, like the Son who killed his father and the Father who killed his son in *3 Henry VI*, the Gardener in *Richard II*, and the ordinary soldiers in *Henry V*. The second is the female characters, such as the Duchess of York in *Richard II*;

---

① The bold characters are original in the text.

Mistress Quickly and Doll Tearsheet in *Henry IV*. What is more, Sir John Falstaff, one of Shakespeare's most famous creations, amuses and amazes us; simultaneously, he aids and immerses in the making of history. Shakespeare's fictional characters have independent lives in the history plays, and they also provide the principal means by which Shakespeare investigates and constructs history.

In conclusion, Shakespeare's history plays occupy an overlapping region between history and literature, challenging the sharp distinction Aristotle in the *Poetics* draw between the imaginative artists or poet who can tell "what may happen" and the historian who is limited to relating what "has happened". Shakespeare's history plays, though based closely on Holinshed and Edward Hall's historiographical writing and thus tied to the realm of verifiable facts, show that there is plenty of room for the fictional use of history. In general, there are two major elements in Shakespeare's fictional use of history, they are "emplotment" and "characterisation", and the "characterisation" can be subdivided into those fictional characters that have historical counterparts and the fictional characters that have no counterparts in history.

1.3.2 Purposes of Shakespeare's Fictional Use of History

According to the "Intention Fallacy" theory of the New Criticism, a literary work is self-contained and self-sufficient because its meaning, structure and value are inherent within itself. The intention—the design and purposes—of its author is not enough to be the criterion for interpreting and evaluating the literary work. Indeed, the author's intention is not equal to the meaning of his works; however, whether the author's intention is equal to the implication of the literary work is one thing, and whether there exists the author's intention is quite another. In fact, the advocation of removing the "intention of the author and the affection of the reader from critical concern" already presupposes the existence of the author's intention (Zhu Gang 33)①. Moreover, the author's intention and the implication of the work are both the

---

① 朱刚.《二十世纪西方文艺批评理论》. 上海:上海外语教育出版社, 2001.

products of interpreting and hermeneutic activities, so the grasp of the author's intention is at least one of the important ways to understand the work of literature.

The dramatic fiction in history plays is a combination of historical and literary narrative, involves both the use of historiography and the fictional creation. It is an ongoing dialogue between history and the writing subject's re-constructional activities. Since it is a process of subjective construction, it would undoubtedly involve the author's intention. Ribner says that a history play is "an adaptation of drama to the purposes of history" (29), but therein lies the interpretive problem.

According to recent critical theories, the idea of history has been pluralised to accommodate the sense in which accounts of past events are different according to the position from where they are viewed, especially in terms of the ideological agendas that may lie behind the presentation of what appears to be an impartial view of historiography. Hayden White's theory of historiography as shaped by the "myth, fable, and folklore, scientific knowledge, religion, and literary art" supports the view of history-writing as a fundamentally ideological practice (1978:94). Traditionally, "ideology" refers to the system of ideas, values, and beliefs common to any social group; in recent years, this vexed but indispensable term has in its most general sense come to be associated with the processes by which social subjects are formed, re-formed and enabled to perform as conscious agents in an apparently meaningful world (Vesser 16). In Althusser's famous essay "Ideology and Ideological State Apparatuses," he points out that "ideology is a 'interpellate' of the imaginary relationship of individuals to their real conditions of existence" (qtd. in Eagleton 142).

For Althusser, written histories are always ideological even though the writers may not be consciously soliciting a particular political or religious point of view. Since Althusser defines ideology as the spontaneous "lived" relationship to the real conditions of existence, writing will always reveals at least certain ideological dimensions, no matter what the author's intention is. Therefore, the central point that needs to be made here is that both the historiography and drama are ideological in the

Althusserian sense.

Old Historicism, as represented by E. M. W. Tillyard, tends to conceive of Shakespeare's history plays as a mostly static and homogeneous background to the historical causation. Tillyard finds in the plays "a universally held" and "fundamentally religious" historical "scheme", which governed by divine providence, beginning with the "distortion of nature's course" in the deposition and murder of Richard Ⅱ and moving purposefully "through a long series of disasters and suffering and struggles" to the restoration of legitimacy and order under the Tudors (1962: 320-321)①. Tillyard's declaration can be construed as Althusserian in its understanding of the deterministic relationship between literature and ideology. Tillyard's understanding, however, is confined to the grand narrative that nonetheless delineates the rigid hierarchical Elizabethan World Picture and the Tudor Myth propagated by the ruling classes.

The fallacy of Old Historicism represented by Tillyard, according to New Historicism, is to view literary works as the autonomous body of fixed meanings that form an organic whole in which all conflicts ideologically resolve. The study of literary works should not universalise cultures and homogenise interpretation, on the contrary, New Historicists claimed, we should focus on the difference of cultures, races, classes, and genders to uncover a diversity of dissonant voices and the subversive forces of the era. Any text, according to New Historicists, although it may seem to present, or reflect, an external reality, in fact consists of what are called **representations**②—that is, the verbal formations which are the "ideological products" or "cultural constructs" of the historical conditions specific to an era

---

① E. M. W. Tillyard, *Shakespeare's History Plays* (London: Penguin Books, 1962), pp. 320-321. See also Lily B. Campbell, *Shakespeare's "Histories": Mirrors of Elizabethan Policy* (London: Methuen, 1964); Irving Ribner, *The English History Play in the Age of Shakespeare* (Princeton U. P. : Oxford U. P. , 1957).

② The bold characters are original in the text.

(Abrams 366-36)①. The striking idea is that historical narratives, as a set of competing stories, the most powerful of which survive at the expense of the less powerful, remark that "History loves only those who dominate her" (Rushdie 124). The relationship between history and power is an area that has been addressed by Michel Foucault, who replaces it with what he calls genealogy. For Foucault, genealogy differs from traditional history in that it tries to take account of the submerged narratives that have been discarded by the prevailing accounts of past. It is also keen to show how history is determined by the systems of what he calls "power/knowledge." Jago Morrison has summarised this well: "For Foucault, traditional history systematically works to suppress evidence of discontinuities, disjunctions and struggles between rival regimes of knowledge, because its overriding goal is to portray the present as the product of clear and traditional development. Genealogy, by contrast, is actively concerned to uncover evidence of alternative and submerged knowledge" (19). As can be seen from this description, the Foucaultian approach to history lends itself well to postmodern and poststructuralist ideas whereby a single unified account of the past is replaced by a plurality of contrasting and competing histories.

Although Foucault's approach to history is mainly discussed in the postmodern context, it is Jean-Francois Lyotard who finally makes explicit in *The Postmodern Condition* precisely what has changed. Lyotard, in the Introduction to his book, defines the postmodern condition as "incredulity toward metanarratives" (xxiv). In his works, the grand narrative is synonymous with metanarrative or master narrative. It refers to all those unified frameworks that presupposed the belief in the doctrine of God, reason, transcendental truth, and science. Lyotard is not opposed to narrative. Narration, after all, constructs objects of discourse, "object to be known, decided on, evaluated, [and] transformed" (18). However, he completely dismisses any totalising narrative. He holds that "the grand narrative has lost its credibility,

---

① M. H. 艾布拉姆斯. 文学术语词典（中英对照）. 北京：北京大学出版社，2009.

regardless of what mode of unification it uses, regardless of whether it is a speculative narrative or a narrative of emancipation" (37). Lyotard supplants the generalisation of grand narrative with "petit récits," the little stories which are in his analysis "the quintessential form of imaginative invention" (60). According to Lyotard, the petit récits lay no claim to extra-discursive authority, to mastery or the absolutism of narrative. They acknowledge the process that Derrida calls "difference," by which signifying practice itself necessarily differentiates and distances all that is extra-linguistic (qtd. in Belsey 29). The postmodern project tells short stories that are nevertheless stories of change and that activate the differences.

In the postmodern context, the authority of the grand narrative, which has meant so much to the over-reaching narrative schema of history, indeed falls and so the falsely static and totalising single-story goes destroyed. Although written at the end of the sixteenth century, Shakespeare's history plays regularly invite the new concerns of representation and analysis. In fact, Shakespeare constantly "makes" histories, and especially in the mature period of his dramatic career. The grand narrative of one unified history is now capable of being replaced by the petit récits of discrete individual texts, which not only indicate the ideological instability of late sixteenth-century culture but also detail the discontinuity and fragmentation under the light of the postmodern condition.

The characterisation as a form of fiction-making, in fact, emerges as a motive force of "petit récit" in Shakespeare's historical universe. In Tillyard's grand narrative of history, characters are subordinated to the paradigmatic expressions of universal rules in history. However, fictional characters, especially the marginal ones including commoners and women, provide petit récits of hybrid histories in Shakespeare's history plays. They play the role of human agencies that motivate the action of history rather than advocate the grand narrative of transcendental teleology.

In Shakespeare's first trilogy, the vivid particularities of Joan of Arc, Jack Cade, and Queen Margaret open many fault lines in the grand narrative of the heroic, poetic and secular history. In the transitional plays, the brilliant characters the Bastard in

King John and the unique mother figure the Duchess of York in *Richard II* oppose to the constraining agenda and pursue their own histories. In the second trilogy, although characters like Falstaff and Mistress Quickly exhibit many of the traits that marked their dramatic antecedents, they are no longer contained by the dramatic hierarchy, and finally occupy the centre-stage in Shakespeare's history plays. All those fictional marginal characters provide a wide variety of viewpoints not only about politics but also about public morals. Examined from a postmodern perspective, they call into question the very instability of ideology and simultaneously make their own histories by themselves. The "petit récits" of those fictional marginal characters provide an interpretative context capable of recognising different histories of the once stable structure. What is more, the inclusion of invented characters in historical plots allows the conflation of various points of view and the orchestration of diverse discourses, conventions, and languages. This hybrid model of fiction highlights discrepancies and conflicts of interest, introducing differences (social, linguistic, and other) of historical experience and thus foregrounding a multiplicity of "histories".

To conclude, the purpose of Shakespeare's ten history plays cannot be concluded merely as a grand narrative of "Tudor Myth" or the "Elizabethan Picture." Instead of producing a notion of historical totality, Shakespeare invites an alternative concept of a fragmentary and discontinuous series of historical differences by producing the dynamic and on-going interactions between history and fiction in his history plays.

1.3.3 Effects of Shakespeare's Fictional Use of History

Written at the end of the sixteenth century, Shakespeare's history plays occupy various sites of contention between older and newer conceptions of history and between the emergent distinctions that define history and drama (literature) in terms of mutual opposition. The very act of adapting historical records for theatrical performance complicates the relationship between literary fiction and historical representation. With the pressures of the cultural changes that given to the appealing dramatic enterprise at that time, it is not surprising that Shakespeare's history plays prove increasingly attractive to the discussions towards the representation and pursuit of "truth".

Thomas Courtenay, for example, proclaims that he could find no "authority for the use of the roses themselves, as an especial and popular symbol" (42) in Shakespeare's history plays. Courtenay proceeds by comparing the events of Shakespeare's plays to the chronicle sources, with the intent of showing that Shakespeare did not dramatise history accurately. Belsey, too, recognising Shakespeare's history plays as brilliant fictions, argues that they are "art, not life, imagination and not the truth" (24). These accounts take for granted that Shakespeare's history plays are only imaginative reports of things that may not even have happened and found them wanting in truth. However, "truth" as disinterested and value-free objectivity is not at this point. One need to judge Shakespeare by standards fitting his profession and time. In order to discuss the question of "truth" in Shakespeare's history plays, one needs to refer back to the critical perceptions dominant at the time which tackles the relation between history and poetry (literature), namely, the classical model for the employment of history in drama established in Aristotle's *The Poetics*, and also Sir Philip Sidney's *Defense of Poesy*, the canonical critical piece in the sixteenth-century.

There seem to be two types of truth, poetic and historical. In Chapter Nine of his *The Poetics*, Aristotle distinguishes the historical truth that the historians aim to have and the poetic truth that the poet treats of:

> It is not the function of the poet to relate what has happened, but what may happen—what is possible according to the law of probability or necessity. The poet and the historian differ not by writing in verse or in prose. The true difference is that one relates what has happened, the other what may happen. Poetry, therefore, is a more philosophical and a higher thing than history: for poetry tends to express the universal, history the particular. By the universal I mean how a person of a certain type on occasion speak or act, according to the law of probability or necessity; and it is this universality at which poetry aims in

the names she attaches to the personages. (2004:17)

What Aristotle wants to express is that the poet does not deal with things as they had happened in the past. To do so would be the work of the historian. Aristotle agrees that poetry presents not facts, but fiction. But this does not make poetry "unreal" or "untrue".

The poet sifts his material, selects the most relevant portions, imposes order and design on the chaotic materials of life and universalises the particular. In this it becomes "ideal"; it presents something as it might have been, or ought to be, according to the law of probability and necessity. What is more, poetry deals with universal, basic elements in human nature, the ever-lasting, permanent possibilities of human life. The historian, on the other hand, is restricted to the particular happenings or the existent facts. Therefore, poetic truth is philosophical in the sense that it is the universal possibility of human nature, whereas historical truth is empirical in the sense that it is only correspondence between singular facts and the dealing of it, and thus poetic truth is higher than the historical truth.

Similarly, Sidney idealises the true poet. Indeed, the poet's manipulation of history is excused for effecting positive change in social conduct. Sir Philip Sidney claims:

> To that which commonly is attributed to the praise of history, in respect of the notable learning is got by marking the success, as though therein a man should see virtue exalted and vice punished—truly that commendation is particular to poetry, and far off from history. For indeed poetry ever sets virtue so out in her best colours, making Fortune her well-waiting handmaid, that one must need be enamoured of her [...] But the history, being captivated to the truth of a foolish world, is many times a terror from well-doing, and an encouragement to unbridled wickedness. (21)

Like Aristotle, Sidney also emphasises the importance of the imagination in the creation of art; poets rely not simply on what they see around them, but also on that inner quality that gives them the capacity to create people, places, situations, and emotions much like those of the everyday world, but in some ways better or worse, to serve as models for human behaviour. So for Sidney, poetic fiction of events in history, rather than a falsification of truth, is essential an action in turning the knowledge of a historical incident into a fruitful lesson that reinstates the poetic truth "in effect another nature, in making things either better than nature brings forth, or quite anew" (7).

The distinction drawn by Aristotle and Sidney between poetry and history may be extended to fictional literature such as the history play. For the history play, although follows history in its outlines even if it departs from facts in details, is about particular persons who live at a particular time and in a particular place. Hence, in reading a history-based literature creation, one should not only focus on the artist's deviation from particular incidents but also pay attention to the overall effects they achieve. Such is a proper ground for the study of Shakespeare's history plays.

Depending on such historical records as Holinshed's *The Chronicle of England* and Hall's *The Union of the Two Noble Families of Lancaster and York*, Shakespeare's ten history plays invariably reconfigure the historiography, transforming the narrative, or a set of narratives into a compressed dramatic representation. His ten history plays are each so different in their use of historical records and explore different ways of narrating and constructing the past. The individual play can hardly be taken as reliable accounts of the historical material they represent. The fact that many passages in the plays are close adaptations of Holinshed and Hall's chronicles, of course, means certain constraints upon the author, who cannot alter facts that are widely known, for example, in a story about King Richard Ⅲ, Richard has to be deposed and replaced by King Henry Ⅶ. Nevertheless, Shakespeare deviates from chronicle resources by the selection, insertion and omission of historical events and by his invention or reinvention of characters with or without precedent in the historical records. The plays are thus full of inaccuracies and anachronisms, which means that the quest for "historical truth"—the exact correspondence between historical facts and Shakespeare's representation would never be achieved. However, the characters and events sometimes appear so authentic in Shakespeare's history plays that the readers or audiences almost take them for real ones. The Duke of Marlborough, as Coleridge relates, was "not ashamed to confess that his principal acquaintance with English history was derived from Shakespeare's plays" (1959:223). So it is significant to realise that Shakespeare's history plays, though not attempting to uncover the truth of the past, achieve another concept of truth by his literary fiction.

There is a playwright George Chapman with his poet's intuition, in his "Epistle Dedicatory" furthers Aristotle's reasoning, and assigns to literary fiction a distinct role in history plays:

> Moreover, for the authentical truth of either person or action, who (worth the respecting) will expect it in a poem, whose subject is not truth, but things like truth? Poor envious souls they are that cavil at truth's want in these natural fictions: material instruction, elegant and sententious excitation to virtue, and deflection from her contrary, being the soul, limbs, and limits of an authentic tragedy. (20-21)

Here, George Chapman highlights the oxymoronic and mixed quality of literary fiction, to which he gives the name of "natural fictions." Such a notion of truth not only implies the exploitation of fictional procedures but also, especially in the practice of postmodernism, what Hayden White called "the fictions of factual representation" (1978:122). And it seems that the function can be attributed to the fictional characters and incidents in Shakespeare's history plays.

One example brings out the humanistic and historical importance is the fictional commoners in Shakespeare's history plays. Some critics argue that Shakespeare's characterisation is mainly about the Tudor rulers, who being the legitimate kings of

England, promotes the monarchy, teaches lessons of political obedience and warns of the evils of rebellion, while the common ones and ignoble ones are largely contained in the grand narrative of monarchies, prescribed in an unfavourable way. Professor W. H, Auden even argues in his *Lectures on Shakespeare* that:

> In fact, Shakespeare rarely presents the people (understood as a collective) in a positive light. The history plays do include exemplary commoners, figures like the Gardener in *Richard II*, Alexander Iden in *2 Henry VI*, the soldiers and gamekeepers in *3 Henry VI* and the English soldiers Bates, Court and Williams in *Henry V*, but these characters, plain, pragmatic and decent, come into focus only to the degree that they resist absorption by their social group. (2000:65)

If one examines these characters carefully, one will find out that all the commoners Auden mentioned are the fictional characters created by Shakespeare. It is incomprehensive to dismiss the fictional commoners (the collective common) as priceless characters in the play. More often than not, it is those fictional commoners, the low-born artisans, gardeners, and scriveners provide the clue to the audience to look sceptically at the actions of high-born kings and royalties. Moreover, Shakespeare's histories, instead of being monolithic propaganda of political intentions, are complex narratives because they demonstrate how history is marked by continuous dissent and discord, betrayal and injustice. One can see kings being too are frail and often simply evil. Richard III cleverly figures himself as a qualified king; however, the fictional Scrivener points out his villainy of killing innocent Lord Hastings. The fictional character Bastard raises questions about political legitimacy that who indeed has the right to rule, and with his brave acts, down-to-earth common sense, the audiences are almost drawn to wish he be the king. Henry V is a troubling one even as he is mostly a charismatic, attractive figure celebrating the glories of England. His fiery patriotic speeches addressing people's nationalist feelings is actually countered by one of his "band of brothers"—the fictional common soldier Williams' accusation on

Henry V's cheating behaviour.

In this sense, it might as well be said that fictional characters' weight is inversely proportional to their numbers: although they appear only sparsely and marginally, on the one hand, they do endanger the singular historical truth of the grand narrative in which they take part and on the other hand, they create a new imaginary world which does not necessarily duplicate what the historical records state; rather, they bring out the possible and probable variations of the historical world to make their own histories. Their presence, therefore, produces a peculiar exchange of validation moving between what is true and what is fictitious, between the prescriptions of historiography and the necessities of poetry.

In general, poetry is more philosophic and deals with the universal truth of human nature, whereas history deals in historical truth; history tells us only what did happen whereas poetry tells us what might happen or what would happen to such characters in such situations as those depicted. Moreover, this is even true of prose and drama no less than of poetry. It may explain the reason why the great novel may often come closer to the reality of a society or a culture than a historical text. The same is true of Shakespeare's history plays with the fictional elements, which throw into relief the dullness of mere empirical historical facts. In Belsey's words, "art is dazzling where history is drab". Holding the mirror up to history, Shakespeare must have realised that history as historiography is insufficient, inferior to, and less true than, history in his plays. Shakespeare's history plays are the "literature of fact", or as Hayden White puts it, "the fictions of factual representation" (1978: 122). In this sense, Shakespeare's history plays have access to a higher and universal form of truth—the poetic truth.

Chapter Two Emergence of the Fictional Use of History: Questioning the Grand Narrative of History

Although Shakespeare's history plays elicit a lot of discussions, they have always been read as constructing an integrated narrative scheme about the "national history of England". Coleridge argued that the English national history aroused "a steady patriotism, a love of just liberty, and a respect for all those fundamental institutions of social life, which bind men together" (165). Tillyard took Coleridge's argument further by proposing that Shakespeare's history plays aim to reveal a universal commitment to the hierarchical order. The order Tillyard described in *The Elizabethan World Picture* was much more than political order, or, "if political, was a part of a larger cosmic order", and he believed the idea of order can be applied to Shakespeare's Histories as well as to Elizabethan literature generally (1943: v). Tillyard argued in another book *Shakespeare's History Plays*: "The picture we get from Shakespeare's Histories is that of disorder", and the only solution to this is the universal acceptance of the great ideal of hierarchy (1962: 15). Shakespeare's history plays, he insisted, look to a grand narrative of the Tudor history which legitimates Tudor rulers' precarious but deeply autocratic rule (1962: 65).

Behind Tillyard's legitimation of order and autocracy in history is the ideological certainty held by the old historicism. In Shakespeare's early history plays, the visual and verbal imageries of the chaos centre on the bloodlines of battle and murder embodied by the mere force of characters. Tillyard tried to use many characters to illustrate his ideas, and his examples include Talbot, Joan of Arc in *1 Henry VI*, Jack

Cade in *2 Henry VI*, and the Son-Father scene in *3 Henry VI* ①. However, if examined carefully, these fictional or semi-fictional figures perform not as straightforward expressions of a unified history, on the contrary, they consistently mock and parody the government's ideological practice on the heroic, political and secular levels, and thus the "continuous and coherent" grand narrative of a national history is radically undermined. The tension between the surface meanings of the historical events and the fictional individual's action deconstructs the unified coherence and opens several fault-lines in the grand narrative.

2.1 *1 Henry VI*: The Interrogation to the Heroic History

Where the historiographies impose order on the chaos of historical facts in the formulations of cause and effect, the dramatists shift the sequence of events around and make changes to achieve specific effects. Shakespeare's history plays not only rewrite the historical past for the Elizabethan present but also invent and revise many ones to fit with his dramatic intentions. In other words, history in Shakespeare's plays is often de-historicised by using fiction: with the addition of fictive characters and events, and an imaginative rearrangement of chronology. Although his primary sources for his history plays are Hall and Holinshed's Chronicles, Shakespeare for his histories appropriates, selects or omits historical events from Hall and Holinshed to dramatise how the past might have been.

---

① See Tillyard, *Shakespeare's History Plays* (1962). pp. 163, "the action revolves round Talbot⋯he stands pre-eminently for loyalty and order in a world threatened by chaos"; pp. 158, "Shakespeare also satisfied the popular taste in setting forth the great popular political theme⋯Joan of Arc is a bad enough woman, Margaret of Anjou an intriguing enough queen"; pp. 76, "there is a terrible sense of the stars' power combined with a precise orthodox doctrine of that power's limit. The problem of fortune and the stars is raised and answered by Jack Cade" and more cases please refer to Chapter One: the Cosmic Background.

J. P. Brockbank makes a general assessment about *Henry VI* plays: "Shakespeare's early histories are addressed primarily to the audience's heroic sense of community, to its readiness to belong to an England represented by its court and its army, to its eagerness to enjoy a public show celebrating the continuing history of its prestige and power" (75). However, if we examine *1 Henry VI* in the light of Shakespeare's dramatic fiction, we would find that the conclusion is hardly convincing. The repeated interruptions, violations, and other undermining of the formality—from the first scene on—bring into question the static conception of history that the chronicles assume as monumental and ceremonial, and map out a deflation of heroism both in and outside England.

2.1.1 Party Politics: The Deflation of Heroism in the Nation

As a playwright, Shakespeare seems more intent upon the imagined working of history than the specific historical chronicles or locations. According to White, historians are concerned with events which can be assigned to specific time-space locations, events which are (or were) in principle observable or perceivable, whereas imaginative writers—poets, novelists, playwrights—are concerned with both these kinds of events and imagined, hypothetical, or invented ones (1978:121). And that is indeed what Shakespeare does with his early history plays—the first trilogy of *Henry VI* plays. Holinshed is freely used in all three parts of *Henry VI*, but *1 Henry VI* is the one which treats Holinshed's narrative most boldly.

Most of the material in the first scene of *1 Henry VI* may come from either Hall or Holinshed, but the writer uses some passages found only in Holinshed. The visible evidence is the number "full scarce six thousand" agreeing with Holinshed's "not past six thousand" (qtd. in Bullough, 1960a: 26). The actual time span of *1 Henry VI* is over thirty years (1422-1453). However, the dramatist deliberately brings together terrible events from many subsequent years to suggest that Henry V's death brings the end of English victories and is the beginning of internal strife. The play begins with the funeral of Henry V (1422) to symbolise the end of an epoch, and this is followed by news from France that many important towns including Paris (1436) have lost, the Dauphin crowned King at Rheims (1429). Bedford goes to strengthen the siege of Orleans (1428-9), and Winchester tells the audience that he intends to seize the new King (1425). Thus the first funeral ceremony, being a fictional ritual which should have celebrated the heroic history of the glorious king, grows into a force that will destroy the basis of English power in France.

In the first scene, we are told that the legendary warrior-king Henry V was "too famous to live long" (*1 Henry VI* 1.1.6)①. The royal successor is notably absent. The infant Henry VI is unseen and rarely mentioned until the third act. In the first sixteen lines, the play is appropriately ceremonial in lamenting the great loss of a hero, yet the other few lines, such as "bad revolting stars,/ That have consented unto Henry's death" (1.1.4-5) introduces a fallen world and "comets, importing change of times and states" (1.1.2) suggests that further disasters would come. Exeter, the uncle of Henry V, tries to direct the ceremony by calling for action: "We mourn in black: why mourn we not in blood? /Henry is dead and never shall revive" (1.1.17-18). This realism is soon cut through by a quarrel between the Bishop of Winchester and the Protector Gloucester. Winchester accuses Gloucester's wife of being too proud, and Gloucester accuses the former of not only refusing to support his wars in France, but seeking power in the secular realm. The solemn ceremony has given way to the open hostility between the aristocratic relatives of the deceased king. Their struggle for power has displaced the concern for the welfare of the nation. Bedford tries to play the peace-maker, but while he prays for civil peace, a sequence of messengers announce progressively more disastrous events in France, and together herald the fears that all that Henry V won might be lost. The glory of English conquest

---

① All quotations of Shakespeare's texts in this book are from the The Third Arden Edition. For detailed information please refer to Bibliography by the entry of "Shakespeare, William". When the quotations are used from the same Shakespeare's text in each section of this book, the name of the text would only appear once and the following in-text citations would omit the name of that text.

is doomed even before its warrior-king has been laid to rest.

The first messenger openly criticise the aristocrats for their inaction—"Awake, awake, English nobility!" (1.1.78). Also, the second and last messenger reports the imprisonment of Talbot, the great English general. The scene ends with a series of activities: Bedford will assemble a new army to fight in France; Gloucester will go to the Tower to examine the artillery and prepare the proclamation of young Henry as King; Exeter will hasten to safeguard young Henry. After the three's exits, Winchester remains onstage to plot:

> Each hath his place and function to attend.
> I am left out; for me nothing remains.
> But long I will not be Jack out of office.
> The king from Eltham I intend to steal,
> And sit at chiefest stern of public weal. (1.1.173-77)

The self-serving soliloquy of the Bishop of Winchester turns the solemn remembrances of Henry V's heroic history to a world of machinations, by which the seemingly honourable aristocrats compete to steal the public wealth. This pattern of dramatic construction will often repeat in the *Henry VI* plays until the dignity and significance of the heroic history being upset in every regard by the aristocrat's struggle for power.

At the end of this fictional scene, the dramatist reintroduces the bitter feud between Gloucester and Winchester. Gloucester's men in blue coats give Winchester's men in tawny coats a beating; the Mayor of London and his officers interrupt, but the fight continues. Finally, Gloucester and Winchester reconciled, but each of them is provided with an aside to underscore the sincerity of the reconciliation. Exeter, with his insight for the gloom and darkness to come, ends the scene with a prophecy of "base and envious discord" (1.187-201).

The Temple Garden scene (2.4), which dramatises the beginning of the Wars of the Roses, has no precedent in the Chronicles and is likely a Shakespeare's invention①. It initiates another set of factions and further trivialises the motives of the aristocrats. In this scene, two powerful men—the Duke of York and the Duke of Somerset, urge the nobles to pluck a red or white rose as a symbol of their political alliance with the York or Lancaster families respectively. We should notice that, historically, the red rose was a Tudor, not a Lancastrian emblem; the white rose belonged initially to the Mortimers. Shakespeare not only assigns the red and white roses to York and Lancaster as the family motifs respectively but also relates the dominant symbols closely to "truth". "The truth appears so naked on my side," declares York, "Than any purblind eye may find it out" (2.4.20-21). "And on my side," replies Somerset, it is "so clear, so shining, and so evident/ That it will glimmer through a blind man's eye" (2.4.22-24). While each party takes his own belief as truth and denounce the other party's badge, the word "truth" shifts emblematically throughout the scene. Somerset insists on a combative definition of truth: wearing the badge of the red rose is the truth or loyalty—loyalty to him, involving assent to his definition of reality. "The truth" in that sense is "the party of the truth" (2.4.32). York is claiming possession of truth as peculiarly his own by introducing the term "true-born" (2.4.27), which will rebound on him later by Somerset's taunt (2.4.90-3) that York's "true" father, genealogically, was "untrue" in being condemned a traitor, and so the cause of York's loss of his "true" title. The Temple Garden scene shows how the War of the Roses might have originated, and it reveals how the shallow noblemen turn a historical moment into a form of party politics, counting roses to decide upon the truth. In the end, both sides assembled their supporters and proceeded to the full-blown faction and feud.

The next time we see the parties at each other's throats is in the royal presence,

---

① According to Bullough's verifications, although there is no record of this scene in the chronicles, the plucking of the roses may be founded on an old legend, perhaps in an allegorical poem. For more information please see Bullough, *Narrative and Dramatic Sources of Shakespeare*, vol.3, pp. 27-28.

where their feud took by their followers, Vernon and Bassett. The two clients demand to be allowed to settle their dispute in violent combat. Only now does King Henry VI join in and he attempts to resolve this dispute by putting on a red rose and by making York and Somerset share the generalship of the English forces in France. The "solution" provides another false reconciliation and aggravates the divisions among the noblemen. The results, of course, are disastrous. England suffers a calamitous defeat because Somerset and York cannot cooperate their movements to come to the relief of the heroic Talbot and his son. As the messenger Lucy laments, the internal divisions amongst the English nobility are more responsible for the death of the two Talbots and the loss of France than the forces and skills of the French.

Throughout the play, the internal dissensions, the rivalries for power, the factions and feuds of the nobility remain unappeased and uncontrolled, and, because they are unappeased and uncontrolled, they undermine the epoch of a glorious heroic history made by Henry V. If the play's fictional arrangement about the noblemen is with political factionalism and scheming at home, the French woman Joan of Arc shows the aristocratic code of heroic virtue is only an illusion in the grand English history narrative.

2.1.2 Joan of Arc: A Radical Challenge to the Heroic Values

Epitomised by the significant volumes of Edward Hall and Raphael Holinshed, the sixteenth-century chronicle was, in Richard Helgerson's words, "the genre of national self-representation" that popularise the nation's past for the reading public (11). But what images of the nation present by these texts? As Rackin argued, women received little attention in "the ideologically motivated discourse" of the Tudor chronicles: "Renaissance historiography constituted a masculine tradition, written by men, devoted to the deeds of men, glorifying the masculine virtues of courage, honour, and patriotism, and dedicated to preserving the names of past heroes and recording their patriarchal genealogies" (1990:147). However, this kind of effort is countered in *1 Henry VI* by the French Woman, Joan of Arc. She subverts the inherited notions of chivalric glory invoked by Talbot and acts as a counterforce against the patriarchal historical record. Specifically speaking, in *1 Henry VI*, Shakespeare invites a reconsideration of the politics of gender by interrupting—and at times even inverting—the anticipated patterns of patriarchal history in which heroic Talbot triumph over the sensual French woman Joan.

1 Henry VI, which is probably the earliest of Shakespeare's English history plays, takes so many liberties with the chronicle account of historical events that Bullough calls it "a fantasia on historical themes" rather than a historical drama (1960a:25). The historical Joan's career (Joan died in 1431) was over long before Talbot's death (Talbot died in 1453), and disaster did not strike England so soon after the death of Henry V. However, Shakespeare deviates from historical time and events purposefully. In *1 Henry VI*, not only is chronological time disarrayed, but the account of historical events is mixed with a good deal of invention. A chronological table① of the historical events indicates the play's manipulation of them:

    1422   Death of Henry V (1.1)

    1429   Talbot captured at Patay. (1.1)

    Henry the Sixth crowned at Westminster. (1.1)

    1430   Joan captured. (5.2)

    1431   Henry crowned in France. Joan burned. (4.1, 5.4)

    1432   Henry returns to England. Peace negotiations at Cambrai. (5.3)

    1436   York appointed regent of France. (4.3)

    1442   Proposed marriage of Henry to the daughter of Armagnac. (5.1)

    1444   Suffolk in France to arrange the marriage of Henry and Margaret, daughter of Reignier, King of Naples. (5.2)

---

① For more information of the table please refer to Shakespeare, William. *King Henry VI Part 1*. Edward Burns ed. The Arden Shakespeare, 2000. pp. 23-25.

1445　Henry and Margaret married. (5.4)

1448　French siege of Le Mans; the English concede Maine to the French. (*2 Henry VI*)

1449　The French take Rouen. Talbot is captured, then released. (3.2, 1.1)

1453　The French recapture Bordeaux. Death of Talbot. (4.4)

As can be seen from the table, the playwright makes Talbot and Joan's careers more closely parallel in time and assigns battles to them. This opposition has been understood by Kittredge as to moralise the national and masculine history. For Kittredge, the editor of *The Complete Works of Shakespeare*, Talbot "represents the forces of England and righteousness," whereas Joan "the forces of demonic malice" (665). The opposition also supports reading of the play as a political-heroic history, in which Talbot "represent English chivalry" and Joan "the forces that threaten the aristocratic ideal of military service and gentle blood" (Riggs 105). However, if examined carefully, one can find the fictive Joan-Talbot opposition is indeed a contest between the masculine English record that Talbot wishes to preserve and the physical reality that Joan invokes to discredit it. Joan's action to erase the English record operates at two levels. On the one hand, her fight drives the English from France at the level of dramatic action. On the other hand, at the rhetorical level, she attacks the English version of heroic values with an earthy iconoclasm and subverts the inherited notions of chivalric glory represented by Talbot.

The play begins with the funeral of Henry V in which Bedford implies that the dead king will occupy a place in history and even more glorious than Julius Caesar's (1.1.56). Bedford's effort at retrieving heroic past is interrupted by Joan, who identifies herself as the "disperser" of Henry V's heroic legacy:

JOAN. Assigned am I to be the English scourge,
Glory is like a circle in the water,
Which never ceaseth to enlarge itself

Till by broad spreading, it disperse to nought.

With Henry's death the English circle ends;

Dispersed are the glories it included.

Now am I like that proud insulting ship

Which Caesar and his fortune bare at once. (1.2.129-39)

Joan's effort at erasing the English heroic history-making operates firstly on a physical level. The historical Joan never fought hand-to-hand and indeed claimed at her trial that she had never killed anyone (Warner 68). However, in *1 Henry VI*, the playwright not only assigns Joan face-to-face encounters with male warriors but also makes her appear as an Amazon.

The Amazons are a mythical race of women warriors in the ancient mythology, mentioned by Homer in the *Iliad* as having fought on the Trojan side at Troy. In the traditional stories, the triumph has always been with the male warrior over the alien Amazons, linking the hero's victory to the defence of the patriarchal historical recording. Borrowing from this tradition, Shakespeare gives it an unusual form by allowing Joan to triumph over her male opponents. Joan's initial entrance onto the stage leads to armed conflicts. Announcing herself as a maid divinely chosen to "free my country from calamity" (1.2.81), this shepherd's daughter invites the Dauphin of France Charles to try her courage by combat. The Dauphin takes up the challenge, but within minutes, he lies at Joan's feet. "Thou art an Amazon," exclaims Charles, "and fightest with the sword of Deborah" (1.2.104-5). Joan is equally formidable in her first encounter with Talbot, again in single combat. The stage direction presents her as "driving Englishmen before her". Like the Dauphin, Talbot attributes Joan's power to her Amazonian physicality. Talbot is disarmed by her "unnatural powers": "My thoughts are whirled like a potter's wheel, /I know not where I am, nor what I do" (1.5.19-20). Not only is Talbot unable to defeat the armed woman in a single combat, but Joan also "scorn[s] [Talbot's] strength" (1.5.15) and leaves him for other conquests. In the battle of Orleans, it is Joan who has "played the m[a]n" (1.

5.16). By contrast, Talbot and his men "cry[s] run away" (1.5.26) from the battlefield.

In staging Joan's confrontations with chivalric warriors, the play revises the traditional images of long-tongued women and physically strong men in Elizabethan time. But what is noticeable is that the play also alludes to Joan as a whore and witch. The re-creation is so libellous (the historical Joan was made Saint Joan after her death) that makes it an uneasy position within the framework of chronicle history.

The most noticeable references are to her sexual liberalism. The innuendos begin when she first meets the Dauphin. She claims that "I must not yield to any rites of love/ For my profession's sacred from above" (1.2.113-14), but later she is openly the Dauphin's mistress. She is known as La Pucelle (the Maid), but Talbot calls her "Puzel or pussel" in a mocking manner(1.4.106). The phrase is generally used to mean "virgin or whore," offering ironic proximity to the double perspectives on Joan—a virgin or a prostitute. Consider, too, the contrasting style of death for Joan and Talbot. While Talbot embraces death heroically with his son on the battlefield, Joan degenerates into a slut before her accusers. Denying her mortal parentage and thereby provoking the curse of her shepherd father, she desperately proclaims herself with a child to save her life, implicating, in turn, the Dauphin, Alencon, and Reignier. However, Joan of Arc's many ignoble deeds are taken over by Shakespeare from Holinshed.

To an enemy, Joan's nickname, La Pucelle (the Maid) was an invitation to crude slander, and Holinshed followed his dry allusion to her "great semblance of chastity both of body and behaviour" with the assertion that to save her life, she "stake[s] not [⋯] to confess herself a strumpet, and (unmarried as she was) to be with child"①(qtd. in Bullough 1960a: 41). The portrait of Joan as a loose woman who

---

① The spellings are rewritten into modern English by the writer of this book. The original lines in Holinshed's texts are "great semblance of chastitie both of bodie and behaviour", "stake[s] not…to confesse herselfe a strumpet, and (unmarried as she was) to be with child".

indulged in "devilish witchcraft and sorceries" and would deny her father because of his low birth is taken from the historiography, whereas Joan's dramatic voices are quite representative of Shakespeare's fictional creation. Joan speaks with distinctive voices that emerge from the undifferentiated blank verse that constitutes most of the dialogue. The lively particularity of Joan's dramatic voices poses most of the threats to the heroic values associated with the national history of masculine fame and glory.

Unable to commit to the convention, Joan is also uncommitted to the ethical stereotypes that structure the consciousness of other characters. Joan's speech constantly invites scepticism at the very moments when values need affirmation. It can be seen in her comment after her eloquent speech has persuaded Burgundy to return to the French: "Done like a Frenchman: turn and turn again" (3.3.85). It is characteristic of her persistent demystification of cherished idealisms. As an iconoclasm, she does not even spare her own achievements once she has finished with her original claim. Her conversation with Burgundy uses a different mode but achieves a similar effect. While Burgundy extols Talbot for his "noble deeds as valour's monuments" (3.2.118), Joan presents a picture that "the cities and the towns defaced/ By wasting ruin of the cruel foe" (3.3.45-46) and forces Burgundy to look at the enemy "as looks the mother on her lowly babe/ When death doth close his tender dying eyes" (3.3.47-48). We should also recall her sardonic response to the conception of heroic chivalry mentioned by Sir William Lucy's epitaph for Talbot. Learning that Talbot has died, Lucy, the messenger who is searching for Talbot, recites Talbot's titles of honour:

> Valiant Lord Talbot, Earl of Shrewsbury,
> Created, for his rare success in arms,
> Great Earl of Washford, Waterford and Valence;
> Lord Talbot of Goodridge and Urchinfield,
> Lord Strange of Blackmere, Lord Verdun of Alton,
> Lord Cromwell of Wingfield, Lord Furnival of Sheffield,

> The thrice-victorious Lord of Falconbridge;
> Knight of the noble order of Saint George,
> Worthy Saint Michael and the Golden Fleece;
> Great marshal to Henry the Sixth
> Of all his wars within the realm of France? (4.4.173-183)

Lucy describes Talbot as a history decked in the titles, and he designates Talbot's patriarchal lineage to heroic military achievements (Rackin 153). Nonetheless, Joan cuts into Lucy's funeral oration with an incisive sarcasm: "Here is a silly-stately style indeed! [...] / Him that thou magnifies with all these titles/ Stinking and fly-blown lies here at our feet" (4.4.184-188). The sarcasm in its rhetorical effects balances the melodramatic excess of the English and at the same time consumes whatever chivalric pretence might remain in the romanticism of war. As Lucy continues his laments of Talbot's death, Joan's scorn to Lucy's request for the Talbot's bodies underlines the iconoclastic nature of the heoric value. Lucy speaks in such a proud and controlling way that Joan feels Lucy is such an arrogant person as "old Talbot's ghost". She lets him have the bodies, because "they would but stink, and putrefy the air" (4.4.199-202).

Again, at the feet of the living French woman Joan lays the lifeless Talbots, the last remnants of the age of chivalry and the faded glories of Henry V. Although Talbot is the play's ostensible hero, it is Joan who expresses most forcefully both the vanity of all heroic values and the unorthodox humanistic perspectives.

In general, the semi-fictional Joan is untraditional. She has so much courage and resources to overcome Dauphin in combat and even quells Talbot momentarily. Beside her, the other French leaders are but shadows. Her physical transgressions dramatically underscore the English effort of history-making. Also, the rhetorical richness of Joan's speech rejects any masculine heroic ideals that a "national self-representation" can invoke. Joan of Arc, therefore, is the proof of fictional elements that ruptures the heroic history.

2.2 2 *Henry VI*: The Interrogation to the National Politics

Shakespeare's ficitonal use of history reproduces historical incidents with alterations here and there. Although Shakespeare does not minimise the force of unexpected events, his emphasis is also on characters, especially those invented or reinvented ones. As mentioned above, Shakespeare starts his revision of history by writing Joan as the rival of Talbot. Because according to the Chronicles, Talbot died in battle some twenty-two years after Joan's execution. And in *2 Henry VI*, Jack Cade is another excellent example of Shakespeare's genius for reinventing figures.

In *1 Henry VI*, there are very few glimpses of those at the bottom. Politics are almost entirely the affair of the elites, who manoeuvre against one another, while the anonymous masses of servants, soldiers, artisans, and peasants remain in the shadows. In *2 Henry VI*, the semi-fictional clothworker Jack Cade with a band of fictional lower-class rebels, coming down to London to overthrow the social order and mimic the political orthodoxy.

2.2.1 Jack Cade: An Inversion of the Political Hierarchy

Continuing the direction of *1 Henry VI*, the ineffectual king is pushed even further towards the margins of history in *2 Henry VI*. Suffolk conspires to control the weak king through the Queen Margaret of Anjou. Humphrey Duke of Gloucester (the Lord Protector) wishes to see himself as the loyal counsellor to the king, yet his continuing battle with the Bishop of Winchester, reveals the ugliness of the naked real politics. York's secret ambitions for the crown and his consistent effort to gain the throne are reinforced all through the play. Finally, the rhetoric of honour and heroism represented by Henry V, Bedford, and Salisbury has been replaced by conspiracies, charges, and murders in the world of Suffolk, Winchester, and York.

The first scenes of *2 Henry VI*, delineate a political and moral landscape dominated by feuds and conflicts between rival nobles. The play opens with the scene that Margaret of Anjou is presented to the king as wife at court by Suffolk. The match is decried by Gloucester. Winchester, Suffolk, and York agree that Gloucester must be brought down. Gloucester rebukes his wife Eleanor for her ambitions to the crown; Eleanor hires a priest, Hume, to bring witches to predict the future; Hume is in the pay of Suffolk. The witches prophesy the downfall of Henry, York, and Suffolk, but the scene is ended by Buckingham and York who arrest Eleanor and sentence her to banishment. Later, when Eleanor in disgrace, "barefoot in a white sheet," meets her husband in the streets, she picks up the image of "liming" to warn Gloucester that Suffolk would betray him (*2 Henry VI* 2.4.54). In the First Scene Third Act, Winchester, Suffolk, and York accuse Gloucester before the king. Seeing his denials are futile, Gloucester describes the trial proceedings as their "complot" (3.1.147) to have his life and a "prologue of chaos" (3.1.142) destined to behave uncontrollably. After Gloucester's futile defence and the exit of Henry VI, Queen Margaret and Suffolk, Winchester (who is now Cardinal) declares an even greater determination to destroy the Lord Protector. Suffolk puts the plot of murdering Gloucester as bluntly as possible: "And do not stand on quillets how to slay him: /Be it by gins, by snares, by subtlety, /Sleeping or waking" (3.1.261-263). The next scene begins with a short exchange between Gloucester's foes. When it is clear that there are no reservations, the worldly Cardinal undertakes to make the necessary arrangements. "Say you consent and censure well the deed," he says to his accomplices, "And I'll provide his executioner" (3.1.275-276). With everyone consenting, the cardinal does what he has promised: Duke Humphrey is strangled in his bed by the Cardinal's two hired murderers.

  The violent murder of Gloucester in his bed dramatises a world of madness and indicates the brutality that ironically overshadows York's rebellion. Although Suffolk and the Cardinal do most of the talking, the real force behind the killing of the Lord Protector is the ambitious York: "My brain, more busy than the labouring spider, / Weaves tedious snares to trap mine enemies" (3.1.339-40). Through his dying uncle

John Mortimer's anti-Lancastrian review of succession from Edward Ⅲ through Henry Ⅵ, York discovers that he is a descendant of King Edward Ⅲ. Priding himself on his right to the throne, York introduces a new element—a clothier, Jack Cade, into the political struggle to rebel in the guise of his dead ancestor John Mortimer.

The Fourth Act of the play is devoted to the insurrection of Jack Cade. Cade as York's pawn is solely Shakespeare's addition to his chronicle sources. The historical Jack Cade is somewhat different from Shakespeare's description. Most of the violence and outrage in Shakespeare's version of the Cade uprising comes from the chronicle story of the Wat Tyler's Peasants Revolt. Shakespeare conflates Jack Cade's rebellion of 1450 with that of Wat Tyler's insurrection of 1381.

Through a meticulous comparison between the play and the chronicle sources, Brents Stirling points out that Shakespeare takes from the Wat Tyler's Peasants Revolt the anti-literacy of the rebels, the wish to kill all lawyers, and the destruction of the Savoy and the Inns of Court. Cade, on the contrary, was impressively personable and articulate, in the words of Holinshed "a young man of goodly stature and right pregnant wit" (qtd. in Shakespeare 2001: 90). What is more, the Cade in history, though a significant symptom of the lack of governance which distinguished the reign of Henry Ⅵ, is a relatively unimportant person. The Cade of Shakespeare, however, is a priceless creation which attracted a great deal of critical attention. The nature of the Cade uprising in 2 Henry Ⅵ has often been debated: whether it is the marginal, dissident and oppressed element to be contained by the society's feudal hierarchy, or whether it can be understood as a radical challenge to such hierarchy? ① To have a comprehensive answer to this question, we need to have a good look at Shakespeare's characterisation of Jack Cade.

It is from York that we first hear of Jack Cade. As the Duke of York claims, he incites Jack Cade and his artisans to rebellion, devising for Cade a false family tree

---

① For an overview of the debate between new historicist and cultural materialists, see Graham Holderness's *Introduction to Shakespeare's History Plays: Richard Ⅱ to Henry V*, 1992.

that mimics York's claims to the throne:

> YORK: I have seduced a headstrong Kentishman,
> John Cade of Ashford,
> To make commotion, as full well he can,
> Under the title of John Mortimer. (3.1.360-5)

The speech makes clear that, "this devil" is to be York's "substitute" (3.1.371). Cade's revolt is not merely a caricature of York's sedition; it is a parody of York's self-promotion. The Duke of York claims that his throne rests on a noble parentage (his mother was a Mortimer; his father a Plantagenet) when he explained earlier at length to his allies Warwick and Salisbury. While Cade exclaims that he also has such a parentage that his father is a Mortimer, and his mother a Plantagenet, Dick the Butcher speaks aside that his father is a good bricklayer and his mother a midwife. The truth-telling Dick confirms that Cade's claims as royal descendant are entirely false. The proletarian mimicry of that genealogical claim affirms class hierarchy, but it may also undermine the position of those nobles such as York who seriously make such pretensions. Most significantly, York cunningly manipulates the action to serve his own political ends. Whether Cade succeeds or fails is of little concern to him, since he plans with his army to "reap the harvest which that rascal sowed" (3.1.381). Thus, Jack Cade's activities grimly reveal a society that, dominated by hypocritical nobles, has virtually collapsed from within.

Encouraged secretly by York, Cade leads the rebels in a revolt. The term "class" is anachronistic in the Elizabethan period, but there is indeed an incipient class-consciousness in Cade's appeal to his followers (Chernaik 36). Social and political hierarchy is presented as the enemy of the people. "It was never merry world in England since gentle came up", claims one rebel (4.2.6-7). So Cade appeals to his followers with an assumption—every "gentleman" is his enemy and all those wearing 'clouted shoon' or 'leather aprons' are his natural allies (4.2.12-13, 174-7).

However, it is not only the gentries who are targeted as the enemy; the rebels are also the enemies of all learning men and the learned profession. Cade executes a clerk because he can read and write. Later, the eloquent humanist Lord Saye who is the spokesman for civilized values and the rule of law confronts Cade face-to-face. No sooner starts Saye his speech of self-defence in Latin than he is greeted with Cade's cry "away with him, away with him! He speaks Latin" (4.7.52-53). One of Jack Cade's accusations against Lord Saye is that Saye has traitorously corrupted the youth of the country by setting up a grammar school, and while their ancestors had no other books but the score and tally to keep accounts, Say has used printing. According to Cade, Saye's behaviour of building a paper mill is also against the crown and dignity of the king (4.7.29-34).

The paper mill and the printing press are anachronisms—neither existed in England at the time of Cade's rebellion—but that does not matter, what matters is the sources of his consciousness—the grammar school took him away from the world of the score and tally and forced him into the world of the printed book. His following words equate education and the processes of law with unjustified privilege, further complicating the situation:

> CADE. Thou hast appointed justices of peace to call poor men before them about matters they were not able to answer. Moreover, thou hast put them in prison, and because they could not read, thou hast hanged them when indeed only for that cause they have been most worthy to live. (4.7.37-39)

It is mad to think that criminals should be spared because they are illiterate, but Cade is making a protest against an actual English law at that time: if a convicted criminal could demonstrate that he was literate—usually by reading a verse from the Psalms—he could claim "benefit of clergy"; that is, he could, for legal purposes, be classified by virtue of literacy as a clergyman and therefore officially be subject to the jurisdiction of the ecclesiastical courts, which did not have the death penalty

(Greenblatt 2004:171). The logic and law are twisted in support of government's condemnation of under-trodden ones. By a privilege known as benefit of upper-class, men who know how to read and write could claim certain immunities when prosecuted for crimes. The result, in most cases, was that the literate thieves or murderers went free. So Cade's speech, which starts as a defence of blind ignorance against learning, turns into a critique of a legal system which perpetuates privilege and injustice. With Cade's parody of the law of courts, we may also feel the justification of Cade's violence.

Against the old world of hierarchical relations between rules and ruled, the landed class and the people, the learned and the unlearned, Cade tries to establish a utopia, a perpetual holiday of festive and feasting guaranteed by the arbitrary rule of Cade himself. With his inventive genius, he has created a fantasy world where his impulses and wishes are laws and that is why he can achieve miracles in a chaotic situation:

> CADE: I thank you, good people. —there shall be no money,
> all shall eat and drink on my score, and I will
> apparel them all in one livery, that they may agree
> like brothers and worship me their lord. (4.2.67-70)

J. A. R. Marriott points out that Jack Cade's description of this utopia has given us "one of the finest portraits of the crafty and 'self-seeking' communist ever painted" (192). Viewed in this light, the dramatist may have gone for the social aims of his rebels—their desire to make all men equal and have things in common, and to cheapen commodities. Besides, Shakespeare's reinvention of Jack Cade and his followers may have also gone for their destructive qualities—their hatred of lawyers and literate people as well as noblemen. Last but not the least, the semi-fictional character Jack Cade represents a grotesque mimicry of the political hierarchy and the barbarism of feudal hierarchy in such a society.

2.2.2 "Infinite Numbers" of Commoners: The Mimicking of the Political Order

In historiography, history is a chronicle of events, and the characters are often subordinated to the action or plot. In drama, the dramatists have more freedom than historians to imagine the possibilities of the interaction between characters. In portraying Cade and his followers, Shakespeare's creative power has gone beyond the chronicle resources. Indeed, Jack Cade and his associates are given more space in the play than their rebellion rightfully claims in the historical sources, and they bring out a large area of life, sweeping forward in a continuous movement. The eruption of the commoners into the dramatic world adds a dimension to the chronicle history. The royalties and nobles' political ambitions are reflected in the paralleling level of ordinary people whose lives unavoidably involved in the politic conflicts. Although without political status, the commoners are not without political influence or political sense.

Apart from Jack Cade, there is a pervasive presence of commoners in *2 Henry VI*, which makes the play "arguably one of the histories that give a substantial voice to the presence of ordinary people in history and their ability to mobilize themselves in sufficient number" (Hampton-Reeves 21). They constitute such a considerable amount of people that Shakespeare's stage directions call for "infinite numbers"①. It seems as if these commoners serve as objects of the lords' insults at the very beginning of the play. They are "base cullions" to Queen Margaret (*2 Henry VI* 1.3.40), "rude unpolished hinds" to Suffolk (3.2.271), "[b]ase dunghill villain and mechanical" to York (1.3.193), the "base-born callet" (1.3.83) to the Duchess of Gloucester, and the "untutored churl" (3.2.213) to Warwick. However, with the progression of the drama, they play an increasingly prominent role to mimic the political order and to

---

① The stage direction "Drum. Enter CADE, Dick [the] Butcher, Simth the Weaver, *and a Sawyer, with infinite numbers [carrying long staves]*" appears between the lines of Nick "Come, come, let's fall in with them" (4.2.27) and Cade's "We, John Cade, so termed of our supposed father" (*2 Henry VI* 4.2.29).

disrupt the conventional notion of history as the story of kings and nobles.

The "infinite numbers" of commoners first appear as petitioners in Scene One Act One. A petitioner claims that Winchester's agent has seized his house, lands, wife, and all; another, says that Suffolk has unlawfully enclosed the commons of Melford for his own use (1.3), but they have such a bad luck that instead of presenting their petitions to the good Duke Humphrey, they go to the corrupt Duke of Suffolk. Suffolk and Margaret tear their petitions. The play continues with the incident of the armourer Thomas Horner and his apprentice Peter Thump (1.3, 2.3). Though being invented by Shakespeare, the quarrel and fight between Thomas and Peter offer a side-note of York's ambitious claim to the throne.

The armourer Thomas Horner and his apprentice Peter Thump are brought before the king to make the conflict between the Yorkists and the Lancastrians come to public. Peter accuses Horner of treason because Horner says the Duke of York is the true heir to the English crown and that Henry VI has no right to the throne. Peter's accusation brings people's attention to the national conflicts caused by York's ambition. Although York calls Horner as "base dunghill villain and mechanical" (1.3.194) who allegedly makes the claims in York's favour, the audience know clearly of the guilt of York who in the previous scene laid out formally to Warwick and Salisbury his genealogical claim to the crown. Just as the noble would deny his true intentions, when questioned by King Henry VI, Horner vehemently denies that he ever says that York is the rightful heir to the throne. Gloucester pronounces a verdict that on a day appointed Peter and Horner will prove the truth of their assertions in single combat.

When the combat takes place, Peter and Horner are accompanied by their neighbours—other commoners, this time enacting a coarse but genuine demonstration of friendship—encourage them to drink to their victory. Horner, who is drunk, boasts an easy victory, while Peter is certain that he would be defeated. But Horner, in his presumption, has drunk too many cups of sack, so that Peter wins the combat, slaying his master, who before dying confesses: "Hold, Peter, hold! I confess, I confess treason" (2.3.96).

Sketching the dispute between Horner and Peter, Shakespeare hints dynastic rivalries penetrating into the life of the ordinary people. The incident of the accusation and the mock trial by combat can be read in different ways. It may be understood as evidence of the disruptive effects of York's ambitions trickling down the social system to the level of armourer and apprentice. However, it may as well suggest "an independent life of those lower orders that mimics and parodies that of their superiors" (Grene 77).

Similarly, the trial of Saunder Simpcox parodies the political instability in the country, for the unsophisticated King Henry is unable to serve as an impartial judge both in the legal proceedings and the national affairs. In Scene One Act Two, the good Duke Gloucester exposes Saunder Simpox for fraudulently asserting that he has been miraculously cured of his blindness by God. Simpcox takes advantage of the king's good faith by claiming that St. Alban has restored his sight. The king himself believes in the "miracle" done by God. According to the sources, Gloucester is also overjoyed at the miracle①, not even to mention Henry's pious credulity "now, God be praised, that to believing souls/ gives light in darkness, comfort in despair!" (2.1.65-66). However, deviating from the account in the sources, Shakespeare transfers Gloucester to a more scrupulous one who exposes the tricks of Simpcox through interrogations. Contrasting the king's naïve credulity with Gloucester's strategic astuteness, the scene can be taken as a metaphor of the paradoxical situation that, Henry and Simpcox, while the latter can see but pretending unable to see, the former cannot see through the political fogs but pretends that he can see. Warwick

---

① The false miracle of Simpcox, originally told in Sir Thomas More's *Dialogue of the Veneration and Worship of Images* (1529) was not in Hall or Holinshed but was added by R. Grafton in his *A Chronicle at Large* (1569). Shakespeare's dramatic version of this story presents no important change save that Gloucester's attitude is changed from "huaynge greate Ioy to see such a miracle, called ye pore man vnto hym" to a deep and wise suspicion. See Bullough. *Narrative and Dramatic Sources of Shakespeare*, vol. 3, 1960. pp. 90-91.

comments ironically on the king's apparent blindness to the guilt of Cardinal and Suffolk who killed Gloucester: "who finds the heifer dead and bleeding fresh/ And sees fast by a butcher with an axe,/But will suspect 'twas he that made the slaughter" (3.2.188-90).

In a way, both Henry and Simpcox shrank from their responsibilities. Henry is unable to rule the country, and Simpcox cannot support his family. However, as a commoner, Simpcox got punished for his behaviour; he and his wife are whipped for their fraud. Once again, Shakespeare adds one line to his source that informs us the motive of the fraud and therefore mitigates the blame. Simpcox's wife states plainly the reason of their deception: "Alas! Sir, we did it for pure need" (2.1.150). The deeply humanising cry is simple but not without eloquence. Compared with the noble's unquenchable ambitions to climb the ladder to collect more fortune and even to be a king, the ordinary people's only wish is to satisfy their basic needs. By tinkling a sympathetic bell in our ears, Shakespeare reasonably justifies the commoners' deeds.

The following episode shows Gloucester's strangled body exhibited in front of the helpless king. After the murder of the good Duke, "many commons" invade the royal presence at Warwick's back and constitute a threatening force amplifying the demand for Suffolk's banishment. The stage device gives a theatrical metaphor of "virtue is choked with foul ambition". Invoked by the murder of Gloucester, the commons "like an angry hive of bees" (3.2.125) beat on the door. The revolt is rendered justifiable by the commoners' rage against the traitorous murder of a nobleman and a "pious" king who is unable to protect the country against the plots of corrupt nobilities. When the King does not defend the right, the people grow muddied, ready to take justice into their own hands or to redress grievances with force. Shakespeare sees the commoners as the victims of disorder and sense that their instinct is for survival, not for giddy change. From this point in the play, the lower orders become increasingly capricious and violent, which finally leads to the climax of the play—Jack Cade and his followers erupt into the stage to mimic the political order and subvert the feudal hierarchy.

Jack Cade rebels in the guise of York's dead ancestor John Mortimer, and with his followers subvert the realm in a deeper and broader scale (4.2). Cade tells his followers that under his rule, "they may agree like brothers" (4.2.69-70). Having taken London, Cade and his "brothers" burn down ancient buildings and destroy everything in their path, turning the land into a "slaughterhouse" (3.2.189). Giving Dick the butcher's patent to continue killing throughout at the fields, Cade invokes the imagery of the "butcher" (3.1.210). The word butchery does not appear in *1 Henry VI*, but by the middle of *2 Henry VI*, it develops into the symbol of barbarism as the country becomes the slaughterhouse of rebellion and the Wars of the Roses, which continue into *3 Henry VI*.

The correspondence between the butchery of the lower orders and that of the nobles finds its emblem in the severed head. After the execution of Lord Saye and Sir James Crowmer, Cade having their heads hoist "at every corner have them kiss" (4.7.127-8). Cade's cruelly delayed sentence and execution of Lord Saye stresses a barbarity which, though less apparent, is no less real in the cruel murder of good Duke Gloucester. Although Shakespeare spares no detail of the atrocities committed by the Cade rebels, he does not make them appear any worse than their aristocratic superiors, who deliberately subvert the law and murder their enemies. Therefore, the depiction of Cade and his followers here is not merely the expression of egalitarianism, but rather a grotesque mimicry of the barbarism of political struggle.

After the riot has been dispersed, Cade flees. He is caught and killed in a garden by a Kent gentry Alexander Iden. Although Tillyard believes that the death scene of Cade is an elaborate sermon on the philosophy of order which Shakespeare is supposed to have embodied in his historical plays①, it definitely cannot be seen as simple and easy as this, and the scene needs further analysis. Iden delivers a speech right before

---

① Tillyard elaborates that "another most explicit version of the same thing (the order is the great principle of degree) is the contrast between the lawlessness of Jack Cade and the impeccable moderation and discipline of the Kentish squire Iden, in *2 Henry VI*". See Tillyard, *Shakespeare's History Plays*. London: Penguin Books, 1992. pp.153.

his meeting with Cade:

> IDEN. Lord, who would live turmoiled in the court,
> And may enjoy such quiet walks as these?
> This small inheritance my father left me
> Contenteth me, and worth a monarchy.
> I seek not to wax great by others' waning,
> Or gather wealth, I care not, with what envy;
> Sufficeth that I have maintains my state,
> And sends the poor well pleased from my gate. (4.10.16-23)

Indeed, what attracts our attention is the name of the gentry, as "Iden" or "Eden" represents a paradise with all the tranquillity and happiness. Being a representative of the genealogical inheritance of land and fortune, Iden seems to be satisfied with all the things he owned now. According to Tillyard, because Iden stands as the symbol of degree, he would not rise at the expense of other people, which is an implication on the rise of York at the expense of Gloucester (1962: 175).

However, when Iden learns who Cade is, he shows no stoic calm any longer as he kills Cade. Although it is Cade who provokes Iden into attacking him, we see a strong man slaughtering a starving one. Iden, having entered to proclaim his abhorrence of the court and courtly ambitions at the opening of the scene, goes off in triumph to court to claim the honour that he knows will be his reward. He never lives up to the pretty charm of the opening speech; moreover, the Kentish garden turns out to be, "another failed paradise in which ideals are vitiated by envy and ambition" (Shakespeare 2001: 34).

In *2 Henry VI*, Shakespeare's fictional representation of the marginal classes not merely acknowledges the boundaries between the aristocracy and the usually invisible artisans and peasants, but also eventually attempts to displace them. Firstly, Cade and the "infinite numbers" of commons undermine the generic unity which Tillyard saw in

1 Henry VI by radically challenging the coherence of heroic history. The characterisation of Joan in *1 Henry VI*, although radically challenges the heroic history, is still confined to a grand narrative with its cast of the royal family, a few prominent nobles and clergy, and the equally aristocratic opponents of the English. But *2 Henry VI*, by introducing Cade and his low-status followers, presents a fundamentally subversive interrogation to the social and political hierarchy. The lower classes by their very presence expand the definition of society to include not only the elites but also all classes in the nation. Therefore, the often invisible populace has become sufficiently worthy of attention to be represented as a part of English history. Secondly, by representing the socially marginal people on stage, Shakespeare deals with a problem that the historiography presents with detachment—the rebellious nobodies that the historians wish to dispatch from the orthodox history. Holinshed and Hall's chivalric kings and princes violently eliminate lower class rebels as just so much criminal nuisance, reasserting the superiority of the noble (Watson 58). However, in *2 Henry VI*, Shakespeare's rebels are named and placed: "Jack Cade the clothier" from Kent, "Best's son, the tanner of Wingham," "Dick the Butcher," "Smith the Weaver" (4.2.4, 21, 25, 28). Although the last three are unhistorical, the mere naming touches them with some humanity to complement their dramatic reality; whatever they might do, they cannot be so easily dismissed as collective villains as in the historical narrative of chronicles.

Finally, the ideological certainties of chronicle history have gone. We confront not the farce of subplot, but the possible forces of history—Jack Cade and his followers invert, distort and burlesque the self-interest, dishonour and barbarism of the social and political order enacted by the feudal hierarchy. This sense of travesty is critical, and we are made both participants in, and spectators of, the historical process, by Shakespeare's fictional use of history in *2 Henry VI*.

2.3 3 Henry VI: The Interrogation to the Secular History

The most thoughtful attempt to define history plays generically (or at least Shakespeare's history plays) is David Scott Kastan's suggestion that they are formally distinct①. He proposed that Shakespeare's history plays have "a unique and determinate shape that emerges organically from the playwright's sense of the shape of history itself" (1982:17).

Kastan's sense of history plays helps us to think about *3 Henry VI*. Throughout all the three *Henry VI* plays, history resists its formalisations. In *1 Henry VI*, Shakespeare has contrasted a hero Talbot to his counterpart, the Amazonian Joan La Pucelle. *2 Henry VI* takes a more ambivalent view of the aspiring mind, depicting the commoners jump out of the formless history and want to form a top-side-down world. However, in *3 Henry VI*, Shakespeare's instinct for the dramatic form is apparently unable to check the rush of historical narrative in the previous *Henry VI* plays. His plot races across the pages of the two Molehill scenes, which are filled with ferocities between the most common human relationships—father and son, mother and son. The narrative in drama provides a chaotic and bloody secular history of both family and state and further develops into the deformed world of Richard III.

2.3.1 Two Molehills: The Subverted Social and Familial Bonds

Compared with the historians, Shakespeare is not interested so much in the complex, actual historical causality responsible for the decline of feudalism as in the human collisions which sprang necessarily and typically form the contradictions of this decline. In *The Historical Novel*, Georg Lukács proposes that the greatness of

---

① See David Scott Kastan, *Shakespeare and the Shapes of Time*. London: Macmillan, 1982.

Shakespeare's plays consisting in his characterisation of the period through his actors. That is, all the qualities of a character, from the ruling passion down to the smallest dramatic subtlety, are coloured by the historical and social circumstances. Not necessarily in a broad or epic historical sense, but certainly in the historical conditioning of the collision; its essence must derive from the specific determinants of the epoch (118). Lukács proceeds to argue that it is a well-known fact that the most notable writers of the period have deep insights into the vital collision of this transitional age. In the tragedies of Corneille or Racine, of Calderon or Lope de Vaga as well as in Shakespeare, a whole set of the inner contradictions of feudalism, pointing inevitably to its dissolution, emerge with the greatest clarity (153).

Shakespeare never simplifies the process of dissolution down to a mechanical contrast between the "old" and the "new". In his plays, the characters of the rising new world which humanely and morally better in many respects and more tightly bound to the interests of people, act as the reflection of the breakdown of the old, ruling-class centred society. Therefore, Shakespeare states every conflict in English history in terms of typical human opposites and concentrates the decisive human relations around these historical collisions. And this is indeed the way with which Shakespeare explores the two Molehill scenes in *3 Henry VI*.

The two "molehill" episodes in *3 Henry VI*—one is of York's being mocked and tortured to death, and the other is divided between Henry's pastoral monologue and the stylised death scene of the fathers and sons—seem to afford a privileged view of the play from the point of the natural parallels between family and state. In both of the two "molehill" scenes, Shakespeare portrays the most general, regulative features of the social and historical collisions and contradictions. The marvellously observed, social-historical conflicts in both family and state create a dramatic effect which is essentially "anthropological".

Ostensibly, the play opens soon after *Part 2* ends, with York and his friends regretting their failure to capture King Henry VI, describing the deaths of enemy leaders, and preparing to hold the Parliament house to depose Henry. Historically, however, this must be dated to 1460, five years after the Battle of St Albans. It was in the Parliament of October 1460 that York made a public claim to the throne. Shakespeare's rearrangement of the chronicle events makes the clash between Red and White roses more intense. The lengthy discussions which preceded the agreement are telescoped and altered in the play after Henry and his party have burst indignantly into the hall.

The contrast between Henry's weakness and York's strength of spirit is shown prominently in the first scene of *3 Henry VI*. Henry enters to find York sitting on the throne. Henry confronts verbally: "Frowns, words, threats/ Shall be the war that Henry means to use" (1.1.72-73). To assert his right to the throne, Henry tries to associate his and Richard's titles with their places in the royal families:

> KING HENRY. What title hast thou, traitor, to the crown?
> Thy father was, as thou art, Duke of York,
> Thy grandfather, Roger Mortimer, Earl of March.
> I am the son of Henry the fifth. (1.1.104-07)

Henry's verbal war, however, lost. His words are ineffective:

> YORK. Twas by rebellion against his king.
> KING HENRY. [Aside] I know not what to say; my title's weak. (1.1.133-34)

Henry fails in his attempt to prove his title to the crown. He can keep the crown only by disinheriting his own son and entailing the crown to the house of York. York's ambitions are supported by his royal ancestry and material preeminence. However, what attracts our attention is that all his son's insistence on their family inheritance to the crown.

The play's early scenes constantly repeat everyone's place in York's family.

"Father, tear the crown from the usurper's head," York's third son, Richard demands (1.1.114); "Sweet father, do so, set it on your head," adds York's eldest son, Edward (1.1.115); "Good brother, as thou lov'st and honorest arms/ Let's fight it out," York's brother, Montague chimes in (1.1.116-17); and York replies, "Sons, peace!" (1.1.119). "Why, how now, sons and brother, at a strife?" York asks in the next scene (1.2.4). The genealogies that link men to one another become the cause and effect of the play's constant wars. While on the King's side, Henry also appeals to the familial relationship as the emblem of revenge and loyalty. "Earl of Northumberland, he slew thy father, / And thine, Lord Clifford, and you both have/ vowed revenge/ On him, his sons, his favorites, and his friends" (1.1.53-56), Henry says. Clifford's proposal—"My gracious lord, here in the parliament/ Let us assail the family of York" (1.1.64-65), identifies bloodshed as a logical effect of blood relation.

When these characters meet at the first Molehill scene at Wakefield, Young Clifford murders the boy Rutland, the young son of York, and then we see Margaret's mockery and killing of York. Being unable to escape, York becomes Queen Margaret's prisoner and is subjected by her to indignities. Margaret makes York stand upon a molehill and crown him with a paper crown. The genealogy that links men to one another being so irresistible that when Margaret taunts York to his death, she recites a list of York's son's names:

> QUEEN MARGARET. Where are your mess of sons to back you now?
> The wanton Edward, and the lusty George?
> And where's that valiant crook-back prodigy,
> Dickie your boy, that with his grumbling voice
> Was wont to cheer his dad in mutinies?
> Or, with the rest, where is your darling Rutland? (1.4.73-8)

To the last question, she knows the answer. Margaret revels in telling York that his youngest son, Rutland, has been slain. She offers York a napkin soaked in the boy's blood to dry his tears. The blood-soaked handkerchief goes beyond the speech to remind us that the family does not end with York and his youngest son's death. York's son Richard promises "Richard, I bear thy name, I'll venge thy death,/ Or die renowned by attempting it," and Edward adds, "His name that valiant duke hath left with thee;/ His dukedom and his chair with me is left" (2.1.87-90).

In such a scene, we may see that all of the important characters are conceived both as a member of an aggrieved family and as a participant in the political struggle of state. The paralleling relations in family and state wave a troubling picture of secular history. York is a legitimate claimant to the throne, but he is also the father of young Rutland. Clifford is the champion of the royalist cause but also a son to a slain father. Margaret is the Queen, but she is also the mother of the disinherited Prince Henry and the outraged wife of King Henry. The characters invoke these magnificent human confrontations in the War of the Roses and find themselves entangled in the historical struggle of the family/state relation.

If the first Molehill delivers the collisions inherited in the state, then the second Molehill scene, by mirroring Henry's wishful innocence, shows the war's destruction to familial bonds of the secular history. At the second Molehill scene at Towton, we see the battle through the King's eyes. Having been chided from the field by the Queen, he takes his stand on a molehill (as York was forced to stand on the molehill after Wakefield) and shows his envy of the simple countryman's life:

> KING HENRY: O God! Methinks it were a happy life,
> To be no better than a homely swain,
> To sit upon a hill, as I do now,
> To carve out dials quaintly, point by point,
> Thereby to see the minutes how they run:
> How many makes the hour full complete,
> How many hours bring about the day,

> How many days will finish up the year,
>
> How many years a mortal man may live.
>
> When this is known, then to divide the times:
>
> So many hours must I tend my flock,
>
> So many hours must I take my rest,
>
> So many hours must I contemplate,
>
> So many hours must I sport myself,
>
> So many days my ewes have been with young,
>
> So many weeks ere the poor fools will ean,
>
> So many years ere I shall shear the fleece.
>
> So minutes, hours, days, months, and years,
>
> Passed over to the end they were created,
>
> Would bring white hairs unto a quiet grave. (2.5.21-40)

Henry's picture of the secular pastoral history amounts to a conceit at the expense of humanity and offers no secure home for humankind. Hall says of the long struggle at Towton:

> This conflict was in a manner unnatural, for in it the son fought against the father, the brother against the brother, the nephew against the uncle, and the tenant against his lord. ①(qtd. in Boswell-stone 306)

Shakespeare gets the hint from Hall's general statement and dramatises the war in a somewhat emblematic way. While King Henry sits on a molehill away from the battle and views from afar the battle, in a moment there enters, a son who bears the

---

① The spellings are modernised by the author of this book. The original spellings are "This conflict was in maner vnnaturall, for in it the sonne fought agynst the father, the brother against the brother, the nephew against the vncle, and the tenaunt against his lord".

body of a man he has slain whom he then discovers to be his father and a father who bears the body of a man he has slain whom he then discovers to be his son. The stage directions tell us: *"Enter a SON that hath killed his father, at one door"*; *"Enter a FATHER that hath killed his son, at another door [with their bodies]"*. Father and Son cannot recognise kinship because they have been fighting on opposite sides in the battle: "Pardon me, God, I knew not what I did! / And pardon, father, for I knew not thee!" says the Son (2.5.69-70); "But let me see: is this our foeman's face? / Ah, no, no, no, it is mine only son!" (2.5.82-3), says the Father. Amid this terrible scene, the son's lament "O heavy times, begetting such events!" (2.5.63) is excelled by the Father's more elaborate denunciation "O, pity, God, this miserable age! / What stratagems! how fell! how butcherly! Erroneous, mutinous, and unnatural, / This deadly quarrel daily doth beget! " (2.5.88-91). The reiterated "beget", echoing in the wailing of Father and Son, is the chaos of civil war that unwrites the most natural relationship in human history. As the son says, viewing his dead father's face: "O heavy times, begetting such events! / From London by the King was I pressed forth;/ My father, being the Earl of Warwick's man,/ Came on the part of York, pressed by his master;/ And I, who at his hands received my life, / Have by my hands of life bereaved him" (2.5.63-8). The patriarchal principle is betrayed at every level since divisions in the state sever the biological ties binding father to son. Revenge and self-interest govern war and politics, distorting the traditional bonds of family and state and ultimately destroying any everyday basis of humanity. In the face of these human tragedies, one cannot help but ask what indeed the meaning of the wars for power in the name of kinship? In case we should miss the point, Shakespeare makes Henry lament: "The red rose and the white are on his face,/ The fatal colours of our striving houses; [···]/ If you contend, a thousand lives must wither" (2.5.97-101).

In the process of Shakespeare's dramatic fiction, the Father-Son scene accomplishes a complexity beyond the distress of the two unnamed soldiers and beyond their representativeness as ordinary Englishmen caught in the savage civil war. The three characters, Father, Son, and King, do not speak to each other. However, all three engaged in a shared enunciation which allegorically dramatises the war's destruction to the familial and social bonds.

The play begins with the first molehill's reiteration of the blood lineage within the family and state and ends with the second molehill's collapse of genealogical order in both the familial and social bonds. The utter lucidity of the collisions brings home the most darkly ironic situation. All these collisions are set within the fictional place where the "gentle" king laments the discords of war and longs for a shepherd's life; ironically he sits upon the "molehill" which figures prominently in York's death, a few scenes previously. Both molehills lead to the tragic recognition that the war not only undermines the social bonds that hold society together but finally tears apart, even the primitive links within the family.

2.3.2 "Natural Mother" Margret: A Threat to Patriarchy in Family and State

Characterisation is a significant concern in Shakespeare's history plays. According to Rackin, characters define their actions as attempts to inscribe their names in the written record. While male characters successfully accomplish that, most female figures are contained in the male domain:

> No woman is the protagonist in a Shakespearean history play. Renaissance gender role definitions prescribed silence as a feminine virtue, and Renaissance sexual mythology associated the feminine with body and matter as opposed to masculine intellect and spirit. (1985: 329)

Indeed most of the protagonists in Shakespeare's history plays are men, while the women who do appear are mostly contained in the domestic scenes. Very often the women and children are only the additions to the chronicle sources. They are a way of offering an alternative perspective to the predominantly male world of politics, battle, and the struggle for power. However, not all female roles are like this in Shakespeare's history plays. Those more assertive or aggressive women who appear in military or power-based scenes, outside the realm of women's work, are given a voice that challenges the logo-centric, masculine patriarchy. For example, Joan of Arc, in *1 Henry VI*, is never portrayed in domestic scenes, but only in scenes of battles. Another assertive and aggressive woman is Queen Margaret of Anjou.

Most notable among the women of the early history plays, Margaret is the only one who appears in all three *Henry VI* and contributes a significant part to the last two plays. She is introduced as a captive led onto the stage at the same time that Joan is led off after Joan's final capture in *1 Henry VI*. In *2 Henry VI*, Gloucester complains that Margaret's marriage to Henry VI will blot noble English "names from books of memory", raze "the characters of [their] renown," deface the "monuments of conquered France" (*2 Henry VI* 1.1.96-100), and thus threatens to erase English history metaphorically. She routinely takes decisive, high-handed, often cruel actions: she tears up the commoners' petitions to Humphrey of Gloucester and fulminates against Henry VI's willingness to submit himself to Gloucester's protection (*2 Henry VI*, 1.3.40-65); she boxes the Duchess of Gloucester's ear (*2 Henry VI*, 1.3.139).

Margaret's disruptive role becomes increasingly prominent as Shakespeare progresses into the unorthodox use of motherhood in her characterisation in *3 Henry VI* Margaret is the Queen, but she is also the mother of the disinherited Prince Edward and the outraged wife of the "unnatural" father King Henry (*3 Henry VI* 1.1.225). Since the "unnatural" father King Henry has renounced their son's right to inherit the throne, Margaret becomes the "natural" mother in two levels: firstly, she is the biological mother of Prince Edward; secondly, she takes the responsibility of retrieving the throne for her son which initially belongs to the father. As a "natural" mother", Margaret divorces herself from King Henry's bed when she finds out he has disinherited their son (1.1.248-51). She taunts Richard of York with a cloth dipped in the blood of his dead son (1.4.79-83). Margaret stabs York and orders his head to be set on the gates of York city (1.4.176-80). Characteristically being represented as raging, cursing, or fighting for her son's rights on stage, she poses a serious threat to the patriarchy in both family and state.

For the Yorkist family, York and his sons repeat again and again their patrilineal relations with each other (1.1). York's sons Edward and Richard constantly call York "Father" and "Sweet father" (1.1.114-5), and York calls them collectively as "sons" (119). York and his sons understand their connections to each other so clearly that there is not any reference to the mother. Male identity in York's family is an absolute fact, a truth about the past that holds them together. To explain that invisible contract, Mary Beth Rose writes:

> Since the mother would remove one from what is conceived as the world of action—the public, socialized world—the best mother is an absent or a dead mother. Thus…we can discern the outlines of what feminist and psychoanalytic criticism have identified as the oedipal plot: the essential separation from the mother (and consequent identification with the father) that proves the enabling condition for a full (i.e. both public and private) adult life. (301)

Paternity in the York family, aggressively resisting the presence of Mother, proves the power of the male genealogies and holds together the familial bonds. However, on the Lancastrian side, Margaret's prominence as a mother suggests a weakness in the patriarchal structures that should have rendered her less visible and less powerful. In this play, Queen Margaret's adultery in *2 Henry VI* leaves little residues, and she has been rehabilitated as a mother: Margaret appears in every scene but one with her son at her side. Her aggression is now associated with the fact that she fights solely to preserve her son's succession. Forming a sharp contrast with the King, she forces "a reconceptualisation of the roles of mother, mistress, queen and wife" (Dutton and Howard 352).

As a symbolic centre of the family and state, King Henry is so meek in his insistence of the genealogical line that he agrees to a self-deprecating bargain with York that allowing York to enjoy the kingdom after his decease (1.1.175). Henry can keep the crown that he inherits as "the son of Henry the Fifth" (1.1.107) only by disinheriting his own son, entailing the crown to the house of York. York's ambitions are supported by the apparent weaknesses of Henry, but we can never forget the strong-willed Margaret, who is the Lancastrian queen, mother of the disinherited Prince Edward.

Margaret, knowing her son has been disinherited by Henry, with a radical disaffection towards Henry, calls Henry as the "unnatural father": "Ah, wretched man, would I had died a maid/ And never seen thee, never borne thee son, /Seeing thou hast proved so unnatural a father" (1.1.214-225). As Prince Edward's "natural" mother, Margaret becomes the family and country's real centre in the sense that she not only assumes authority in the family but also takes upon herself the burden of guaranteeing Prince Edward's succession to the English throne. With her son at her side, she stands before Henry to issue her ultimatum of divorce:

> QUEEN MARGARET. But thou preferr'st thy life before thine honour.
> And seeing thou dost, I here divorce myself
> Both from thy table, Henry, and thy bed,
> Until that act of parliament be repealed
> Whereby my son is disinherited. (1.1.246-50)

With this divorce, the Northern lords that have sworn their loyalty to King Henry turn to follow Queen Margaret's lead. For Margaret, she believes that she will disgrace the King and utterly ruin the House of York. She asserts once again, "Thus do I leave thee. / Come, Son, let's away. / Our army is ready; come, we'll after them" (1.1.255-256). In separating herself from Henry's bed and taking on the responsibility of championing her son's rights to the throne, Margaret is in a contradictory position within the patriarchal structures of family and state, but she is also a vehicle for exposing the controversial nature of many of the patriarchy's claims.

The first one is her challenges to the traditional feminine role in the domestic domain. Instead of being a docile figure that carries on the service of everyday living and maintains the bonds of family, Margaret tells Henry she wants to stay away from him and take care of herself and her son. With the divorce declaration, Margaret becomes the *de facto* leader of the royal family and the Lancastrian party. According to Holinshed, Margaret has in her company the Prince, all the lords of the North parts, and eighteen thousand men. They march from York city to Wakefield. At Wakefield, the queen's forces bring York to his knees in battle. The chronicle account of York's death is "within half an hour slain and dead, and his whole army discomfited" ①(qtd. in Bullough 1960a:124).

The chronicle account of York's death at the Battle of Wakefield is not sensational enough, so the dramatist fictionalises this historical event into a famous dramatic scene, in which we see Young Clifford's murder of the boy Rutland, and then the mockery and elaborate killing of York himself. Margaret revels in telling York that his youngest son, Rutland, has been slain. She offers him a napkin soaked in the boy's blood to dry his tears. In a perversion of the coronation ceremony, Margaret sets a paper crown on York's head. She taunts him, "Ay, marry, sir, now looks he like a king! / Ay, this is he that took King Henry's chair/ And this is he was his adopted heir" (1.4.96-98). York tries to attack Margaret's femininity with insults. York attempts to paint Margaret as a "she-wolf of France" (1.4.111), "inhuman" (134), having a "tiger's heart wrapped in a woman's hide" (137). These images of "unruly woman" can be seen as men's reaction to the threats to male authority and their patriarchal world, for Margret's "carnivalesque punishments of mocking enthronement partake of the inverted structure of 'world-upside-down' rites" (Gupta 54). While York accuses Margaret of unruly and unseemly behaviour for a

---

① The spellings are modernised by the author of this book. The original text is "within half an hour slaine and dead, and his whole armie discomfited".

woman, it is he who is humiliated. Rather than allowing York to undermine her control of the situation, Margaret projects the qualities of a weak woman onto York, who is reduced to tears and cries for vengeance (1.4.147-179). York's attempts to attack Margaret by challenging her femininity are futile; he is silenced and stabbed by the Queen and his head is set upon the gates of York City (1.4.179-180).

Henry is shaken by the incident, crying "Withhold revenge, dear God!", "Tis not my fault/Nor wittingly have I infringed my vow" (2.2.7-8). Henry's emotional reaction to York's death shows the second inversion of patriarchal stereotypes: the man is masculine and brave; the woman is weak and vulnerable. Here the King is wailing and lamenting, and the Queen has assumed complete control of the army. The inversion is reinforced later in the same scene when Clifford says to his king: "I would your Highness would depart the field. /The Queen hath best success when you are absent" (73-74). Henry is feminised to the point where he is dismissed from the field, and Margaret, the "natural mother" assumes the traditionally masculine roles of soldier and ruler.

In this sense, Prince Edward has virtually become Margaret's son instead of following the patrilineal line of Henry. From Margaret's symbolic devoice with Henry until his death, the Prince stays in Margaret's company and echoes her warlike words and manner. The final scene indeed offers a prominently affectionate picture between mother and son:

> QUEEN MARGARET. And, though unskilful, why not Ned and I
> For once allowed the skilful pilot's charge?
> We will not from the helm to sit and weep,
> But keep our course, though the rough wind say no,
> From shelves and rocks that threaten us with wreck. (5.4.19-23)

The prince, for his part, valiantly takes up his mother's charge and praises his mother:

> Methinks a woman of this valiant spirit
> Should, if a coward heard her speak these words,
> Infuse his breast with magnanimity
> And make him, naked, foil a man at arms. (5.4.39-42)

Later, Oxford remarks and praises the "women and children" (actually mother and son). It is indeed the mother's courage that restores the son's valour. However, the touching scene is tragically brief, and the prince is soon taken captive by the Yorkists. York's son stabs the prince in front of his mother, Margaret. The revised patriarchy figured in mother and son is remarkably short-lived, but its memory lingers.

Generally speaking, Margaret's "natural mother" role threatens to dismantle the patriarchal assumptions in both family and state. Margaret not only performs excellently well the role of a mother, but also shows herself as the model for women's participation in politics. Both as a mother and a ruling woman, Margaret poses a threat to the law and custom of the patrilineal succession inherent in the patriarchy system. What is more, the "natural mother" image is so persisting that it grows into Shakespeare's later plays *King John* and *Richard II*.

In conclusion, Chapter Two focuses on Shakespeare's fictional use of history in *1 Henry VI*, *2 Henry VI*, and *3 Henry VI*. The first trilogy is not inculcation of what Tillyard termed as "Tudor myth". The religious scheme and monarchical rights are relevant but not the main focus of the first trilogy. The book suggests that Shakespeare's history plays, though still very much concerned with the endless political oscillation of "great men", undercut and revise the Tudor propensity of order and hierarchy. Behind the compressed dramatic representation is Shakespeare's exploration of the rendezvous between historical past and fictional reinvention. What is important is that, through the exploration, there emerges Shakespeare's fictional use of history, which comprehends all classes of people and different genders. His marvellous first try on reshaping historical characters and inventing new characters, such as Joan and Cade, and the "infinite numbers" of commoners, if not imitations of reality, has the vividness of living characters. His selection and compression of historical materials into the dramatic plots are at work, too. On the whole, the many fictional elements are at work and pose severe interrogations to the grand narrative of history on the heroic, political and secular levels.

Chapter Three Further Exploration of the Fictional Use of History: The Possibility of Constructing a Different History

    The first trilogy, in which the fictional elements act as the fault-lines in the seemingly smooth appearance of history, calls attention to the failure of a grand narrative which designed to keep disorder at bay. But then, is there no alternative to the inexorable and teleological development of history? It is possible to read Shakespeare's history plays otherwise under the light of the postmodernism, the ways which have explicit resonances for us in the present era.

    The postmodernism calls into theoretical question all realities, all certainties, and with them the certainty of history. The work of Saussure puts in doubt the possibility of the extra-linguistic reality in language. There is, Saussure's work implied, no sure place beyond language to draw from. History is consequently linguistic too, precisely a narrative of story, and thus no longer able to guarantee our readings of a singular truth. One of the postmodernist interrogations of history is Derrida's "différance." Derrida insists that "différance is literally neither a word nor a concept" (1982:3). Instead, it can only be recognized as a play of differences that is both a spacing of signifiers in relation to one another and a deferral of meaning when they are read. It is Lyotard who puts Derrida's notion further by rejecting all dominant ideologies as grand narratives, and extols the minorities and the heterogeneous nature of history. Lyotard's account of history, then, is not a grand narrative but only about change, not as extra-discursive explanation but a guarantee of textual difference. In general, the postmodernist practice sheds light on the possibilities of uncovering a different story in the seamless history-as-myth.

Written after the first trilogy, *Richard III*, *Richard II* and *King John* can be counted as the transitional plays between Shakespeare's early trilogy of *Henry VI* series which belongs to the period of Shakespeare's apprenticeship and the late trilogy of *Henry IV-V* series which are much more mature and popular. We can see a progressive development of Shakespeare's fictional use of history in these transitional plays. In the first trilogy, the fictional or semi-fictional characters—aristocratic traitors, peasant rebels and female characters, try to raise radical challenges yet still caught up within the binary opposition between the legitimate authority and the historical subversion. In the transitional plays, the characters become increasingly prominent and clash individually and competitively to define how different their histories can be.

Gradually, we can see the focus of Shakespeare's dramatic fiction has been shifting from the official histories of the royalties and nobles to the unofficial histories such as the Bastard and the mother figures which though altogether unhistorical, act as the audience's window on understanding a different past. What is more, Shakespeare deals with two unresolved mysteries of history—the death of two young Princes in *Richard III*, and the death of Arthur in *King John* so delicately as to raise the question towards the undetermined truthfulness of history. From this perspective, it is possible to read Shakespeare's transitional plays as his further exploration of fictional use of history, which discloses the possibilities of constructing a different history.

3.1 Reinvention of History: The Historical Characters Being Refashioned by the Poetic Treatment

Constructing history underscores its fictional quality. Louis O. Mink once proposes that the narrative form in history as well as in fiction is an artifice, or in other words, the product of individual imagination (145). This notion deconstructs the seemingly unbridgeable gap between historical events and fictional events.

Although historians and writers of fiction may be interested in different kinds of events, the forms of their respective discourses and their aims in writing are often the same. Besides, the techniques or strategies that they use in the composition of their discourses can be shown to be substantially the same, however different they may appear on a purely dictional level of their texts.

In *Tropics of Discourse*, White contends that "history as a discipline is in bad shape today because it has lost sight of its origins in the literary imagination" (99). When considered as "verbal artifacts" or to put accurately, "verbal fictions", modern historical narrative, despite their aims and claims to be scientific and objective, share some very fundamental features with literary narrative (1978:82). One of the features is that both history and literature are highly conventionalised in their narrative forms, and not at all transparent either in terms of language or structure. Given the fact that similar structuring devices exist in both history and literature, there are many standard features shared between historian's recording historical events and writers' fictional use of the pasts. For Hayden White, the deep structural content is "generally poetic, and specifically linguistic, in nature, and which serves as the precritically accepted paradigm of what a distinctively 'historical' explanation should be" (1973: ix).

Into the cultural debate about the demarcation of history and literature—or, the blurring of history and fiction—Shakespeare had already stepped several centuries earlier. In fact, Shakespeare regularly explores "the literature of fact" or, in Hayden White's words "the fictions of factual representation" (1978: 122) by his poetic reinvention of the historical legacy, especially in his transitional plays. By the poetic reinvention of historical characters, the dramatist reshapes history into a different past.

3.1.1 *Richard III*: The Deformed Shape of King's Body

Historiography is the writing of history, which is often sponsored, authorised, or endorsed by its government. In the historiography of Shakespeare's time, we are most likely to find the descriptions of kings. However, this kind of description is only the historical legacy to which the dramatist refers. Shakespeare poetically reworks his sources to develop the figure of Richard III as a degenerate monster. Back in *2 and 3 Henry VI*, Richard was still the Duke of Gloucester who was a leader of the Yorkist faction and the assassin of Henry VI. In *Richard III*, Richard, or more precisely the "new" Richard, emerges with his deformed shape of the body and exuberant cry for self-recognition, bursting fully into life. What he promises is nothing less than the ability to shape "history" into his own liking, in his own image: the hunch-back villain transfigures the landscape of history.

Although certainly a usurper and probably a murderer, the historical Richard is, according to Oscar Campbell's *A Shakespeare Encyclopaedia*, a competent administrator and a skilful and brave soldier (695). The latter fact makes it unlikely that his physical deformity is as significant as Shakespeare seems to indicate. A portrait now in the Society of Antiquaries of London, painted about 1505, shows a Richard with straight shoulders. However, a second portrait, possibly of earlier date in the Royal Collection, seems to problematise the whole controversy. For in it, X-ray examination reveals an original straight shoulder line, which was subsequently painted over to present the raised right shoulder silhouette so often copied by later portraitists.① What is more, in Edward Hall's *Union of the Noble and Illustrate Families of Lancaster and York*, Hall's account of Richard's youth emphasises his courage, war-like skill, and notable services to Edward at battles (qtd. in Bullough 1960a: 226).

So why Shakespeare depicts Richard like this—a malevolent hunch-back monster? In order to have a clear picture of the transmission, we need to document briefly the line in which Richard's deformity being successfully instated. The legend of Richard III's wickedness began during his lifetime and spread during the sixteenth century not only because every supporter of the Tudor regime wished to attack him but also because of the circumstantial details provided by the hostile historiography. The

---

① The Information is provided by Pamela, Tudor-Craig, *Richard III* (1973); quoted in Watt, *Shakespeare's History Plays*, pp. 99.

narrative material of *Richard Ⅲ* comes straight from the historical sources, in particular, the historiographies of Polydore Vergil's *Anglica Historia* (1534), Thoams More's *History of Richard Ⅲ* (1513), *The Mirror for Magistrates* (1559-96), and the chronicles of Edward Hall (1548) and Raphael Holinshed (1587). For Plydore Vergil, whose *Anglica Historia* had been initially commissioned by King Henry Ⅶ (Richmond in the play), Richard embodies the culminating example of transgression within a scheme of usurpation and betrayal, bringing about the disruption of moral and political order (Bitot 107). Thomas More provides an even more revealing physical and political portrait, a probable source of inspiration to Shakespeare:

> Richard Duke of Gloucester […] was little of stature, evil-featured of limbs, crook-backed, the left shoulder much higher than the right, hard-favoured of visage […] He was malicious, wrathful, and envious, and, as it is reported, his mother the Duchess had much ado in her travail, that she could not be delivered of him uncut, and that he came into the world the feet forward, as men be born outward and, as the fame ran, not untoothed. (qtd. in Bitot 108)

What is more, Thomas More produces a concentrated, eventful record of Richard's reign. More's entirely hostile account transforms Richard Ⅲ's nature, increases the tyrant's villainy at all points and sets Richard Ⅲ as an ultimate emblem for human degradation, which goes against the idealised and the divine purpose represented by Richmond.

Shakespeare's fiction must have based upon these Tudor historiographies. Nevertheless, Shakespeare's Richard escapes from historical boundaries and becomes a stylised, larger than life demonic figure. It seems that the greatness of Shakespeare's poetic reinvention does not lie in its political motivations but in foregrounding the very fascination exerted by Richard's power to shape and control the history. Therefore, the focus should then be on exploring textually the outcome of a creative process which transforms these historical legacies of historiography into the compound, repulsive, and attractive figure that is Richard Ⅲ.

Shakespeare allows himself some unusually drastic rearrangements of historical material to model Richard effectively in the early stages. Into the opening episodes come the funeral of Henry Ⅵ in 1471, Richard's marriage with Anne Neville in 1472, the imprisonment of Clarence in 1478, and the last illness of Edward in 1483. The drawings together of these events and their presentation to us through the perspective of Richard give us the impression that Richard himself is controlling the making of history, just as he seems to be controlling the shape of the play.

Richard's control of his own play is remarkable. He has nearly a third of its text and all its significant soliloquies. By turning his chaotic physical condition into a rhetorical benefit, Richard suggests that he can "change shapes with Proteus for advantages" (3.2.192). Indeed, since most of his soliloquies are grouped near the beginning, we are early conditioned into accepting his view of the event. Richard Ⅲ's self-proclaimed deformity is established when the demonic presence of his body emerges from the famous opening speech:

> But I, that am not shaped for sportive trikes,
> Nor made to court an amorous looking—glass;
> I that am rudely stamped and want love's majesty
> To strut before a wanton ambling nymph,
> I that am curtailed of this fair proportion,
> Cheated of feature by dissembling nature,
> Deformed, unfinished, sent before my time
> Into this breathing world scarce half made up,
> And that so lamely and unfashionable
> That dogs bark at me as I halt by them,
> Why, I, in this weak piping time of peace,
> Have no delight to pass away the time,
> Unless to spy my shadow in the sun

And descant on mine own deformity. (1.1.14-27)

Since his deformities prevent him from tasting the wanton pleasures in which the king delights, and make him not to court an "amorous looking-glass", Richard is "determined to prove a villain". On the face of it, Richard identifies his being in entirely negative terms—shadow being the opposite of substance and his deformed shape being alien to the pleasures of the court. However, in the distinction between the "amorous looking-glass" and the "shadow in the sun", we find a contrast of two modes of reflection. On the one hand, the "flattering glass" is "amorous" and seems to endorse Richard's self-compliance, as well as invites the self-absorbed superficial representation. On the other hand, the shadow enhances deformity, adding a further dimension of devilishness to an already twisted physical and psychological substance. Indeed, the very fascination exerted by the historical Richard Ⅲ's substance seems to grow in direct proportion to the fictional Richard's effort of refashioning the shadowy world.

Characteristically, Richard sees himself, and roots his self-consciousness, in the externalised image of his own shadow. His confidence, coming from looking at his shadow from the amorous looking glass, reminds us of Jacques Lacan's "mirror stage". Lacan writes:

> The view I have formulated as the fact of a real specific prematurity of birth in man[⋯] This development is experienced as a temporal dialect that decisively projects the formation of the individual into history. The mirror stage is a drama whose internal thrust is precipitated into insufficiency to anticipation—and which manufactures for the subject, caught up in the lure of spatial identification, the succession of phantasies that extends from a fragmented body-image to a form of its totality that I shall call orthopaedic—and, lastly, to the assumption of the armour of an alienating identity, which will mark with its rigid stricture the subject's entire material development. (4)

Out of his anticipation of the throne in the "mirror", Richard steps forward to command a corrupt and exhausted language, and to renew the credibility of his radical claim. He claims his destiny not as a deserving hero, but as the fabricating freak: "Then, since this earth affords no joy to me / […] I'll make my heaven to dream upon the crown" (3.2.165, 168). Richard has so much creative power that he energetically imposes his ordering upon the shape of history, and thence we may say that he makes the world of *Richard III* play "mine".

However, when Richmond (the future Tudor King who is going to unite Lancaster and York) approaches, the play begins running to its predetermined conclusion. As a Plantagenet king, being unhandsome in person as in personality, Richard III is destined to be defeated by a Tudor King (Richmond later crowned as Henry VII, and he is Elizabeth's grandfather). On the night before the final battle with Richmond, Richard is haunted in his sleep by the ghosts of his victims. Henry VI, Clarence, Rivers, Grey and Vaughan, Hastings, the two young Princes, Lady Anne, and Buckingham rise to lay their curses on Richard. The tension at the heart of the dramatic fiction, between, on the one hand, Richard's illusory freedom and capacity to refashion the history and, on the other, the "preordained" patterns of history which have cast him merely as the last King of the Civil War, makes him engrossed in his crimes of the past. So when that happens, his identity collapses: "Richard loves Richard; that is, I am I. / […] Is there a murderer here? No. Yes, I am / […] I am a villain: yet I lie. I am not" (5.3.183-191). No matter he is a villain or not, Richard arises from the historical legacy to exclaim his own fate and is ready to perish in battle so as to win immortal shame.

In conclusion, as attractive a character as the Richard in historiography, Shakespeare's Richard III refashions himself by his histrionic vitality, his command of sarcasm and irony, and his artist's capacity for manipulation of materials. The figure that emerges so decisively in the later stages of *3 Henry VI* to ride the chaos that follows the social disintegration we have been observing, takes control theatrically as well as politically in *Richard III*. In the final scene of *3 Henry VI* an ambitious and disgruntled Richard murmurs aside, "yet I am not looked on in the world. / This shoulder was ordained so thick to heave, / And heave it shall some weight, or break my back" (5.7.22-4). Richard's deformed shoulder is what "shoulders" the deformed shape of history. Deformity, as a self-augmenting textual effect, contaminating the telling of Richard's body as well as Richard's story, has always been associated with his literary presence. Not only does Richard theorise his own deformity, but he also generates and theorises deformity as a form of historical narrative. However, no matter which kind of shape he wants to take, his deformity, transmitted through historiography, is the dramatic focus of the play and refashioned poetically by Shakespeare.

Utilising the sources of Tudor historical legacies, Shakespeare poetically refashions the figure of the king as a hunch-back monster. What we shall see in *Richard III* is a contrast between the dynamism and energy of the character's confidence in his act and in his ability to control the play, and the unalterable patterns of historical progression—a conflict for controlling the shape of history.

3.1.2 *Richard II* : The Different Modes of King's Language

Under the perspective of postmodernist philosophy of history, there is no unbridgeable gap between history and literature. Both history and literature are linguistic construction, which is realised through narrative. Although historical and literary narratives are similar when it comes to their interpretation at the suprafactographic level, there are also differences between them. One of the differences is the language of narratives. The literary narrative shows the mechanisms of decision-making by human beings; it includes dialogues and penetrates human consciousness. The historian would probably be willing to enliven his narrative, for instance, with dialogues, but he is not allowed to do so because he is not allowed to invent things (Domanska 132). In this way, a historian can never penetrate the human psyche in the way Shakespeare does.

Shakespeare's rhetoric skills of narrating history are unique and eliciting in

Richard II. Marion Trousdale fruitfully examines *Richard II* as "a rhetorical exercise" (65). As Trousdale explains, Shakespeare's method is to "open up the history" of a famous monarch by considering its possibilities from varied standpoints and with different modes of perception—the King as judge, the King as tyrant, the King as a man deposed—and then "unfold" the narrative by "suggesting some of the topics that lie within" (79). The topics that lie within the three modes of King's image are realised through different rhetorical techniques. If we take a closer look at *Richard II*, we would find that the prominent talks of name and meaning, title and self, mirror and truth constitute the language of the King's three images respectively. Under this light, the character's physical activities become less critical than the character's different rhetorical techniques in *Richard II*. Contending attitudes towards weak legitimate kings and strong illegitimate rulers call for different techniques; Richard's courage as anointed king and despair in the face of adversity draw upon various rhetorical techniques. Thus, the play emerges as a fabric of thematic and perspectival interconnections woven together by rhetorical techniques, which provides different modes of "understanding and even constructing history" (Trousdale 79).

The primary source of Shakespeare's *Richard II* is Holinshed. From Holinshed, Shakespeare takes most of the names and incidents in his play and follows in the main the chronicler's sequence of events. But Shakespeare still reshapes some of the characters and their speeches. One of the most significant changes from Holinshed is the new prominence accorded to Richard's uncle—John of Gaunt. In the chronicle from which Shakespeare draws his facts, Gaunt is scarcely a presence at all. Indeed he enters Holinshed's narrative briefly at only two points: first, in a sentence recounting his death and, second, in Carlisle's speech reminding Parliament that Bolingbroke (Gaunt's son) had been banished partly on the advice of "his own father" (qtd. in Shakespeare 2013: 128). On this slender foundation, Shakespeare makes Gaunt an essential figure in the episode of "the King as Judge", invents his grief as Richard's motive for commuting Bolingbroke's sentence, and constructs an entire episode out of the leave-taking of the father (Gaunt) and son (Bolingbroke).

The rhetorical technique of "name" versus "meaning" figures very prominently in the first mode of "the King as Judge". The emphasis of name and meaning is manifested in the opening lines when Richard addresses Gaunt by the name of Lancaster:

> KING RICHARD II. Old John of Gaunt, time-honoured Lancaster,
> Hast thou, according to thy oath and band,
> Brought hither Henry Hereford thy bold son,
> Here to make good the boisterous late appeal—
> Which then our leisure would not let us hear—
> Against the Duke of Norfolk, Thomas Mowbray? (1.1.1-6)

It is invoked in Richard's first words his most potent subject: Henry Bolingbroke—the future Henry IV. Bolingbroke and Mowbray come before Richard "to appeal each other of high treason" (1.1.27). Bolingbroke tries to name Mowbray as "traitor"—"thou art a traitor and a miscreant" (1.1.39) and also accuses Mowbray of conspiring to murder the king's uncle, the Duke of Gloucester. Mowbray's speech dismisses language as an inferior and unreliable medium, through which the name-giving accusation can too quickly become denounced:

> MOWBRAY. Not my cold words here accuse my zeal.
> 'Tis not the trial of a woman's war,
> The bitter clamour of two eager tongues,
> Can arbitrate this cause betwixt us twain. (1.1.47-51)

"Cold words" of the name "traitor" hovering in the air waits for its justice; however, to call someone traitor falsely is to be a traitor himself, which is evident to Richard II, since he may be the real progenitor of the cause. Though the debate begins in the realm of language, after Richard's words fail to calm the men down,

Bolingbroke and Mowbray agree to settle the matter by physical combat. The name "traitor" is going to be applied to one of the combatants at his death.

Gaunt's visit to the widowed Duchess of Gloucester is another invented episode by Shakespeare. In the short dialogue between Gaunt and the widow, Gaunt appears to be sure that Richard is responsible for the death of Duke of Gloucester who is Richard's severest rival for the throne. However, Gaunt urges Gloucester's widow to "put our quarrel to the will of heaven" (1.2.6). In her reply, the widow repeatedly touches on the idea of naming: "Call it not patience, Gaunt; / it is despair. / In suffering thus thy brother to be slaughtered" (1.2.29-30). It is as though the principle of the applicability of names has been generally unbalanced in the realm. The name "traitor" floats in the air, and it is Richard who ultimately at fault. Yet the name cannot be applied to him, for as a king, Richard himself is the Judge.

The next scene begins with the ceremonious presentation of the combatants, whose names are so important that Richard instructs to "ask him his name, and orderly proceed to swear him in the justice of his cause" (1.3.10). All seems about to be resolved until Richard halts the ceremony in its midst. He banishes Mowbray and Bolingbroke and instructs them to swear "never shall embrace each other's love in banishment" (1.3.84), which is in contradiction to his earlier command that they are friends. Through Richard's self-contradiction, we can see his main object: the name "traitor" should not stick, and he needs to keep the name's ambiguous meaning. By doing so, he robs both Bolingbroke and Mowbray of their names from "the book of life" (1.3.202) that would have manifested the truth and justice of their cause. Mowbray bitterly laments that "if ever I was traitor, / My name be blotted from the book of life, / And I from heaven banished as from hence!" (1.3.201-203). It is much more bitter for Bolingbroke because the banishment represents a double disappointment: a lost opportunity for testing and proving family honour, and a thwarted aspiration to register his name as a chivalric hero.

After the sentence of Bolingbroke's banishment, Gaunt attempts to ease the pain of his son's exile by playing the meanings of the name. Gaunt advises Bolingbroke not to take his banishment literally that "think not the king did banish thee, but thou the king" (1.3.280). However, Gaunt's effort provokes an instant reply: "My heart will sigh when I miscall it so, / When finds it an enforced pilgrimage" (1.3.262-4). Bolingbroke instinctively recognises that changing the name of a thing does not change its reality. The corporeal or mystical substance of words is mostly illusory for Bolingbroke. Because Bolingbroke does not intend to play with names, instead, he wants to grasp the chance of making himself a real king.

Compared with the pragmatic Bolingbroke, Richard enjoys the privilege of assigning names and is deeply involved in the naming process. However, the essential link between name and meaning has been broken when Richard meets the dying Gaunt. John of Gaunt, approaching death after his son's banishment, restates the "loss of names":

> KING RICHARD II. What comfort, man? how is't with aged Gaunt?
> GAUNT. O how that name befits my composition!
> Old Gaunt indeed, and gaunt in being old.
> Within me grief hath kept a tedious fast,
> And who abstains from meat that is not gaunt?
> For sleeping England long time have I watched;
> Watching breeds leanness, leanness is all gaunt.
> The pleasure that some fathers feed upon
> Is my strict fast—I mean my children's looks,
> And therein fasting hast thou made me gaunt:
> Gaunt am I for the grave, gaunt as a grave,
> Whose hollow womb inherits nought but bones. (2.1.72-83)

The affirmation of plenitude and truth in the signifier of "Gaunt" by name and nature is made an absence by Richard. John Baxter suggests that Gaunt's name embraces three aspects of his identity—brother to the murdered Gloucester, father to the banished Bolingbroke and counsellor to the English throne; Richard has killed all three "in so far as Gaunt's essence subsists" in each of them (91). Gaunt is dying of grief for a land which has no heirs, a realm whose lineage is coming to an end as Richard fails to live the name of King and the meaning of sovereignty: "Landlord of England art thou now, not King" (2.1.114).

Behaving like a "King of Tyrant" after Gaunt's death, Richard II seizes Gaunt's property that Bolingbroke should have inherited. So Bolingbroke returns from exile to claim his rights. It is from here that Richard II enters from Gaunt's rhetoric realm of name and meaning into Bolingbroke's realm of title and power. Bolingbroke's talks are less about the property than about something else he inherits from his father—the title Duke of Lancaster. Bolingbroke insists on being addressed by his title Lancaster rather than his old title of "Hereford":

> LORD BERKELEY. My Lord of Hereford, my message is to you.
> HENRY BOLINGBROKE. My lord, my answer is—to Lancaster;
> And I am come to seek that name in England;
> And I must find that title in your tongue,
> Before I make reply to aught you say. (2.3.69-73)

What may seem perverse fastidiousness in Bolingbroke begins to look more like legalistic shrewdness when we see him replying to York's condemnation of his return with: "As I was banished,/ I was banished Hereford/ But as I come, I come for Lancaster" (2.3.112-13). Compared with Bolingbroke, Richard's conceit is more radical. The title means so much to Richard that by abandoning his title, he loses not only his name but also his identity. When Bolingbroke asks whether he is willing to give up the crown, Richard replies with puns and paradoxes, "Ay, no; no, ay; for I must nothing be. / Therefore no 'no', for I resign to thee" (4.1.201-2). Richard, in his narcissistic distress, toys with ambiguous significances of language. There are at least two ways of understanding these lines: (1) Yes, no. No, yes. Have lost my title, I am now nothing. (2) "I, no. No, I", which in delivery can sound like "I know no I"; in this reading, we may paraphrase: "Since I am now reduced to nonentity, I cannot even know who I am, and therefore whatever I say is meaningless."①

In Richard's view, the title "king" is part of his proper name—inherently legitimate, inviolable, and unquestionable. Richard must assume that his title is indistinguishable from his identity. Since Richard seems to treat equivalent the title "king" as the man "Richard" so that to lose the former is also to lose the latter. For Richard, ceasing to be king is equivalent to non-existence. If he resigns to Bolingbroke his title, there is nothing left of him to be content or discontent. Richard's fanciful and impassioned speeches have an undeniable power, but they obviously cannot save him from his inevitable tragedy "the King being Deposed".

After being captured by Bolingbroke, Richard is isolated in Pomfret Castle. Self-indulgently anticipating total defeat, Richard is the first person after Bolingbroke's return to pronounce the word "deposed":

> RICHARD: What must the King do now? Must he submit?
> The King shall do it. Must he be deposed?
> The King shall be contended. Must he lose
> The name of King? I' God's name, let it go. (3.3.143-6)

Losing the name and title of King, Richard loses everything. Cast out of his world of power and significance, Richard wants to view his own natural face and his "bankruptcy of majesty", so he orders a mirror. The mirror into which Richard narcissistically looks and smashes can be seen as an iconographic symbol which reflects the truth of history. As "the looking glass of man's life", history is an exact

---

① For further discussion of this complicated passage, see *King Richard II*, the Arden Shakespeare, 2013. pp. 399.

imitation of reality which in turn produces "wisdom". According to Cicero, the metaphor of the "looking glass" seeks to establish an unproblematic continuity between appearance and knowledge: on the one hand, accurate reflection or precise imitation of the object, and on the other hand, a wisdom or understanding acquired via that process of reflection on human experience (qtd. in Holderness 2000:205). In this sense, the mirror is assumed to be capable of not merely reflecting a surface reality, but of disclosing a hidden truth, depicting an underlying reality and presenting human conditions as accurately as possible.

However, when Richard calls for a looking-glass to reflect a climactic moment of his own history, what he sees is not an accurate reflection, but a distortion, or even inversion, of the truth. Bolingbroke refers with contempt to Richard by saying "the shadow of your sorrow hath destroyed/ the shadow of your face" (4.1.291-292). The dark shadow cast by Richard's fancied sorrow is unreal and induces illusion. The mirror, instead of being an agent of reflective wisdom, acts as a confessional record of Richard's own soul, and reflects the very opposite of what Richard feels himself to be. The brittleness of the mirror symbolises for Richard the fragility and impermanence of life, which links thematically to the "hollow crown" speech (3.2.144-177). Thus, the distortions, fragmentation of subjectivity involved in Richard's personal tragedy help to expand consciousness and deepen perception on conflicts between word and meaning, title and self, mirror and truth.

Richard has often been called a poet-king, not because he speaks excellent verse—as the "unpoetic" Bolingbroke does—but because his attitude toward language is poetic. Instead of applying to physical forces, the only thing Richard Ⅱ can resort to is a metaphorical language, which is a manifestation of his powerless control on history. The three different rhetorical modes of "name and meaning", "title and self", "mirror and truth" help to realise Richard's highly intellectual, emotional language in his entire journey through "the King as Judge", "the King as Tyrant", and "the King being Deposed". Also, he experiences the whole metamorphosis of language in which the marriage of word and thing, signifier and signified, is put asunder and man's thought divorced from the actual world.

All in all, Shakespeare poetically reinvents the chronicle sources through the verbal medium in *Richard II*. By using the various rhetorical techniques, Shakespeare fictionalised Richard II's history into a rhetorical game which finally falls into the different signifiers of language. Shakespeare's combined, varied and repeated permutations of rhetoric skills make the whole dramaturgy so unique and the history so different and eliciting. It is his creative energy and poetic reinvention makes us realise that the "true" representation of history resides, not in the objective imitation of material fact, but in the intuitive apprehension of a verbal reality.

3.2 Becoming of History: The Fictional Elements Being Historicised into Plays

Under the light of postmodernist philosophy of history, both history and literature are narratives, and both of them involves the same techniques of "emplotment" and "characterisation", so many barriers separating history from the literature have been removed, but there are still some differences. One of the differences is that the writer of fiction can invent rousing speeches and dialogues in the literary narrative. However, the historian is not allowed to do so in the historical narrative because he is not allowed to invent things. Apart from the differences between the languages of narratives, there is another essential difference which Jerzy Topolski quite neatly points out:

> The essential difference between historical and literary narratives is that the historian cannot invent individual facts. He cannot deliberately include in his narrative fiction pertaining to what originates from the empirical base. A man of letters, on the contrary, may include the description of such facts in his text. This kind of facts is realized through a narrative organisation of the past—an organisation that is not intrinsic to the past itself. (qtd. in Domanska 131)

That is to say, the historians could not intentionally fabricate a single event based on experience. The "emplotment" and "characterisation" in the historiography should at least have some "traces" of the historical events, such as the archived materials, government documents, narratives of the witnesses. Although a historian cannot "invent individual facts", a dramatist can do, and that is indeed what Shakespeare does in his history plays. Like Topolski says: "The historian reports on history, while the man of letters shows the becoming of history" (qtd. in Domanska 133). By inventing fictional characters and historicising them into history plays, Shakespeare reveals the universal human psyche and furthermore shows the mechanisms of the "becoming" of history. Those fictional figures, with a psychological feature, go beyond the dialectical necessity of the dramatic collision to inscribe their own records and broaden the scene of history.

3.2.1　Bastard in *King John*: "A Bastard to the Time"

King John, covering a much earlier historical period (John reigned from 1199 and died in 1216), was probably written by Shakespeare in 1596 between *Richard II* and *1 Henry IV*. It is generally thought that *King John* was based not directly on chronicle history, but on an anonymous play entitled *The Troublesome Raigne of King John of England*, which took its material from Holinshed's *Chronicles* and was partly influenced by John Bale's morality, *Kynge Johan*. ① Our views about Shakespeare's fictional use of the historical material must depend upon the comparisons between *King John* and *The Troublesome Raigne*.

Almost every consideration of the relationship between *King John* and *The Troublesome Raigne* comments on how Shakespeare's version plays down the papacy's power over Christian nations. In *the Troublesome Raigne*, the author's purpose was to

---

①　For more information please refer to Bullough, Geoffrey. *Narrative and Dramatic Sources of Shakespeare*. Vol. 4. *Later English History Plays*: *King John*, *Henry IV*, *Henry V*, *Henry VIII* London: Routledge & Kegan Paul, 1960. pp. 1-25.

modernise John as an opponent of Church abuses the papal power. There was much repetition in the working-out of anti-papal expressions. Compared with his predecessor, Shakespeare's *King John* makes very little use of anti-papal material. Instead, Shakespeare makes Philip the Bastard a much more prominent figure than that of *The Troublesome Raigne*.

Philip the Bastard (also known as Philip Faulconbridge, half-brother to Robert Faulconbridge) is a fictional character inserted into the narrative by the author of *The Troublesome Raigne*. In creating him, the anonymous playwright interweaved suggestions from all his sources. Holinshed mentioned one "Philip, bastard son to king Richard [···] killed the viscount of Limoges, in revenge of his father's death", and this suggestion could very well be enriched by what Hall said of the Earl of Dunois, who preferred the brand of bastardy to be known as the legitimate son of a cowardly lord (qtd. in Bullough 1960b:7). *The Troublesome Raigne* was in all probability Shakespeare's immediate source and supplied him with all the materials of his plot. However, Shakespeare's Bastard is much more complex and possesses more life than the sketchy portrait he finds in *The Troublesome Raigne*.

In *The Troublesome Raigne*, the Bastard has a romantic and heroic quality, which is indicated in his determination to retrieve from Austria the lion skin. Besides, when John collapses, he takes command and tries to encourage John against his clerical enemies. However, the author of *The Troublesome Raigne* was willing to embroider historical facts but not to romanticise them so far as to turn the Bastard into the complete hero (qtd. in Bullough 1960b:8). While in Shakespeare's *King John*, Philip the bastard is the most attractive character in the play. Next to all the moral and political corruption, the Bastard emerges as the influential spokesman for the clear-eyed people's common sense.

Take the two Bastard's attitudes towards the death of Arthur as an example. The death of Arthur is of cardinal importance. In *The Troublesome Raigne*, the Bastard puts up a strong plea on behalf of John, saying:

> For Arthurs death, King John was innocent,
> He desperate was the deathman to himself,
> Which you to make a colour to your crime injustly do impute
> his default. (*The Troublesome Raigne* II. iii. 456-8)①

However, in Shakespeare's *King John*, the Bastard does not defend John as the Bastard in *The Troublesome Raigne* tries to do. He suspects Hubert grievously and knows:

> From forth this morsel of dead royalty,
> The life, the right and truth of all this realm
> Is fled to heaven, and England now is left
> To tug and scamble, and to part by th'teeth
> The unowed interest of defence-swelling state. (*King John* 4.3.143-147)

Although he never overtly accuses John, he is intelligent enough to realise who is really responsible for the crime. He pronounces a heavy curse on John's agent Hubert. Confronted by the body of Arthur and the prospect of a world ruled by self-interest and blind contingency, the Bastard declares himself perplexed: "I am amazed, methinks, and lose my way/ Among the thorns and dangers of this world" (4.3.140-141).

From the above comparison, one can see that although Bastard is a character Shakespeare borrows from *The Troublesome Raigne*, Shakespeare's aims are thoroughly different from those of the latter play. In *King John*, instead of choosing his legalised position, the Bastard chose his bastardy at the beginning of the play. By doing so, he denies himself full access to the lineal history that would guarantee him a

---

① For the whole text of *The Troublesome Raigne of King John Part One and Part Two* (1591), please refer to Bullough, Geoffrey. *Narrative and Dramatic Sources of Shakespeare*. Vol. 4. *Later English History Plays: King John, Henry IV, Henry V, Henry VIII* London: Routledge & Kegan Paul, 1960. pp. 72-119.

position and declares his own fictionality. Thus the Bastard is a perfect emblem of "bastard to the time" (1.1.207) being "historicised" in the narration. Through Shakespeare's reinvention, the Bastard becomes a far more complex and attractive figure who join in King John's political poise and rub elbows with political leaders to interrogate the imperfections of the world. What is more, the Bastard raises questions about political legitimacy that who indeed has the right to rule, he or King John without really answering them.

The Troublesome Raigne begins with Queen Eleanor regretting the death of Richard I and welcoming the accession of John. *King John* starts at once when the new king is faced with the lawful claim brought by Chatillon, on Arthur's behalf, to the Kingdom of England and the territories of Ireland, Poitiers, Anjou Touraine, Maine (1.1.10-11). King John refuses Chatillon's request by declaring both possession of the crown and lineal right of succession the throne: "Our strong possession, and our right for us" (1.1.39).

The unhistorical dispute between Philip Faulconbridge and his brother Robert Faulconbridge over Philip's identity of bastardy follows. Robert does not want Philip to inherit his dad father Sir Robert's land because he believes Philip has a different biological father—Richard I, Coeur-de-Lion (1.1). King John is called upon to judge the dispute over Philip's inheritance. King John decides the case according to law, pointing out that, whomever Philip's biological father may have been, as the child of Sir Robert's wife, born in wedlock, he must be accepted by his mother's husband as his child. This is an infrangible legal tie, the king explains; a bond so strong that it could withstand even the will of a king. For even if Coeur-de-Lion himself had subsequently tried to claim Philip as his own, Sir Robert could quite legitimately refuse him. To the younger brother Robert's charge against Philip, King John's verdict is: "Sir, your brother is legitimate. Your father's wife gave birth to him after marriage and if she was unfaithful, that is her fault. That is a risk all husbands take who marry wives. Even if he were my brother's, my brother could not have claimed him. And your father never raised any suspicion about it. It follows, then, that my mother's son conceived your father's heir. Your father's heir must have your father's land."①(1.1.116-129)

John's verdict serves to tie the Bastard to his father's inheritance. However, John's claim to the English throne shown resting, in part at least, on the same sort of testamentary basis as Robert's claim to his father's estate. Although John in the opening scene declares his strong possession and right of the throne, his mother Queen Eleanor admits privately that his rule depends on "strong possession much more than right" (1.1.40). It is a clear admission of John's status as a usurper. John may possess the crown but has an inferior claim to the throne than Arthur's. Therefore, the Bastard's case of legitimization unveils King John's own illegitimacy to the throne, indicating that the King's rule, after the death of his brother Richard I, rests more upon "possession" than on "right" (1.1.40), and that Arthur's claim, as the son of John's older brother, is as good or better. Not only the Bastard helps to addresses the problem of King John's legitimacy to the throne, but he also acts as an interrogation to the reigning king, who relies more on the performance of role-playing than on true noble mind.

In Scene One Act Two, King John and Arthur (with French King Philip as spokesman), confront one another before the besieged town of Angiers. Each of the two opposing kings addresses the citizens of Angiers with the same formula of loyalty and obedience:

KING JOHN. England, for itself.
You men of Angiers, and my loving subjects—
KING PHILIP. You loving men of Angiers, Arthur's subjects,

---

① This part is translated from the original texts by the writer of the book. The original text is: "Sirrah, your brother is legitimate;/ Your father's wife did after wedlock bear him/ then, if he were my brother's,/ My brother might not claim him; nor your father,/ Being none of his, refuse him: this concludes;/ My mother's son did get your father's heir;/ Your father's heir must have your father's land." (1.1.116-129)

Our trumpet called you to this gentle parle—(2.1.203-206)

Confronted with the two contesting claims, the citizens of Angiers refuse to surrender to either of the rival armies but begin to wait for "right" to reveal itself and the appearance of "the worthiest king" (2.1.282). Although both claimants have substantial rights to the throne, the claimant who is "worthier" resists determination. When the citizens of Angiers continue refusing to surrender to either of the rival armies, King John and King Philip, following the "wild counsel" of the Bastard, agree to "lay this Angiers even with the ground,/Then after fight who shall be king of it" (2.1.399-400). But a hastily arranged marriage between Blanche (King John's niece) and Lewis (the Dauphin of France) patches up John and Philip's differences. They immediately abandon their former vows and loyalties to reach a self-interested deal. Reading it as a proof of the hypocritical realpolitics, Kastan argues that the world of political activity here is a theatre where the emphasis has moved away from the fixity of meaning into the arena where kingship is a performance of role-playing and "him who plays it best that proves the king" (1999:11). Neither John nor Arthur plays it well. Arthur, the "true king", can muster no power without European allies; John maintains the throne by "strong possession much more than right" (1.1.40). The better claim comes to Bastard, who, as "a bastard to time" (1.1.207), understands the unstableness of commitment in a muddling world more thoroughly than the others.

At Angiers, the Bastard is rapidly becoming educated in the ways of the world, and he shares with us in soliloquy his contempt for the hypocrisy of those in power. The eager to gain is dismissed in Bastard comments on "commodity" (2.1.573-590). The Bastard's list of commodity incorporates an encompassing use of the word: self-interest, advantage, expediency and gain. All parties are involved in this worship of "gain", which is another name for self-advantage—including John who has traded a part of his kingdom to "stop Arthur's title in the while" (562). It is through his understanding of "commodity" that Bastard learns his first lessons of "the bias of the world" (2.1.574). Comparing himself to "a poor beggar", the Bastard ends his soliloquy with a declaration to gain: "Since kings break faith upon commodity, / Gain, be my lord, for I will worship thee" (2.1.598-599). This declaration, of course, recalls his earlier promise made to himself. After being declared the illegitimate son of Richard Coeur-de-Lion, the Bastard delivers soliloquies on his new station as "a bastard to the time" (1.1.207) and summarises his way forward to "smack of observation" (1.1.208). Despite his repeated resolutions to take advantage of the "sweet poison" (1.1.213) and to take on the personal gain, there is no evidence he can quite bring himself to "practise to deceive" (1.1.214). On the contrary, as the seriousness of events undermines his detachment, the Bastard matures rapidly throughout the play and turns out to be the de facto leader of England, an authority he does not hold in historiography and never could have held.

After John's death, the Bastard rallies the loyal English nobles for an attack on the French. He kills Austria and helps English to win over French. Serving as the political and military commander of the English forces, the Bastard becomes the de facto king of England as the play reaches its conclusion. It is one of the unique tricks in Shakespeare's use of history that he keeps from his audience until the last scene that King John has an heir. The audience's imaginations, freed from chronicle fact, are lured into foreseeing Bastard as the King until the inevitable moment we learn that "the lords are all come back, / And brought Prince Henry in their company" (5.6.33-4).

In the end, the Bastard turns to his final rhetorical and dramatic task, the loyal endorsement of Prince Henry as king and the great patriotic effusion of the play's final lines. He is altogether freed from the historical context and brought forward to deliver the final rousing speech: "This England never did, nor never shall/ Lie at the proud foot of a conqueror" (5.7.112-113).

In general, although Shakespeare draws from *Troublesome Raign* the character of Bastard, there is no reason to doubt that Shakespeare's sophisticated reinvention of Bastard has produced a heightened sensitivity to the effect of fiction. King John's dying declaration—"I am a scribbled form, drawn with a pen/ Upon a parchment" (5. 8. 32-33) is, according to Kastan, an acknowledgement that "both the 'historical' John and the fictional Bastard are 'scribbled' form, characters in a play created with Shakespeare's pen" (1999:15). Hence the Bastard is a "Bastard to the time" in the sense that he "born" in the play by Shakespeare's dramatic representation (he changed his parentage and name in the first scene) and "reborn" within the nominally sphere of aesthetic creation (a "scribbled" form, characters created by Shakespeare's pen) (Braunmuller 313).

The Bastard serves Shakespeare well. Through selection, emphasis, and fabrication of the historical legacy, Shakespeare makes the Bastard shatter the limitations of history and loom much more abundant than history. The "Bastard to time" invites us to acknowledge the possibility of the character, through appearing in the medium of the fiction, being historicised into the narrative and indicating the becoming of history. What Shakespeare does hesitantly when invents the fictional character of the Bastard, he does with magisterial freedom in his fictional characterisation of Falstaff in *Henry IV* plays.

3.2.2 Duchess of York in *Richard II*: The Culmination of Women's Role as Mother

It has often seemed that the places where history is made—the royal court and the field of battle are exclusively reserved for men, and the business of making history is conducted almost entirely by men. No wonder Rackin argues that of all the dramatic genres that were popular on the Elizabethan stage, the English history play was the least hospitable to women (1985:329). In the first trilogy, although the prominent female character such as Joan of Arc appears as the severe challenge to the patriarchal history, she is killed and punished for stepping the line. However, in the transitional plays *Richard III*, *Richard II* and *King John*, the feminine voices dispute and threaten the patriarchal myths, implying that validity of history should include the voices of women and especially the subversive forces of women as the mothers. In the plays, a group of mothers shake the constraints of patriarchal society and break out from the domestic domain to the public court to make their voices heard. The culmination of the mother image is the Duchess of York in *Richard II*, who with her assertiveness and spiritedness saves her only son's life and finally wins her subversive status in the perceived conflicts centring on paternal power and authority.

In a well-ordered patriarchal world, women are silent or invisible. First, as daughters, then as wives, they are subject to male control, and men speak and act on their behalves. In *King John*, the only traditional female figure is Blanche, who is the niece of the King. According to Boswell-stone's comparison of Holinshed and Shakespeare, Blanche of Castile was not present at the interview between John and Philip—which took place on August 1199, or at their later meeting described in the play; and the circumstances of her subsequent betrothal—on May 23, 1200—bore no resemblance to those imagined by the dramatists (53). That is to say, Blanche is a fictional character who was imported into the play to fulfil her ill-fated marriage in the Battle of Angiers. When the citizens of Angiers refuses to surrender to either of the rival kings, John and Philip, following the "wild counsel" of the Bastard, agree to "lay this Angiers even with the ground, /Then after fight who shall be king of it" (*King John* 2.1.399-400). At this point, the spokesman for the citizens of Angiers proposes a way of keeping the peace and reconciling the enemies: Blanche, John's niece, should be married to the French Dauphin with a substantial dowry to be paid by England to France, thus to unite the two "warring nations in amity" (2.1.482) by "a friendly treaty" (2.1.538). Blanche obediently accepts her role in a patriarchal society. Recognising that she has no will of her own, she will accept her fate willingly.

> BLANCHE. My uncle's will in this respect is mine:
> If he sees aught in you that makes him like,
> That anything he sees, which moves his liking,
> I can with ease translate it to my will. (2.1.510-14)

To the two kings, Blanche is the medium in which they would negotiate their peace treaty. Also, to all three men, she represents a "site for the inscription of a patriarchal historical narrative" (Howard 122). However, very soon, the two countries ignore Blanche's betrothal and restart the war. Blanche pleads desperately for the peace her marriage was designed to secure. Having failed in her plea, Blanche cries:

> Which is the side that I must go withal?
> I am with both. Each army hath a hand,
> And in their rage, I having hold of both,
> They swirl asunder, and dismember me. (3.1.327-30)

Blanche, as a niece to the English king as well as a wife to the French Dauphin, fails in her traditional feminine role and thus being "dismembered" by the patriarchal power. The dismembered Blanche sheds light on the images of docile daughters who are treated as blank pages awaiting the inscription of patriarchal text.

If we turn from the images of women as daughters to the images of women as wives, *Richard II* provides a convenient starting point. Richard II's Queen Isabel is a figure so different from the historical queen—a child-wife who figures hardly at all in Holinshed's account of the period. So the Queen in *Richard II* is virtually an invention of the dramatist. Shakespeare does not make much of Richard's love for his wife, perhaps because he knows that in fact, she was only a little girl (qtd. in Bullough 1960a:377-378). Instead, he makes her a pitiful sufferer, who suffers a lot due to Richand's decay. We do not see their farewell, but she has taken the parting sadly. Very soon, in a garden, she learns that her husband is captured and she is advised to go to London.

The famous Garden-scene is located in the Duke of York's garden. The Gardener's man wanders why they should keep their garden in order while the whole land falls to ruin for want of such attendance, but the Gardener informs him that

Bolingbroke has taken charge of the kingdom's garden and moralises on Richard's decay. He instructs the man to pluck up and root all the disordered plants as Richard should have done those of his kingdom. According to some critics, this scene is a parable that compares the elements of disorder in a state to weeds that must be rooted out and plucked away; however, this interpretation cannot explain fully the great importance of the very constrained and peripheral perspectives embodied in the King's wife—Queen Isabel. Shakespeare notably allows the audience to observe Queen Isabel venting her exasperation on a gardener. Significantly, the gardener seems to have even more knowledge of events at the centre than the Queen, who does not even learn that Richard is to be deposed until she eavesdrops on the gardeners' conversation. Hiding amidst the "shadow of trees" (3.4.25), powerless and voiceless, Isabel is, as she exclaims, "pressed to death through want of speaking" (3.4.72). Significantly, the Queen is not the only female character in *Richard II* to voice her dissatisfaction with the impotence accorded by her gender role; the Duchess of Gloucester, having urged her brother-in-law [John of Gaunt] avenge her husband's murder by Richard II, is refused by Gaunt ruthlessly. When begging to know "where then, alas, may I complain myself?" (1.2.42), she only has her frustration compounded by Gaunt's retort, "To God, the widow's champion and defence" (1.2.43). The powerless Duchess of Gloucester leaves the stage to die of grief.

These fictional female characters as daughters and wives elaborate on the silencing of women in the patriarchal culture. However, when it comes to the representation of mothers in Shakespeare's drama, we may get a different implication. In Shakespeare's history plays, there are very few mothers in contrast with the frequently represented fathers and their sons. Mothers, however, perform a significant role in history. Mothers bring forth future kings, they produce daughters who marry kings, and they lose their children to battle, sickness, or murder. One curious scene with probably most mothers of Shakespeare's history plays is in *Richard III*, where three mothers come together in unlikely unison, all grieving for sons lost to violent deaths.

The scene opens with old Queen Margaret alone, returns from exile in France "to watch the waning of mine adversaries" and hopes to enjoy the revenge of seeing "bitter, black and tragical" consequences come upon her enemies (*Richard III* 4.4.4-7). The return of Margaret contradicts fact; she died in 1482 and never came back to England after she was ransomed. Her memories and curses are just a means of drawing the three mothers together. Queen Elizabeth (wife of Edward IV and mother of the young princes in the Tower) then appears too. As Elizabeth weeps for her lost children, Margaret speaks aside, reminding the audience of her own losses. Finally, the Duchess (the mother of Edward IV and Richard III) comes to mourn with Elizabeth, wishing that England could "as well afford a grave / As [···] yield a melancholy seat" (*Richard III* 4.4.25-6). As their mourning continues, Margaret comes forward to add her woes to theirs.

Margaret, though she does cease to be the enemy of the Queen and the Duchess of York, becomes an active participant in their mourning, drawing out clear parallels between all three of them as mothers:

> MARGARET. Tell over your woes again by viewing mine.
> I had an Edward, till a Richard killed him.
> I had a Harry, till a Richard killed him.
> (To the Queen) Thou hadst an Edward, till a Richard killed him.
> Thou hadst a Richard, till a Richard killed him.
> DUCHESS OF YORK. I had a Richard too, and thou didst kill him.
> I had a Rutland too, thou holp'st to kill him. (*Richard III* 4.4.36-42)

Motherhood here becomes an especial curse for the Duchess of York to bear, who has not only sons and grandsons but who also produced the very Richard that killed most of them. The scene rises to climax as Queen Elizabeth begs Margaret to teach her how to curse "My words are dull. Enliven them with yours", and Margaret exits with the assurance that Elizabeth's own grief will be the teacher—"Thy woes will make them sharp and pierce like mine" (*Richard III* 4.4.124-25).

Grief is not always so cruel in its depiction, until now, the mothers, except Margaret, are constructed almost entirely in terms of a private world of individual grief. Even Margaret, as discussed above (see Chapter One 1.3.2), is punished by stepping the line of patriarchal power restriction. However, there are more prominent mother figures emerge in *King John*, where the fathers and husbands are dead, reduced to the merely printed names in history books, and the "mothers survive to dispute the fathers' wills and threaten their patriarchal legacies" (Rackin 1990:178).

In *King John*, each of the three potential heirs to the throne—John, Arthur, and the Bastard—appears with his mother. Their mothers are Eleanor, Constance and the Lady Faulconbridge respectively. Although none of them is the principal character, they play essential roles in the potential subversion of the genealogical line. Jacques Derrida argues that "the birth of writing (in the colloquial sense) was nearly everywhere and most often linked to genealogical anxiety" and "the genealogical relation and social classification are the stitched seam of arche-writing" (1974:124-125). In *King John*, it is through the three mothers' persistent effort to subvert the genealogical line of the masculine historical record that they exercise the power of writing a fictional history of mothers.

The play begins with a scene that takes up a crucial problem in a patriarchal society—the nature of genealogical succession. According to Rackin, the written historiographic narrative suppressed women because it had to suppress the knowledge that all men have of the physical impossibility of ever discovering a sure biological basis for patriarchal succession. Hence the association of women with nominalism and their characterisation are subverters of the historiographic record (1985:337). Because an adulterous woman at any point could make a mockery of the whole story of patriarchal succession, women are inevitably threatening to the patriarchal historiographic enterprise①(Rubin 188). In the play's opening sequence, when King John tries to claim his legitimacy to the crown, Eleanor had, in fact, already privately conceded her son's illegal right in a "whispered" aside: "Your strong possession much more than your right" (*King John* 1.1.40).

The similar thing occurs when the Bastard—here called Philip Faulconbridge—and his younger brother Robert come before the king to dispute the Faulconbridge legacy. Robert claims that Philip is not their father's son and should not inherit the Faulconbridge legacy. King John believes in Robert's story, but he disagrees about the legal consequences. He cites a law that states that once a woman is married, her husband is technically considered the legal father of any child she bears, no matter who the biological father actually is. John's attempt to make the judgment exposes a contradiction in patriarchal law.

According to the law expounded by John, a wife, like a cow, is the possession of her husband. Any child she bears is his, even if her husband is not the biological father. Eleanor is the first to guess the Bastard's true father, for she can read his physical nature being similar to Coeur-de-Lion's face. But without Lady Faulconbridge's testimony, the Bastard is still going to inherit the legacy. Thus, the very absoluteness of patriarchal right provides for its own subversion, for Lady Faulconbridge's infidelity as a mother has created a nightmare situation in the patriarchal genealogies—a son not of her husband's being destined to inherit her husband's land and title. Lady Fauclonbridge is an unhistorical character, but she is the only one who knows the truth about the Bastard's paternity. It takes one mother to guess it and another mother to verify it. Thus, this episode makes explicit the fault line that lies beneath the patriarchal claims and repressions—the repressed knowledge

---

① Lacan also discusses the legitimacy by quoting Levi-Strauss's argument that the structures of language are implicated "with that part of the social laws which regulate marriage and kinship," i.e., with legitimacy and patriarchal succession, mythologies that serve male interests. For more information, please refer to Gayle Rubin. "The Traffic in Women: Notes on the 'Political Economy' of Sex,". *Towards an Anthropology of Women*. Ed. R. Reiter. New York: Monthly Review Press, 1975.

of mothers' power to subvert men's genealogical continuity and their genealogical claims.

Constance is another complex mother figure who threatens to subvert the patriarchal world. Shakespeare changes Arthur from a valiant young man to a child and ignores Constance's historical husbands①. So modified, Constance is all the more threatening to the logocentric, masculine historical record. Rather than sitting back to let the men control all the action, Constance tries to change the course of history by driving political careers. She tries to ally with King Philip of France to regain the throne for her son Arthur. After she learns there is going to be a peace treaty and a wedding between England and France, Constance points to the falsehood behind King Philip's royal exterior: "You have beguiled me with a counterfeit" (3.1.25-6). Exercising a traditional patriarchal right by marrying his son to the blank and docile Blanche, the French king makes his claim to leaving a mark on history: "The yearly course that brings this day about", he declares, "shall never see it but a holy day" (3.1.81-2). Rejecting the French King's effort at masculine history-making, Constance wails:

> A wicked day, and not a holy day!
> What hath this day deserved? what hath it done,
> That it in golden letters should be set
> Among the high tides in the calendar?
> Nay, rather turn this day out of the week,
> This day of shame, oppression, perjury. (3.1.83-88)

Refusing to allow the marriage a place in the historical record, Constance rejects the news of it as a "tale" "misspoke, misheard" (3.1.4-5) and demands the day on

---

① Arthur, historically about 15 years of age, but in the play is made much younger, perhaps eight or nine; Constance, widow of Geoffrey Plantagenet but historically twice more married.

which it took place removed from the calendar. Howard neatly points out here, by denying the men's story and demanding the literal erasure of the date, Constance speaks for "the forces that make the writing of patriarchal history impossible in the world of this play" (123).

When the men ask her to hold her tongue, Constance calls out for war instead of accepting the traditional role of a docile and pathetic woman. Moreover, even in the extremity of her grief, she can be witty, as when she mocks the false heroism of Austria, who had vowed so pompously to fight till Arthur is set on the English throne. Referring to Austria's lion-skin of bravery①, she says: "Thou wear a lion's hide? / Doff it for shame, / And hang a calf's skin on those recreant limbs" (3.1.135-6). When Pandulph claims that Constance lacks the "law and warrant", Constance replies by challenging the law itself. She says, when the law cannot do right, let it be legal to do wrong. Since the law itself is completely wrong, how can the law keep people from cursing? By doing so, she speaks out against the patriarchs and their falling system in words which can be dismissed lightly: "O, that my tongue were in the thunder's mouth! / Then with a passion would I shake the world" (3.4.38-42).

Constance, finding herself betrayed, refuses to accept the men's view of history. After Arthur being captured, she renders invalid the men's dismissal of her grief as madness. She proves her self-knowledge in her role as a mother, "my name is Constance, I was Geoffrey's wife, / Young Arthur is my son, and he is lost" (3.4. 46 - 7) and confronts the men who urge her to control herself with a moving and convincing speech.

> CONSTANCE. He talks to me that never had a son
> Grief fills the room up of my absent child

---

① The Duke of Austria in France is wearing the dead King Richard I's lion-skin coat and it is alleged in the play that it is he who killed Richard I. In real life, Austria didn't kill Richard. The King was shot by some people with a crossbow during the siege of a castle in France.

Lies in his bed, walks up and down with me,

Puts on his pretty looks, repeats his words,

Remembers me of all his gracious parts,

Stuffs out his vacant garments with his form.

Then have I reason to be fond of grief? (3.4.91, 93-8).

Constance accuses the men of their inability to empathy and gives a defence of how her actions are, in fact, totally reasonable. There is nothing ritual about her complaints, and she is alone in her suffering, surrounded by a group of hypocritical and cynical men. At the end of the play, with the death of Arthur and John successively, the crisis of patriarchal authority ends with Salisbury's idiom of historical faith in the accession of Prince Henry, who will "set a form upon that indigest/ Which he [John] hath left so shapeless and so rude" (5.7.25-27). It seems that Constance had already responded to this "form" allegorically: "I will not keep this form upon my head, / When there is such disorder in my wit" (3.4.101-102). Constance would never compromise to the patriarchal history and society.

Although Constance stands out prominently in the political conflicts, she still could not have a real influence on the male, patriarchal world. As her sons died, she is kept out of politics and remains silent until the end. However, there is a mother who finally makes her voices heard. The Duchess of York, who is the only prominent female figure other than the Queen in *Richard II*, is the most mature mother character in Shakespeare's history plays. The Duchess of York can take drastic and decisive action in the face of male rebuttal, and she successfully saves her son from being killed by the King.

The story of York's discovery of his only son Aumerle's intended treason is derived from Holinshed. But Holinshed never mentioned such a person as Duchess of York, and the quarrel between the Duke and Duchess of York about their son did not get a mention in both Holinshed and Hall. York's first wife, Aumerle's mother, Isabella of Castile, died in 1394, five years before the action dramatised here; his second wife, the one presented in this scene, was historically Aumerle's stepmother. The doting mother role of the Duchess of York is invented wholly by Shakespeare① (Bullough 1960a: 411-412). However, it is this fictional mother figure that not only threatens to upset the patriarchal historiographic enterprise but also finally deconstructs the male-dominated political world.

At the beginning of the scene, the Duchess asks York to continue his account of the new King Bolingbroke's entry into London—an account the old man had broken off because of his weeping. "Where did I leave?" asks York. The Duchess replies: "At that sad stop, my Lord,/ Where rude misgoverned hands from windows' tops/ Threw dust and rubbish on King Richard's head" (5.2.5-6). What is ironic is that, although Old York is moved by Richard II's sad fate, he actually will also throw "dust thrown upon his [Richard II] sacred head" a few lines later. When his son enters, and the Duchess says "here comes my son Aumerle," York's response is:

> Aumerle that was,
> But that is lost for being Richard's friend.
> And, madame, you must call him Rutland now.
> I am in parliament pledge for his truth
> And lasting fealty to the new-made king. (*Richard II* 5.2.41-45)

Compared with the Duchess's simple understanding of what Aumerle essentially is, a son, York's designation of Aumerle's public titles is trivial. There is even a touch of hollow self-importance in York's phrasing of "I am in parliament pledge" of

---

① Bullough documented Holinshed's description of York's discovery of Aumerle's treason. In the original texts, there is no such a person as the Duchess of York. And the reason why Aumerle (historically the Earle of Rutland) was pardoned is because he himself came before the King's presence, knelt down on his knees, beseeched the King of mercy and forgiveness, and declared the whole matter of conspiracy unto the King to obtain pardon. See Bullough, *Narrative and Dramatic Sources of Shakespeare vol* 3. pp. 411-412.

"lasting fealty" with "new-made king". The Duchess persists. It is not Aumerle or Rutland she greets. Again she says simply, "Welcome, my son" (5.2.465). A moment later, York discovers Aumerle's participation in the conspiracy to assassinate the new king.

Following the chronicles, Shakespeare makes the discovery depend on Aumerle's carelessness in allowing the seal of the indenture to protrude from his bosom. After discovering Amuerle's conspiracy, York is so furious that he vows to report Aumerle's treason to the new king. Terrified by her husband's anger, the duchess assumes, wrongly, that he is motivated by doubts about his son's paternity.

> DUCHESS OF YORK. But now I know thy mind, thou dost suspect
> That I have been disloyal to thy bed,
> And that he is a bastard, not thy son.
> Sweet York, sweet husband, be not of that mind,
> He is as like thee as a man may be
> Not like to me, or any of my kin. (5.2. 104-9)

Neither York nor the audience has any reason to doubt what the duchess says. Howard wrongly assumes that: "the Duchess's anxious suspicion that York doubts his son's paternity is ludicrous, and instead of empowering the duchess as a sexual threat to the authority of her husband and the legitimacy of her son, her reference to the possibility of her adultery is designed to elicit dismissive laughter" (139). The fact is, no one feels that the Duchess's action is ludicrous. Instead of eliciting dismissive laughter, it makes us see a sensible mother who manages to call on the genealogical relation to influence the political action and finally saves her son.

Obviously, York wants to report his only son to the king to protect himself from the oncoming troubles. While the duchess, portrayed as an "unruly" scold and subjected to York's abuse ("foolish woman", "fond mad woman", "frantic woman", "old dugs", 5.2.80-95; 5.3.87-8), takes the decisive action to save her son. When York struggles to get his boots, the Duchess clambers onto a horse, rides off to the centre and gets things done: she compels the King to spare her only son's life. Therefore, the Duchess of York, instead of being frantic and ludicrous, is actually clever and shrewd.

On the contrary, the meek York, determining to report his only son's conspiracy in order to save his own life, shows how hypocritical and unmanly a political father can be. In York's pleading for the death of his own son, there is a suggestion of personal moral loss, the collapse of natural human feeling. The division in the family between the Duke and Duchess is just a reflection of the opposition between the patriarchal order and the mother instinct. As a mother, the Duchess of York is surrounded by male "put down" terms and stigmatised as an unruly shrew. However, she refuses to accept the extreme marginalisation and powerlessness that is thrust upon her gender. She speaks and acts in ways which threaten the dominance of the patriarchal world and, indeed, of Elizabethan society. Thus, her rejoinder to her husband's "Peace, foolish woman", is, notably, "I will not peace" (5.2.80-81).

In the following scene, the domestic quarrel resumes in the royal presence, and this time the tense atmosphere is explicitly identified with the eloquence of the duchess's intervention. "Speak with me, pity, open the door!" she cries, "A beggar begs that never begged before" (5.3.76-77). When Bolingbroke, the new King Henry IV, pardons Aumerle, the King comments "our scene is altered from a serious thing, / And now changed to 'The Beggar and the King'" (5.3.77-80). Howard comments: "It is the woman who is blamed for initiating both the generic lowering of the drama and the social lowering of the action" (141). However, the Duchess of York is the only woman in the play who influences the public and political concerns of men. It is her action that saves her only son's life, and indeed, what kind of action should be termed as "lowering" when it actually saves a life? Besides, the beggar and king scene is just another paradox of Bolingbroke's usurpation, after all, "a thief passes for a gentleman when thieving has made him rich", if not for his success in seizing the crown, it would be hard to say who is the beggar, who is the king.

Therefore, the solemn dignity of the court (and of the history play) has not only places for domestic quarrels but also shows the mother's power to subvert the men's self-righteousness and the patriarchal history. The fictional mother figure of Duchess of York subjects male roles to radical scrutiny and finally deconstructs them by highlighting the considerable distance between male vocalisation about manliness—a frequent occurrence in patriarchal history—and the actual behaviours they perform.

In conclusion, Shakespeare's fictional female roles, no matter they are Princesses or Queens, daughters or wives, without children, are merely shadows of the patriarchal history. Only as mothers, can they subvert the patriarchal world and voice their voices. The unique images of a group of mothers, following the line from the "a tiger's heart wrapped in a woman's hide" Queen Margaret, to the wailing mother Constance and finally develops into the "untruly" mother Duchess of York. They not only overwhelm all protocols of normal political behaviours but also subvert the genealogical line of patriarchal history. Also, it is the Duchess of York, who breaks out from the domestic domain to the public court and with her assertiveness and spiritedness saves her only son, represents Shakespeare's culmination of fictional mother character that shakes the constraints of historical sources and looms larger than the history.

3.3 Meditations on Truth: The Undetermined Truthfulness of History

In the opening scene of *King John*, Robert Faulconbridge, the younger brother of the Bastard, speaks somewhat incredulously: "But truth is truth" (1.1.105). Shakespeare explores the province of history by wrestling with this question, raising doubts about the undetermined truthfulness of history in his plays.

It has always been claimed that the fundamental purpose of history is to record the truth about the past. In order to anticipate some of the objections with which historians often meet in the argument that follows, one needs to distinguish at the outset the historical truth from poetic truth. It has been conventional to characterise their differences since Aristotle. According to Aristotle, historians are concerned with events which can be assigned to specific time-space locations, events which are in principle observable or perceivable, whereas imaginative writers—poets, novelist, playwrights—are concerned with both these kinds of events and imagined, hypothetical, or invented ones. It is the imaginative power which makes poetic truth different from historical truth. Moreover, it is the effort of the imagination, and the intellect involved in the poetry universalises the particular and renders poetic truth a higher position than the historical truth.

In *Richard III*, Shakespeare's aims are thoroughly different from those of the writers of historiography in that he corrupts the substance of the historical tradition, and continually questions the historical truth of the two princes and Lord Hastings' deaths. Besides, in *King John*, by sifting the material, selecting the most relevant portions, imposing a design on the chaotic material of historical records, Shakespeare relates what may happen in Prince Arthur's custody and mysterious death, which then achieves the poetic truth in his literary fiction.

3.3.1 Deaths of Two Princes and Lord Hastings in *Richard III*

The historiography of the early modern period, firmly based on classical models, invoked as its main principles the sixteenth-century historical thinking. The sixteenth-century theorists of historiography were preoccupied with the problems of "truth", that's to say, truth to the historical record and historical recollection. Under this light, One needs to avoid false and forged versions of historical narration. This development of a positivist and objective conception of history, draws on the power of evidence to capture and reveal the truth of the past.

Nevertheless, the reliability of the historiography is quite dubious. A historical event consists of the actions of a human individual that has been left behind in the past. What is more, telling the past, or even one's domestic past is unavoidably a narrative organisation which effects a violation of the verbal image of "reality". To provide a specific verbal image of "reality" is to change a reality "as such" into a reality that is adapted to our aims and purposes of history (*Tropics of Discourse* 121). Therefore, the written account that has survived is tainted by the perspective and intentions of the writer. There is no such thing as a neutral history book. Historiography, or the written history, always arises out of the particular individuals' writing in particular contexts. In this sense, the privileged position of historiography as the record of the historical truth is undermined.

It is Shakespeare who regularly introduced such questioning into his history plays, especially in *Richard Ⅲ*, where Richard, as an excellent self-fashioned figure, distorts the shape of history and changes the verbal image of "reality" to suit his aims. Although Richard believes that he can hide the truth implicitly behind his own "crooked" record, the murder of the two princes and Hastings will comment eloquently on such perversions of key theoretical issues as the historical truth in both oral and written history.

In the Tower of London, the two young Princes see the substance of historical truth lies in the oral history of myth and legend. The point is made precisely by the younger Prince Richard of York, who says he heard that his Uncle Richard (known also as Duke of Gloucester, the later King Richard Ⅲ) was born with teeth. Pressed to identify the source of this biographical detail, the boy first invents a witness—the nurse of Gloucester (2.4.32), one who could be imagined as both professionally qualified, and in a position to observe the infant Gloucester's premature teething. Then, when the reliability of his source is questioned (2.4.33), he tries to validate the story by referring to those most generalised sources, popular memory and oral tradition (2.4.34). Not only the myth of character but the history of the tower is theoretically interrogated in an exchange between the Prince Edward who is the heir to the throne, and the governing magnate Buckingham:

PRINCE EDWARD. I do not like the Tower, of any place.

Chapter Three Further Exploration of the Fictional Use of History: The Possibility of Constructing a Different History

> Did Julius Caesar build that place, my lord?
> BUCKINGHAM. He did, my gracious lord, begin that place;
> Which, since, succeeding ages have re-edified.
> PRINCE EDWARD. Is it upon record, or else reported
> Successively from age to age, he built it?
> BUCKINGHAM. Upon record, my gracious lord.
> PRINCE EDWARD. But say, my lord, it were not registered,
> Methinks the truth should live from age to age,
> As 'twere retailed to all posterity,
> Even to the general all-ending day. (3.1.68-78)

The young prince is sufficiently expert in the historical study to be able to differentiate between oral and documentary history, between historical interpretations grounded in the physical record, and those perpetrated by oral tradition. His sophistication is strikingly impvessive that he actually points out the difficulty of recovering the past and the need to check written records and to compare it with oral tradition. The Prince argues that historical truth ought to be trans-historical as well as manifest in the oral history, which even though without physical record, can survive unaltered through the ages and pass consistently to successive generations, even to the "general all-ending day" (3.1.78).

Nonetheless, the difficulties and complexities in retrieving the historical truth are exposed by the Duke of Gloucester (the future King Richard Ⅲ, hereinafter is referred to as Richard) with a dismissive aside that is then corrected to an expression of apparent agreement. The juxtaposition of these two statements, one being covert and the other deceptive, reveals the controversy:

> GLOUCESTER: [Aside] So wise so young, they say, do never live long.
> PRINCE EDWARD: What say you, uncle?

> GLOUCESTER: I say, without characters, fame lives long.
> [aside] Thus, like the formal vice, Iniquity,
> I moralise two meanings in one word.
> PRINCE EDWARD: That Julius Caesar was a famous man;
> With what his valour did enrich his wit,
> His wit set down to make his valour live
> Death makes no conquest of this conqueror;
> For now he lives in fame, though not in life.
> I'll tell you what, my cousin Buckingham. (3.1.79-89)

  The "one word" in question is the fundamental dimension of history—the historical truth in oral history. Ironically the figure being chosen to exemplify this is a vital representative of the heroic tradition form which Richard also claims descent, Julius Caesar. Caesar's greatness is not tied to physical existence any more than his reputation for heroism and intelligence ('valour' and 'wit' [3.1.85]) depending upon oral tradition. "Death makes no conquest of this conqueror" in a double sense: to being with, Caesar is still, as a historical character, very much alive and continually resurrected in people's oral tradition; but he "lives in fame", because the purity of his honour survives the detraction and manipulation of historical reconstruction. "Fame", Richard agrees, can live long "without characters" because historical truth is not dependent on the documentary inscription or physical record. However, the initial semi-humorous aside poses an opposite view: too smart for his own good, the young prince's life must be terminated, if only to confound his theory. Indeed, Prince Edward's theory of history is of course wholly unacceptable to Richard, who depends precisely on history's attachment to physical records he can adjust and manipulate for his own ends. His manipulation of the indictment of Lord Hastings is one example.

  The odd little scene in *Richard III* in which a Scrivener (a scribe, particularly of legal documents – never seen again in the play) speaks of what he sees on the very matter of historical writing. This scene is based on an episode in Sir Thomas More's *History of Richard III*, as recorded in Holinshed's Chronicles, where More cites a schoolmaster and a merchant exchanging words about the apparent fraudulence of the proclamation, which was produced a mere two hours after Hastings had been beheaded and obviously the result of a much longer process than the time could have allowed (qtd. in Dillon 18). In changing the dialogue between a schoolmaster and a merchant into a monologue by the Scrivener, who is invented and bestowed a job of writing, Shakespeare calls historical truth into question and makes the audience see the undetermined truthfulness in the written account of history.

The Scrivener, who writes out the indictment (a legal document to be read out in public justification of one's execution outside St. Paul's Cathedral) against Lord Hastings, knows very well that it is a faked document and complains that he has spent eleven hours writing the indictment of good Lord Hastings, which "in a set hand" is fairly engrossed. He traces back this sequence of events: Catesby brought the indictment to him last night, and then the Scrivener spent eleven hours copying it. The first draft or "precedent" took just as long as eleven hours to write out, so that is twenty-two hours. And yet five hours ago, Lord Hastings was alive, untouched, and at liberty. The Scrivener laments the duplicity of the legal record:

> Here's a good world the while. Who is so gross
> That cannot see this palpable device?
> Yet who so bold but says he sees it not?
> Bad is the world, and all will come to nought
> When such ill dealing must be seen in thought. (3.6.10-14)

The Scrivener has spent the last eleven hours writing out the incitement of Lord Hastings, yet Hastings was free and not accused of any crime up to five hours age; so the document was prepared in advance of even the accusation, far less any trial. The Scrivener's indignation is both moral and professional, for his task of scriptwriting begins before the incident and ends too late to authorise—although it will retrospectively "legitimise"—the death of Hastings. This scene demonstrates at once the play's preoccupation with history writing. Because this scene focuses on a written document that the Scrivener literally holds in his hand, it is easy to prompt an audience to consider the way history is constructed.

Since the previous scene has already presented the spectacle of Hastings' severed head carried by Lovell and Ratcliffe and the readiness of Richard's decision to execute Lord Hastings in the scene before that:

> RICHARD: Thou are a traitor.
> Off with his head! Now by Saint Paul I swear
> I will not dine today until I see the same. (3.4.73-75).

Richard has shared most of his crimes and deceits directly with the audience. However, what this scene does is to make people pause to reflect on the nature of history writing. The Scrivener suggests that any fool can see through "this palpable device", but none dares say it aloud, and the "palpable device" of the long-prepared indictment questions the authority of historical truth in history. History itself is highly-edited and based on the evidence of precisely such written account as the indictment of Hastings.

It seems that Shakespeare, like Sir Philip Sidney, realises that the historian bases his own authority "upon other histories, whose greatest authorities are built upon the notable foundation of hearsay" (Sidney 13). Therefore, the reports (hearsay) from other people he believes, is of dubious reliability and hardly a satisfactory foundation for a supposedly accurate and authoritative record. Taking the questioning stance towards the deaths of two princes and Hastings, the play seems to indicate that history is constructed more on the temporal and social site rather than on the historical truth they purport to represent.

3.3.2 Custody and Mysterious Death of Arthur in *King John*

For both playwright and historian, they need to select the actions that are most profitable to be known, although the playwright will allow fiction a more significant role than the historian should. When playwrights upset the raw historical sources that not only seemed uninteresting but are also deficient, they write history plays that are, in Chapman word's, "not truth, but things like truth" (qtd. in Braunmuller 311). When the test of historical truth becomes secondary, dramatic invention flourishes. No longer following the chronicle closely nor seeking only to achieve its effects, the playwright independently creates persuasive agents-in-action and a plausible causal sequence. With *King John*, Shakespeare rewrites chronicle resources in such a way that he dramatises the interaction of conflicting views of historical reality and achieves a kind of aesthetic truth. There are two examples—the invented problems of Arthur's legitimacy and the handling of Arthur's torture and death.

The focus of *King John* is the legitimacy of the king. As far as the play concerned, the issue of legal heritage is in Arthur's favour, who is the son of Richard I. Until replaced at the urging of Eleanor in Richard I's will by John, Arthur is genealogically the heir to the English throne. The clarity of this issue, rather than providing a firm basis for the right view of the conflict between John and Arthur, only intensifies the problems of history and raises the challenge to the nature of "truth" as the play presents it. Because in history, the fact is that John's claim to the throne is better than that of his nephew Arthur. John is the legitimate heir named by his dying brother—Richard I, and because "primogeniture was only one legal route to the crown" (Courtney 122).

The ignorance of these facts in *King John* invites an interrogation to the nature of "truth". The Faulconbridge brothers' arguments over the elder's legitimacy can also be taken as an exemplification of the problematic "truth". Robert, the younger, voices his simple faith when he tries to blemish his brother as a bastard: "But truth is truth" (1.1.105). The terminology of this word is so crucial as to understand all the situations in the play. For one thing, Robert means truth as fact. For the other, when the Bastard shortly afterwards acknowledges Eleanor as his grandmother "by chance but not by truth" (169), the word "truth" nevertheless takes on a different meaning. As Coeur-de-Lion's illegitimate son, he is not truly Eleanor's grandson, even though in fact he is so. The Bastard's ambiguous case of "truth" points to the fundamental conflicts between "fiction" (the textual legitimacy of fictional arrangements) and "truth" (the historical legitimacy of the chronicle resources). The opposition is further exemplified in Shakespeare's dramatisation of Arthur's custody and mysterious death.

The historical Prince Arthur of Brittany, as the son of John's elder brother—the late Richard I, had a claim to the throne. The throne was claimed by Arthur with the military support of Philip II of France. When fighting to regain the Angevin lands, King John managed to capture him in France in the summer of 1202. Arthur was imprisoned at a castle in Falaise belonging to John's chamberlain, Hubert de Burgh. In 1203 Arthur disappeared in captivity, no one knows for sure what happened to him, but rumour blamed John for his murder.

A lot of rumours about Arthur's death were spread through all France in the late spring of 1202, and various nobles began to criticise sharply against King John. It is said that Hubert de Burgh and one of the executioners, moved by Arthur's "lamentable words", spared their prisoner. However, "in the course to sent Arthur abroad through the country, the king's commandment was fulfilled, and Arthur also through sorrow and grief was departed out of this life" (qtd. in Bullough 1960b: 32).

In order to describe Arthur's death, Shakespeare borrows from Holinshed's Chronicles. However, Holinshed himself does not know how to solve the myth and he jumbles together a series of inconsistent explanations of Arthur's death. Collecting all the rumours, Holinshed summarises several "manners" of Arthur's death:

> Some have written, he climbed over the walls of the castle, and fell into the river of Saine, and so was drowned; Other write he died of natural sickness due to a long time of grief and languor; But some affirm, that King John secretly caused him to be murdered. ①(qtd. in Bullough 1960b:33)

So for the death of Arthur, Holinshed depicts it in a remarkably ambiguous, even open-ended treatment. In Holinshed's account, John's responsibility for Arthur's death is quite confused. Lacking confessions from the murderers themselves, the episode produces a fundamental irresolution between fact and truth, a gap that cannot be definitively closed. Did John command murder orally? Did he seal a warrant for Arthur's murder? In approaching the custody and death of Arthur, Shakespeare works with Holinshed's material that has already revealed its adaptability to varied interpretation, and which gives him the opportunity of composing with dramatic explanation and innovation.

Referring back to Holinshed's account of Arthur's death, Shakespeare chooses one assertion that King John gave Hubert a warrant and ordered that Arthur's eyes were burned out to build his dramatic plan. In Scene Three Act Three, King John appeals to Hubert to kill Arthur. John uses intensely personal, very sensuous, and even affectionate imagery:

---

① This paragraph is rewritten into modern English by the author of this book. The original text goes like this: "But now touching the maner in verie deed of the end of Arthur, writers make sundrie reports. Neuerthelesse certeine it is, that, in the yeare next insuing, he was remooued from Falais vnto the castell or tower of Reouen, out of the which there was not any that would confess that euer he saw him go aliue. Some haue written, that, as he assaied to haue escaped out of prison, and proouing to clime ouer the wals of the castell, he fell inot the riuer of Saine, and so was drowned. Other write, that through verie greefe and languor he pined awaie, and died of of naturall sicknesse. But some affirme, that king John secretile caused him to be murthered and made awaie, so as it is not throughlie agreed vpon, in what sort he finished his daies; but verelie king John was had in great suspicion, whether worthilie or not, the lord knoweth".

> KING JOHN: Hear me without thine ears, and make reply
> Without a tongue, using conceit alone,
> Without eyes, ears and harmful sound of words;
> Then, in spite of brooded watchful day,
> I would into thy bosom pour my thoughts:
> But, ah, I will not! yet I love thee well;
> And, by my troth, I think thou lovest me well. (3.3.49-55)

John has done the entire thing necessary by this time, and he does not need to reveal his wishes any further to Hubert. Still, he does. After several vain efforts, he finally manages to speak plainly and inveigles Hubert into agreeing to kill Arthur: "He shall not live" (3.3.67). John promises Hubert a reward, but what exactly is unspecified. More ambiguous is the irony of John's words to Arthur that Hubert will attend on him "with all true duty" (3.3.73). Only John, Hubert, and the audience know what the true duty is.

In Scene One Act Four, Hubert is to kill Arthur in the castle. Wholly invented by Shakespeare, the scene is another excellent dramatic rewriting of history. The intense psychological conflicts in the castle scene between Arthur and Hubert exemplifies that Arthur is in his greatest danger with Hubert's executioners and hot irons. Hubert shows Arthur a paper, evidently a royal warrant (4.1.6), commanding that his eyes be put out with hot pokers on the table. Arthur tries to persuade Hubert not to blind him. He asks whether it is Hubert's heart to kill him, and he recalls how he, when Hubert's head ached, wrapped his best handkerchief around Hubert's forehead. The handkerchief was made for Arthur by a princess, and he never asked Hubert for it back. Arthur continues to plead:

> And with my hand at midnight held your head,
> And like the watchful minutes to the hour,
> Still and anon cheered up the heavy time,

Saying, 'What lack you?' and 'Where lies your grief?'
Or 'what good love may I perform for you?' (4.1.45-49)

Deeply moved by the child's eloquence, Hubert spares Arthur from the fear of being blinded. Indeed, everybody would be moved when they hear these touching words. Shakespeare writes Arthur into such a pitiful boy who says so moving words that no one can resist the boy's pleading. Although he escapes being blinded, Arthur cannot escape the fate of death. At the beginning of Scene Three Act Four, we see Arthur, inexplicably disguised in a "ship-boy's semblance", jumped to his death from a "wall" onto "stones". However, even knowing what we know, what is the truth about Arthur's death and John's or Hubert's guilt or innocence concerning it? In the play, the actual difficulty of providing a valid answer is exposed when Hubert rushes in with his previous report that "Arthur doth live" (75). When the lords threaten to punish him as a "murderer", Hubert protests his innocence in terms that recall the "innocent" Robert Faulconbridge, the younger brother of the Bastard, who taught that truth is the truth:

ROBERT FAULCONBRIDGE. Do not prove me so.
Yet I am none. Whose tongue soe'er speaks false,
Not truly speaks; who speaks not truly, lies. (4.3.90-92)

Hubert himself has just disproved the over-simplified logic of that defence by speaking falsely (Arthur does live) without lying (he supposed he spoke the truth). Moreover, his claim of innocence only emphasises the difficulty of speaking truly as things now stand. John's nobles, Pembroke, Salisbury, and other nobles assert that it was Hubert, at the king's command killed Arthur. They "burn in indignation" (103) over the legitimate heir Arthur's death and the concentration of play must inevitably extend into the doomed future of John's reign. Finally, on his deathbed, John exclaims "I am a scribbled form, drawn with a pen/ Upon a parchment" (5.7. 32-

33). The episode produces a darkly ironic vision of history marked by the unintended consequences of establishing historical truth. Nevertheless, it also provides an insight into the fact that the fictional use of history in the drama is an aesthetic project which may achieve the poetic truth instead of the historical truth.

In *King John*, Shakespeare probes the possible reinvention of Arthur's death and custody from the various reports. The reinvention presents plausible account which aims not to recapture "historical truth", but to produce aesthetically satisfactory text. The warrant, instead of being as a prop, links John's command to kill Arthur with the dying king's description of himself as "a scribbled form, drawn with a pen", Anticipating John's "form upon a parchment", Philip the King of France describes young Arthur:

> Look here upon thy [John's] brother Geoffrey's face.
> These eyes, these brows, were moulded out of his;
> This little abstract doth contain that large
> Which died in Geoffrey, and the hand of time
> Shall draw this brief into as huge a volume. (2.1.99-103)

The textual legitimacy manifests itself explicitly in the imaginary dramatic representation. Instead of using some of everything and thereby gives a puzzling picture, Shakespeare's literary invention avoids the blurring and unconsciousness in history, describes the actions as a coherent whole.

In general, the fiction of Arthur's custody and death in *King John*, although based not on a photographic presentation of historical events, draws on the essential elements of human nature, the everlasting, universal aspects of human life—compassion and benevolence. The literary fiction creates the possibility of filling the gap between fact and history with a poetic truth in a metaphorical level, which transforms the historical resources into a perpetual writing form and dramatic presence.

In conclusion, history, as the grand narrative of an implicitly orthodox or conservative national history, suppresses difference. However, in the transitional plays *Richard III*, *Richard II* and *King John*, Shakespeare's more radical fictional use of history uncovers the differences within the rationality and thus writes history otherwise. In these plays, Shakespeare serves the two masters, the nominally factual chronicle and the dramatisation of that chronicle more skilful than he does in the early history plays. He manages invention into the rifts chroncle history left.

The manipulation of the historical legacy is so effective in *Richard III* and *Richard II* that these two plays offer almost inexhaustible complexity, prohibiting the absolute belief in kings' images. In *Richard III*, the deformed shape of King Richard III is ultimately controlled by the patterns decreed by history; while in *Richard II*, a tide of rhetoric language swallows even the most certain referents of words that would have fixed the King's history. Besides, Shakespeare invents the Bastard's very existence in *King John* and the unique mother figure Duchess York in *Richard II* to expand history broader than that of the grand narrative can encompass. Criticising dirty politicians who make decisions based on self-interest, the Bastard is the most complex and common-sensed character who also embodies the hope of England. We feel that the Bastard is a solution to the dilemma between history and fiction and anticipates Shakespeare in his mastery of styles in the second trilogy, especially in his characterisation of Falstaff. What is more, in *Richard III*, Shakespeare raises the perplexing dilemma in determining and recovering the historical truth in the two Princes and Hastings' death. In *King John*, Shakespeare touches the teases the problem of the legitimacy of the fictional reworking of chronicle resources. History is such a highly edited past that raises people's concern towards the validity of the historical narrative, thus calling into question the historical truth in history.

Chapter Four Maturity of the Fictional Use of History: Making "Petit Récit" of Hybrid Histories

If the first trilogy is an introduction to Shakespeare's fictional use of history, the transitional plays mark the advancement towards maturity in his dramatic fiction, the second trilogy which is written by Shakespeare in a later period can be seen as the utmost exploitation of the formal possibilities in his fictional use of history. In the second trilogy, Shakespeare's fictional use of history achieves its fullest complexity through the intermixture of fictional elements with material adopted from historical records.

In his *Postmodern Condition*, Lyotard radically defines "postmodern" as "incredulity toward metanarratives" (xxiv). He dismisses any totalising discourse of history-as-myth and holds that "the grand narrative has lost its credibility" (37). In order to achieve the delegitimation of the totalitarianism, he calls for a plurality of competing little narratives—the petit récit (60). The petit récit tells short stories which are nevertheless stories of change. Under the light of this contemporary literary interpretation, Shakespeare's fictional characters in the second trilogy implicate the postmodern values and cultural connotations explicitly. Moreover, there are many histories to be made, meanings to be differentiated, and dissensions to be made. Instead of hailing the large-scale version of the unified grand history, the fictional characters hold their voices to make their own petit récit of hybrid histories. The many subversion, reversal, and fragmentation of those histories thus make unlikely the possibility that a single historical truth can be attained.

4.1 "There is a History in All Men's Lives": Three Related Strata of Histories in *1 , 2 Henry IV*

By summoning hybrid details of the past, and shaping the particular fiction to give it a dramatic present, Shakespeare constantly writes history. Writing itself, as Michael de Certeau's book *The Writing of History* indicates, produces history①. And that is indeed what Shakespeare does—making histories in his history plays. His characters provide the principal means by which Shakespeare makes histories. They have independent lives in the fictive world of drama, but they also assist the investigation and production of history. The richness of these characters' fictional lives renders suspects to any attempt on limiting their functions or impact. Their presences and actions in Shakespeare's narrative dwell on, in Lyotard's phrase, "petit récit" of short stories. Anyone familiar with Shakespeare's use of his sources would know that *1 , 2 Henry IV* stands out prominently in this kind of postmodern project.

King Henry IV's speech in *2 Henry IV* has particular importance to unlock the "petit récit" of histories in time. He says: "O God, that one might read the book of fate, / And see the revolution of the times" (3.1.45-46), that is to say, if only one had the power of a particular, privileged historical perspective, then one could divine the future. Warwick responds: "There is a history in all men's lives/ Figuring the nature of the times deceased" (3.1.80-1). While this sentiment hints at a predictive value of history, it still unconsciously hints at the ways how the dramatist explores the several versions of history and constructs a tapestry of "histories" in all men's lives. I would argue that there are at least three strata of histories operating in the two *Henry IV* ② plays, namely, the conspicuously invented and subversive "ahistory" in Falstaff,

---

① Here the writer of this book used the surface meaning of the book's title. For strong points of view on this issue, see Certeau, *The Writing of History*. New York: Columbia University Press, 1988.

② In this chapter, *Henry IV* is use to refer to the two history plays *1 Henry IV* and *2 Henry IV* collectively.

the Royal Party's selective and self-serving national history and the commoner's construction of quotidian history, and these strata of histories collectively paint a colourful picture of English society more inclusive than one finds in any other Shakespearean history play.

4.1.1　Falstaff's Invented and Subversive "ahistory"

Written during 1596 to 1597, *1 Henry IV* was first published in 1598 with the original title: "*The History of Henrie the Fourth; With the Battle at Shrewsbury, between the King and Lord Henry Henry Percy, Surnamed Henrie Hotspur of the North. With the Humorous Conceits of Sir John Falstaffe*". At first, Falstaff's name was "Sir John Oldcastle", and although the change was made before the publication, the character was so well known under its first title that for many years allusions were made to it.

Historically, Sir John Oldcastle was a tragic and pious religious man. He was a Herefordshire landowner. A useful supporter of Henry IV in the Welsh Marchers, Oldcastle was a friend of Henry IV's son, perhaps when the Prince was his father's lieutenant in Wales. He martyred for his pious Protestant beliefs during the reign of Henry V (1417). The substitution of "Falstaff" for "Oldcastle" has often been ascribed (though without any real evidence) to complaints by the Oldcastle's descendants—7th Lord Cobham, William Brooke who was the Lord Chamberlain at that time (Bullough 1960b: 155). William Brooke was offended at the dramatist's presenting his martyred ancestor in so disreputable a guise and was powerful enough to force Shakespeare to change the old rogue's name.

Shakespeare, responding to the protests of the Cobham family, changed the name from John Oldcastle to John Falstaff. According to Oscar Campbell, Shakespeare took this substitute from *1 Henry VI* the name of a cowardly character called Sir John Fastolfe and "by a shift of vowels came up with Falstaff" (314). Despite all this, vestiges of Oldcastle remain in Hal's speeches when he refers to Falstaff as "many old lad of the castle" (*1 Henry IV* 1.2.34), and in the Epilogue to *2 Henry IV*, which assures us that "Oldcastle died martyr, and this is not the man" (Epilogue 2:32). Indeed it is not the man, for Falstaff is anything but an embodiment of those ancient religious and aristocratic beliefs. Being unable to find a place in chronicles, Falstaff is not in history and is "ahistoircal" in nature. Falstaff is "ahistorical" in the sense that he could float freely not only of historical scenes in life but also of the narrative fiction in art.

The juxtaposition of the fictional and factual, of the "ahistorical" Falstaff and the restrictive framework of the historical context to which he is doomed to yield, create depth and poignancy of an "ahistory" more vibrant than anyone can find elsewhere in Shakespeare's history plays. While the noun "ahistory" commonly referring to the lack of concern to history or ignorance to history, this unique "ahistory" provided by Falstaff is the transformation of orthodox history into Falstaff's own version of history. In this sense, Shakespeare's fictional use of history is at its most profound when he uses the "ahistorical" Falstaff freely to create the "ahistory"—"A" history of Falstaff's timeless comic world and his power of inversion.

4.1.1.1 Falstaff's Timeless Comic World

The historical action in *1 Henry IV* is, of course, based mainly upon the account of the reign which Shakespeare finds in Holinshed's chronicles. However, Shakespeare's play conspicuously compresses and selects events of the reign, ignoring a lot of other historical events, making the revolt of the Percys and their defeat at Shrewsbury the play's central historical action. Historically, Henry Percy, also known as Hotspur①, was over twenty years older than Prince Henry (usually called Harry

---

① Hotspur is the son of Sir Henry Percy (Earl of Northumberland). Originally called Harry Percy, later surnamed Hotspur for his energetic campaigns against the Scottish border clans. As son and heir of the Earl of Northumberland, he was also known by the courtesy title of Lord Percy. He was killed at the battle of Shrewsbury, although not (as in Shakespeare) by Prince Hal. The dramatist makes him a youth; historically, he was senior to Bolingbroke's son Prince Henry by twenty-two years. Bolingborke is Henry Bolingbroke (Earl of Derby and Duke of Hereford) in *Richard II*, in *Henry IV* he is King Henry the Fourth.

and, by Falstaff alone, Hal), the future King Henry V (Bate 1). With his dramatic fiction, Shakespeare alters history and makes them rival youths of the same generation. What is more, Shakespeare makes Hotspur the contemporary of Hal to act as a foil to him, and the young Prince emerges, against the evidence of the historiography, as the hero of the decisive battle Shrewsbury, which in fact is King Henry IV's actual military success. These non-historical reshapings mark the difference between history and history play and give the narrative a shape only dimly perceivable in the historical sources. Besides, the changes turn Holinshed's account of the troubled reign of King Henry IV into a "bildungsroman" drama that concentrates on Prince Hal and his development through rebellion and uneasiness to kingship.

Shakespeare's limited commitment to his resources is quite evident in *Henry IV* plays, but what is even more demonstrable is that Shakespeare invents the character of Sir John Falstaff and creats around him a comic world which provides a constant alternative to the chronicle events. In *1 Henry IV*, the "ahistorical" Falstaff is probably prominent or arguably, the most compelling character apart from Prince Hal. Much of the play is dedicated to the non-historical comic scenes; indeed, less of this play is dependent upon the historical material than the writer's fictional narrative. One measure of the play's attenuation of its relation to history is that six of the play's nineteen scenes are wholly devoted to Falstaff's comic action, and Falstaff appears additionally in three of the thirteen "historical" scenes (Shakespeare 2002:14).

The "ahistorical" Falstaff is an essential narrative tool in *1 Henry IV*. He appears in both the comic and the "historical" scenes. Moreover, his comic action in Eastcheap tavern creates and constitutes some kinds of internal opposition to the ethical conventions, political priorities and hierarchal power embodied in the royal court. The physical vitality embodied by the exuberant Falstaff refuses to be dominated by any authority and resists to be contained by the hierarchies of orthodox history.

As the prime embodiment of the ahistorical comic world, Flastff is impecunious and pleasures of flesh number his days. At the very beginning of *1 Henry IV*, When Falstaff at his first appearance asks: "Now, Hal, what time of day is it, lad?"

(1.2.1), Prince Hal incredulously asks why Falstaff should care what time it is since time only means "cups of sack", "capons", and "wenches in flame-coloured taffeta" (1.2.5-10) for him. The time of the day, the week, the month, the year are not Falstaff's business as he lives in a perpetual enjoyment of drinking, eating and visiting brothels. The conflict which pervades the play is thus set up at once between a timeless, comic, physical world and a time-dominated, political, historical world: it is the battle between Falstaff and his comic world with physical enjoyments on one side, and Prince Hal and his political world with historical imperatives on the other side.

Throughout the two *Henry IV* plays, Hal attempts, again and again, to use the fat knight to construct his time-dominated political world. *1 Henry IV* opens at the palace in London, where a "shaken" and exhausted King Henry IV speaks to his council about recent civil strife in England. Meanwhile, we see Prince Hal carousing all night in the Boar's Head tavern which is located in the Eastcheap of London and planning a robbery with his loser pals, Falstaff and Ned Poins. But then, alone on stage, Prince Hal surprises us with a shocking soliloquy. In this play's only soliloquy (famously known as "I know you all" soliloquy), which sets the tone for all the play, Hal is revealing his political calculation in using his tavern life as an instrument of policy, and "redeeming time" when men think least he will (1.2.207).

There is a lot to be said about this great "I know you all" soliloquy. Prince Hal claims that he is not as degenerative as he appears to be. He is just acting that way and pretending to be a sordid wild child. Eventually, he is going to stage a dramatic "reformation" (from wild child to honourable prince) that will shock and amaze his countrymen and his father. The change of Hal, who is going to be a central character in the *Henry V* plays as a charismatic king, is not a miraculous transformation but a conscious self-fashioning. He announces that he will "awhile uphold/ The unyoked humour" of Falstaff's "idleness" (1.2.185-6). To the Prince, Falstaff is a threat to order. What is more, Falstaff is a threat that is purposefully conjured to necessitate the exercise of rule, an example of authority's "constant production of its own radical subversion and the powerful containment of that subversion", in Greenblatt's formulation (1988:41). However, Greenblatt's inference only suggests a royalist fantasy of power. It is to accept Hal's version of events identical with Shakespeare's or, rather, it is to presume that the tavern world represented by Falstaff exists only for the production of aristocratic pleasure and value. Nevertheless, as the editor of *1 Henry IV* points out "neither the history play nor history itself, in fact, gives much evidence that containment is ever as efficient or complete as this reading insists" (Shakespeare 2002:38). If subversion is always produced by and for power, power would always remain unchallenged and intact; but Falstaff's very comic and physical presence on the scene argues otherwise.

Even in the soliloquy that closes the scene, Hal foresees himself "redeeming time" (1.2.210); what we watch, with constantly renewed delight, is Falstaff's valiant endeavour to defend himself against the intrusions of time, history, and reality. Still in the soliloquy, Hal's use of the "sun" metaphor in "symbols, imagery, allegory" represents the exact fantasy of order in the time-dominated political world. That is to say, Hal sees himself as "sun", the ultimate representation of time and justice. He declares that he wants to redeem the time; Falstaff is the disorder, irrelevant ahistorical one. So by redeeming the time, Hal does not only redeem the prodigal time but also the comical companion. Falstaff, however, will not submit to the power of redeeming so easily. He embodies the massive evidence of the heterogeneity that will not be made one. Revealingly when he imagines his life in the impending reign of Henry V, Falstaff turns the world upside down in fantasy.

> FALSTAFF. Marry, then, sweet wag, when thou art king, let not
> us that are squires of the night's body be called
> thieves of the day's beauty: let us be Diana's foresters,
> gentlemen of the shade, minions of the moon,
> and let men say we be men of good government,
> being governed, as the sea is, by our noble and chaste mistress

the moon, under whose countenance we steal. (*1 Henry IV* 1.2.22-28)

The "squires of the night's body" are boisterous festivity. Falstaff absurdly implies that the king's breath has the power to invert the system of meanings. The concluding pun on "steal" specifies the subversive nature which Falstaff identifies himself with: the transformation of the sun leads on to reversals of order under the governance of the moon, in which the reality of the world is to be sought in darkness rather than in light, ruled by the moon rather than the sun. And the crime of stealing is a refusal of control, of legality, and most of all, of the sovereign's authority.

The riotous and disorderly world invented by the timeless Falstaff may be interpreted as the world of festive comedy, the Bakhtinian carnival. Carnival is a religious festival season that celebrates the inversion of social order and the indulgence of unruly and riotous behaviour, and it is a temporary way for people to cut loose and thumb their noses at authority, without getting into trouble①(Bakhtin 2009: 158). The prince's orderly political world with hierarchy and inequality is carnivalised in Falstaff's fictive world. Once being carnivalised, Hal's time-dominated, political world of the historical reality is no different from Falstaff's timeless comic world of the physical vitality.

For Falstaff, what actually happens does not matter in his timeless, ahistorical comic world; all that matters is how he wittily constructs it. His comic exaggeration when he is baited into relating the events at Gad's Hill is evidence of his improvisatory genius in "redeeming" events. He does not know that Hal and Poins are the masked robbers and lies that a hundred thieves robbed him and his crew. He even boasts that the thieves "have peppered two of them" (*1 Henry IV* 2.4.184). As Falstaff continues with the story, the number of robbers doubled into four. Hal reminds him: "What, four? / Thou sadist but two even now" (2.4.190). He insists that "four,

---

① For more elaboration of "carnival", see M. M. 巴赫金. 巴赫金全集(第五卷). 石家庄: 河北教育出版社,2009:158-170.

Hal; I told thee four"—"These four came all affront and mainly thrust at me. I made me no more ado, but took all their seven points in my target, thus". Falstaff miraculously turns four into seven in the same sentence, and when faced with other people's interrogation, he asserts emphatically: "Seven, by these hilts, or I am a villain else" (2.4.193). Started with two imaginary enemies, he multiplies the number of robbers until the above numbers refreshed by the latter ones immediately. For the "ahistorical" Falstaff, he just lives in the moment. Before that moment, he has forgotten all about his words and deeds, refused to acknowledge the accounts. After that moment, he has no time to think, nor does he care. With regard to the timeless world he inhabited, historical time is no longer a sequence of causes and effects being unable to cut, but the independent existence being incoherent in every second.

When his actual behaviour at Gad's Hill, his running in fear from the Prince and Poins and roaring like a bullcalf is exposed, the real issue, even for the Prince, is not his cowardice but against his wit. "What trick, what device, what starting-hole canst thou now fine out to hide thee from this open and apparent shame" (2.4.255-7), says Hal, confident that he has him cold. However, Falstaff escapes one more time in his audacious insistence that he knew him all along. "By the Lord, I knew ye as well as he that made ye/ was it for me to kill the heir-apparent? / Should I turn upon the true prince?" (2.4.259-261). Falstaff cannot be humiliated; he is resilient, always able to recover his poise and regain his mastery of the situation. Falstaff's wit does mark his consistent challenge to the focused, political dominated world. At one's most rigorous, one might say with Dr Ben Johnson "that no man is more dangerous than he that with a will to corrupt hath the power to please" (355).

Falstaff's comic exuberance reaches a climax when he performs the role of King Henry IV, and Hal plays as his son. Having heard about the news that the Percy family became partners with the Welsh, the Scots, and Mortimer to overthrow King Henry IV and anticipates his father's wrath the next day, Hal decides to play out the interview in jest with Falstaff in the tavern.

Chapter Four Maturity of the Fictional Use of History:
Making "Petit Récit" of Hybrid Histories

> RINCE HENRY. Do thou stand for my father, and examine me upon the particulars of my life.
> FALSTAFF. Shall I? content: this chair shall be my state, this dagger my sceptre, and this cushion my crown. (*1 Henry IV* 2.4.366-369)

Here the majesty of the monarchy is parodied by Falstaff: a stool becomes a throne, a dagger a sceptre, and a cushion a crown. Although the Prince immediately questions the conventions of theatre, Falstaff accepts the cheap props as the objects they represent (2.4.370-372). Falstaff, taking up and extending the explicit references to the fact that this is the extempore play, even vows to move Hal: "Well, an [if] the fire of grace be not quite out of thee/now shalt thou be moved" (2.4.373).

Falstaff begins to make the ultimate comic move: he delivers a long prose speech as King Henry, chastising Hal for wasting his youth and defiling himself with the disgraceful company, of which Falstaff is the only "virtuous" exception. Prince Hal demands they change places on the grounds that Falstaff does not sound like King Henry. Playing the king, the prince sternly berates Falstaff. Playing Prince Hal, Falstaff advises the prince to banish all his companions except the virtuous and goodly Falstaff. "No, my good lord," pleads Falstaff for Hal's personal feelings, "Banish Peto, banish Bardolph, banish Poins, but for sweet Jack Falstaff, kind Jack Falstaff, true Jack Falstaff, valiant Jack Falstaff" (2.4.462-464). To which quest, Hal chillingly replies: "I do, I will" (2.4.466).

The Prince's answer is so clear-cut that it leaves no room for tenderness. However jovial in the delivery, the comic plea can scarcely avoid sounding the ring of truth, for being aware that rule depends upon the exclusion of those anarchic energies that resist the strategies of incorporation and subjugation, Hal would inevitably banish Falstaff. Though the words can be spoken light-heartedly, Hal delivers it with a sense that we almost know the inevitability of Falstaff's eventual rejection. There is no surprise that in *Henry V* , the new King Henry V rejects Falstaff: "I know thee not, old man" (*Henry V* 5.5.47).

Through the rehearsal of Falstaff being banished by Hal in the Tavern scene, we can see the prince's tactics of absorbing Falstaff-like man in the history while to deny him totally when he is in the position of King. The theatrical games of role-playing not only evacuate the representation of monarchy by reducing it to its literal components, but also make visible other dark thoughts as well: kingship is a theatrical performance by a gifted scoundrel; Hal's father, King Henry IV, has no more legitimacy than Falstaff, because Henry IV usurped the throne from Richard II. Therefore, the impromptu play may have seemed to reverse the authoritarian the Prince so early tries to enact, and Falstaff indeed gives his compelling voice to what aristocratic history would repress. Hierarchy in this view gives way to variety, a ceremony to festivity, containment to the carnival.

Falstaff's comic world grows into the next two plays—*2 Henry IV* and *Henry V*. In *2 Henry IV* , his being ahistorical is because he is a fictional adjunct in the nostalgia for the comic tavern world dramatised in *1 Henry IV*. The only tavern scene in *2 Henry IV* is suffused with a longing for Falstaff's merriment but darkened by the recognition that the festive spirit may be irrecoverable.

The climax of this play is the scene in which Falstaff appears with Hal, newly crowned as Henry V. The new king is determined to construct a new history by erasing what has already been written about him. He readies himself to confront Falstaff in a final battle of competing histories. On the other hand, the "ahistorical" Falstaff, delighted in news that the old King is dead and assumes a royal privilege naively, makes his way to London for the coronation ceremony. Aware that he is inappropriately dressed for the occasion, his clothes "stained with travel" (5.5.24), he convinces himself that "this poor show doth better" because it "doth infer the zeal [he] had to see" his minion crowned (5.5.13-14). More audaciously, his calling out to "King Hal" as "my sweet boy" (5.5.42) stops the royal procession of the coronation, which is presumptuous. Falstaff's interruption of the new King's coronation procession presumes on a privilege that the audience knows is no longer his. As a significant embodiment of the ahistorical time and riotous disorder, Falstaff must finally be rejected and imprisoned. Brutally smashing his friend's wild expectation of favour, the new king begins his rejection with an ironic echo of his "I know you all" soliloquy: "I know thee not, old man. Fall to thy prayers. / How ill white hairs becomes a fool and jester!" (5.5.46-47)

Falstaff is banished from the royal presence. Yet a moment later Falstaff seems already to be slipping free from this strike—"Go with me to dinner. Come, Lieutenant Pistol; come, Bardolph. I shall be sent for soon at night" (5.5.87-88)—and at the play's close, Shakespeare announces that he will bring him back once again. "One word more, I beseech you," says the speaker in the Epilogue of 2 *Henry IV*, "If you be not too much cloyed with fat meat, our humble author will continue the story with Sir John in it" (Epilogue 2: 27-28). It is as if Falstaff himself refuses to accept the symbolic structure of the play that has just ended. His irrepressible comic vitality refuses to be dominated by any authority, resisting incorporation into any containment by the stabilising hierarchies of the illusionistic representation of history. D. Traversi writes:

> This variety in his [Shakespeare] traditional and popular derivations, indeed, largely accounts for the unique fascination exercised by Falstaff; it is as though many anonymous figures, consecrated by established custom and related to living popular tradition, were brought together, at once united and transformed, in this great figure of swelling, if unregulated, vitality and comic vigour. (qtd. in Bullough 1960b:175)

From participation in this wealth of life, Prince Hal is, by the very responsibilities of his position, largely excluded. Falstaff's timeless comic vitality finally challenges and subverts the time-dominated political world of Prince Hal.

Generally speaking, Falstaff serves as a connecting link between two worlds, the timeless comic tavern world in which he is at home and the time-dominated world of politics and military world to which he also has access. The comic world neither dominates nor subordinates to the historical world. It is, rather, to say something even more radical: that the very existence of the "ahistorical" Falstaff's comic world serves to create an ahistory which raises questions about the nature of history. The ahistory provided by Falstaff is a part of the very fabric of history, exposes the exclusions and biases in the political and historical world.

4.1.1.2 Falstaff's Power of Inversion

In the recent critical theories, the notion of history has been pluralised to accommodate different accounts of past events according to the position from where they are viewed, especially in terms of the ideological agendas that may lie behind the presentation of what appears to be an impartial interpretation of the past. No historical investigation revealed by the historian or historical sources is complete without historical context, and sometimes the significance of history is hard to determine. Furthermore, many purported "histories" can be shown to have been invented; at the same time, however, these fabrications still tell us much about a society's beliefs and dreams. All in all, the idea of history as a set of competing stories, the most powerful of which survive at the expense of the less powerful, remarks that history loves only those who dominate her. The relationship between history and power is an area that has been addressed by Michel Foucault in his system of "power/knowledge". For Foucault, power differs from tantalisation of history in that it tries to take account of the submerged narratives that have been discarded by the prevailing accounts of past. The Foucauldian approach lends itself well to the understanding of how Falstaff creates "ahistory" by using his power of inversion.

In history plays otherwise stiff with heavy politics and men fighting for power, Falstaff serves as an inversion: he inverts values through interesting discourse and inverts the play's otherwise deafening seriousness. Falstaff's first appearance in Scene Two Act One of *1 Henry IV* elicits Prince Hal's twelve lines of insults berating him for his laziness, his gluttony and his fondness for whores and alcohol. Falstaff acts like a drunken slob who ought to be the object of Prince's jesting scorn. However, the tone goes away when Falstaff delivers a subtle and poetic defence of his position that demands a second thought.

"Indeed, you come near me now, Hal," Falstaff tries to identify with the Prince by categorising both of them as thieves of the night, living under the moon and the stars, not under the beautiful sun, "for we that take purses go by the moon and the seven stars, and not by Phoebus" (*1 Henry IV* 1.2.14-16). By saying that he and Hal going by moon and stars, Falstaff suggests that Hal has joined him in the alternative values—do not go by Phoebus, but the other, rival deity, the wine-god Dionysus and therefore turns the traditional morality to the amorality. "When thou art king"— Falstaff continues skilfully to theorise the toppling of morality by kicking away any appeals to absolute ethic—"let not us that are squires of the night's body be called thieves of the day's beauty; let us be Diana's foresters, gentlemen of the shade, minions of the moon" (1.2.23-25).

Falstaff identifies himself and the Prince with a culture of inversion: the transformation of the sun leads on to reversals of order under the governance of the moon, in which the reality of the world is to be sought in darkness rather than in light, ruled by the moon rather than the sun; and in which the official justice is reversed to surrender to natural appetite ("being governed as the sea" [1.2.27]) in a kingdom of thieves. The world is turned upside-down in this culture of inversion.

Falstaff's power of inversion is also reflected in his humanistic perspective and comments. Although most people think that *Henry IV* plays deal primarily with the fortunes of princes, *Henry IV* plays actually insist that history must be recognised as something more capacious than merely the record of aristocratic motives and actions. Like *King John*, its immediate predecessors among Shakespeare's historical plays, *Henry IV* plays develop the Bastard's position as a fictional commentator on political and historical episodes much more thoroughly in Falstaff. What the Bastard in *King John* called "commodity" gives way to a common sense embodied in Falstaff's fat body.

As a presenter and commentator, Falstaff offers an alternative, though probably not objective perspective. Falstaff's comments on politics and chivalry honour wave a paralleling line to Prince Hal and his rival Hotspur's political and military history. Falstaff's perspective makes Hal and Hotspur's aristocratic attitudes, especially those towards honour, look like posturing. Falstaff's speech powerfully points to the deflating perspective on honour, and the fact that honour is just another word of being "powder" and "ate" in the war, a thing of air with no power to "set a leg" or "take away the grief of a wound" (*1 Henry IV* 5.1.131-32). He who has it, Falstaff wryly remarks, is very likely to be dead. It is, he concludes, "a mere scutcheon" (5.1. 139-140). In order to understand his down-to-feet common sense, we need to take a closer look at Prince Hal, Hotspur, and Falstaff's behaviours respectively.

Hotspur is the embodiment of an old-style chivalric warrior. He lives by the code of honour and is scornful of the courtly manners embodied by the trimly dressed, clean-shaven lord who comes to demand Hotspur's prisoners. The clash of styles between the battlefield and court is enough to turn him into a rebel. Being a rebel who tries to embellish his rebellious action, Hotspur desires to prove the value of "honour" embodied in him. Talking about honour just like talking about some human being, Hotspur suggests he can grab "honour" by "her" hair ("locks") and rescue her from the bottom of the ocean ("the deep") (1.3.202, 204). He also sounds a bit like a treasure hunter, who is more interested in the prize than the principles behind the action. Hotspur continues with the way by saying the man who rescues her (Honour) does not have to share the glory with anyone. And finally, he asserts that nobody wants to share the glory.

No matter how honourable Hotspur's pretensions may sound like, the reason why Hotspur behaves like this is that he is eager and ambitious for power. Pretending to be honourable and chivalric, one can be more able to seize power. Therefore, Hal, being compared bitterly by his father to Hotspur as the embodiment of "riot" and "dishonour", promises to redeem himself by defeating Hotspur in battle. He believes that he can make up for everything that he has done by killing Hotspur at the triumphant end of some battles. Hal claims, "when I wear[s] a garment all of blood/and stain my favours in a bloody mask" that he would be able to wash the shame away with it (*1 Henry IV* 3.2.132-141). What interests us most about this passage is Hal's notion that his "shame" and dishonour will be "scour[ed]" and "washed away" along with the blood of battle when all is said and done.

So for Hal, the "honour" is not earned from doing noble and beneficial things for people, but only by killing people to reshape his image that was contaminated in his prodigious lifestyle. Falstaff exposes both Hal and Hotspur's cynical self-interest of seeking after power and honour by commenting aside. Hotspur's extravagant chivalric commitments are countered by Falstaff's devastating common sense that common foot-soldiers are but "food for powder" (*1 Henry IV* 4.2.65).

Falstaff's common sense also anticipates the way he will perform during the battle at Shrewsbury. In the battlefield, Prince Hal finally kills Hotspur, but Falstaff resurrects from his faked "death" and stabs the already dead Hotspur. The presence of the very live Falstaff, lying on the ground and playing dead as the Prince kills Hotspur, not only reflecting Falstaff's own refusal to respond to the demands of war but makes the chivalric earnestness of the Prince and Hotspur look somewhat pointless and ridiculous. No sooner has the Prince taken an emotional farewell of Falstaff whom he supposes dead that the "Poor Jack" raises himself. Then Falstaff launches into a comic comment on the virtues of counterfeiting:

> Counterfeit? I lie, I am no counterfeit: to die, is to be a counterfeit; for he is but the counterfeit of a man who hath not the life of a man: but to counterfeit dying, when a man thereby liveth, is to be no counterfeit, but the true and perfect image of life indeed. (5.4.114-118)

Falstaff's remarkable ability to think practically and realistically saves his life and forms a sharp contrast with the hypocritical chivalry spirit of "honour". The honour carries serious weight, but Falstaff does not buy it. For Falstaff, "honour" is revealed to be a thin concept that some men use in a fruitless attempt to elevate the gruesome realities of warfare to something noble. So not surprisingly, Falstaff's perspective on this subject offers a soliloquy on the concept of honour.

> FALSTAFF. 'Tis not due yet. I would be loath to pay him before
> his day. What need I be so forward with him that
> calls not on me? Well, 'tis no matter; honour pricks
> me on. Yea, but how if honour prick me off when I
> come on? How then? Can honour set to a leg? No; or
> an arm? No; or take away the grief of a wound? No.
> Honour hath no skill in surgery, then? No. What is
> honour? A word. What is in that word honour? What
> is that honour? Air. A trim reckoning! Who hath it?
> He that died o' Wednesday. Doth he feel it? No.
> Doth he hear it? No. 'Tis insensible, then. Yea,
> to the dead. But will it not live with the living?
> No. Why? Detraction will not suffer it. Therefore
> I'll none of it. Honour is a mere scutcheon; and so
> ends my catechism. (*1 Henry IV* 5.6.127-140)

Here, the old knight discusses the concept of "honour" in his famous "catechism" (this means his speech is delivered in the form of a question and answer session). Falstaff says "honour" is nothing but "air". It cannot heal battle wounds ("set to a leg" or perform a "surgery"), and those who pay for "honour" with their lives cannot even enjoy it because they are dead. Unlike other characters (such as Hotspur and Hal), Falstaff points out the meaninglessness of "honour" and refuses to elevate the concept of honour (which, as we have seen, seems to come out of the violence of warfare) to anything other than a mere "word". He sharpens the utter opposition between the empty words and the only thing that matters, at least to him, the life. Falstaff's philosophy is a simple "give me life" (*1 Henry IV* 5.3.58) and never mind about ethical and political codes of behaviour ("I like not such grinning honour as Sir Walter hath" [5.3.57]). Falstaff's comments and voices stand outside the prevailing political spirit and draw its cogency from a common sense of life philosophy, that is to say, history is made not only of big speeches and dramatic events but also of the daily lives of people who eat, drink, sleep and die.

Falstaff's power of inversion also lies in his holding a line between the political march of history and the humanistic virtues of friendship, loyalty, good humour and self-mockery. In order to illustrate this, we need to think of the difference between Falstaff's jokes and Hal's jest with Francis in the tavern "to drive away the time till Falstaff come" (*1 Henry IV* 2.4.27). Accompanied by Falstaff, Prince Hal gains access to an urban cast of characters far removed from anything he has known before, and he takes particular delight in having learned their language: "They call drinking deep 'dyeing scarlet'". Hal soon becomes "so good a proficient in one quarter of an hour" that he will be able to "drink with any tinker in his own language" for the rest of life (2.4.13-17). Hal definitely shows his remarkable ability to master the commoner's language and successfully "command all the good lads in Eastcheap". Francis the drawer falls prey to him immediately.

To kill time before Falstaff arrives, Hal plays a trick on Francis the drawer. Hal gets Poins to stand in some other room and call the Drawer, while the Prince holds him there with his questions. The scene is occupied by Hal's ungenerous jest towards Francis. All Francis can do is call out to Poins, "Anon, anon, sir". Hal has a good laugh at the expense of Francis, who does not know which way to go. Even Poins does not quite get the joke. He asks hopefully, and Hal replies only that Francis has "few words than a parrot" and that Francis' whole life is running up and downstairs and totalling up bills (2.4.87-98). If "the issue" for Hal is that Francis is exposed as unimaginative and inarticulate, "the issue" for the audience is that Hal is exposed as condescending and cruel as a snob and a bully. What he accomplishes with his jest is merely to discomfort a waiter in a tavern, paralysing him in confusion and fear.

Hal's final comment that Francis has "fewer words than a parrot" triggers the contrasts between Hal and Falstaff. In comparison with Hal's attitude towards social lowering, Falstaff's is more humane. Compared with Prince Hal's narcissistic pose to "redeem" himself as a "glittering" monarch by using his downtrodden friends as foil, Falstaff continuously reinvents himself as an irrepressible everyman: "sweet Jack Falstaff, kind Jack Falstaff, true Jack Falstaff, valiant Jack Falstaff", one with "every man jack" (*1 Henry IV* 2.4.463-4). Unlike Hal's, Falstaff's jokes are not at the expense of others but generally at his own expense. Falstaff speaks to and for those who understand him. His mimicry exposes the narrow self-interests of those in power and those who seek it, and, unlike Francis, he is a man of a great many words and one who will not be fixed in the Prince's designs. Being an "ahistorical" character that possesses the power of inversion, Falstaff possesses a mysterious inner principle of vitality. He inhabits, creates and constitutes some kinds of internal opposition to the ethical conventions and political priorities embodied in the sovereign hegemony of king and prince in their state or court. Refusing to be "redeemed" and "absorbed" by Prince Hal and being represented as wit and humane, Falstaff presents a culture of inversion and the orthodox history must broaden itself to incorporate his voice and the tavern world he inhabits.

Falstaff is the most conspicuously fictional character in *Henry VI* plays. However, Falstaff never quite fits into the restrictive frames of the historical scenes in which he appears. His common sense, good humour and self-mockery present a unique historical perspective, endowing him a power of inversion that lessens whatever the illusion aristocratic ethics may have on us. "The better we come to know Falstaff", writes W. H. Auden, "the clearer it becomes that the world of the historical reality which a Chronicle Plays claims to imitate is not a world which he inhabits" (1962: 183). But of course he does—at least in the two *Henry IV* plays; there he inhabits not the political world of historical reality but the comic world of physical vitality and inversion. And he inhabits it so thoroughly that he becomes the mark of resistance to the centralisation of power and the evidence of history play's heterogeneity.

In conclusion, if most of the history plays centre on the significant figures, *Henry IV* centres on one too, that is Falstaff who is not great in the political or national sense, but in his subversive intelligence, carnivalesque exuberance, and resistance to all orthodox values. His very existence and willing to take what it offers, always as its critic, is an unruly presence challenging the fundamental assumptions that motivate the political world. Just like the time's Bastard in *King John*, but performs even much better than the Bastard, Falstaff transcends his "ahistorical" status to create his own history. His "ashitorical" voices not only speak out social elements absent from the so-called "historical" main plot but also speak the reality of class differentiation and domination that the aristocratic, historical plot ignores or idealises. Moreover, the history, like the history play itself, can no longer be the story of great men and matters of state but has to expand itself to include the "ahistory" represented by Falstaff and other figures like him.

4.1.2 King and Royal Party's Selective and Distorted National History

Shakespeare makes histories in *Henry IV* plays. Through the plays, Shakespeare conflates the history narrated in Holinshed, compressing time and anticipating events with such slick causality that, as Bullough observes, ten years of King Henry IV's reign are telescoped into only a few weeks (1960b: 253). Holinshed reports that following the defeat of the rebels at Shrewsbury, the King moved his army against the Earl of Northumberland, who was conspiring to revolt (qtd. in Bullough 1960b: 524). Shakespeare reverses the chronology, turning a consequence of the defeat of the rebels—Northumberland's fleeing to Scotland—into an ignominious cause of that defeat. Moreover, all the events which in Holinshed occur up to Northumberland's death play out in Shakespeare as a direct and immediate result of the death of Hotspur at Shrewsbury. The radical change of historical events allows a rich fiction of the political and military past in national history. Finally, as the King and Royal Party's problematic process of constructing national history—the selective use of detail and distorted memory of the military and political life make fiction out of the historical events, we can see the fact that the national history is just a partial view of the past.

In *1 Henry IV*, Falstaff asks somewhat incredulously: "Is not the truth the truth?" (2. 4. 222) Shakespeare's *Henry IV* plays, in a radical departure from chronicle resources, raise doubts about the very truth of the narrative of national history by making the Rumour as the king and royal party's ally. Rumour in the Induction of *2 Henry IV* acts as a device to reveal the competing narratives of the battle. "Painted full of tongues", Rumour is not a human character; instead, it is a personification of hearsay—the stories that are circulated without any confirmation or certainty.

Any play that opens with the appearance of Rumour invites consideration of how one can know what really happened in the past. Rumour opens his speech by attracting audience's attention: "Open your ears; for which of you will stop/ The vent of hearing when loud Rumour speaks? / I from the orient to the drooping west/ Making the wind my post-horse, still unfold/ The acts commenced on this ball of earth" (*2 Henry IV*, Introduction, 1-5). It might seem reasonable that Rumour functions as a reminder of the outcome of the Shrewsbury battle. There is here, though, a mixture of partly true, mostly false items. Rumour continues to say that it is he who comes to "stuff" men's ears full of lies about the recent war between the king's forces and the rebel army. Through the misrepresentation that Rumour offers, history is both created and distorted. As Rumour boasts:

> Upon my tongues continual slanders ride,
> The which in every language I pronounce,
> Stuffing the ears of men with false reports. (*2 Henry IV*, Induction 6-8)

History is implicitly redefined in this speech as carried in reports. False reports lead to false history, as it is Rumour who "unfold[s]/ The acts commenced on this ball of earth" (Induction 5), most of the play's opening scene will be devoted to assessing conflicting evidence about the battle.

Rumour proceeds to tell the news of Henry IV's victory at Shrewsbury and how Prince Hal defeated young Hotspur and his troops in a bloody battle near Shrewsbury. The King and Hal's victory ended the rebellion and quenched the fire of revolt with the rebel's own blood. But hastily Rumour says he has been spreading the news to the contrary:

> But what mean I
> To speak so true at first? My office is
> To noise abroad that Harry Monmouth fell
> Under the wrath of noble Hotspur's sword,
> And that the king before the Douglas' rage
> Stooped his anointed head as low as death. (Induction 27-32)

The misreport reminds us of what really took place at the end of *1 Henry IV*: several of the King's lookalikes were killed by Douglas; the King himself was in danger before being saved by Hal. Also, of course, it was Hotspur who was killed by Hal, not the other way round. However, Rumour boasts that he has been spreading the rumour about the King and Hal's deaths from Shrewsbury to the place where he now stands—in front of the castle where Northumberland, Hotspur's father, lies within.

The false version of events continues in the first scene where Northumberland receives contradictory information about the outcome of the Shrewsbury battle. The messengers are coming one by one, and every single one of them will report nothing but what he has heard from Rumour. Lord Bardolph is the first one who arrives at Northumberland's castle to bring the news from the front. Lord Bardolph, dependent on the rumour-based information, excitedly reports that King Henry IV has been wounded at the battle and is about to breath his very last breath. Besides, Bardolph gets things the wrong way around not only by having Hotspur killed Hal but also making Falstaff Hotspur's captive. In fact, of course, as we see at the end of *1 Henry IV*, Falstaff having feigned death to avoid being killed or captured, and claimed the death of Hotspur as his achievement.

Before he expresses his joy at such news, Northumberland pauses to ask how Bardolph knows this: "Saw you the field? Came you from Shrewsbury?" (1.1.24-5). That is, what is the source; where is the evidence for such presumed fact? Northumberland has dispatched his own servant Travers to learn about the battle, who then enters with a contradictory report that the "rebellion had ill luck, / And that young Harry Percy's spur was cold" (1.1.41-42). Lord Bardolph questions the reliability of Travers' source. Bardolph believes the outcome of the battle as the Rumour reported so firmly that he even swears that if Hotspur has not been successful, he will give up everything he has, in exchange for a piece of lace. The truth cannot be gained until Morton enters. Unlike either Lord Bardolph or Travers, Morton has actually witnessed the Shrewsbury battle.

> MORTON. But these mine eyes saw him in bloody state,
> Rendering faint quittance, wearied and out-breathed,
> To Harry Monmouth; whose swift wrath beat down
> The never-daunted Percy to the earth. (1.1.107-110)

Morton reports many other details of the battle and concludes: King Henry has won. The king has sent a speedy force led by young John of Lancaster and Westmoreland to seize Northumberland. Eyewitness drives out the rumour, thereby making possible a credible report of the past.

Despite its uniqueness, this particular Induction may seem somewhat surprising as an introduction to a history play because it is eminently and overtly destabilising. With the function given to Rumour, this character initiates the exploration of a national history where one of the principal activities is to ascertain what really happened. However, what Rumour seems to trigger is a feeling on the instability of meaning in

Chapter Four Maturity of the Fictional Use of History: Making "Petit Récit" of Hybrid Histories

the national history: what has already been reported about the historical events may have suffered from falsification and may stand in need of revision. Then a different reading of Rumour is possible, that is to say, Rumour is, in fact, suggesting the instability, change and uncertainty as an unavoidable part of the pursuit of historical awareness. For this kind of historical awareness, Shakespeare joins the links between history and fiction by reproducing his fictionalised versions of national history from earlier dramas.

The dramatist makes histoty by using his narrative in other plays, providing thereby an intertextual understanding of what the natioral history really looks like. Under this light, the national history introduced by Rumour allows various types of fictionalised narratives, among which the most conspicuous two are Hotspur's distorted narration of his conspiracy for rebellion and King Henry IV's highly selective memory about how he seized the throne with abounding references to *Richard II*.

The first and most striking instance is Hotspur's recollection of his first meeting with Bolingbroke (now King Henry IV) in Scene Three Act One of *1 Henry IV*)①. This is a scene brilliantly worked up by Shakespeare out of Holinshed's statement about Hotspur's initial conspiracy and his co-rebels being "not a little fumed" with King Henry IV (Bullough 1960b: 185). Because King Henry IV demands Hotspur's prisoners and refuses to ransom Mortimer, Hotspur is so angry that he cannot be got to listen to his uncle's plans for rebellion and constantly interrupts Worcester with another burst of indignant anger. The last lash of Hotspur's rage is devoted to remembering his first encounter with "this vile politician Bolingbroke". The first meeting and exchange between Hotspur and Bolingbroke are so satirically recalled by Hotspur.

> HOTSPUR. In Richard's time—what do you call the place?
> A plague upon it, it is in Gloucestershire.

---

① Bolingborke is Henry Bolingbroke (Earl of Derby and Duke of Hereford) in *Richard II*, in *Henry IV* he is King Henry the Fourth.

> Twas where the madcap duke his uncle kept,
> His uncle York, where I first bowed my knee
> Unto this king of smiles, this Bolingbroke.
> NORTHUMBERLAND. At Berkeley castle?
> HOTSPUR. You say true.
> Why, what a candy deal of courtesy
> This fawning greyhound then did proffer me!
> 'Look what his infant fortune came to age',
> And 'gentle Harry Percy', and 'kind cousin'.
> O, the devil take such cozeners! (*1 Henry IV* 1.3.240-252)

It is there that Hotspur joins Bolingbroke. The whole passage naturalises the passing of time and the action of memory. Hotspur is ingenuously reproachful to Worcester and Northumberland that they conspired to get rid of Richard II—the sweet, lovely rose—and helped to plant "the thorn", "the wild rose" Bolingbroke (*1 Henry IV* 1.3.174-175), as though he had been in no way involved. However, the fact is that it is he and his father, who upheld Bolingbroke to the throne of the king. In *Richard II*, Hotspur offers Bolingbroke with a respectful submission.

> HOTSPUR. My gracious lord, I tender you my service,
> Such as it is, being tender, raw and young,
> Which elder days shall ripen and confirm
> To more approved service and desert. (*Richard II* 2.3.41-44)

It is in response to this submission that Bolingbroke responds in kind: "I thank thee, gentle Percy, and be sure/ I count myself in nothing else so happy/ As in a soul remembering my good friends, / And as my fortune ripens with thy love" (*Richard II* 2.3.45-48). Now the rebels under Henry IV badly need to distort history because their real part in the forced deposition of King Richard II does not suit their present purposes – to dispose of the present King Henry Ⅳ, whom they now term as a usurper. On the eve of the battle of Shrewsbury, Hotspur quite cursorily recollects the initial motive for their support of Bolingbroke and his restricted and conditional narration is quite digressive and self-interested.

Trying to make it appear that they have nothing to do with Henry Ⅳ's illegitimate seizure of Richard Ⅱ's crown, Hotspur accounts why they helped Bolingbroke: "My father, my uncle, and I were the ones who made him King (Henry Ⅳ) in the first place! When he barely had twenty-six men fighting with him, when he was weak and no-one cared about him, just a poor, unnoticed criminal trying to get home, my father welcomed him back. When my father heard him swearing a promise to God, weeping and speaking with a passion that he had only come back to claim his title from his father's inheritance and reconcile himself to King Richard, he felt sorry for him and offered to help him"①(*1 Henry Ⅳ* 4.3.59-65). This, according to Hotspur, creates a mass appeal because Northumberland's name attracts the support of all "the lords and barons of the realm".

The oath sworn by Bolingbroke at Doncaster that he came for nothing beyond his entitlement to the Duchy of Lancaster, figures largely in the sources. But we hear nothing of that oath as such previously, and no one is more assiduous in taking Bolingbroke's benefit throughout the takeover of the kingdom by the same Northumberland and Hotspur. Distortedly recollecting what "actually" happened as their reasons for the rebellion, Hotspur shows the very unreliability of the way he retells the story in changed circumstance. The truth of just how Bolingbroke came to seize power may be as yet undecidable, but the effect is to allow a reflection on the duplicity of the rebels' distorted versions of their conspiracy for rebellion.

---

① This part is translated from the original texts by the writer of the book. The original texts goes like this: "My father gave him welcome to the shore. /And when he heard him swear and vow to God/ He came but to the Duke of Lancaster, /To sue his livery, and beg his peace, /With tears of innocency and terms of zeal,/ My father, in kind heart and pity moved,/ Swore him assistance, and performed it too" (*1 Henry Ⅳ* 4.3.59-65).

In Scene One Act Four of *2 Henry IV*, the Archbishop of York says of King Henry IV: he will "keep no tell-tale to his memory/ That may repeat and history his loss/ To new remembrance" (4.1.202-204). Shakespeare uses "history" as a verb only in this time in the entire canon. This exclusive focus on the word "history" corresponds to an unusually rich concern for the King's highly selective narration of national history based on his false memorial reconstruction.

With a radical departure from the chronicle resources, Shakespeare banishes the royal presences of the King and the Prince to the outskirts of *2 Henry IV* for much of its first four acts. The King makes his appearance only in Act Three, in a scene which introduces the Prelate's Rebellion. It depicts the ailing King—now at his palace in Westminster—and his nobles as political strategists who are trying to cope with the uncertainties of war and the "revolution of the times" (3.1.46) which defeat even the best-laid plans. "How chances, mocks/ And changes fill the cup of alteration/ With divers liquors!" laments the king (3.1.51-53). Henry IV lives in constant fear that his usurpation of Richard II will be punished by the rebellion of those who once helped him to the throne.

In discussing the unhealthy state of the nation with his nobles, the King is full of despair and launches into a lengthy speech that is full of gloom about the future of the kingdom. Rumour plays a significant role in exacerbating the King's distress. Calculating the number of enemy troops, the King falls victim to the unreliable reportage that "they say the Bishop and Northumberland/ are fifty thousand strong" (3.1.95-96). Warwick disputes the figure by reminding the King of the danger of listening to the false reports, which Rumour warned against in the Induction: "It cannot be, my lord. / Rumour doth double, like the voice and echo, / The number of the feared" (3.1.96-98). Yet just a few lines later, in an attempt to bring comfort to the King, Warwick himself appears to have fallen victim to the rumour by reporting that he receives "a certain instance that Glendower is dead" (3.1.103), when in fact Glendower is still very much alive.

Furthermore, King Henry IV indulges in a revisionist history in which rumour and memory become faulty allies. In recounting Richard's prophecy that civil war will be the result of usurpation. He looks to the Earl of Warwick and says: "O God, that one might read the book of fate, / And see the revolution of the times" (3.1.45-46), and he proceeds to turn to a memory of the past when a mere eight years ago Richard, Northumberland, Hotspur, and himself were all friends. Pursuing this train of thought, Henry then recalls a specific moment in which Richard predicted Northumberland's future treachery. Trying to seek from Warwick a confirmation, Henry continues as though he recollects from his memory that Richard II, with his eyes brimming with tears because of Northumberland's rebellion, spoke words that now seem prophetic.

> KING RICHARD II. 'Northumberland, thou ladder by the which
> My cousin Bolingbroke ascends my throne'
> Though then, God knows, I had no such intent.
> 'The time will come that foul sin, gathering head,
> Shall break into corruption' so went on,
> Foretelling this same time's condition
> And the division of our amity. (*2 Henry IV* 3.1.66-79)

Here Henry quotes a confrontation scene from which he was absent. Besides, the lines themselves are misquoted: Richard's reference to "the mounting Bolingbroke" (*Richard II* 5.1.56) here becomes the affectionate "my cousin Bolingbroke". What is more, Henry's calling on Warwick as a witness, however, is a fiction, for no Earl of Warwick appears in *Richard II*.

King Henry IV has already revised the history from his perspective, yet he still wishes to have the power of an individual, privileged historical perspective. If that were possible, he says, people "would shut the book and sit him down and die" (3.1.55). While this sentiment hints at the predictive value of history, the dramatist stops short of accepting it. In Act Four, the past is recalled again on giving an account of the reign of Richard Ⅱ. In Scene One, Mowbray remembers the long-ago exile of his now-deceased father—Norfolk, during King Richard Ⅱ's reign. Mowbray and Westmorland become absorbed in a dispute over their conflicting recollections of the aborted trial-by-combat between Mowbray's father and the as-yet-uncrowned Bolingbroke. Mowbray offers a glorious account of the tournament of the earlier play: "And then, at Coventry, my father and Harry Bolingbroke met in a formal challenge. They were both mounted on their horses and ready to charge. Their horses were neighing, anxiously waiting for their riders' spurs to drive them forward. Their steel-tipped lances were ready for the attack. The visors of their helmets were down. Their eyes were on fire behind the steel slits. The trumpet sounded, and then—when there was nothing that could have stopped my father from killing Bolingbroke—the King prevented the fight by throwing down his royal sceptre. That sceptre was a symbol of his life; when he threw it down, he threw down his life and the lives of every man that has since died at war under the leadership of Bolingbroke"①(2 Henry Ⅳ 4.1. 117-126).

Mowbray summons this superb description of the tournament at Coventry in memory of his father. The young Mowbray, who could not have been present, nevertheless has stored up a history of his father and now tells a crucial moment of the story. However, such history is subject to ongoing and sometimes contradictory interpretation, a process that assists in distinguishing reliable account from rumour. Westmoreland, the leader of the King's army, contradicts Mowbray's interpretation of the Coventry tournament: "You speak, Lord Mowbray, now you know not what" (4.1.130). So he proceeds to remind the listeners that Bolingbroke's reputation was

---

① This part is translated from the original texts by the writer of the book. The original text is "Henry Bolingbroke and he, /Being mounted and both roused in their seats, /Their neighing coursers daring of the spur,/ Their armed staves in charge, their beavers down,/ Their eyes of fire sparking through sights of steel,/ And the loud trumpet blowing them together,/ Then, when there was nothing could have stayed/ My father from the breast of Bolingbroke—/ O, when the king did throw his warder down,/ His own life hung upon the staff he threw." (2 Henry Ⅳ 4.1.117-126)

Chapter Four Maturity of the Fictional Use of History:
Making "Petit Récit" of Hybrid Histories   · 159 ·

very high at the time of the Coventry tournament and offers an alternative view of that remembered scene: "Who knows who would have won the duel? But if your father [Norfolk] had won in that duel, he would never have made it out of Conventry alive. For the country hated him, while they loved and prayed for Bolingbroke. They blessed him and worshipped him more than they did King Richard at that time"①(4. 1. 133-139).

Westmoreland and Mowbray's intricate, petty argument demonstrates how absurd and complicated the tensions surrounding King Henry IV's throne have become and also shows how differently history is remembered by different characters. This squabble about history brings into focus the function of evidence, memory and the recurrence of such moments when there is an urge to rehearse the past. The exchange does not indulge some grand scheme of history, such as a providential view; rather, it underlines the absurdity of the royal party's self-serving and selective use of memory.

Moreover, the King's last words give another indelible mark to the selective construction of memory. Shortly before his death, he wishes to be carried to the Jerusalem Chamber. This reminds us of his first plan of a crusade against the infidels to atone for the murder of King Richard: "I'll make a voyage to the Holy Land/ To wash this blood from off my guilty hand" (*Richard II* 5. 6. 49-50). While it is postponed by civil unrest in *1 Henry IV* (1.1. 47-8), in *2 Henry IV*, he reiterates his penitential desire to go the Holy Land (3. 1. 107-8) and later indicates that the preparations have been made (4.3. 1-7). However, in his advice to the Prince shortly after, undertaking a crusade has become a political strategy that casts suspicion on his earlier protestations of penitence: "[I] had a purpose now/ To lead out many to the Holy Land… Be it thy course to busy giddy mind/ With foreign quarrels, that action

---

① This part is translated from the original texts by the writer of the book. The original text is: "Who knows on whom fortune would then have smiled? / But if your father had been victor there, / He ne'er had borne it out of Coventry;/ For all the country in a general voice/ Cried hate upon him; and all their prayers and love/ Were set on Hereford, whom they doted on/ And blessed and graced, indeed more than the King." (*2 Henry IV* 4. 1. 133-139)

hence borne out/ May waste the memory of the former day" (*2 Henry IV* 4.3. 338-9, 342-44). In this cynical light, his dying wish to be carried to the Jerusalem Chamber can be seen as another case of his selective reconstruction of memory. While one might assume that the King is knowingly revising events in order to exculpate himself, the fact is that his refashioning of history is self-serving and based on faulty memorial reconstruction. This misrecollection of military and political events contributes to the network of the report by which *Henry IV* interrogates the nature of historical truth and invention. By dramatising the unreliability of historical narration in the King and royal party's selective and distorted national history, Shakespeare subjects the stories of those in power to public scrutiny.

In conclusion, beginning with Rumour's false report of what happened at Shrewsbury and ending with the King's reporting the prophecy that he would die in Jerusalem, *Henry IV*, for the most part, summons selected details of the past, shapes the particulars of telling, and complicates chronicle national history with the dramatic immediacy of personal reminiscence. This exclusive focus on the retellings and reshaping corresponds to an unusually rich concern for the issues of history, that is to say, the King and royal party's selective and distorted adaptation of the military and political past that finally leads to a national history fostering rumours and hearsay.

4.1.3　Commoners' Social History of Quotidian Existence

Gathering groups of people whose unwritten histories rival in importance, the two parts of *Henry IV* are so mixed dramas that cast a wide net over England. By drawing on oral traditions and popular nostalgia, the plays create a comprehensive social history rich in the quotidian life which populated by commoners—the "vital commoner" Falstaff, Tavern Hostess Mistress Quickly, Country Justices Shallow and Silence, and those characters around them.

The tavern scenes of Eastcheap of *Henry IV*, in both its parts, introduce a lower stratum of society with commoners who collectively paint a picture of what London might have been like at that time. As a prime embodiment of the tavern world,

Falstaff is Shakespeare's primary means of access to those whom Thomas Edward called as the "the vital commoners" (qtd. in Bate 209). Formerly a knight, Falstaff has decayed from the gentry and is back among the commoners. He possesses no property, being always on debt and on the run from the law. If he has a home and a family, it is in the alehouse among his drinking companions.

As a vital commoner, Falstaff's perspective offers an alternative to the power-seeking aristocratic nobles and reminds us of ordinary everyday life. When Falstaff tells Hal in the tavern that "Worcester is stolen away tonight", the reference is of course to the rebellion that is at the centre of the historical action, but he judges its effect in a measure impossible to imagine in the official history: "Thy father's beard is turned white with the news. / You may buy land now as cheap as stinking mackerel" (2.4.349-51). It throws matters of rebellion and deposition into an entirely new light. Howard Erskine-Hill remarks, this "is not only a sign of human distance from these events: it is a mark of a new kind of interest in them" (79). Falstaff has immediately seen the possible financial influences exerted by the breakdown of government on ordinary people. Falstaff's concern opens out a relatively realistic portrayal of life other than the high politics appears in the aristocratic circle. Thus, the present argument concerning the succession of the king takes on a more significant substance of ordinary people's material interest. Those people are not directly involved in shaping the serious military and political histoty but their daily lives inevitably reflect the historical events that go beyond their control.

Another example is Falstaff's withering insight into the war aroused by the Hotspur rebellion at the end of Scene Three Act Three in *1 Henry IV*:

>PRINCE HENRY. The land is burning; Percy stands on high;
>And either we or they must lower lie.
>FALSTAFF. Rare words! Brave world! Hostess, my breakfast, come!
>O, I could wish this tavern were my drum! (*1 Henry IV* 3.3.202-205)

The imminent war begins to turn the Prince away from his low-life pursuit to thoughts of victory and glory, but both war itself and the Prince's sudden shift into heroic mode have the opposite effect on Falstaff who dismisses "rare words" and a "brave world" of honour in favour of breakfast and more ale. Falstaff is at once the vital commoner and the great truth-teller, who reduces war to its bottom line: common foot-soldiers are but "food for powder" (*1 Henry IV* 4.2.65). He proves a pause and reflection on the seemingly aristocratic attitudes towards war. His voice of ale and safety is a way of saying that history is made not only of big speeches and events but also of the daily lives of people who eat, drink, sleep and die.

Through the delineation of the vital commoner Falstaff, Shakespeare describes the social life nearly two hundred years ago and treats the quotidian life with the delight in vigorous language and robust humour. Like Falstaff, another commoner who blooms in Shakespeare's plays and is not the least proof of Shakespeare's dramatic originality is Mistress Quickly. Mistress Quickly's innovative construction of the past reveals a social richness that official history cannot reach.

The Boar's Head tavern hostess Mistress Quickly has a complex evolution over the three plays—*1 Henry IV*, *2 Henry IV*), *HenryV* in which she appears. She is the nameless Hostess in *1 Henry IV*), acquiring a name only from the greeting of the Prince at his entrance: "What sayest thou, Mistress Quickly? How doth thy husband? I love him well, he is an honest man" (3.3.73-4). In *2 Henry IV*), she not only has lost the offstage honest husband to make possible the constantly renewed promises of marriage by Falstaff but also acquired a new comic image of her own that allows her to sketch a whole social scene of London life.

A widow past her prime, Mistress Quickly has lived in hope for the past twenty years that Falstaff would marry her and offer her social advancement by making her "my[Falstaff's] lady" (2.1.91). Failed by Falstaff several times, Mistress Quickly attempts to have him arrested for non-payment of his tavern debt. In the midst of petitioning the Lord Chief Justice to support her "action" against Falstaff, Quickly is unexpectedly diverted into reminiscing about the occasion when Falstaff allegedly made her a marriage proposal.

> MISTRESS QUICKLY. Marry, if thou wert an honest man,
> thyself and the money too.
> Thou didst swear to me upon a parcel-gilt goblet,
> sitting in my Dolphin chamber at the round table
> by a seacoal fire upon Wednesday in Wheeson week,
> when the Prince broke thy head for liking his father to
> a sinning man of Windsor—
> thou didst swear to me then, as I was washing thy wound,
> to marry me and make me "my lady",
> thy wife. Canst thou deny it? Did not goodwife Keech,
> the butcher's wife, come in then and call me gossip Quickly?
> coming in to borrow a mess of vinegar;
> telling us she had a good dish of prawns;
> whereby thou didst desire to eat some;
> whereby I told thee they were ill for a green wound?
> And didst thou not, when she was gone down stairs,
> desire me to be no more so familiarity with such poor people;
> saying that ere long they should call me madam?
> And didst thou not kiss me and bid me fetch thee thirty shillings?
> I put thee now to thy book-oath:
> deny it, if thou canst. (*2 Henry IV* 2.1.84-102)

No one is better at recounting the past than the Hostess. Her memory of Falstaff's proposal is marked by details of the material surroundings—he was sitting in her "Dolphin chamber" by a "seacoal fire" and swore "upon a parcel-gilt goblet". The list of goods she must pawn in order to pay for his new wardrobe. Falstaff's promise to improve the Hostess's condition by marrying her is given shape and substance by the mundane details of its retelling. The mundane trivialities bring vividly to life the selective memory of a woman for whom the only history matters is to get married to Falstaff. Out of this tale emerges a life of novel-like density: the rough-and-tumble of Falstaff and Hal's continuing relationship, Falstaff's knightly airs, the social advancement that marriage to him would mean for Quickly. To some degree, Mistress's anecdotal and self-serving recollections almost come to a historian's construction of history. Her memorial construction of history contributes to people's understanding of her life, which is a low English life, with a company of such persons as may well be supposed to frequent a London tavern in those days.

What is more, as a socially marginalised character, Mistress Quickly's dynamic language provides alternatives to the official speech of the court. The popular energies of Mistress Quickly lie in her original way of speaking by using malapropism. At first sight, Mistress Quickly is naming or misnaming something; however, when scrutinised, we find that Mistress Quickly has a metamorphosis power. When Mistress Quickly cries out to Falstaff "Ah thou honey-suckle villain!" and again "Thou art a honey-seed", she means, not "honey-suckle" and "honey-seed", but "homicidal" and "homicide" (*2 Henry IV* 2.1.55, 59). So she admits that Falstaff has "stabbed" her most beastly in her "house", which suggests her sexual history with Falstaff and punctures her pretence for respectability. The wordplay by Mistress Quickly finally points at a social issue that rarely mentioned by the chronicle history—prostitution, which is of central importance to *2 Henry IV*. Doll Tearsheet, one of the "parish heifers" (2.2.153), whom Mistress Quickly brings to Falstaff for a last night of merriment before he goes off to war, lives on the lowest rank of the social ladder. As a prostitute, she is a woman of meagre means, as she reveals when she confronts Pistol for "tearing a poor whore's ruff in a bawdy house" (2.4.144-5). The large ruff is an item commonly worn by Elizabethan prostitutes (Rackin 1990:138-9). With the astonishing circumstantial details and the vital bawdy wordplay of the mundane, everyday life, Mistress Quickly's memorial construction of her history offers an insight into the everyday existence of ordinary folks in London.

The common folks in *Henry IV* also assume the mantle of unofficial historians in their accepted capacity as "time's doting chronicles" (*2 Henry IV* 4.3.126). With political events shunted to the margins of the play, individual acts of remembrance or, more specifically, the stories which they tell themselves and others about their past lives become the principal source from which history is generated. At the centre of this world are two county justices Shallow and his cousin Silence in Gloucestershire. The two county justices, with their appropriate provincial speech patterns and idiosyncratic memories, are among the most indelible portraits Shakespeare ever painted.

The first appearance of Shallow and Silence is after Warwick has uttered a speech on time and history: "There is a history in all men's lives/ Figuring the natures of the times deceased" (*2 Henry IV* 3.1.79-84). Shallow is an old man vainly reminisces about his days as a student at Clement's Inn, where, he imagines, "they will talk of mad Shallow yet" (*2 Henry IV* 3.2.14-15). He names his friends there as if they were present; he recounts their rowdy escapades and visits to the "bona robas" (3.2.23); and with a memory of details as keen as the Hostess's, he brags about "a merry night" he spent "in the Windmill in Sanit George's Field" (3.2.195-197) and about an epic fight he once had with one "Samson Stockfish, a fruiterer, behind Gray's Inn" (3.2.32-3). He also recalls that "Jack Falstaff" was then just "a boy and page to Thomas Mowbray" (3.2.25-6). Shallow's yokefellow of equity, Justice Silence, unlike Shallow, is a man of few words. Silence is familiar with Shallow's history at Clement's Inn, no doubt from having been regaled with his exploits repeatedly: "You were called lusty Shallow then, cousin" (3.2.16). What characterises their conversation is Shallow's memory of past—"Jesu, jesu, the mad days that I have spent! And to see how many of my old acquaintance are dead" (3.2.33-4)—and, in the next breath, his blunt knowledge of the present reality: "How a good yoke of bullocks at Stamford fair" (3.2.37-8). By playing with the time-scales so that distant memory is set with vivid clarity alongside the immediate facts of the price of ewes and bullocks at the local fair, a sense of timelessness is achieved. It is Falstaff's role to prick the rosy bubble of their reminiscences in his soliloquy at the end of the scene:

"Lord, Lord, how subject we old men are to this vice of lying!" (3. 2. 289-90). However, the cynical appraisal does not erase the fact that the search for a golden world, where time and history can be kept at bay, is almost fulfilled at Justice Shallow's establishment in Gloucestershire.

The strong sense of bucolic ideal is regained at the beginning of Act Five, where Shallow appears again on the stage. Rebels may be defeated, kings may die at Westminster, but the appropriate variety of ideally old time is realised by Shallow. Shallow, as one of His Majesty's Justice of the Peace, is even unaware of under which king he serves. Also, one has the feeling that he might never find out, and that it would scarcely alter the principles of his jurisprudence if he does, but for the arrival of Pistol with "happy news of price" (*2 Henry IV* 5. 3. 95) that one king has succeeded another. And there, in the simplest form of historical progression, images of a more stable England is replete with farming references and its reminders of everyday England in "pippins" and "small beer", and where life's problems appear to be no greater than the decision to dock a servant's wages for losing a sack. The immemorial quality of the rural world animated by Shallow's ramblings summons up an England that is older and more stable than anything possible in the court world of intrigue, innovation and reversal.

With characters such as Falstaff, the Hostess, Shallow and Silence, *Henry IV* plays move from court to tavern, council chamber to battlefield, city to country and paint a panorama of England, embracing a more comprehensive social range than any previous historical drama present. The common folks' personal anecdotes and reminiscences are kept alive by an oral tradition that makes their stories more ephemeral and less regulated than the stories recorded by chroniclers.

The commoners' quotidian existence shows the basic elements of human nature, the everlasting, universal aspects of human life. What might be construed as an irrelevant account from the linear syntax of chronicle history thus reveals itself, from a different standpoint, as "a door opening briefly on to areas of social history that were largely occluded by the state-centred focus of most Tudor historiography but that we have since come to value" (Cavanagh et al. 58-59). In this sense, the histories of commoners stand independent of, and rival in importance, the chronicle history in which the Tudors tried to forge a national grand narrative. And as Dillon persuasively argues, the vital point of adding their stories is "to complicate the chronicle narrative, to reverse the perspective of top-down history temporarily so that the shell of glamour and inevitability falls away from the doings of monarchs and aristocrats, allowing the spectators to consider history as a set of contingent circumstances that could have been different" (25).

In conclusion, most of the "high" political history centres on issues of dynastic succession, affairs of state and military conflict. In *Henry IV* plays, the political history that constitutes the main content of the Tudor chronicles and Shakespeare's previous English history plays is displaced by the popular tradition of storytelling in which the history is typically reconstituted through the commoner's quotidian reference of the past. By tapping into alternative sources of histories within common folk's subculture, *Henry IV* could be seen as participating in an enquiry into dynastic historiography and its adequacy. Hence we might speculate that Shakespeare places these competing models in contention with one another precisely to pose the question of what constitutes "history".

4.2 *Henry V*: Representing History on the World Stage

Henry V is one of England's greatest and most successful warrior kings and remains one of England's national heroes. The reign of Henry V has long been regarded as one mainly of "victorious acts". The sixteenth-century historians regarded his French claims as just, and his actions as altogether admirable both before and during his invasion. Besides, they believed that Henry V always behaved in the best chivalric tradition, and his youthful escapades (when he was still Prince Hal) seemed all the more endearing when he became, as Holinshed declared, "a majesty[…] that both lived and died a pattern in princehood, a lode-starred in honour, and mirror of magnificence"①(qtd. in Bullough1960b:349).

Holinshed's chronicle underlies the whole historical action of *Henry V*, though Shakespeare picks materials from Holinshed's numerous details, limiting himself mainly to the French business, omitting most happenings in England and ignoring the conflict with the Lollards and the execution of Sir John Oldcastle. The other primary source for *Henry V* is an anonymous play printed in 1598 with the title *The Famous Victories of Henry the Fifth: Containing the Honourable Battle of Agincourt*. Nevertheless, this title applies only to the play's second half, because its first half mainly deals with the hero's wild doings in London as Prince Henry, his conversation at his father's deathbed and his dismissal of his former companions (Shakespeare, 2015:7-8). On the available evidence, Holinshed and *The Famous Victories* provide all the material from which Shakespeare creates the dramatic action of *Henry V*, but he selects and reshapes his historical material with his usual dramatic fiction.

Shakespeare not only reinvents his own form of history play when he creates the hybrid modes of the *Henry IV* plays, he reinvents it again in *Henry V*. The seemingly epic subject of the glorious warrior king requires a different sort of understanding under the foresight of the Chorus' performance, and at the same time, a change in the narrative mode phases out of the Eastcheap lowlifes and is in favour of ordinary soldiers' quaint comments on the King.

4.2.1 Drama vs. History: The Chorus' Theatrical Representation of History

Choric② scenes occupy a central place in *Henry V*. The choric is a dramatic

---

① The spellings are modernised by the author of this book. The original spellings are " a majestie… that both lived and died a paterne in princehood, a lode-starre in honour, and mirrour of magnificence".

② Choric means "of, relating to, or being in the style of a chorus and especially a Greek chorus". Examples are conveniently available in Online Webster Dictionary 〈http:// www. Merriam-webster. com/dictionary/choric〉.

strategy not available to historians. Because for historians, they need to record what happened without any comments so as to present history objectively. Shakespeare makes full use of choric scenes. He not only emphasises the self-reflexivity and the theatricality of the drama, but he also elaborates the problems of trying to represent history on the stage.

The chorus is the most direct and closest form of the choric scenes a playwright can use, except perhaps by including a character by his or her own name, to reveal an authorial voice. Because Shakespeare particularly uses the Chorus in *Henry V* to hide ironically behind to offer comments and to explore the difficulty of representing history, we shall concentrate more on the Chorus here than on any other aspects in this play.

Shakespeare is conscious of the need for "a Muse of fire, that would ascend/ The brightest heaven of invention" (Prologue 1-2). Since the form imposed upon him is drama, he calls for a theatre with "a kingdom for a stage, princes to act/ And monarchs to behold the swelling scene" (Prologue 3-4). As it is he must do his best with the Globe or Curtain stage, Shakespeare regrets that his play and stage could not include enough, with its "turning the accomplishment of many years/ Into an hourglass" (Prologue 30-31). Accordingly, he inserts the Chorus before each Act and adds an Epilogue. According to Bullough, the insertion of the choruses is Shakespeare's experiment in drama to:

> Arouse a sublime feeling of patriotic exaltation and urgency in the audience, to apologize for the stage's shortcomings and at the same time to remedy them by linking the episodes (adding also descriptions of places and incidents not to be represented), to excite suspense about future events, and generally to dignify and elevate the action with heroic glamour. While recognizing the limitations of the theatre, he overcame them by employing a compere to supply epic spaciousness, detachment and sublimity. It rose indeed nearer to epic-tone than anything Daniel or Drayton ever wrote. (1960b:351)

Although we may confirm that the choruses before each act link the episodes and offer extra descriptions of Henry V's actions, we cannot come to a simple conclusion that the effect of their presences is to elevate Henry V with heroic glamour. Because there is a contrast between what the Chorus says and what the actions really are. The Chorus in *Henry V* performs a vital function of commenting nearly all the acts in the play, giving the audience a slide-show of tension in the play itself between narrative and representation, comment and action, and heroism and anti-heroism (Hart 148). Challenging the imagination of the audience directly, the Chorus, while being represented, is a narrative media between the audience and the representation of the main historical action. While the Chorus exalts Henry's heroism, the action shows him to be both a great soldier and a schemer, and the parallel contrast is evident all through the play.

The opening Chorus, in his prologue to the play, compares the magnificence of the historical action and the theatre's inadequacy to imitate it and calls on the audience to use their imaginations in a collaborative enterprise. Aiming to present an epic drama, the Chorus begs to be excused for the inadequacy of the stage for the representation of the material that is complex and majestic: "But pardon, gentlemen, / the flat unraised spirit who dares /to act out such a great subject matter on this unworthy stage. / Can this stage the size of a cockfighting ring hold/ the huge fields of France?" (Prologue 8-12) The Chorus continues to figure itself in the "wooden O" and laments that it cannot stuff the helmets that terrified even the air itself at the Battle of Agincourt into this meagre wooden O: "Oh pardon, since a crooked figure may/ Arrest in little place a million, / And let us, ciphers to this great account, / On your imaginary forces work" (Prologue 15-18).

Admitted itself as a crooked figure or the wooden O, the Chorus in *Henry V* brilliantly articulates its proposition that the historical representation and historical action are the same things unless the audiences should use their imagination to close the gap between sign and substance. The real purpose of the Chorus is not so much to give unity to the play as to indicate the perspective from which the events and personalities are to be viewed. So the stage is an O, a gap to be filled. The play is a play of desire to fill the blank with some imaginative confirmation. Since it is impossible literally "to bring forth/ So great an object" as "the vasty fields of France" or the troops massed for battle at Agincourt on the stage, the Chorus then asks the audience to pretend, to "suppose":

> CHORUS. Suppose within the
> girdle of these walls
> Are now confined two mighty monarchies,
> Whose high upreared and abutting fronts
> The perilous narrow ocean parts asunder:
> Piece out our imperfections with your thoughts;
> Into a thousand parts divide on man,
> And make imaginary puissance;
> Think, when we talk of horses, that you see them
> Printing their proud hoofs I'th' receiving earth.
> For 'tis your thoughts that now must deck our kings,
> Carry them here and there, jumping o'er times. (Prologue 17-29).

Full of phrases in the imperative mood, the Chorus is in the play to demand the audience's attention and command them to be imaginative as well as patriotic. He also represents the perspective of the ordinary Englishman: "Piece out our imperfections with your thoughts". The Chorus is also invoking the power of representation to recreate the very content of history and the past, and to make historical writing and historical event identical—"Admit me Chorus to this history, / Who prologue-like your humble patience pray, / Gently to hear, kindly to judge our play" (Prologue 32-34). The Chorus in *Henry V* helps broaden the focus of the play by introducing theatrical elements on the stage and promises to tell a different story of history.

The centre of this representation is not the country but the king—Henry V, who is a heterogeneous character with different traits inextricably intermingled. It is on him that the play displays a polyphonic political picture which sheds light on audiences' understanding of the crucial issues. The Chorus hails Henry as the "mirror" or exemplar of "all Christian kings" (2.0.6), a description both accurate and ironically inaccurate. On the one hand, Henry, limited to a particular kind of kingship by the political circumstance inherited from his father, is the best of his kind, a soldier and leader without parallel. On the other hand, Henry, as the once wayward Prince Hal he was, is a schemer who continues to play the elaborate game of play-acting. The comparison between the Chorus' description and Henry's handling of the traitors and his behaviour towards Falstaff in Act Two demonstrates him as both a qualified king of political pragmatism and high principle, and a planner who draws up self-interested scheme of cheat and betrayal.

Act Two begins with Henry V's claim to invade France. The Chorus voices the universal enthusiasm for the war, his hyperboles enlivened with wit ("They sell the pasture now to buy the horse" [2.0.6]). The following scene allows Eastcheap to exert into the play. Bardolph, Nym, Pistol and the Hostess, are present on the stage. With the Boy's message about Falstaff's sickness, the mood changes. The Hostess's return gives a sombre tone by providing a detailed narrative of death. "Ah, poor heart," Mistress Quickly memorably recounts, and she says, "he is so shaked of a burning quotidian tertian that it is most lamentable to behold" (2.1.117-119), which confirms that Falstaff is dying. Given Falstaff's manner of life, the official cause of death may be overindulgence, but the play makes clear that it is a "murder": "The King has killed his heart" (2.1.88). At the end of 2 Henry *IV*, the newly crowned King sententiously disclaims Falstaff, who has boisterously saluted him in his coronation procession and forbids Falstaff to come near him in future. It is evident to this rejection of Falstaff that the Hostess is referring when she declares that the King has killed his heart. The reference reminds us that Henry has killed Falstaff in order to undertake the responsibilities of kingship, especially in his case the waging of war. The judgment that Nym and Pistol made of Henry captures some ambivalences. "The

King is a good king" (2.1.125), but he "hath run bad humours on the knight" (2.1.121). The comic distance thereby gives us a perspective different from that of the Chorus. The earlier scene of Henry's killing of traitors might reveal the perspective clearly.

While the traitor Scroop hails the King's mercy, Henry criticises Scroop on his disloyalty and condemns them to death. The execution of Scroop, the traitor with whom Henry believes he shared "dear care and tender preservation" (2.2.58), sadly complete the severance of personal ties which reminds us of what is, from Falstaff's perspective, Henry's equal betrayal of Falstaff. When Henry asks Scroop, "wouldst thou have practised on me for thy use?" (2.2.99), we remember that Hal "practised" on Falstaff too, using him as a mask behind which to hide his real character. Here, we might find Henry, less noble than the Chorus would have us believed because he lacks ethical integrity and human warmness.

Act Three traces events from the landing and invasion of Harfleur to the eve before Agincourt. Once again, the Chorus to Act Three challenges the imagination of the audience: "Thus with imagined wing our swift scene flies/ In motion of no less celerity/ Than that of thought" (3.0.1-3). After an imaginative picture of the ships sailing to Harfleur, the Chorus announces the war is now ready to begin: "Work, work your thoughts, and therein see a siege" (3.0.25). It is against a background of "Alarums" and soldiers carrying scaling-ladders that King Henry makes his rallying speech: "Once more unto the breach, dear friends, once more" (3.1.1). Harfleur is proving a hard nut to crack, and the King on stage will be disappointed. The scene follows is Fluellen and the other captains discuss military matters. Their argument is neatly brought to an end when "the town sounds a parley", which, in the next scene, brings the King before the walls of Harfleur. The dreadful threat of the King calls the soldiers to imitate the action of the tiger: "[S]tiffen the sinews, conjure up the blood, /Disguise fair nature with hard-favoured rage. / Then lend the eye a terrible aspect; / Let it pry through the portage of the head/ Like the brass cannon" (3.1.7-11). It can be argued that if the defenders who have called for the parley are going to surrender anyway, then there is no need for the speech, but to stage the surrender without it would have been an anticlimax. This climax, on the other hand, presents a ruthless king with real politics.

Act Four includes the Agincourt battle and King Henry V's victory. The chorus to Act Four serves several functions. It builds up suspense with the outcome of the forthcoming battle in uncertainty, emphasising the odds against "the low-rated English" (4.0.18) that are outnumbered by "the confident and over-lusty French" (4.0.19). In his vivid description of the camps on the eve of the battle, the Chorus insists on providing the sad state of "the poor condemned English" (4.0.22). With evocative scene-painting, the Chorus encourages audiences to see and hear what a danger the ordinary soldiers would face.

> CHORUS. The poor condemned English,
> Like sacrifices, by their watchful fires,
> Sit patiently and inly ruminate,
> The morning's danger; and their gesture sad,
> Investing lank-lean cheeks and war-worn coats,
> Presenteth them unto the gazing moon,
> So many horrid ghosts. (4.0.22-28)

The portrayal of King Henry V in this Chorus is heroic: he is depicted as the ideal prince, doing precisely what a military leader should do in such circumstances. Though passing among his men like a god disguised, he treats all men alike. "Mean and gentle" are the same to him, as he speaks to his soldiers as "brothers, friends and countrymen" (4.0.34). And the Chorus convinces us that he sincerely promises a "little touch of Harry in the night" (4.0.47). Yet the scene that follows affords a parallel contrast to the popular activities of Henry, who as Prince Hal had been over-familiar with commoners and deliberately confounded expectation. As a King, he has realised the common touch, but his incognito preserves the right stance between him and his subjects. While obtaining the common soldiers' support on him, Henry plays a prank on foot-soldier Williams. What he appears to be is very different from the conventional praise in the Chorus, and the encounter between Henry and Williams ends not with solidarity or courage, but with disharmony—a quarrel, a challenge, and a box on the ear. Therefore, the Chorus creates the irony of saying one thing and meaning the opposite (or something different). And any audience would become victims of this theatrical stance if he or she takes the Chorus's representation at face value, particularly the rhetorical games the Chorus plays. As Hart would put it, this is a history play, and history asks for a "literal, as well as a literary, connection" to the world (155).

Act Five presents the peace conference at Troyes, the King's wooing of Princess Katharine, and the preparation for the union of the two crowns. The Chorus to Act Five explicitly states one of his dramatic functions, which is to pass over the events of the five years between Agincourt and the peace treaty. As the Chorus explains: "I humbly pray them (those who have not read the story) to admit th'excuse/ of time, of numbers and due course of things/ Which cannot in their huge and proper life/ Be here presented" (5.0.3-6). Nothing is said of King Henry's second campaign in France: Agincourt, the decisive victory, is here the end of the war, and "Harry's back returning again to France" (5.0.42) is a peaceful one, taking place after a decent interval to allow the French to mourn their dead. The other business of the Chorus is to consciously call attention to a dramatic aim of the history play: "and myself have played/ The interim, by remembering you 'tis past" (5.0.43-44).

At the centre of the final act is Henry's wooing of Katherine as the prelude to a politically motivated marriage. Henry, scornful of courtiers' elegance and rhetoric, is proud of his physical power and of his martial exploits: "when France is mine, and I am yours, then yours is France, and you are mine" (5.2.175-6). Towards the end of the courtship he reverts to this theme, without any disguise this time, of his own acquisition of France.

KING HENRY V. Take my by the hand, and say "Harry of England, I am thine": which word thou shalt no sooner bless mine ear withal but I will tell thee aloud "England is thine, Ireland is thine, France is thine, and Henry Plantagenet is thine". (5.2.234-238)

The bargain is sealed with a kiss. The scene ends with hopes of peace as the French King and Queen look forward to "neighbourhood and Christian-like accord" between the two peoples, and such a union is sealed with another kiss. This second kiss, taken with due formality, leads into the prayer for every sort of harmony: "God, the best maker of all marriages, / Combine your hearts in one, your realms in one!" (5.2.353-354). Ironically, Henry's marriage to Katherine will not produce a "spousal" of the kingdom. Nor will the marriage produce the "boy, half French, half English, that shall go to Constantinople and take the Turk by the beard" (5.2.205-207). Anyone familiar with the history and Shakespeare's first trilogy would know that the marriage produces a king who leads the country into the War of Roses. And the subtle complexity increased when the Chorus plays the Epilogue.

In the Epilogue the Chorus transfers the now-familiar image of the dramatist to the "bending author" and the ironic complexity increases. "Our bending author" has him discussed the story that has been pursued "with rough and all-unable pen". "Confining" men to a "little room", "mangling by starts the full course of their glory", the Chorus tells his tale that moves from order to chaos.

> CHORUS. Small time, but in that small most greatly lived
> This star of England: Fortune made his sword;
> By which the world's best garden be achieved,
> And of it left his son imperial lord.
> Henry the Sixth, in infant bands crowned King
> Of France and England, did this king succeed;
> Whose state so many had the managing,

That they lost France and made his England bleed;

Which oft our stage/ hath shown; and, for their sake,

In your fair minds let this acceptance take. (Epilogue 5-15)

The Chorus telescopes historical time in the extreme, and calls attention to the difficulty of representing history on the stage. As an abrupt turn of events, the Chorus moves from a description of Henry V's triumph to a lament of waste under Henry Ⅵ. The loss of France and the War of Roses are duly mentioned, with regret, but the final emphasis is not on the disappointing historical events but on the plays which have so acceptably staged them.

In conclusion, the Chorus mediates between the audience and past events, helping to interpret and shape history. By eliciting the audience's imagination and presenting an ambiguous picture of the main character—King Henry V, the Chorus realises the complexity of historical shaping on the stage. To seek out the inconsistencies between what the Chorus says and what the stage action shows, one may sense Shakespeare's concealed uneasiness over his story or his hero, and Shakespeare's deliberate insinuations that his story and his hero were not what they might seem. The contradiction pushes at the confines of the history play and finally makes us more aware of the coexisting dilemmas between the dramatist's representation of the king on stage and the chroniclers' official history of the king.

4.2.2 Rabbit or Duck?: The Ambiguous Image of the King Presented by His "Band of Brothers"

The critical reception of *Henry V* indicates that the play may be considered one of the most ambiguous or ambivalent works of world literature. It seems impossible to write or speak about *Henry V* without taking side in the king's trial, and almost all such trials end by the usual arguments: those in favour of Henry (patriotic and nationalistic sentiments embodied in the King) and those against (his banishing and "killing" Falstaff, the violence of his speech before Harlfeur, the killing of the French prisoners after Agincourt, his sending his old friend Bardolph to death, etc.). Pugliatti sharply points out that it is not only on Henry that a verdict is pronounced, but also "part of the critical energy is spent in connecting the judgment of the most celebrated English king to what we may guess about Shakespeare's political attitude" (137).

E. M. W. Tillyard's account of Shakespeare's purpose in the history plays is "to dramatise the whole stretch of English history from the prosperity of Edward Ⅲ, through the disasters that succeeded, to the establishment of civil peace under the Tudors" (304). A purpose, which Tillyard derives from Hall's chronicle, leads him to find the last play of the series and the presentation of its hero, unsatisfactory. Henry V could not be made "the symbol of some great political principle", nor could his complex personality in the *Henry IV* plays be simplified into the perfect king that the tradition required (305-6).

However, Tillyard's general view of Shakespeare's history plays as embodiments of orthodox Tudor historical thought has met with much opposition and the most recent developments in this area are the new historicist and cultural materialism criticism. The oft-cited commentary on the play is Greenblatt's *Shakespearean Negotiations*. In his New Historicist reading "Invisible Bullets: Renaissance Authority and its Subversion", the critic juxtaposes the *Henry IV*, and *Henry V* plays with Thomas Harriot's account of Virginia and Thomas Harman's exposure of the practices of rouges and vagabonds. Greenblatt applies the moral and psychological implications of these two works to the plays. As regards *Henry V*, he concludes:

> The play deftly registers every nuance of royal hypocrisy, ruthlessness, and bad faith-testing, in effect, the proposition that successful rule depends not upon sacredness but upon demonic violence—but it does so in the context of a celebration, a collective panegyric to "This star of England", the charismatic leader who purges the commonwealth of its incorrigibles and forges the martial national state. (1988:56)

Greenblatt is bitingly ironic at the expense of the conventional ideological attitudes he finds in the play, seeing Shakespeare as not himself being ironic, but as registering a fundamental ambivalence inherent in the exercise of power, which the critic is able to deconstruct. Among the paradoxes Greenblatt cites is Fluellen's praise of the "gallant-king" for having killed his "best friend", as Alexander the Great had done (*Henry V* 4. 7. 22-38, 44-7). As Greenblatt says, this reminder of Falstaff's rejection is "potentially devastating": "Hal's symbolic killing of Falstaff—which might have been recorded as a bitter charge against him—is advanced by Fluellen as the climactic manifestation if his virtues" (1988:58). Moreover, he continues to argue, "the very doubts that Shakespeare raises serve not to rob the king of his charisma but to heighten it, precisely as they heighten the theatrical interest of the play" (63). Thus, according to Greenblatt, the authority fosters the subversion in order to control it.

Sinfield and Dollimore discuss the working of ideology in Shakespeare's representation of history from a different perspective. In their cultural materialist essay "History and Ideology, Masculinity and Miscegenation: the Instance of *Henry V*", Sinfield and Dollimore invert Greenblatt's emphasis of "containment" thesis, argue that: "even in this play, which is often assumed to be the one where Shakespeare is closest to state propaganda, the construction of ideology is complex—even as it consolidates, it betrays inherent instability" (114). Pointing to the conflicting attitudes in late Elizabethan England towards foreign war, they look beneath the national unity affirmed in *Henry V* and find that "its obsessive preoccupation is insurrection", so that though "systematically, antagonism is reworked as subordination or supportive alignment. It is not so much that these antagonisms are openly defeated but rather that they are represented as inherently submissive. Thus the Irish, Welsh, and Scottish soldiers manifest not only their countries' centrifugal relationship to England but also an ideal subservience of margin to center" (118). Pugliatti puts it in a simple way of understanding: "Here again we get the picture of somebody (consciously?) supporting the dominant ideology (epic celebration of

Henry V) who nevertheless unconsciously incorporates here and there unfavourable elements which are introduced as the physiological antibodies of ideology"(138).

No matter it is from Greenblatt or Sinfield and Dollimore's perspectives, the ideologies under working are so complicated that no deliberate intention can be ascribed to the dramatist. However, there is a position that we may need to take into consideration. Norman Rabkin starts from Gombrich's well-known description of the picture of an ambiguous zoomorph being (rabbit or duck?) and concludes that, like that drawing, *Henry V* is constructed in such a way as to seem either one thing or the other. Rabkin argues that "Shakespeare's habitual recognition of the irreducible complexity of things has led him, as it should lead his audience, to a point of crisis" (296), but the fact is that the two versions may not be contradictory and that the point of crisis may well consist in the fact that Shakespeare is trying to present a polyphonic political picture, namely, both a rabbit and a duck. Norman Rabkin has written: "One way to deal with a play that provokes such conflicting responses is to try to find the truth somewhere between them" (279). So the "truth" he finally found in *Henry V* is that "Shakespeare creates a work whose ultimate power is precisely the fact that it points in two opposed interpretations it requires of us" (279). Therefore, he concludes, "in this deceptively simple play Shakespeare experiments, perhaps more shockingly than elsewhere, with a structure like the gestaltist's familiar drawing of a rare beast" (279). In other words, perhaps Shakespeare intends to cover the underlying disparate ideologies up with the ambiguous image of the King, there is no need to assert that a choice must be made to have a clear-cut portrait of Henry. Under this light, the reading is postmodern in its assertion of differences. Early in *Henry V* the Chorus speaks highly of a warrior king with no comparison in history, but by the end of *Henry V* the legitimacy of kingship itself is in question. The play charts a fall into difference which generates a world of uncertainties. Therefore, the text reveals marks of the struggle to fix meaning, and simultaneously of the excess which unavoidably renders the image of Henry and the nationalism he represents unstable.

Both the Chorus and King Henry V hail the brotherhood between the King and the common soldiers. The Chorus before Act Four tells us that the King bids the downtrodden poor ("poor condemned English" [4.0.22]) good morning before the battle of Agincourt and calls them "brothers, friends and countrymen". The King in his "Saint Crispin's Day" speech also speaks of glory, honour, and brotherhood- all ideals that aimed to inspire "we few, we happy few, we band of brothers" (4.3.60). However, the King's "band of brothers", some of them as degraded as Nym, some of them being officers from different parts of the country, some being the agent of action, present perspectives that are different from the chorus's glorifying praise on the King's patriotic behaviours and the unified picture of nationalism presented by the King.

As early as in Scene Two Act Two, Bardolph and Nym recall the King's rejection of Falstaff, who is now sick of heart (2.1). The rejection is not revisited until the Agincourt battle, where Fluellen is praising King Henry V by comparing him to Alexander the Great. Fluellen refers to one well-known story of how, in a drunken passion, Alexander killed his friend Clytus. Gower objects, "Our king is not like him in that: he never killed any of his friends" (4.7.39-40). However, this statement is countered by Fluellen's reference to Falstaff:

> FLUELLEN. As Alexander killed his friend Cleitus, being in his
> ales and his cups; so also Harry Monmouth, being in
> his right wits and his good judgments, turned away
> the fat knight with the great belly-doublet: he
> was full of jests, and gipes, and knaveries, and
> mocks; I have forgot his name.
> GOWER. Sir John Falstaff. (4.7.44-50)

Fluellen's very mode of thinking exposes cracks in the king's moral armour and actually reminds us that the King turned off his old friend. King Henry V is compared to Alexander the Great of Macedon not only because they are both great warriors, but also because as Alexander, being drunk, killed his friend Cleitus, and so did Henry V, being in his right mind, turned away the fat knight and actually killed him. After Fluellen's damaging reference to Henry's symbolic killing of Falstaff, Henry makes a triumphant entrance. This entrance, with its military "Alarum" followed by a royal "Folurish"①, according to Greenblatt, "is the perfect emblematic instance of a potential dissonance being absorbed into a charismatic celebration" (1988:58). It calls audiences' attention to that Henry behaves in ways that oddly cruel to his former companions.

The play registers another death of Henry's old companion—Bardolph. In Scene Six Act Three, Henry, entering with his soldiers, asks Fluellen if there have been any casualties in the recent fighting, and Fluellen answers "the Duke hath lost never a man, but one that is like to be executed for robbing a church, one Bardolph, if your majesty know the man" (3.6.100-101). Though the King, of course, does "know the man", his next speech "we would have all such offenders so cut off" (3.6.106) makes no mention of any previous association with Bardolph and has no element of personal warmth. Henry's inexplicable betrayal of Falstaff and his old acquaintance being so "cruel/Ingrateful, savage, and inhuman" (2.2.94-95) deftly registers Henry's royal hypocrisy, ruthlessness, and duplicity.

It is not just that Henry fails to establish contact with his old acquaintance; he does not even seek it. He is now a qualified hero, and wages war on an allegedly reasonable excuse to the Harfleur. Henry's rallying speeches addressed to the soldiers at the siege of Harfleur ("once more unto the breach, dear friends" [3.1.1-2])— reveals sharp political pragmatics at work. The "dear friends" is carefully modulated into three parts. It begins with the king's immediate kinsmen and closest followers. They set the lead example. Attention then turns to the aristocracy and gentry, the

---

① Both the "Alarum" and "Flourish" are in the stage direction after Gower's declaration: "Here comes his majesty" (4.7.52). The stage direction is "*Alarum. Enter* KING HARRY [with] BOURBON [as his prisoner, WARWICK, GLOUCESTER, EXETER, a Herald and others,] *with Prisoners. Flourish.*"

"noblest English" (3.1.17), whose role is to "be copy now to men of grosser [i. e. less high-class] blood/ And teach them how to war" (3.1.24-25). Then come the "yeomen" and finally "the mean and base" (3.1.25, 29). The speech thus enacts the chain of command down the ranks. It offers a textbook image of the officer ranks leading from the top to the down by class differences.

Henry's rallying speech inspired the soldiers to die for the king. However, Nym, Pistol and Falstaff's boy are not. Although at first aroused by the national heroism, within fifty lines Nym, the Boy and Pistol are wishing they were in London. In a sense, Nym and the others refute the words of King Henry: they are the ordinary soldiers, who are not in the least motivated by heroism but would instead save their own lives. The effects are double-sided: they make Henry's rhetoric, by contrast, seem more magnificent and necessary if men like Nym, Pistol, and Bardolph are to be led into war; but they also give us some comic distance from Henry and remind us that, like Hotspur's rhetoric of war, Henry's rallying speech is inhumane. The response of Nym, Pistol, and the Boy directly attack Henry's appeal to honour— "Dishonour not your mothers" (3.1.22)—in ways reminiscent of Falstaff's attacks on honour throughout the *Henry IV* plays.

The King's "band of brothers" not only includes Nym, the Boy and Pistol, those degraded foot soldiers, but also the officers in the King's army. The most noticeable are four captains, the Welsh Captain Fluellen, the English Captain Gower, the Scottish Captain Jamy, and the Irish Captain Macmorris. In the same scene where the foot soldiers like Nym appears, Fluellen flaunts his Welsh nationality with an extravagance that almost is half-comical, and the Irish Mac Morris is so sensitive on the subject of his nationality that the slightest reflection on it would make him roar.

> MAC MORRIS. Of my nation! What ish my nation? Ish a villain,
> and a bastard, and a knave, and a rascal. What ish
> my nation? Who talks of my nation? (3.2.124-126)

The defiance is so fierce that even the sturdy Fluellen is eager for a compromise. Nevertheless, sensitive as the Irishman is, Morris is passionately devoted to the King, and in the siege of Harfleur, the Duke of Gloucester, the King's brother, is "altogether directed" by him. Fluellen is attached equally profoundly to the King and makes comprise between his loyalty and his nationalism by claiming that Henry V himself is a Welshman.

> FLUELLEN. All the water in Wye cannot wash your majesty's
> Welsh plood out of your body, I can tell you that:
> God bless it and preserve it, as long as it pleases
> his grace, and his majesty too! (4.7.105-108)

Some critics interpret this scene as evidence of Henry's becoming a prophetic harbinger of the union of different people—Englishmen as well as Irishmen, Scotsmen and Welshmen (Patterson 88). Some other regard the scene as proves the four captains' fine, vehement spirits and devotion to the war in hand (Humphreys 18). However, I would like to argue the scene serves as a parody of Shakespeare's vague idea on nationalism, that is to say, the different perspectives on nationalism being not so easily to be contained in the ambiguous image of the King.

The issue of the English domination of Wales appears in the play to be more containable—Welsh must have seemed the most tractable issue, for it had been annexed in 1536 and the English church and legal system had been imposed (Holderness 1992b:195). Henry V and the Tudors could indeed claim to be Welsh, though over the centuries it may have caused more suffering and injustice than the subjection of the lower classes. Most attention is given to Fluellen. The jokes about the way Fluellen pronounces the English language are, apparently, just reminders of Katherine's English lesson in the next scene. At the heart of the lesson are words in English for Katherine with sexual and military referents: "foot" and "gown" in English sound like "foutre" and "count" in French, which is almost the same as

Welsh people need to learn English after being annexed.

Although Fluellen "cannot speak English in the native garb" (5.1.76), there is no incomprehension between him, the Welsh, the Scottish and the English captain. Indeed, unlike what happens with the French, all these characters speak English, though in a remarkably different form. It may be agreed that, as Sinfield have remarked, "The jokes about the way Fluellen pronounces the English language are, apparently, for the Elizabethan audience and many since, an adequate way to handle the repression of the Welsh language and culture" (125). However, the situation is not as simple as that: in Fluellen, Jamy and Macmorris's "disfigured" English, a way of speaking where the difference is made explicit, a form of resistance to cultural integration is objectively represented. If the process of unification tends to kill the native tongues, nevertheless the marginal cultures still express some form of centrifugal force, if nothing else, by corrupting the "garb" of the prescribed unitary language. The process, which becomes polyphonic, is explained as a recurrent cultural phenomenon by Bakhtin in his "Polyphonic Discourse in the Novel":

> The victory of one reigning language (dialect) over the others, the supplanting of languages, their enslavement, the process of illuminating them with the True Word, the incorporation of barbarians and lower social strata into a unitary language of culture and truth, the canonization of ideological systems, philology with its methods of studying and teaching dead languages [...] all this determined the content and power of the category of "unitary language" in linguistic and stylistic thought. But the centripetal forces of the life of language, embodied in a "unitary language", operate in the midst of heteroglossia. At any given moment of its evolution, language is stratified not only into linguistic dialects in the strict sense of the word ... but also ... into languages that are socio-ideological: languages of social groups, "professional" and "generic" languages, languages of generations and so forth. (271-272)

The word "polyphonic" is a musical term, referring to simultaneous lines of independent melody which makes a whole. But here, it is a feature of narrative, which includes a diversity of views and voices. In *Henry V*, neither the English tongue nor the ideologically saturated discourse succeeds in eliminating differences by imposing a "unitary language" of culture and truth. The four captains' voices may be taken as a polyphonic picture rather than a monolithic nationalism.

The next group of common soldiers are three yeomen—Court, Williams, and Bates, who offered as the fantasy of the "band of brothers". Although fulfilling the promise of "a little touch of Harry in the night" offered by the fourth Chorus, they add to it a mockery so great as to not only rebuff the self-deluding populism Henry V's image bears, but reveal the King himself as a betrayal of the effective rules.

On the eve of Agincourt, the climactic battle of the play, Henry encounters three yeomen soldiers Court, Williams, and Bates accidentally in his "little touch" with the "band of brothers". Faced with the necessity of talking with plebeians, Henry tries to use the time to prepare them for death. He advocates that if the king's cause is good, and the soldiers' consciences clear, death is no real threat to them. However, Williams challenges on behalf of the ordinary soldiers the justice of the king's war. He raises the issue that the king has no moral entitlement to risk people's bodies, their lives and the security of their families in his war. From the perspective of ordinary soldier, death is not simply a question of conscience, an affair of the soul, but a matter of "legs and arms and heads, chopped off in a battle", of mutilated bodies on the battlefield, "some swearing, some crying for a surgeon, some upon their wives left poor behind them, some upon the debts they owe, some upon their children rawly left" (4.1.138-140). If Williams' voice is the voice of the people, his final sentence specifies the nature of the challenge he delivers: "Now, if these men do not die well, it will be a black matter for the king that led them to it; who to disobey were against all proportion of subjection" (4.1.143-145).

Williams' charge so deeply troubles Henry that he reaches to the extreme of sophistry to evades the issue. The fact that Henry fails to answer the question at the heart of their encounter indicates the justice of the war is not as glorious as the king advocates. Another profound proof that Williams' reproach is legitimate can be seen when the shallowness of Henry's populism is revealed. Henry V and Williams exchange the gloves the night before Agincourt in token of their quarrel. Each takes the other's glove to wear in his cap (4.1). Williams, of course, does not know that his quarrel is with the king who is in disguise. The gloves seem at that point, to Williams at least, to be mere markers of their identity for future mutual recognition. After the great victory of Agincourt, Henry sees Williams wearing the glove in his cap and summons him to explain it. On hearing that Williams has sworn an oath to fight with the possessor of his glove, Henry and Fluellen, who is with him, agree that he should keep his oath. Henry then constructs another layer of deceit to add to his earlier disguise by giving Fluellen the glove that Williams gave him and telling Fluellen he plucked it from the French Duke of Alencon's helmet in battle. He asks Fluellen to "wear this favour for me [Henry]" and to apprehend any man that challenges it as a friend to Alencon and an enemy to Henry.

When Williams and Fluellen meet, Williams recognises Fluellen's glove, but Fluellen does not recognise the glove that Williams wears:

> WILLIAMS. Sir, know you this glove?
> FLUELLEN. Know the glove? I know the glove is a glove.
> WILLIMAS. I know this, and thus I challenge it.
> *Strikes him.* (4.8.6-9)

Tempers follow the blow, but the quarrels are quickly intervened first by the Earl of Warwick and the Duck of Gloucester, then by King Henry and the Duke of Exeter. Williams and Fluellen give their accounts of the fight as they promised to do when they saw the respective gloves; but for Henry, this is a moment of pure theatre: "Give me your glove, soldier. Look, here's the other in the pair" (4.8.40-41). He continues briefly accusing Williams of offences against him: "It was me you promised to hit, and you insulted me terribly" (4.8.42-43). However, since the King maintains his incognito until this moment, Williams rightly replies: "Your Majesty came not like yourself. You appeared to me but as a common man" (4.8.51-52). Again, the occasion allows Henry to create a further moment of pure theatre, by which the glove and, supposedly, the offence are both magically transformed. Henry asks his uncle Exeter to fill the glove with gold coins and give it to Williams. Henry asks Williams to keep it, and "wear it for an honour in thy cap/ Till I do challenge it" (4.8.60-61).

This scene creates a slightly queasy effect. On the one hand, it seems to seek audience's approval for a gesture of regal magnanimity, but on the other hand, Williams' speech of justification is inserted to make an audience see that Henry's talk of "offence" is out of order. Henry thus "forgives" an offence that was never truly committed. Characteristically for this play, the effect is dialogic, leaving audiences uncertain whether this is evidence of a man worthy of being king or one who knows how to play with a cheap trick.

Williams voices the repository of the popular voice, and he demonstrates that the meanings of both the sovereignty and law do not go uncontested. The audience is left to consider the ideological density. Has the national leader the right to demand obedience to the point of death? What are the rights of the people? What is justice? Who is entitled to define them, to impose them? Is it the king? Ultimately, outside the fictional world of the history plays, the people are to ruminate on the law of justice and the monarchy.

In the *Henry IV* plays, it is Falstaff who consistently represents the refusal of monarchic order. While in *Henry V*, it is his presumable "band of brothers" challenge the King's moral and legal entitlement to the throne. As a King, Henry V surrounded by men of all types and classes: nobles, an army of ordinary folks, soldiers willing and unwilling, brave and cowardly, Welshmen, Irishmen and Scots, who participate variously in his war. To present this varied picture of a dutiful monarch and a people on the march the dramatist draws not only from Holinshed and other chroniclers but also fictions. Henry does penance for his father's crime, brings treason remorselessly to justice, and displays at Agincourt that he has secured the victory that he thus so richly deserves. Act Five of *Henry V* also celebrates the victory of the ideal Christian king. However, the king's band of brothers, instead of presenting a heroic image of Henry V and the monolithic nationalism, present a disillusioned representation and not a very happy picture of the national history. Besides, those common soldiers, produce peculiarly an amphibology of the King as both "Rabbit" and "Duck"—an appealing person but simultaneously an ethically repulsive king.

All in all, the "both-and" paradox allows us to follow Shakespeare's deviation from the historiographical norms, and to abandon conventional criticism's desire to explain the plays either in the "rabbit" way of great men or in the "duck" way of a cruel Machiavellian king. Shakespeare, through a lengthy exploration of dramatic fiction of history, is more willing to express an independent view of English history, a view of history that differs factually, conceptually, and ideologically from versions endorsed by the culture's hegemonic forces.

In conclusion, Chapter Four turns to Shakespeare's fictional use of history in *1 Henry IV*, *2 Henry IV*, and *Henry V*. Telling different stories of their histories, the ordinary people reject the Tudor absolutism and show that the world belongs to those who are prepared to take it. The juxtaposition of all kinds of histories, such as the ahistorical Falstaff in the literary history, Mistress Quickly selective and self-adaptive oral history in *Henry IV*, and the Chorus's theatrical representation of history in *Henry V*, creates a depth and poignancy of interaction between history and fiction richer than anywhere else in the history plays. Extraordinarily enough, the second trilogy, read from the present, might perfectly adapt to an epigraph Lyotard's strongly appeals at the end of his essay "What is postmodernism?":

> Let us wage a war on totality; let us be witnesses to the unpresentable; let us activate the differences and save the honour of the name. (82)

Although Shakespeare makes free with his sources in a way that no serious historian could now approve, his fictional use of history, despite the historical difference, displays some of the concerns which impel our own postmodern understanding of "petit récits". The "petit récits" of histories can be most clearly exemplified by the fictional characters. The Mistress Quickly, amusing and amazing us with her recollection of the past hybrid details, simultaneously shapes that particular fiction and gives it a dramatic present; the county Justices Shallow and Silence, recapturing their past experiences and issues of death, aids and immerges in the production of history; not to mention Falstaff, the most special artifice of Shakespeare's construction of history, the one who brings history and fiction face to face, is the culmination of all stands of history. Even the most historical scene which is seen as the articulation of the grand nationalist narrative—Henry V celebrates of the glories of England in fiery patriotic speeches—is actually dissented by vibrate voices of his "band of brothers". Shakespeare's fictional use of common people propels the possibility of histories made by the people and indicates in the process the uttermost possibilities of "there is a history in all men's lives". Shakespeare, in other words, makes histories.

Chapter Five Destination of the Fictional Use of History: An Understanding of the Nature of Truth

In choosing "All is True" as the subtitle of *Henry VIII* and fictionalising the Prologue that constantly reminds us about "finding truth" and "chosen truth" in the play, Shakespeare himself transforms its subject matter—the nature of truth—into a proverbial sayings, like "All's Well That Ends Well," whose meaning required interrogation. It seems that Shakespeare is not only mocking the claims for superior veracity in the title but also is showing the destination of the fictional use of history in his last English history play.

Probably written in 1613, *Henry VIII* is a history play written by Shakespeare and John Fletcher at the end of Shakespeare's career. *Henry VIII*, as the subtitle under which it was first performed—*All is True*—suggests, is obsessed with the truth. According to statistics provided by Mcmullan, not only the word "true" itself appears no fewer than twenty-five times, but there are six occurrences of "truly", one of "true-hearted" and eighteen of "true". The Prologue alone offers two occurrences of "truth" and one of "true" in thirty-two lines, first of all locating the concept within faith, hope and expenditure—"Such as give/Their money out of hope they may believe/May here find truth" (7-9) – then connecting it with a sense of deliberate selectivity or, to be precisely, election—"our chosen truth" (18)—and finally addressing the relationship between artistic intention and representation—"the opinion that we bring/ To make that only true we now intend" (20-1) (Mcmullan 2-3). Yet, despite its consistent engagement with "truth" and "true", a clear understanding of the nature of "truth" and how to achieve the ideal of "being true" remains elusive in *Henry VIII* due to the play's problematic handling of the historical representation.

On the one hand, it is a play depends on its visible pursuit for the truth of its historical representation (this play is obsessed with the "truth"). On the other hand, it seems wilful to undercut the historical truth, because even the briefest glances at the Henry VIII reign ought to make it appear that the play's engagement with "what actually happened" in that reign is very limited. The primary source of *Henry VIII* is Holinshed's *Chronicles*, which are followed very closely in some parts of the play, with occasional verbal echoes (Bullough 1960b: 443). Incidents from the *Chronicles* have been selected with particular reference to six main historical situations: the conflict between Buckingham and Wolsey in which the Cardinal triumphs; the tragedy of Katherine of Aragon; Wolsey's fall; the marriage with Anne Bullen; Gardiner's plot against Cranmer; the birth of Princess Elizabeth. To concentrate the events of some twenty years into the play, Shakespeare disrupts chronology and selects historical events. Only a portion of Henry's life, for example, we see only two of the six wives, is dealt with. Also the break with Rome—surely the most significant political event in Henry VIII's reign—is treated only obliquely. Moreover, on closer inspection, the order of historical events is freely varied, usually by anticipating time. The Field of the Cloth of Gold meeting was held in 1520. Buckingham was executed in 1521. Henry did not marry Anne Bullen until 1532, but his meeting with her was placed before Buckingham's condemnation and his marriage before Wolsey's fall and death (1530). Katherine of Aragon died in 1536, but this was made to occur before Princess Elizabeth is born (1533), as is the plot against Cranmer, which may have occurred in 1540.

The sophisticated treatment of history found in *Henry VIII* aims, in Gordon McMullan's words, to elicit "productive anxiety about the nature of historical and political truth" (7). There is, however, one significant precedent for thinking in this way. Judith H. Anderson published a long essay entitled "Shakespeare's *Henry VIII*: The Changing Relation of Truth to Fiction" in which she suggested the Prologue is at variance with the title, or the play that follows turn out to have ambiguous or contradictory contents, "the very notion of objective truth [will be] thereby subjected to examination". "In this last case," she added, "the claim that 'all is true' becomes not false, bur ironic" (149).

Far from sustaining a sense of "truth" as an absolute, the play requires the audience to establish their own individual or communal interpretations of the truth of those significant historical events. We hear characters offering personally biased oral reportages and testimonies or commenting events from radically different perspectives due to their disparaging self-interests. The play's emphasis on the concept of truth, then, signals not only its engagement with the fascination of truth but also with the much broader issue of how truth is debated and established within the history. Viewed under this light, in choosing "All is true" as *Henry VIII*'s title, Shakespeare himself invites a radical understanding of the nature of truth in history.

5.1 "May Here Find Truth": The Scepticism about the Historical Truth in the History Plays

For Aristotle, as for Sir Philip Sidney, history records the historical truth about past events which "actually happened". Nevertheless, Sidney readily admits too that the historian also bases his own authority "upon other histories, whose greatest authorities are built upon the notable foundation of hearsay" (13), that is to say, reports from other people of dubious reliability, are hardly the satisfactory foundation for a supposedly true and authoritative record. The same questioning stance towards historical truth is replicated in *Henry VIII*. Because people can only gain knowledge through the second-hand narration, and see history as if one were looking at flowers in the fog, there emerges the scepticism towards historical truth which permeates through the play. By examining Shakespeare's fictional representation of historical events and characters in *Henry VIII*, we would find that the historical truth of an event or action is not clear and is distorted by the second-hand narration.

Most of the events of *Henry VIII* are reported after having passed through distorting filters of the personally biased oral reportages or testimonies. Moreover, the fact that various characters present incidents from their own versions and thus form multi-perspectives indicates perplexing and even contradictory interpretations. The examination of Shakespeare's unique dramatic mode of *Henry VIII* can tap into the equivocal interpretations. In his critical essay, "Dramatic Mode and Historical Version in *Henry VIII*", Paul Dean neatly observes that the play offers "no organic and cumulative movement toward a single concluding point" (178).

The most apparent difference between *Henry VIII* and Shakespeare's earlier history plays is its lack of a double plot. For example, there are two storylines in *Henry IV* plays, the one is serious and the other is light-hearted. These two storylines are perrectly balanced. Howerer, the Prologue in *Henry VIII* specifically rejected this kind of double plot:

> I come no more to make you laugh: things now,
> That bear a weighty and a serious brow,
> Sad, high, and working, full of state and woe,
> Such noble scenes as draw the eye to flow,
> We now present. (Prologue 1-5)

To omit a comic subplot is to omit opportunities for diversification of mood and to distance the audience from the play by giving them no characters with whom they can easily identify. We, as readers and audience, are made to feel remarkably far from the action in much of the play; repeatedly, we eavesdrop on reports of events rather than witness the events themselves. Still, the Prologue asks the audience to locate their concept within occurrences of faith and expenditure—"such as give/ Their money out of hope they may believe/ May here find truth" (7-9). While this succeeds in making the thematic point that we apprehend history mainly in the effort to find the truth, the following appeal to deliberate selectivity . "Only they/ That come to hear a merry, bawdy play, / a noise of targets, or to see a fellow/ will be deceived" (Prologue 13-16), indicates a detached or even aloof atmosphere. Any artistic work of course "interprets" through necessary selectivity and compression, but Shakespeare has dramatised the essential limitations in our knowledge of "truth" through a "second-hand nature of our acquaintance with historical events" (Dean 182).

Even before the appearance of the King, the first scene sets up a world in which the "truth" would be exceedingly complicated. Prior certainty repeatedly dissolves in the face of later revelations. The scepticism about the possibility of access to the truth is introduced through Norfolk's oral reportage of the famous meeting between Henry VIII and Francis I of France at the Field of Cloth to Buckingham.

Initially, we get to take Norfolk's glorious description at face value as he describes himself to Buckingham as "ever since a fresh admirer" (1.1.3) of the spectacle put on by the Kings of England and France during their meeting at the Field of the Cloth of Gold. Norfolk reports it in appropriate terms, referring to the English and French kings as "suns of glory" (1.1.6), whose alliance unites their separate majesties into a single image of magnificence, "pomp was single, but now married/ To one above itself" (1.1.15-16). He gives an unusually long speech to describe the scene.

> NORFOLK. They did perform
> Beyond thought's compass, that former fabulous story
> Being now seen possible enough, got credit
> That Bevis was believed. (1.1.35-38)

The spectacle seems to offer a picture of the power of the kings and the significance of the occasion as the establishment of peace between two great nations. But it is indeed within a few dozen lines we learn that the whole thing was a waste of time, producing only a temporary peace which "not values/ The cost that did conclude it" (88-9), and that the French have already broken the pact. As a result, looking back at the speech, we realise that it expresses a kind of relativism. Also, Norfolk's speech describes a flamboyantly artificial event that turns out to be utterly meaningless. The English and French are each viewed in light of the other, with no firm ground for judgment: "The two kings, / Equal in lustre, were now best, now worst, / As presence did present them" (28-30). So we are forced to acknowledge the emptiness of the grand gesture that only a moment before had seemed both convincing and appropriate.

Lee Bliss observes, "[I]n the beginning all had seemed true to Norfolk and, in his report, to us; only in retrospect can we see how false, how truly unstable…that appearance was" (3). We realise, too, that Norfolk's assertion that he is still an "admirer" (3) of what he saw in France is itself a loaded comment. Bliss rightly points out:

> "Admire" did not signify wonder in the sense of approbation, but rather an ironic sense of amazement at the disparity between a dream of transcendent and transforming harmony and the disconcertingly mutable political realities of an impoverished nobility and a broken treaty. (3)

Norfolk turns out to be much less impressed than he had sounded initially. In his reportage, judgment and the truth on which judgment must be based are both entirely contingent, as is Buckingham's reaction. Buckingham voices incredulity and mocks the high rhetorical style that Norfolk has been using—"O you go far"—but Norfolk argues "the tract of everything would by a good discourser lose some life/ Which action's self was tongue to" (1.1.40-42). Norfolk's answer indirectly points out the fact that no matter how well told, any account of what took place would fall short of capturing the event as it was experienced by those present at that time. The scene thus emphasises that the historical events would be inevitably distorted through the verbal transmission. Buckingham then continues to ask:

Chapter Five　Destination of the Fictional Use of History:
An Understanding of the Nature of Truth

> Who did guide—
> I mean, who set the body and the limbs
> Of this great sport together, as you guess? (1.1.45-47)

On being told it was Wolsey, Buckingham provides an alternative perspective from which to view the ceremonies as "fierce vanities" (54) whose costliness has ruined many noblemen and all for "minister communication of/ A most poor issue?" (1.1.86-87). Norfolk himself, having made the occasion sound so spectacular and so convincing, happily takes up Buckingham's theme, and instantly dismisses the celebrations as a kind of thing done by someone who lacks noble blood. "There's in him stuff that puts him to these ends," he sneers, "being not propped by ancestry" (58-59).

The splendid scene of pomp reported by Norfolk proves to be hollow and ironic. The withheld information and shifting perspectives in the personal reportage offer a characteristic questioning towards the truths established by individuals. Personal bias in this play generally undermines people's trust and invites sceptical interpretation of events. The subsequent trial scenes also promote this scepticism towards the grand appearance of the moment in history or any single person's assertion.

In Scene Two Act One, the case against the Duke of Buckingham is preceded by King Henry VIII's learning, via Katherine, of the taxation Wolsey is imposing on the country in Henry's name. Wolsey himself points out that language report distorts facts, which he considers to be because "sick interpreters or weak ones" make irresponsible remarks. He says: "Traduced by ignorant tongues, which neither know/ My faculties nor person yet will be/ The chronicles of my doing" (1.2.72-74). Wolsey's admission of the possible distortion of historical interpretation should warn King Henry to attend circumspectly to the Surveyor, but it does not. During the following pre-trial hearing held at Cardinal Wolsey's instigation, Henry seals the Duke Buckingham's fate on the basis of a single character's testimony, that of the Duke's former Surveyor. In the pre-trial of the Duke Buckingham, the former Surveyor, gives testimony against the Duke before the King. His only attempt to prove his credibility is to relate how the Duke was incited to these villainous thoughts by a "vain prophecy" (1.2.149), which promised that "the duke / Shall govern England" (1.2.170-1). Queen Katherine is obviously disturbed by the developments, and she intervenes. "If I know you well," she says, "[y]ou were the Duke's surveyor, and lost your office/ On the complaint o'th' tenants" (1.2.171-3), which points out that the Surveyor may well be motivated by a desire for revenge against his former master. The Queen's observation also recalls the earlier complaint against Wolsey, who, like the Surveyor, was charged with wrongdoings by anguished subjects (1.2.56-7). Protesting that he will "speak but truth" (1.2.177), however, the Surveyor offers no material or corroborating evidence. The rest of the testimony, though very fragmentary, is enough to convince the King to pronounce the Duke a "traitor to th'height" (1.2.214), but the audience is surely left much less convinced. On closer inspection, this uncertainty stems not only from the fact that Wolsey is involved, nor from Katherine's observations about the possible motivation of revenge, but the dubious meanings of the second-hand narratives—the Surveyor's reports of the Buckingham's ambition for the crown. The Surveyor reports Buckingham as having threatened to play "the part [his] father meant to act upon/ Th' usurper Richard" (1.2.195-6). The Surveyor's oral testimony, despite the self-consciously dramatic detail of the narration, almost likes a scriptwriter's visualisation.

> SURVEYOR. After 'the duke his father', with the 'knife',
> He stretched him, and with one hand on his dagger,
> Another spread on's breast, mounting his eyes
> He did discharge a horrible oath. (1.2.205-6)

Since we are overhearing rather than witnessing this, we are denied the superior knowledge of facts: Did Buckingham really mean to usurp power? Did the surveyor tell the truth or not? Did the King kill Buckingham because he knows Buckingham's real intention? The result of this oral testimony is to make the historical truth hard to determine. Buckingham's last speech before execution seems to offer a formal occasion for us to learn the truth—traditionally, convicted criminals would confess their crimes and ask the King's forgiveness, and Buckingham claims that he is "richer" than his "base accusers,/ That never knew what truth meant" (2.1.105-5)—yet his public testimony remains ambivalent.

> BUCKINGHAM. I am the shadow of poor Buckingham,
> Whose figure even this instant cloud puts on
> By darkening my clear sun. (1.1.224-26)

Buckingham's closing comment echoes the imagery of the scene's opening only to reverse it (the English King is referred to as "sun of glory" by Norfolk 1.1.6). He claims to forgive his enemies, yet looks forward to haunting them. He claims he will "cry for blessings" (90) on the King, yet he craftily describes himself not just as Duke of Buckingham, but also as Lord High Constable which quietly hints that the real reason for his execution is the threat he could post to the King if he claims his hereditary rights①:

> BUCKINGHAM. My state now will but mock me.
> When I came hither, I was Lord High Constable
> And Duke of Buckingham; now, poor Edward Bohun.

---

① Lord High Constable originally, one of the principal officers of the royal household, whose powers included being commander-in-chief of the army in the absence of the monarch and supreme arbiter of issues of chivalry. The post had become a purely ceremonial one by the early sixteenth century, but Buckingham viewed it as his hereditary right ever since Henry Ⅳ's marriage to one of the Bohun heiresses. In this context, "Buckingham's claim to the throne was no worse than Henry Ⅷ's, …. [and] the fact that Buckingham's claim to the great constableship also emphasized his royal connection probably did not greatly please the king". For more information on this aspect of issue, see McMullan, *King Henry Ⅷ*, Cengage Learning, 2000. pp. 274

Buckingham's last words turn on a series of antithetical perspectives: he is either innocent or guilty; his fall is due either to his treason or to the frame by Wolsey; the surveyor either gives true or false testimony. It is impossible for the audience to judge whether he is rebellious or whether he has the aristocratic pride that motivated his attack on Wolsey, which leads to his being framed and killed. Therefore, the downfall of Buckingham revolves around a series of conflicting interpretations and makes us experience the impossibility of knowing any definite "truth".

Wolsey's downfall, when it comes (Scene Two Act One), exhibits a strongly similar uncertainty. Wolsey tries to prevent Henry VIII from divorcing Queen Katherine and marrying Ann Bullen. It is reported how Wolsey's letters to the Pope fell into Henry's hands. Then Henry hands over the letters and asks Wolsey to explain. We are told that Wolsey's intercepted letter to the Pope has enraged the king, though Wolsey's estimation of his sovereign's position is quite accurate: "My king is tangled in affection to/ A creature of the queen's, Lady Anne Bullen" (3.2.35-36). Henry's indignation at Wolsey's interference is perhaps justified by the threat Wolsey poses to England and its autonomy, but the "truth" is that after five lines, we learn that Henry is already married to Anne. Almost immediately, Henry chides Wolsey for being a bad manager of his earthly affairs and adds "sure in that/ I deem you an ill husband, and am glad/ To have you therein my companion" (3.2.141-43). Wolsey claims that he has endeavoured to match his performance to his professions, and the king replies: "[this] is a kind of good deed to say well, /And yet words are no deeds" (3.2.153-54). We may justly wonder the conscious irony in Henry's righteous maxim, for Henry himself certainly offers occasions to doubt the credibility of the second-hand narrative, which is a divorce between word and deed, appearance and intent.

We are more certain of Wolsey's guilt than that of others accused, for he confesses the truth of some of the charges (3.2.210); yet he too refuses publicly to acknowledge what he will in private admit. When the four plotters (the scene begins with Norfolk, Surrey, Suffolk, and the Lord Chamberlain plotting against Wolsey) arrest him and demand the Great Seal, Wolsey refuses to surrender it "words cannot carry/ Authority so weighty ···/ Till I find more than will or words to do it/···/ I dare, and must deny it" (3.2.233-38). With a rich irony, he again appeals to more than second-hand evidence of the truth, showing the respect for properly constituted authority which he scorned in Buckingham: "so much fairer/ And spotless shall mine innocence arise, / When the king knows my truth" (3.2.300-02). The words "true" and "truth" dominate the rest of the scene, but by this time, we have been prevented from any simple reception of these concepts.

Despite the subtitle "All is True" and the references to "truth" in the Prologue constantly claim that what the play is showing must be true, the fact is that we are denied access to the truth of historical events due to the second-hand narrative of personally biased reportage and testimony. "Tis most true: These news are everywhere—every tongue speaks'em" (2.2.36-37), the effect of this filtering of events is to sustain a sense of radical uncertainty throughout the play. Moreover, the reference made by the prologue to "find truth here" is subjected to profound scrutiny in the play, too.

5.2 "Our Chosen Truth": The Multiple Perspectives of the Political Motivation

Any artistic work contains necessary selectivity and compression, but Shakespeare capitalises on the inconsistencies of the chronicles and with them enhances his use of multiple sympathetic perspectives. McMullan observes that the play is permeated by "a thoroughgoing scepticism about the possibility of access to the truth of motivation of historical event" (96). If the oral reportage and testimony visualise the process of history revision and display the distortion of historical truth, then displaying the same event from multiple perspectives reveals the inconsistencies of the political motivations through a proliferation of explanations within the play itself.

Although it seems impossible to realise what the Prologue says "may here find truth", the Prologue still progresses to indicate its references to "truth" being loaded to "our chosen truth" (Prologue 18) of those deaths and births, rises and falls of "the very persons of noble story" (Prologue 26). However, instead of focusing on a single central figure, no single character is allowed to be the focus of "our chosen truth" in *Henry VIII*. Buckingham falls at the hands of a surveyor manipulated by Wolsey; Henry finally divorces Queen Katherine; Wolsey declines and suddenly dies. Attempts to identify Wolsey, Anne Bullen, Katherine or even Henry as the "central" character are misguided. Since no single character is indispensable, the dramatist is free to explore the more significant movements of history to which all are subjects. Dean points out that the play "emphasises the uncertainties of history in order to question the availability of an omniscient perspective on historical events" (178). In this sense, the omniscient perspective of one narrator or presenter is replaced by the multi-perspectives embodied by different characters. This multi-perspectivism makes it difficult for us to have a clear view of the political motivation and not to mention "to rank our chosen truth with such a show" (Prologue 18).

Boris Uspenskij has argued that multi-perspectivism in historical narratives is a way to show and illustrate the non-monologic nature of history. According to the Russian scholar, the variety of possible interpretations of a historical event is not to be seen as contradictory, but as merging into one another:

> If a historical event can produce different explanations, one can think that this is due to the fact that diverse impulses converge in it which has all led to the same outcome (creating, so to speak, an effect of resonance or of reciprocal strengthening). Thus, the very possibility of offering different explanations may mirror the real, objective, non—accidental nature of the event. (qtd. in Pugliatti 45)

However, what does this multi-perspectivism suggest in the representation of history in *Henry VIII*? It is worth noting that in describing different characters' multiple perspectives, Shakespeare has multiplied our doubts about the real intention towards the historical events. Since the King's divorce is a constant topic within the play, it can be taken as a case for us to explore the uncertainties of different people's real motivations. Besides, the various perspectives provided to torn the truth of motivations are not only exemplified by the noble people but also by the fictional presences of the Gentlemen and the Old Lady in the play.

Historically, Queen Katherine's trial occurred four years before Henry's secret marriage to Anne Bullen. Thus Henry's obvious impatience to be rid of Katherine is given additional significance by the compressed time scheme: Henry has secretly married Anne while the question of Henry's divorce is still "unhandled" (3.2.58). Since this dramatic situation results from conscious changes in historical chronology, its implications can hardly be fortuitous. Henry's impatience renders his motivation ambivalent.

At Scene Two Act Two, Henry dismisses the noble in order to discuss with Wolsey and Campeius their "impartial judging" of the legality of Henry's marriage to Katherine. Henry's final public comment reflects his ambivalent posture:

> KING HENRY VIII. Would it not grieve an able man to leave
> So sweet a bedfellow? But conscience, conscience;
> O, tis a tender place, and I must leave her. (2.2.140-43)

Henry here offers the judges a veiled order to comply with his wishes. Perhaps most striking is Shakespeare's juxtaposition of Henry's plea of "conscience" with Ann's comment in the first line of the next scene. As if continuing a previous conversation with the Old Lady, Anne caps Henry's statement with "Not for that neither" (2.3.1). Since we do not know the referent of her remark, we take the line as an evaluation of Henry's remorse of conscience. Henry's stated reasons are questionable, and the extent of his hypocrisy, however, is left open.

At Katherine's trial, Henry offers a touching history of his prick of conscience, carefully marked as the official version by his narrative with a peremptory nervousness absent from Holinshed: "Then mark the inducement. / Thus it came: give heed to it" (2.4.167) (McMullan 310). Henry stresses his concern for religious rectitude and the national effects of his lack of a male heir. Such a political motivation might be readily acceptable, although Shakespeare certainly exploits the different perspectives in both Katherine's references to her fidelity and her daughter, and the Gentlemen and Old Lady's equivocal irony of Anne's sexual relationship with the King.

Claiming to have been a "true" wife to Henry, Katherine grounds her self-defence partly on Henry's private knowledge of her fidelity, partly on matters of public record. She reminds Henry that she has been his wife, obedient to him for more than twenty years and has been blessed in becoming pregnant with many children. Besides, she offers Henry the chance to recall the record that it is Henry's father who is reputed for being most prudent and her own father, King of Spain that arranged the marriage and thought it would be legal for them to marry. Henry has remained silent during the trial. His praise of Katherine's wifely virtue occurs only after Katherine has swept indignantly out of the court. When the cardinal suggests that Katherine commit her cause to the "king's protection", her answer strikes at the sincerity of Henry's profession of love as well as the Cardinal's hypocritical assurance of the king's love:

> QUEEN KATHERINE. Would you have me—
> If you have any justice, any pity,
> If ye be anything but churchmen's habits—
> Put my sick cause into his hands that hates me?
> Alas, has banished me his bed already,
> His love, too long ago. (3.1.115-20)

Katherine accuses the king and the cardinal of their duplicity and associates their personal hypocrisy with the more extensive moral corruption which pervades England. Katherine wishes she had never set foot on the English land or been flattered by the people in England. She accuses that people have angles' faces there, but heaven knows what they are really like (3.1.143-45). While Katherine may defy this world and refuse to accept its rules, she cannot change its nature. The conflicting perspectives are also evident in the Gentlemen's acceptance of Buckingham's downfall and Anne Bullen's rise.

The Gentlemen's first appearance is at the opening of the second scene when the Second Gentleman is on his way to Westminster Hall to hear sentence pronounced on the Duke of Buckingham, who is on trial for treason. The first Gentlemen considers how terrible this would be if Buckingham is indeed not guilty of treason (thereby also inviting the audience to consider this possibility), then continues their conversation to discuss the "slander" of the "buzzing of a separation/ Between the King and Katherine" (2.1.148-9) and to voice suspicion of Cardinal Wolsey's possible involvement and motivation. Communication becomes a process which simultaneously transmits and degrades truth, like an organic and inescapable infection: "it grows again/Fresher than ever it was". The clause "held for certain" clearly captures the tone here: realities and opinions have become indistinguishable from each other. The build-up to this exchange of rumour is both revealing and complex. The Second Gentleman drops a broad hint of knowledge: "[y]et I can give you inkling/ Of an ensuing evil, if it fail, / Greater than this" (2.1.139-41). His friend's eager reply is a masterpiece of contradiction, desiring while denying the desire to know the truth, or, rather, the rumour. It also emphasises faith, not just as trustworthiness but as belief: "Good angels keep it from us. / What may it be? You do not doubt my faith, sir?" (2.1.142-143), to which the Second Gentleman responds, teasingly, "This secret is so weighty 'twill require/ A strong faith to conceal it" (143). Hence the two gentlemen fail to cut through the confusion of events, or offer an anchor of objectivity, on the contrary, they are more like the biased presenters, spreading the events with "attitude". Their dialogues, as Bliss notes, "pointedly fails to resolve the kinds of questions—truth or deception, guilt or innocence—which the play repeatedly raises" (5). The truth of the motivations, in this context, occupies the same space as slander: the two seem interchangeable and dependent solely upon the succession of events and the way things are viewed from moment to moment.

The very fact that the two gentlemen of middling status passing on discussions doubting the good governance of the state, together with the fact that the scene ends with the First Gentleman becoming uneasy with their openness and his suggestion that they should talk about this more in private (4.1.168-9), encourages the speculation on how people's various perspectives work on to provide different explanations to the same political event. What becomes apparent is the isolated nature of the Gentlemen's perspectives, defined not merely as one person's perspective on a coherent truth, but instead as only one facet of events seen by one person which may share little or nothing with the perspective of other persons. It is undoubtedly the case that, far from offering objective clarification, the play dwells on the multiple perspectives different characters have on the same event to the point that provokes "our chosen truth" rather than dispels confusions.

The difficulty to establish any fixed and stable perspective on the political events is clearly illustrated when the two Gentlemen meet again, on which occasion they provide their commentaries on Anne's coronation procession. This procession is described in an exceptionally glamorous way (4.1.36). However, its majesty is significantly hampered by the framing of the second Gentleman's informative dimension of remarks. He appears at first to be wholly caught up in the ceremony and calls the new Queen, as an "angel", having "the sweetest face I ever looked on", but then quickly turns into the suggestion that the King's sexual desire is the real motive underlying his discard of first Queen for this younger beauty.

> SECOND GENTLEMAN. Our King has all the Indies in his arms,
> And more, and richer, when he strains that lady.
> I cannot blame his conscience. (4.1.45-7)

When a third Gentleman joins them, coming from the coronation at Westminster

Abbey, the discourse becomes even more pointedly fleshly and sexualised. He has been, the third Gentleman says:

> Among the crowd i'th'Abbey, where a finger
> Could not be wedged in more. I stifled
> With the mere rankness of their joy. (4.1.58-60)

"Rankness", besides carrying the meaning of "crowding", also implies the excitement and odour of bodies. The transparent and unrestrained sexuality of the commentaries gives sidelines of Anne's perceived route to power through sex.

Another character who offers different perspectives is the Old Lady. The Old Lady, who appears to be a court lady-in-waiting, enters into direct dialogue with Anne Bullen rather than comments from the margins. In Scene Three Act Two, the Old Lady mocks Anne's apparent surprise at being made Marchioness of Pembroke, hinting that Anne is already embarking on the course of making herself Henry's Queen. As Anne denies any interest in being a queen, the scene becomes deeply ironic. Since although Anne appears to be shy, modest and very concerned about Queen Katherine's fate, we have seen her in wantonness at Wolsey's banquet and the Lord Chamberlain reminds us that she may be pregnant. Was Anne not willing and eager to become Henry VIII's wife, the King would have no reason to divorce Katherine. This is equally clear to the Old Lady, who openly accuses Anne of hypocrisy and points up her knowledge of Anne's intention to have the King with several obscene double entendres.

> ANNE. By my troth and maidenhead,
> I would not be a queen.
> Old Lady: Beshrew me, I would,
> And venture maidenhead for't; and so would you,
> For all this spice of your hypocrisy.

> ANNE. Nay, good troth.
>
> Old Lady. Yes, troth, and troth;
>
> You would not be a queen?
>
> ANNE. No, in truth. (2.3.34-41)

Anne uses troth as loyalty when pledged in a solemn agreement; however, the Old Lady twists it slightly to mean "truth". The Old Lady taunts Anne about the splendours which "the capacity/ Of your soft cheverel conscience would receive, / If you might please to stretch it" (2.3.31-33). Also, the Old Lady plays the extended sexual pun to indicate Anne's real intention of being "quean" (i. e. whore) and finally to be "queen" as the scene progresses. ① Besides, the pun on queen/quean calls Henry's real motive in question and degrades Anne, especially when we learn of her reward (in the form of a title and funds) "for pure respect," as the Old Lady sarcastically terms it (2.3.95). From the Old Lady's perspective, Anne is simply "fresh fish" capitalising on her physical attraction and Henry's lust (2.3.86).

The fact that we need to hear the Gentlemen's commentaries and the Old Lady's puns in order to establish a different perspective on the real motivation of King's marrying Anne undercuts all the glorious and pretending excuses the King finds for himself and reveals the uncertainties of people's narrative. Also, the uncertainties foreground the radical and unbridgeable differences between the characters' multi-perspectives in a surprisingly subtle way. As Pierre Sahel notes:

> Most of the events of *Henry VIII* are echoed—more or less unfaithfully—within the play itself. They are not dramatized but reported after having passed through distorting filters. Characters present incidents and occurrences—or,

---

① Gordon McMullan notes that "queen" is a pun here, as throughout this scene, on the early modern word "quean", that is to say, a whore. For more information see McMullan, *King Henry VIII*, Cengage Learning, 2000. pp. 292.

often, their own versions of incidents and occurrences. (145)

However, why people only believe in what they themselves believed? It is because, from different perspectives, different people think themselves seeing the only truth. Obviously, the reason why they filter incidents from their own version is people's self-interest. In the play, no one is presented as wholly innocent or without self-interested motives. The play seems to dwell on the diverse characters' sharply disparaging self-interests.

Take, for instance, the contradictive descriptions of Wolsey given by Katherine and Griffith in Scene Two Act Four as an example. Katherine has learnt of Wolsey's death, and she says she will speak a "frank epitaph" of him (4.2.103). Katherine generalises Wolsey as a man with boundless appetites and ambitions, who was fine with buying and selling public offices. Plus, he was just a bad example of a clergyman: he lied and took bribes, and that is not right for a religious man to do.

Griffith, Katherine's gentleman usher, responds with an alternative epitaph, one which the Cardinal would presumably have preferred: Wolsey was a good man who came from a humble background but grew into a scholar. Griffith also reminds Katherine that when Wolsey died, he was a God-fearing man.

Rhetorically, the two speeches are roughly proportionate; yet as far as motivations are concerned, there is presumably a wealth of difference, since Katherine's venom has been prompted by the savagery of Wolsey's behaviour toward her. What we hear from Griffith is rhetoric: he feels the need to offer both sides of any debates with equal fluency and conviction. The effect is to present us with two quite distinct pictures of Wolsey which hardly overlap at all. We have no reason to think that Griffith believes Wolsey to have been the exemplary figure he describes, but this scene strikingly reduplicates our experience of the history—what we are given is from a limited perspective, with heavy fog that no one can peer through. Although the reporter or the recorder claims that it is true, who knows they reports or records from which perspective, and can we really have the truth?

In the last scene, Archbishop Cranmer baptises the baby Elizabeth—the future Queen Elizabeth I and delivers a long speech about how prosperous the country will be under the rule of Elizabeth. Although at Scene Two Act Five, the king highly praise Cranmer for his "true heart", and the Archbishop himself asserts people would find the words he utters "truth", audiences know his description is inconsistent with the historical facts:

> His [Cranmer] seamless genealogy is silent about the reigns of both Catholic Mary (1553-1558) and Edward Ⅵ (1547-1553). But the ultimate irony is of course that Cranmer himself was burned at the stake by Bloody Mary for his heretical Protestant beliefs. The Archbishop's history of England erases his own tragic death. (Kamps 210-211)

Shakespeare's arrangement of this passage in the final scene delivers an essential message to the audience: History is not an objective fact, but a selective or, to put it in Prologue's words, the "chosen" one constructed by people for different purposes from different perspectives.

Henry Ⅷ not only demonstrates the unreliability of the direct and indirect oral testimony in the shaping of history but also points out how the multiple perspectives of explaining history challenge the so-called historical and political truth in the history. Far from sustaining a sense of "truth" as an absolute, the play makes truth indeterminate. Requiring the audience to establish their own individual or communal interpretations of those significant historical events, the play's emphasis on the concept of truth, then, signals not only its engagement with the fascination of truth but also with the much broader issue of the ways in which truth is debated and established within the conception of history. From the self-mocking subtitle "All is true" to the opening lines declaring that "may here find truth", the dramatist has been suggesting to the audience that history is artificially created and purposefully constructed as "our chosen truth".

5.3 "To Make That Only True We Now Intend": The Ringing Assertion of the Poetic Truth about the Future to Believe

Shakespeare's history plays, going beyond Holinshed and Hall's chronicles, show an explicit, additionally self-conscious concern with the nature and varieties of truth. Regularly inviting our interrogation towards the historical objectivity in the representation of history, *Henry VIII* presents a self-conscious relation between history and history play and more generally between historical truth and poetic truth. To understand this relation between historical truth and poetic truth, we need to take a closer look at one significant precedent—Aristotle's *The Poetics*.

In connection with other terms belong to the same semantic field, Aristotle pertains poetic truth to poetry and the historical truth to history. The latter is constituted by the contingent, by the "actual" events as they happened, whereas poetry arranges "such things as might or could happen in accordance with probability or necessity" (1958: 18). Therefore, poetic truth is the universal truth of human nature, whereas historical truth is only the correspondence between singular facts and the dealing of it. Aristotle also argues that:

> The poet must be a maker of plots rather than of verses, since he is a poet by virtue of his representation, and what he represents is actions. And even if he writes about things that have actually happened, that does not make him any less a poet, for there is nothing to prevent some of the things that have happened from being in accordance with the laws of possibility and probability, and thus he will be a poet in writing about them. (2004:18)

Explaining the creative reproduction by poetry, Aristotle establishes at the same time connection between poetic feigning and truth. The very fact that the poet selects his material and imposes order on it, and produce an effect of "possibility" and "probability" about the representation, embodies the essence of poetic truth. It is through the fictional use of material into a cohesive whole that a poet achieves the idealisation of appearances. A great poet is to incorporate history selectively in that "first constructs the plot on the lines of probability, and then inserts characteristic names" (Aristotle 2004:17). In this sense, poetic feigning or the fiction transcends the empirical historical truth and achieves a possibility of universal truth, or to put it in another way, the poetic truth.

Generally speaking, it is not the poet's job to tell history, though it is important that they employ it in their comments on human life. It is not their task to report historical incidents truly but to truly manipulate those incidents in shining the poetic truth of human nature—the eternal emotions, thoughts, feelings, and actions of human beings. This might be the function which can be attributed to Shakespeare's history plays, and his last history play just proves to offer the final destination of his fictional use of history—the poetic truth.

Henry VIII thoroughly undermines our trust in the existence of historical and political truth, yet it ends with a ringing assertion of poetic truth about the future which we are expected to take on trust. In part this is a kind of trick: the play's future was its original audience's past, and they were bound to assent to Cranmer's prophecy because they had seen its fulfilment. Nevertheless, in another sense, the final scene—and in particular Cranmer's prophecy on the birth of Elizabeth—redeems the previous action without rationalising it: the entire fictional plot seems calculated to demonstrate the future rather than looking back on the past events. Cranmer's speech is thoroughly prepared for, especially in its retreat from historical time to poetic eternity.

After Wolsey's fall, the play turns to Katherine's peaceful death, and Henry's vindication of Cranmer, whose function in the play is to reverse Wolsey's and to put a halt to the consecutive dying falls we have previously heard. At the end of *Henry VIII* Cranmer's prophecy of the happy reigns of Elizabeth Tudor and James Stuart seems to relate poetic vision to historical fact, yet in doing so, it invites our asking how vision itself relates to the rest of the play and how the play's ending relates to history.

Disclaiming any suspicion of "flattery", Cranmer initiates a dynamic movement of prophecy at Elizabeth's christening and insists that his words are divinely prompted "truth" (5.4.16). "Let me speak, sir," Cranmer urges the King, "For heaven now bids me; and the words I utter/ Let none think flattery, for they'll find' em truth" (5.4.14-16). The infant Elizabeth, he claims, will be the cause of national blessings "Which time shall bring to ripeness"; she will be "a pattern to all princes living with her,/ And all that shall succeed," all the graces and virtues appropriate to monarchy "Shall still be doubled on her," and "good grows with her" (5.4.20-2,30,32). Finally, in this time of revelation, he assures us:

> CRANMER: Truth shall nurse her,
> Holy and heavenly thoughts still counsel her:
> She shall be loved and feared: her own shall bless her;
> Her foes shake like a field of beaten corn,
> And hang their heads with sorrow: good grows with her:
> In her days every man shall eat in safety,
> Under his own vine, what he plants; and sing
> The merry songs of peace to all his neighbours:
> God shall be truly known; and those about her
> From her shall read the perfect ways of honour. (5.4.28-32, 36-7)

Moreover, he goes on to foretell James' accession as a time of peace and hope, treating "truth" as a key attribute bequeathed to her successor by Elizabeth:

> Peace, plenty, love, truth, terror,
> That were the servants to this chosen infant,
> Shall then be his, and like a vine grow to him:
> Wherever the bright sun of heaven shall shine,

His honour and the greatness of his name

Shall be, and make new nations. (5.4.47-52)

"Truth", then, personified as a critical attribute of the elect ruler is emphasised in the prophecy as the foundation of the future reign. Just as the plot of *King John* ends with the assurance that Prince Henry will "set a form upon that digest/Which [John] hath left so shapeless and so rude" (5.7.26-27), and the Bastard's ringing declaration that England will never be conquered so long as it "to itself do rest but true" (5.7.118), the birth of the Princess Elizabeth ends a similar narrative with similar assurances. Elizabeth, who likes the maiden Phoenix:

CRANMER. The bird of wonder dies, the maiden phoenix,

Her ashes new create another heir,

As great in admiration as herself;

So shall she leave her blessedness to one,

When heaven shall call her from this cloud of darkness,

Who from the sacred ashes of her honour

Shall star-like rise, as great in fame as she was,

And so stand fixed: peace, plenty, love, truth, terror,

That were the servants to this chosen infant,

Shall then be his, and like a vine grow to him. (5.4.39-49)

The Phoenix, being both a single creature and a part of an endless cycle of regenerations which inhabits both time and eternity, is a symbol that has been foreshadowed throughout the structure of the play.

At first glance, it seems as if the events in the play unfold sequentially. Buckingham's fall at the hands of a surveyor manipulated by Wolsey; Anne Bullen's rise and Katherine of Aragon's gradual decline; the eventual divorce of Henry and Katherine; the sudden decline and death of Wolsey; the death of Katherine; the birth of Elizabeth; and the attempt by the Privy Council to remove Cranmer. However, if scrutinised carefully, the sequence of historical events is not a pure sequence but a cycle. We see each subsequent event in its past and future relations with others in *Henry VIII*. We hear of earlier events which take place in the theatrical present (for example, Wolsey's finding 'evidence' against Buckingham) will play back upon their successful perpetrators (thus, Henry's finding 'evidence' against Wolsey), and our knowledge of Henry VIII's life means that we know the way Henry behaves towards Katherine and Anne will be replayed several more times with subsequent wives. Like the Phoenix who can emerge from its ashes with renewed youth to live through another cycle of years, the plot exists not as an organic and cumulative movement toward a single concluding point, but as a frieze in which the sequence of events being more cyclical than sequential. Each subsequent event in the play plays back their previous perpetrators, and the history will be replayed several times in the theatrical present and future.

By the end of the council scene, Henry claims to be "grow stronger and more deserve to be honoured", and Cranmer's prophecy appears to come as a final revelation that offers Elizabeth's birth as the fulfilment of the historical narrative. However, in an analysis of the effect of dramatic structure, Clifford Leech argues that despite the fact that the play ends with Elizabeth's christening and Cranmer's apocalyptic prophecy, the dominant impression of the play is:

> There could be no tight structure in this play, for it is truly a chronicle, beginning arbitrarily with the fall of Buckingham and ending arbitrarily with Anne's moment of splendour. Moreover, our attention is repeatedly drawn to events outside the time of the play, and these (apart from the sanguine references to England's condition under Elizabeth and James) concern events of the same kind as we have witnessed in the action. Of all the last plays, it is the one that most clearly indicates the cyclic process. Nothing is finally decided here, the pattern of future events being foreshadowed as essentially a repetition of what is

here presented. (Leech 21)

It is true that, if we regard history, as merely "chronicle", or as a series of rises and falls, there is no reason why it should ever stop. However, Shakespeare knows from the beginning the difficulties posed to the playwright by the lack of teleology in the chronicle form. Looking back from Cranmer's vision to the rest of the play, even in the absence of an intentional signal from the playwright, we should have difficulty not remembering history. Anne Bullen, Elizabeth's mother, beheaded by Henry Ⅷ; Cranmer himself burned by Catherine's and Henry's daughter Mary, Queen Elizabeth's death, James Stuart's immoral court which lends an odd resonance to Cranmer's prophesying that James will flourish "and like a mountain cedar, reach his branches/ To all the plains about him" (5.4.53-54). Certainly when Cranmer says that "Truth shall nurse her," we cannot forget our experience of a world in which it is impossible to determine the "truth" of even simple, purportedly factual statement. Therefore, to regard *Henry Ⅷ* as an amorphous or open-ended work seems wilfully perverse. The appalling political motivations and ugly human nature are too mostly realistic and compel one to shift the attention from the contingent, ambiguous world to an idealised one in which truth can be known. Viewed under this light, the final scene, instead of being an escapist fantasy of the vain repetition, offers an aesthetically satisfying experiment in providing a suggestion of resolution and finality to resolve the endless repetitions in history.

This final scene contributes to a resolution between the history and the truth, that is to say, the "golden world" of Cranmer's vision exists only in a transcendental aesthetic world. An apocalyptic realisation, the phoenix born and reborn in the golden world remains a goal of all men's desires. Going beyond the limits of the radically changing world, the Phoenix imagery grasps the ever-lasting values in the truth of the poetic vision. Precisely because it is metaphorically as well as literally "visionary", we can accept and believe the prophecy's perfection of men and language: the words which have echoed throughout the play—"truth"—seem no longer ironic but suddenly restored to full dignity by the image of a world in which they would be simple statements of fact. At the same time, the sense in which Cranmer describes things hoped for, and prays for what he "sees", allows his words to bridge the division between prediction and history's fulfilment of that prediction without compromise of falsification. Therefore, Cranmer's prophecy offers "an aesthetic rather than a logical sense of resolution and finality" (Bliss 22). Moreover, Bliss argues that this vision encourages and explores the play's framework to create a world where humanity's endless cycle of rising and fall can be translated into the more miraculous image of the death and rebirth of "the maiden phoenix" (23). The division between the temporal, physical world of history and the atemporal realm of truth is thus finally united and transcended.

Generally speaking, *Henry VIII* demonstrates a fascination with technical experimentation which has been variously regarded as an exaltation from the promise of "may here find the truth" to the deliberately "our chosen truth" and finally to the only ever-lasting truth—the poetic truth we now intend. Here we have Shakespeare's last word on a problem with which he had been grappling throughout his career: the problem of the accommodation of the open, expansive truth of history within the closed, concentrated and intensified poetic feigning of drama. While the historiography deals with particular events, here Shakespeare's dramatic fiction ignores the nonessentials, removes irrelevances, and concentrates on the essentials in keeping with the law of logicality, probability and necessity. The particular object taken by the dramatist is transfigured to reveal the essential elements of human nature, the everlasting, universal aspects of human life, which makes the characters and events appear so authentic in his plays that the readers or audiences take them for real ones. The Duke of Marlborough, as Coleridge relates, was "not ashamed to confess that his

principal acquaintance with English history was derived from Shakespeare's plays". ①
No doubt there are many more now (especially those not from the United Kingdom)
whose acquaintance with England's past comes via Shakespeare. So the poetic truth,
the idea of the universal, shines through Shakespeare's fictional use of history in his
history plays. That is, as the Phoenix reborn from the fire, Shakespeare's history
plays, in a recycling and renewing process, give us the timeless poetic truth in human
history.

In conclusion, Chapter Five is about *Henry VIII*, which is the last history play
written by Shakespeare in a much later time. Moving further into the history and
retreating from the jovial resolution he imposed in the second trilogy, Shakespeare
reopens the question of historical causation with an increasingly intense interrogation of
the "truth" in history. In *Henry VIII*, the quest for "historical truth" is destabilised by
the personally biased oral reportages and the multi-perspective embodied by the
fictional figures such as the Gentlemen and the Old Lady in the text. Besides,
Cranmer's final reference to Elizabeth as Phoenix cannot be confined to literally "true"
predictions of her actual reigns, or be taken as flattery merely satisfying the reigning
monarch's taste. It is a ringing assertion of the artistic future one can believe in.
Shakespeare's history plays like "the maiden Phoenix", born and reborn in the
vicissitudes of numerous historical moments, are always in search of self-renewal in
people's reading and performance and therefore, present to readers and audiences with
the poetic truth of the universal human nature.

---

① For a sampling of materials that reflect Coleridge's comments related to this, see "Writings on Shakespeare: A Selection of the Essays, Notes, and Lectures of Samuel Taylor Coleridge on the Poems and Plays of Shakespeare"/ Newly Edited and Arranged by Terence Hawkes. With an Introduction by Alfred Harbage. 223.

Chapter Six Conclusion

Old Historicism understands history to be outside literature and believes that history is an independent social and ideological system, which is complete and stable in a specific historical era. E. M. W. Tillyard, the representative of Old Historicism, enunciates that Shakespeare's ten history plays form, from the outset, a unified and cohesive totality of historical writing which articulates the "Tudor Myth" and "the Elizabethan Picture". Although many critics accept the concepts, this grand narrative of the feudal ideology is no longer valid in the light of the contemporary conditions of cultural production. More intricate explorations of these dramas draw on a much wider range of narrative possibilities.

New Historicism, in the growing calls to the "textuality of history" and "historicity of text", breaks down the barriers between literary works and other non-literary social-cultural practices and hence explains the dynamic process of the interaction between literature and other social practices in the cultural system adequately. Discontinuity becomes the object and the tool of research, that is to say, the matter for literature analysis does not consist in finding conventions and traditions, but in pondering in rifts and limits.

It is the postmodernism that furthers this kind of recognition. The postmodernist theory emphasises the decentring and fragmentation of the categories of experience and the subject in the name of difference which crystallised in Lyotard's famous definition of postmodernism as "incredulity towards metanarratives". Moreover, it is Lyotard's "petit récits", the little stories which are in his analysis "the quintessential form of imaginative invention" (Lyotard 18), supplant the grand narrative. If the theory is so understood it is clear that postmodernism entails a decisive loosening or weakening of the epistemological certainties which once made "history" unproblematic. These concerns, the products of a post-Shakespearean discursive tradition and our historical moment, determine the primary concern of the current study—the fictional use of history in Shakespeare's English history plays.

With the centrality of the fictional elements given to the ten history plays, the research method is necessarily two-fold and involves situating Shakespeare's fictional use of history in relation to two fields of references that are themselves unstable and contradictory. The fifteenth-century past, as recorded in the historiographical writings (Holinshed and Hall's chronicles) constitutes one field, while the fictional elements which include "emplotment" and "characterisation" make up the other. By comparing the two fields, one can see Shakespeare's ten history plays, from the outside each individually and independently shaped by its unique narrative, are from the inside a continuous series which collectively shows Shakespeare's growing maturity in the historic-dramatic exploration.

In the first trilogy, Shakespeare taps into the fictional use of history in dramatic writing. In these three plays, a phase of English history which is unrivalled in the chronicles for its complexity and violence of incidents is confronted and converted into dramatic form through the extensive use of fictional elements. By selecting details of the past and rearranging them into particular telling, and also in creating fictional characters, with or without suggestions from history, Shakespeare poses series challenges to the Tudor Myth on three levels—heroic in *1 Henry VI*, political in *2 Henry VI* and familial in *3 Henry VI*. The greatness of Shakespeare's fictional use of history in these three plays is that it succeeds in subverting the power relations in each area and opening the fault lines of the grand narrative of Tudor history. Once every kind of social and human bond—chivalric, political and familial—has thus been whittled away, there emerges Shakespeare's more mature consciousness towards the fictional use of history in the next three plays.

If Shakespeare only tries his hands at the fictional use of history in the first trilogy, the next three plays, *Richard III*, *Richard II* and *King John*, are Shakespeare's daring experiment in which he shows an ability to construct the different histories of both the kings and marginal characters. In *Richard III* and *Richard II*, the historiography as a text subjected to reinvention allows Shakespeare to reconstruct the historical legacies of king's images from unique perspectives. In *Richard II*, Shakespeare uses his imagination to create the different modes of Richard II's language that suit the different stages of the King's reign. In *Richard III*, Richard III's deformed body, which transmitted through the malicious Tudor historical legacy, is the dramatic focus of Shakespeare and refashioned by him poetically. Shakespeare not only changes the shape of history but also enlarges history by his characterisation of the Bastard as a "Bastard to time" and the Duchess of the York as a culminated mother figure in *King John* and *Richard II* respectively. Finally, in *Richard III* and *King John*, there emerges a perplexing dilemma in determining and recovering the historical truth of several undetermined deaths in history. Through the Scrivener's indignation at copying a previously fabricated indictment against Hastings after Hastings' death, we see the unreliability of historical writing in *Richard III*. By raising the perplexing dilemma in determining and recovering the truth of Arthur's custody and death, *King John* touches the teases the problem of its own historical authenticity and historical fiction. These two episodes produce a darkly ironic vision of history marked by contingency and unintended consequences, but they also sound a sceptical note regarding historical narrative and its attempt to establish the truth of the past.

Among the features which distinguish Shakespeare's second trilogy from previous plays is the effort to represent the various levels of English society dramatically, and this may also be taken as a sign of Shakespeare's maturity in his fictional use of history. *1 Henry IV* and *2 Henry IV* present a low English life that comprises a company of such persons as may well be supposed to frequent a London tavern in those days. This is the world from which emerges the dominant figure of Falstaff, the extraordinary artifice of Shakespeare's construction of "ahistory", the one who brings historical narrative and literary fiction face to face. His physical vitality, comic criminal romance, and power of subversion become inscribed in the genealogy of submerged histories. The nostalgic histories of Mistress Quickly and the country Justices Shallow and Silence nevertheless resist incorporation into a grand narrative and strive, in their oral traditional and popular nostalgia, to realise the histories of commoners. In *Henry V*, the theatrical representation of history continues to expand and from which emerges the Chorus's and the ordinary soldiers' comments that collectively show an ambiguous image of the King. With those characters, Shakespeare depicts a truly England rich in the commoners who collectively provide petit récits of their own hybrid histories more inclusive than one can find in any of Shakespeare's early history plays.

In the last English history play *Henry VIII*, the question of "truth" is raised again. By reopening the question of historical causation and complicating the conflicts it involves, *Henry VIII* destabilises history in a whirling dialectic that increasingly calls into question the "historical truth". In *Henry VIII*, we constantly hear characters offering personally biased oral reportages and testimonies or commenting events from radically different perspectives due to their disparaging self-interests. It is due to this kind of perspectives that Shakespeare poses an increasingly intense interrogation of the historiographic project and the possibility of the realisation of the historical truth. Moreover, Cranmer's final prophecy of Elizabeth as Phoenix raises the question of the credibility of fiction and the incredibility of fact—Elizabeth's reign as a lasting promise of peace and the end of the reign, irrevocable and non-regenerating. Viewed under this vision, by referring to Phoenix, Shakespeare invites an aesthetic reconciliation between fact and truth, history and fiction, and offers, in the form of an ideal solution—the poetic truth, as the escape from the endless historical repetitions of the political world's sickness and corruption.

Taking Shakespeare's fictional use of history as its central concern, the book combines the diachronic research of the ten history plays with the synchronic grasp of the contemporary interpretation. Vertically speaking, Shakespeare's ten English history plays, instead of being a grand narrative of a Tudor history, are a series of historic-dramatic exploration, which presents a diversified, discontinuous, hybrid histories each individually and independently shaped by its unique narrative. Although the constituent plays of Shakespeare's history series are separate entities, they relate to each other in the series as part of a wider organism which reflects a systematic and progressive maturity in Shakespeare's fictional use of history.

What is more, Shakespeare's fictional use of history, if not imitations of reality, succeeds in endowing the dead skeletons of history with flesh and bold, and also in creating, with or without suggestions from historiography, fictional female and common characters such as the Duchess of York, Mistress Quickly and the common soldiers. The fact that Shakespeare uses the emplotment and characterisation to explore the histories of different cultures, classes and genders not only fragments the grand narrative into hybrid "petit récits", but also provides an interpretative context capable of recognising unstable units of the once stable structure to which history nominally belonged. Through the diachronic analysis, this book proposes that Shakespeare fabricates a lot of fictional female characters and common people in the ten history plays. By interrogating the grand narrative of English national history, those fictional characters raise radical challenges to the grand narrative of feudal ideology and develop into their unique "petit récits" of all men's histories.

Horizontally speaking, this book explores the relationship between history (historiography) and literature (fiction), a correlative of what narrative fullness may become when translated into dramatic form. The study of this kind of relationship offers us a new perspective to view the thesis so insistently lay down and retroactively imposed upon any kind of historical writing—the dilemma between literature and history, fiction and truth. The book proceeds on the assumption that in calling attention to the complexities and difficulties involved in representing history, the one story of single "historical truth", is no longer authoritative for Shakespeare. However, Shakespeare accepts history as true even if it only slightly resembles the truth of the past ages. In other words, the principal features of his characterisation and employment are exhibited with such fidelity; their causes, and even their secret springs, are such hybrid mode of histories that by pitching them together, we may not attain the knowledge of history in all its truth, but we may get the universal truth of humanity which can never be effaced. In this way, Shakespeare's history plays claim a kind of poetic truth and achieve authenticity in the aesthetic rather than the empirical sense.

  Although this study is rather suggestive in many ways, owing to the limited time and knowledge, the book unavoidably has limitations and needs further improvement. First of all, this book does not analyse *King Edward III*, which is the sole play absent from the Shakespeare First Folio of 1623 to find a place in modern collections of his works. One of the main methods this book uses is to compare history plays with the historical sources. Since this play is newly established as Shakespeare's works, there is very few evidence of its sources, so the analysis of Shakespeare's history plays does not include *Edward III*. Although the book does not mention *Edward III*, *Edward III* is essential for our comprehensive understanding of Shakespeare's fictional use of history in the history plays. Secondly, although this book tries to make a comprehensive investigation of Shakespeare's history plays, due to the complexity of the many concepts involved in the interpretations, it still leaves some important issues unexplored. Therefore, the future studies need not only to conclude *Edward III* in the canon but also to make a more in-depth and systematic analysis.

  Generally speaking, history in the Shakespeare's history plays is often de-historicised by means of fictionalisation: with the reinvention of historical characters and the addition of fictitious characters, and an imaginative rearrangement of events in chronology. The fabricated plots and characters stand centrally in signifying relations of power in the plays, but often in radically different ways. While the high-born monarchs and noblemen are seeking to fix a glorious national history, the fictional female and common figures, defined in part by their "petit récits" of hybrid histories, undermine the authority of the once stable grand narrative. In this sense, Shakespeare's fictional use of history in the ten history plays produces consultation and circulation within and outside the cultural, political life and finally gives voice to the multivocal and hybrid histories that aid our understanding of how comprehensive the histories of all men's life in England at that time can be.

What is more, Shakespeare adopts many things from the chronicle resources, but he also fictionalises a bunch of characters and plots, which mean the quest for historical truth would never be met with a satisfying answer. However, Shakespeare's unique way of exploiting unofficial histories and incorporating peripheral characters into historical narrative achieves a kind of polyphonic perspectives which renders the history of being more real and credible in the plays than in the historiography. No matter how paradoxically it may sound, Shakespeare fictional use of history contributes to his histories' truthfulness in the history plays.

To conclude, Shakespeare's fictional use of history acts as a counteracting force against the historiography, which not only seemed uninteresting but is also deficient, and his history plays, though being not true, achieves, paradoxically, the truth about the human experience. As the Phoenix reborn from the fire, Shakespeare's history plays have been recycling and renewing and finally permeate the poetic truth in eternal time and space. This kind of poetic truth is the only reason why Shakespeare's history plays are remembered and played in the ever-lasting human history.

Bibliography

Anderson, Judith H. "Shakespeare's *Henry VIII*: The Changing Relation of Truth to Fiction". *Biographical Truth: The Representation of Historical Persons in Tudor-Stuart Writing.* New Haven & London: Yale University Press, 1984.

Aristotle. *Aristotle's Poetics.* Ed. John Baxter and Patrick Atherton. Trans. George Whalley. Montreal Buffalo: McGill-Queen's University Press, 1997.

—. *On Poetics and Style.* Trans. G. M. A. Grube. New York: Bobbs-Merrill, 1958.

—. *The Poetics.* Coradella Collegiate Bookshelf Editions. 2004. 4 June. 〈thewritedirection.net〉

Auden, W. H. *The Dyer's Hand, and Other Essays.* New York: Random House, 1962.

—. *Lectures on Shakespeare.* Ed. Arthur C. Kirsch. Faber & Faber, 2000.

Bakhtin, M. M. "Discourse in the Novel". *The Dialogic Imagination: Four Essays by M. M. Bakhtin.* Ed. Michael Holquist. Trans. Caryl Emerson and Michael Holquist. Austin: University of Texas Press, 1981.

Baldo, Jonathan. *Memory in Shakespeare's Histories: Stages of Forgetting in Early Modern England.* New York and London: Routledge, 2012.

Bates, Jonathan. *The Genius of Shakespeare.* London: Picador, 2008.

Bate, Jonathan, and Eric Rasmussen, eds. "The First Part of Henry the Fourth". *William Shakespeare: Complete Works.* Beijing: Foreign Language Teaching and Research Press, 2014.

Baxter, John. *Shakespeare's Poetic Styles: Verse into Drama.* London:

Routledge & Kegan Paul, 1980.

Belsey, Catherine. "Making Histories Then and Now: Shakespeare from Richard II to Henry V". *Uses of History: Marxism, Postmodernism, and the Renaissance.* Eds. Francis Barker, Peter Hulme, Margaret Iversen. Manchester and New York: Manchester University Press, 1991.

Bitot, Marie-Helene Besnault Michel. "Historical Legacy and Fiction: the Poetical Reinvention of King Richard III ". *The Cambridge Companion to Shakespeare's History Plays.* Ed. Michael Hattaway. Cambridge: Cambridge University Press, 2002.

Blanpid, John W. *Time and the Artist in Shakespeare's English Histories.* Newark, London: University of Delaware Press, 1983.

Bliss, Lee. "The Wheel of Fortune and the Maiden Phoenix of Shakespeare's King Henry the Eight". *ELH: A Journal of English Literary History*, 42 (1975): 1-25.

Boswell-Stone, W. G. *Shakespeare's Holinshed: The Chronicle and the Historical Plays Compared.* New York: Dover Publications, INC, 1968.

Braunmuller, A. R. "King John and Historiography." *ELH* 55.2 (1988): 309-322.

Brockbank, J. P. "The Frame of Disorder—Henry VI". *Early Shakespeare: Stratford-upon-Avon Studies*, No. 3. Eds. John Russell and Bernard Harris. London: Edward Arnold, 1961.

Bullough, Geoffrey. *Earlier English History Plays: Henry VI, Richard III, Richard II.* Ed. Geoffrey Bullough. Vol. 3 of *Narrative and Dramatic Sources of Shakespeare.* 8 Vols. London: Routledge & Kegan Paul; New York: Columbia University Press, 1960a.

—. *Later English History Plays: King John, Henry IV, Henry V, Henry VIII.* Ed. Geoffrey Bullough. Vol. 4 of *Narrative and Dramatic Sources of Shakespeare.* 8 Vols. London: Routledge & Kegan Paul; New York: Columbia University Press, 1960b.

Butcher, S. H. *Aristotle's Theory of Poetry and Fine Art with a Critical Text and Translation of the Poetics*. London: Macmillan and Co., Limited, 1911.

Campbell, Lily B. *Shakespeare's "Histories": Mirrors of Elizabethan Policy*. London: Methuen, 1964.

Campbell, Oscar James. *A Shakespeare Encyclopaedia*. Eds. Oscar James Campbell, Edward G. Quinn. London: Methuen & Co Ltd, 1966.

Cavanagh, Dermot et al. *Shakespeare's Histories and Counter-Histories*. Eds. Dermot Cavanagh, Stuart Hampton-Reeves and Stephen Longstaffe. Manchester: Manchester University Press, 2006.

Certeau, Michael de. *The Writing of History*. Trans. Tom Conley. New York: Columbia University Press, 1988.

Chapman, George. *Bussy D'Ambois and The Revenge of Bussy D'Ambois*. Ed. Frederick S. Boas. Boston and London: D. C. Heath & CO., Publishers, 1905.

Chernaik, Warren. *The Cambridge Introduction to Shakespeare's History Plays*. Cambridge: Cambridge University Press, 2007.

Coleridge, Samuel Taylor. *Notes and Lectures Upon Shakespeare and Some of the Old Poets and Dramatists: With Other Literary Remains of S. T. Coleridge*. Ed. Henry Nelson Coleridge and Sara Coleridge Coleridge. Vol. 2. London: William Pickering, 1849.

—. *Coleridge's Writings on Shakespeare*. Ed. Terence Hawkes. Intro. Alfred Harbage. Capricorn Books, 1959.

Courtenay, Thomas Peregrine. *Commentaries on the Historical Plays of Shakespeare*. Vol. 2. London: General Books, 1840.

Dean, Paul. "Dramatic Mode and Historical Vision in *Henry VIII*". *Shakespeare Quarterly*, 37 (1986): 175-189.

Derrida, Jacques. *Margins of Philosophy*. Trans. Alan Bass. Chicago: University of Chicago Press, 1982.

—. *Of Grammatology*. Trans. Gayatri Spivak. Baltimore: Johns Hopkins University Press, 1974.

Dobson, Michael, and Stanley Wells, eds. *The Oxford Companion to Shakespeare*. Oxford: Oxford University Press, 2001.

Dolezel, Lubomir. "Fictional and Historical Narrative: Meeting the Postmodernist Challenge." *Narratologies*. Ed. David Herman. Columbus: Ohio State University Press, 1999.

Domanska, Ewa. *Encounters: Philosophy of History after Postmodernism*. Charlottesville and London: University Press of Virginia, 1998.

Dillon, Janette. *Shakespeare and the Staging of English History*. Oxford and New York: Oxford University Press, 2012.

Dutton, Richard, and Jean E. Howard. *A Companion to Shakespeare's Works*. Eds. Richard Dutton and Jean E. Howard. Vol. 2. The Histories. Blackwell Publishing, 2003.

Erskine-Hill, Howard. *Poetry and the Realm of Politics: Shakespeare to Dryden*. Oxford: Clarendon Press, 1996.

Eagleton, Terry. *Ideology: An Introduction*. London & New York: Verso, 1991.

Greenblatt, Stephen. *Will in the World: How Shakespeare Became Shakespeare*. New York and London: W. W. Norton & Company, 2004.

—. *Shakespearean Negotiations: The Circulation of Social Energy in Renaissance England*. Berkeley: University of California Press, 1988.

Greenblatt, Stephen, and Giles Gunn, eds. *Redrawing the Boundaries: The Transformation of English and American Literary Studies*. New York: The Modern Language Association of America, 1992.

Grene, Nicholas. *Shakespeare's Serial History Plays*. Cambridge: Cambridge University Press, 2002.

Hart, Jonathan Locke. *Theater and World: The Problematics of Shakespeare's History*. Boston: Northeastern University Press, 1992.

Hampton-Reeves, Stuart and Carol Chillington Rutter. *The Henry VI Plays*. Ed. Carol Chillington Rutter. Manchester: Manchester University Press, 2006.

Helgerson, Richard. *Forms of Nationhood: the Elizabethan Writing of England*. Chicago and London: University of Chicago Press, 1992.

Herman, David, ed. *Narratologies: New Perspectives on Narrative Analysis*. Columbus: Ohio State University Press, 1997.

Hertel, Ralf. *Staging England in the Elizabethan History Play: Performing National Identity*. Ashgate, 2014.

"History." *Merriam-Webster. com Dictionary*. Vers. 2019. Merriam-Webster, Inc. 8 May 2019 〈https://www. merriam-webster. com/dictionary/history〉.

Hodgdon, Barbara. *The First Part of Henry Ⅳ Texts and Contexts*. Ed. Barbara Hodgdon. Basingstoke: Macmillan Press Ltd. , 1997.

Holderness, Graham. *Shakespeare History Plays: Richard Ⅱ to Henry V*. Basingstoke: Macmillan Educ. , 1992a.

—. *Shakespeare Recycled: The Making of Historical Drama*. New York, London: Harvester Wheatsheaf, 1992b.

——. *Shakespeare's History*. New York: St. Martin's Press, 1985.

—. *Shakespeare: The Histories*. Basingstoke: Macmillan, 2000.

Holinshed, Raphael. Preface. *Holinshed's Chronicles of England, Scotland, and Ireland*. Vol. Ⅱ. ENGLAND. September 24, 2005. The Project Gutenberg EBook. 5 Sept. 2019 〈https://www. gutenberg. org/files/16738/16738-h/16738-h. htm〉.

Howard, Jean E. *Engendering a Nation: A Feminist Account of Shakespeare's English Histories*. Ed. Phyllis Rackin. London: Routledge, 1997.

Humphreys, A. R. , ed. *Henry V*. By William Shakespeare. Harmondsworth : Penguin, 1968.

Hutcheon, Linda. *A Poetics of Postmodernism: History, Theory, Fiction*. New York and London: Routledge, 1988.

Jameson, Fredric. *The Political Unconscious: Narrative as a Socially Symbolic Act*. London: Metheun, 1981.

Jonson, Ben. Introduction. *Ben Jonson*. By Brinsley Nicholson and C. H. Herford. Eds. C. H. Herford et al. London: Benn, 1930.

Kamps, Ivo. "Possible Pasts: Historiography and Legitimation in *Henry VIII*". *College English*, 58(1996): 192-215.

Kastan, David Scott. *Shakespeare and the Shapes of Time*. London: Macmillan, 1982.

—. "To Set A Form upon That Indigest: Shakespeare's Fiction of History". Eds. Stephen Orgel and Sean Keilen. *Shakespeare and History*. New York & London: Garland Publishing, Inc, 1999.

Kittredge, George Lyman, ed. *The Complete Works of Shakespeare*. Microform. Oxford: Microform International, 1986.

Lacan, Jacques. "The Mirror Stage as Formative of the Function of the I". *Écrits: A Selection*. Trans and Ed. Alan Sheridan. London: Tavistock Publications, 1977.

Lake, Peter. *How Shakespeare Put Politics on the Stage: Power and Succession in the History Plays*. New Haven and London: Yale University Press, 2016.

Leech, Clifford. "The Structure of the Last Play". *Shakespeare Survey* II: *The Last Plays (with an Index to Surveys 1-10)*. Ed. Allardyce Nicoll. Cambridge: Cambridge University Press, 1958.

Lukács, Georg. *The Historical Novel*. Trans. Hannah and Stanley Mitchell. Lincoln: University of Nebraska Press, 1983.

Levin, Richard. "The Problem of 'Context' in Interpretation." *Shakespeare and the Dramatic Tradition*. Ed. Elton and Long. Newark: University of Delaware Press, 1989.

Levy, F. J. *Tudor Historical Thought*. San Marino & California: The Huntington Library, 1967.

Louis, Montrose. "New Historicisms". *Redrawing the Boundaries: The Transformation of English and American Literary Studies*. Eds. Stephen Greenblatt, Giles Gunn. New York: The Modern Language Association of America, 1992.

Lyotard, Jean-Francois. Introduction. *The Postmodern Condition: A Report on Knowledge*. By Lyotard. Trans. Geoff Bennington and Brian Massumi. Minneapolis:

University of Minnesota Press, 1984. Vol. 10 of *Theory and History of Literature*. Ten vols. 1979-84.

Marriott, J. A. R. *English History in Shakespeare*. London: Chapman & Hall, 1918.

McMullan, Gordon, ed. *King Henry VIII*. By William Shakespeare and John Fletcher. Cengage Learning: Arden Shakespeare, 2000.

Mink, Louis O. "Narrative Form as a Cognitive Instrument". *The Writing of History*. Eds. R. H. Canary and H. Kozicki. Madison: University of Wisconsin Press, 1978.

Morrison, Jago. *Contemporary Fiction*. New York: Routledge, 2003.

Ornstein, Robert. *A Kingdom for a Stage: The Achievement of Shakespeare's History Plays*. Harvard: Harvard University Press, 1972.

Patterson, Annabel. *Reading Holinshed's Chronicles*. Chicago & London: The University of Chicago Press, 1994.

Pugliatti, Paola. *Shakespeare the Historian*. New York: Palgrave Macmillan, 1996.

Quint, David. "'Alexander the Pig': Shakespeare on History and Poetry". *Boundary* 10 (1982): 50.

Rackin, Phyllis. "Anti-Historians: Women's Roles in Shakespeare's Histories". *Theatre Journal*, 37 (1985): 329-44.

—. *Stages of History: Shakespeare's English Chronicles*. Ithaca, N. Y.: Cornell University Press, 1990.

Rabkin, Norman. "Rabbits, Ducks, and Henry V". *Shakespeare Quarterly*, 28 (3), 279-296.

Reese, M. M. Preface. *The Cease of Majesty: A Study of Shakespeare's History Plays*. By Reese. London: Edward Arnold, 1961. vii-ix.

Ribner, Irving. *The English History Play in the Age of Shakespeare*. Princeton University Press: Oxford University Press, 1957.

Ritter, Harry. *Dictionary of Concepts in History*. Reference Sources for the

Social Sciences and Humanities. Number 3. New York: Greenwood Press, 1986.

Riggs, David. *Shakespeare's Heroical Histories*: "*Henry VI*" *and Its Literary Tradition*. Cambridge Mass. : Harvard University Press, 1971.

Rose, Mary Beth. "Where Are the Mothers in Shakespeare? Options for Gender Representation in the English Renaissance." *Shakespeare Quarterly*, 42 (1991):219-314.

Rossiter, A. P. *Angel with Horns*: *Fifteen Lectures on Shakespeare*. Ed. Graham Storey. London: Longman, 1989.

Rubin, Gayle. "The Traffic in Women: Notes on the 'Political Economy' of Sex". *Towards an Anthropology of Women*. Ed. R. Reiter. New York: Monthly Review Press, 1975.

Rushdie, Salman. *Shame*. London:Cape, 1983.

Sahel, Pierre. "The Strangeness of a Dramatic Style: Rumour in 'Henry VIII' ". *Shakespeare Survey*, 38(1986): 145-152.

Sanders, Wilbur. *The Dramatist and the Received Idea*: *Studies in the Plays of Marlowe &Shakespeare*. Cambridge: Cambridge University Press, 1968.

Gupta, S. C. Sen. *Shakespeare's Historical Plays*. London: Oxford University Press, 1964.

Shakespeare, William. *King Henry IV Part One*. Ed. David Scott Kastan. Bloomsbury Arden Shakespeare, 2002.

—. *King Henry IV Part Two*. Ed. James C. Bulman. Bloomsbury Arden Shakespeare, 2016.

—. *King Henry V* . Ed. T. W. Craik. Oxford & New York. Bloomsbury Arden Shakespeare, 2015.

—. *King Henry VI Part One*. Ed. Edward Burns. Thomson Learning: Arden Shakespeare, 2000.

—. *King Henry VI Part Two*. Ed. Ronald Knowles. Thomson Learning: Arden Shakespeare, 2001.

—. *King Henry VI Part Three*. Eds. John D. Cox and Eric Rasmussen.

Bloomsbury Arden Shakespeare, 2001.

—. *King John*. Eds. Jesse M. Lander and J. J. M. Tobin. Bloomsbury Arden Shakespeare, 2018.

—. *King Richard II*. Ed. Charles R. Forker. Bloomsbury Arden Shakespeare, 2013.

—. *King Richard III*. Ed. James R. Siemon. Bloomsbury Arden Shakespeare, 2013.

Shakespeare, William and John Fletcher. *King Henry VIII (All is True)*. Ed. Gordon McMullan. Cengage Learning: Arden Shakespeare, 2000.

Sidney, Philip. *The Defense of Poesy*. Ed. Albert S. Cook. Ginn & Company, 1890.

Sinfield, Alan. *Faultlines: Cultural Materialism and the Politics of Dissident Reading*. Oxford: Oxford University Press, 1992.

Smallwood, R. L. "Shakespeare's Use of History". *The Cambridge Companion to Shakespeare Studies*. Ed. Stanley Wells. Shanghai: Shanghai Foreign Language Education Press, 2000.

Smidt, Kristian. *Unconformities in Shakespeare's History Plays*. London: Macmillan, 1992.

Southgate, Beverley C. *History Meets Fiction*. Harlow: Longman, 2009.

Tillyard, E. M. W. *Shakespeare's History Plays*. London: Penguin Books, 1962.

—. Preface. *The Elizabethan World Picture*. By Tillyard. London: Chatto & Windus, 1943. v-vii.

Trousdale, Marion. *Shakespeare and the Rhetoricians*. Chapel Hill: University of North Carolina Press, 1982.

"Truth." *Merriam-Webster. com Dictionary*. Vers. 2019. Merriam-Webster, Inc.. 8 May 2019 〈https://www.merriam-webster.com/dictionary/truth〉.

Ure, Peter, ed. *King Richard II*. The Arden Shakespeare. London: Methuen, 1961.

Vesser, H. Aram, ed. *The New Historicism*. New York: Routledge, 1989.

Warner, Marina. *Joan of Arc: The Image of Female Heroism*. New York: Alfred A. Knopf, 1981.

Watson, Donald G. *Shakespeare's Early History Plays: Politics at Play on the Elizabethan Stage*. London: The Macmillan Press LTD, 1990.

Watt, R. J. C. *Shakespeare's History Plays*. London and New York: Routledge, 2014.

Wells, Stanly, ed. *The Cambridge Companion to Shakespeare Studies*. Shanghai: Shanghai Foreign Language Education Press, 2000.

White, Hayden. *Tropics of Discourse: Essays in Cultural Criticism*. Baltimore London: The Johns Hopkins University Press, 1978.

——. *Metahistory: The Historical Imagination in Nineteenth-century Europe*. Baltimore & London: The Johns Hopkins University Press, 1973.

Wilders, John. *The Lost Garden: A View of Shakespeare's English and Roman History Plays*. London: Macmiallan, 1978.

埃娃·多曼斯卡. 邂逅:后现代主义之后的历史哲学[M]. 彭刚译. 北京:北京大学出版社,2007.

戴卫·赫尔曼. 新叙事学[M]. 马海良译. 北京:北京大学出版社,2002.

F. R. 安克斯密特. 历史表现[M]. 周建漳译. 北京:北京大学出版社,2011.

高继海. 读《俗世威尔—莎士比亚如何成为莎士比亚》. 史学月刊,2009(3):130-134.

桂扬清. 伟大的剧作家和诗人——莎士比亚[M]. 上海:上海外语教育出版社,2010.

郭剑敏. 文学与叙事之维的历史存在——论海登·怀特的后现代历史叙事学[J]. 内蒙古师范大学学报(哲学社会科学版),2018(1):93-96.

哈拉尔德·韦尔策. 社会记忆:历史、回忆、传承[M]. 季斌、王立君等译. 北京:北京大学出版社,2007.

海登·怀特. 后现代历史叙事学[M]. 陈永国、张万娟译. 北京:中国社会科学出版社,2003.

——叙事的虚构性:有关历史、文学、和理论的论文(1957-2007)[M]. 罗伯特·多兰编,马丽莉、马云等译.南京:南京大学出版社,2019.

——元史学:19世纪欧洲的历史想象[M].陈新译.南京:译林出版社,2013.

华莱士·马丁.当代叙事学[M].伍晓明译.北京:中国人民大学出版社,2018.

华泉坤,洪增流,田朝绪.莎士比亚新论——新世纪,新莎士比亚[M].上海:上海外语教育出版社,2007.

柯林伍德.历史的观念[M].扬·冯·德·杜森编,何兆武、张文杰等译.北京:北京大学出版社,2010.

李艳梅.莎士比亚历史剧研究[M].北京:中国社会科学出版社,2009.

——莎士比亚历史剧与元代历史剧比较研究[M].北京:中国社会科学出版社,2014.

刘炳善.英汉双解莎士比亚大词典[M].郑州:河南人民出版社,2002.

刘岳红.从莎士比亚历史剧看中世纪后期英国的有限王权[J].湖南大学博士论文,2008.

M. H. 艾布拉姆斯.文学术语词典(中英对照)[M].北京:北京大学出版社,2009.

M. M. 巴赫金.巴赫金全集(第五卷)[M].白春仁、顾亚铃译.石家庄:河北教育出版社,2009.

迈克尔·斯坦福.历史研究导论[M].刘世安译.北京:世界图书出版公司,2012.

宁平.莎士比亚英国历史剧研究[M].北京:外语教学与研究出版社,2012.

——中国莎士比亚历史剧研究之滥觞[J].大连民族学院,2006(2):34-37.

彭刚.叙事、虚构与历史——海登·怀特与当代西方历史哲学的转型[J].历史研究,2006(3):23-38.

盛宁.新历史主义·后现代主义·历史真实[J].文学理论与批评,1997(1):48-58.

斯特凡·约尔丹.历史科学基本概念词典[M].孟钟捷译.北京:北京大学出版社,2012.

苏珊·S.兰瑟.虚构的权威:女性作家与叙述声音[M].北京:外语教学与研究出版社,2018.

W. H. 沃尔什. 历史哲学导论[M]. 北京:北京大学出版社,2008.

王宁. 作为历史主义者的莎士比亚——兼论莎士比亚历史剧对我们的启示[J]. 外国文学研究,2016(6):8-15.

王维昌. 论莎士比亚历史剧创作的艺术原则[J]. 安徽师范大学学报(人文社会科学版),1999(3):362-368.

王霞. 在诗与历史之间:海登·怀特历史诗学理论研究[M]. 北京:中国社会科学出版社,2014.

卫丽杰. 莎士比亚历史剧中的篡位君王形象研究[J]. 华中师范大学硕士论文,2009.

威廉·莎士比亚. 莎士比亚全集·第七卷·历史剧(卷一)[M]. 方平主编,屠岸、方平等译. 上海:上海译文出版社,2014.

——莎士比亚全集·第七卷·历史剧(卷二)[M]. 方平主编,覃学岚、方平等译. 上海:上海译文出版社,2014..

温潘亚. 历史剧:作为一种历史叙事[J]. 江苏社会科学,2017(5):180-187.

吴玉杰. 新历史主义与历史剧的艺术建构[M]. 北京:中国社会科学出版社,2005.

辛雅敏. 二十世纪莎评简史[M]. 北京:中国社会科学出版社,2016.

雅克·德里达. 书写与差异(上、下册)[M]. 张宁译. 北京:生活·读书·新知三联书店,2001.

叶凯. 历史"虚构"与文学虚构——对新历史主义的一个批评[J]. 浙江大学硕士论文,2008.

翟恒兴. 走向历史诗学——海登·怀特的故事解释与话语转义理论研究[M]. 杭州:浙江大学出版社,2014.

张进. 新历史主义与历史诗学[M]. 北京:中国社会科学出版社,2004.

张京媛. 新历史主义与文学批评[M]. 北京:北京大学出版社,1993.

——当代女性主义文学批评[M]. 北京:北京大学出版社,1993.

张泗洋. 莎士比亚大辞典[M]. 北京:商务印书馆,2001.

赵志义. 历史叙事中的"真实"与"虚构"问题[J]. 青海师范大学学报(哲学社会科学版),2007(6):52-56.

朱刚. 二十世纪西方文艺批评理论[M]. 上海:上海外语教育出版社,2001.